2

The Time
of Roses

"It was the Time of Roses;
We plucked them as we passed."

"Florence, winter comes in every year, but it is followed by spring, and spring is followed by summer, and in summer the roses bloom again, and the time of roses comes back, Florence, and it will come back even to you."

The Time of Roses

L.T. MEADE

EDITED BY
Heather Harpham Kopp

HARVEST HOUSE PUBLISHERS
Eugene, Oregon 97402

Cover by Koechel Peterson and Associates, Minneapolis, Minnesota.

Interior illustrations by Joneile Emery, derived from original illustrations from the Victorian period.

THE TIME OF ROSES

Copyright © 1998 by Harvest House Publishers
Eugene, Oregon 97402

Library of Congress Cataloging-in-Publication Data

Meade, L. T., 1854–1914.
    The time of roses / L.T. Meade.
        p. cm. — (Victorian bookshelf series)
    Edited by Heather Harpham Kopp.
    ISBN 1-56507-784-9
    I. Kopp, Heather Harpham, 1964– . II. Title. III. Series.
PR4990.M34T56   1998
823'.8—dc21   97-31381
                                 CIP

Printed in the United States of America.

98   99   00   01   02   03   / DC /   10   9   8   7   6   5   4   3   2   1

A Sweet Discovery

"You are the one woman on God's earth for me. Do you hear me, Florence? I love you! I didn't mean to speak, but the truth has been wrung from me."

Romantic declarations, adventurous heroines, and timeless lessons of the heart . . .

Welcome to a world where beauty is virtue, and virtue promises a life of love. Though many of its charms have disappeared, the essence of the Victorian era is still fondly recalled today. We are fascinated by the sophisticated manners, customs, and ideals of only a century ago. And we are wistfully certain that something quite wonderful has been lost.

Antique romances such as the one you're holding offer a delightful opportunity to revisit the past and recapture some of its charm. *The Time of Roses* is part of a new series called The Victorian Bookshelf—old books rescued from dusty shelves or attics and rendered beautiful again.

Beware, however, the beauty of this book. Yes, it will look lovely on a side table or fire mantel. But between its gorgeous covers it is also a captivating read to rival most popular present-day novels.

Written by Elizabeth Thomasina Smith, *The Time of Roses* was originally published around 1890. Known by her pseudonym, L.T. Meade, the author was beloved on both sides of the Atlantic for several decades. The daughter of a minister, her novels not only capture the imagination but enrich the spirit.

The Time of Roses is set, for the most part, in London. Our heroine, Florence, is determined to make money for herself and her widowed mother. But employment is hard to come by, and Florence's funds threaten to run out. Desperate to not return home a failure, she reluctantly takes part in a dishonest scheme proposed by a corrupt young woman from her past.

Soon, Florence gains fame and fortune posing as a brilliant writer of short stories. But in the process she loses faith in her own potential for goodness. Confused, and feeling unworthy of the man she really loves, Florence becomes engaged to yet a different man—a calculating editor who wants to share in her literary success.

Because Elizabeth Thomasina Smith lived in the time she wrote about—versus a modern author creating a historical romance—her books reward us with the unmistakable ring of authenticity. While *The Time of Roses* has been slightly condensed, details of period charm have been preserved whenever possible.

Readers will also appreciate the occasional passages excerpted here from popular etiquette books of the day, such as *Etiquette for Ladies and Gentlemen* (1877), *The Modern Hostess* (1904), and *The Book of Good Manners* (1923). We gain perspective, and we smile, when we read tips such as, "It is not good form—as some girls do—to carry small animal pets, guinea-pigs, lizards and the like, in the pocket of your cloak or wrap."

How much has changed in our society! And yet, any woman will recognize a part of herself in the story that follows. So curl up in your favorite cozy corner, and join Florence as she discovers the frailties of the human heart, and the redeeming power of true love.

—*Heather Harpham Kopp*

❧ I ❧

Home at Last

t was on a summer's evening early in the month of August that the little Mum was once again seen on the platform at Dawlish.

She wore somewhat rusty widow's black, and her face had that half-anxious, half-comical expression, which made people turn to look at her with something between a smile and a sigh. She was commonplace and plain, and yet in one sense she was neither commonplace nor plain. She had a character, and that character had developed during the last few years, and rather for the better.

There were very few passengers on the platform, and the little woman paced up and down, thinking to herself. "My Florence is coming home at last! But I wonder what sort of girl Miss Sharston is. She has been very kind to Florence, but it was rash of Florence to invite her. Still, I suppose we shall be able to manage all right."

Just then the signal announcing the approaching train was lowered, and a moment or two later the train drew up at the platform and one or two passengers alighted. Among these was a tall, well-built, dark-eyed girl, and accompanying her was another girl, not so tall and very slender, with an ethereal sort of face and large, speaking gray eyes.

The tall girl rushed up to where the little Mum was standing.

"Here I am, Mum," she said, "and this is Kitty, and we are both tired and hungry and glad to see you again."

"The cottage is just as small as ever it was, Florence," replied the little Mum.

"Oh, I am so glad to see you, Miss Sharston." Here she shook hands with Kitty Sharston.

"We like things small," said Kitty, "we want to have a real charming time in the country. It is very good of you to consent to take me in, Mrs. Aylmer."

A porter appeared. Florence bustled off to see to the luggage, and Mrs. Aylmer and Kitty slowly left the station. Florence ran after them in a moment or two. "Well," she said, "here we are! Both of us have done with school forever and a day. We are grown-up girls ready to take our place in the world and to give you a right good time, Mum. Isn't that so, Kitty?"

"Yes," said Kitty, in that gentle voice which always had a pathetic ring in it. Then she added after a moment's pause, "But I don't know that I am glad to have left school. I must confess that I enjoyed the last few years at Cherry Court School immensely."

"Don't talk to me of Cherry Court School," said the widow with a slight shudder.

She glanced round in an inquiring way at Florence, who colored faintly and then said in a stout voice, "I have repented of that old sin long ago, and I do not in the least mind having Cherry Court School alluded to. I have had a right good time, and it was a very lucky thing for me I did not win that scholarship, for if I had I should have been eating the bread of dependence now,

8

whereas—" Here she drew herself up, uttered a quick sigh, and looked ahead of her.

Her face was not handsome, but it was bright and taking. And her red-gold hair made it impossible to call her plain. She was head and shoulders taller than the little Mum, who gazed at her with something of her old expression of mingled affection and fear.

They reached the tiny house, where Sukey was standing on the steps, looking not a day older than she had six years ago. She dropped a curtsy when she saw Florence, but Florence ran up and wrung her hand.

"How do you do, Sukey?" she said. "I am very glad to come home, and this is my great friend Miss Sharston."

Sukey stared up at Kitty, then she glanced at Mrs. Aylmer and slowly shook her head. "It's a very, *very* small house," she said, "and how we are to fit you two young ladies in is more than I can tell."

"Never mind, Sukey," said Mrs. Aylmer, "I have it all arranged."

Here Mrs. Aylmer shook her hand with a playful gesture at Sukey, and then the entire party found themselves in the house. Florence had not been home for three years. Kitty had never seen the cottage at Dawlish before. Certainly the one sitting room was very tiny.

"How it has dwindled!" said Florence, looking around. "Good gracious! Why, the ceiling nearly reaches my head, and as for the walls"—she stretched out her long arms playfully—"I can almost touch from wall to wall. But never mind, it's home. It's your house, Mum, and you are good to take us girls in and look after us for a whole delightful fortnight."

"There is a very nice supper waiting for you," said Mrs. Aylmer, "and quite in the old style—crabs and a watercress salad. I thought you would appreciate that. You remember them, don't you?"

"Nothing could be more appetizing," replied Florence. "Would you like to come upstairs now, Kitty?"

Mrs. Aylmer had given up her wee bedroom to the two girls. Where she was to sleep was a mystery known only to herself. But, as she seemed quite cheerful and happy over it, Florence advised Kitty not to investigate matters too closely.

"They say he is a very pushing and a very designing young man, and that he twists poor Susan round his little finger."

"It's the Mum's way," she said. "She quite adores the thought of having us both with her in this little dull house. Can you put up with it, Kitty?"

"The place is quite lovely," replied Kitty, "and I would put up with anything after the news I told you this morning."

"Oh, that your father is really coming back, and that you don't have to go to India after all! And you are going to live here and take a beautiful house and be a real mistress of a home," said Florence.

"I don't know anything about the beautiful house, nor being mistress of a home," replied Kitty. "But I am going to be with Father wherever he is, and that," she added, "will be home to me."

"Of course," answered Florence in a somewhat wistful tone.

"But what are you going to do, Flo?"

"I am going to earn my living," replied Florence stoutly.

"Of course. But how?"

"I shall talk things over with you and the Mum. I have left school at last for good. What a blessing it is that I shall not have anything to do with Aunt Susan! I feel so jolly independent, but I should like to meet her and—"

"Girls, supper is ready," called out Mrs. Aylmer from below, and the two ran downstairs.

The meal was very merry, and the old schoolfellows were glad to be together. Mrs. Aylmer chatted in very much the way she had chatted six years ago. She could not help constantly alluding to her sister-in-law, Mrs. Aylmer the great.

"I have not seen her," she said, "but she sends me my money regularly once a quarter—twelve pounds ten shillings. She never misses a day, I will say that for her, and I think I am a very good manager not to be one farthing in debt."

"You are perfectly splendid, Mother," replied Florence.

"She has never once asked for you; she said she would not, and she has kept her word," continued Mrs. Aylmer.

"Well, Mother, does it matter?" replied the daughter.

"They say, too," continued the little Mum—and here she heaved a heavy sigh—"that she has adopted a young man as her heir. I have never seen him, but his name is Maurice Trevor. He is no relation of any sort, and goodness knows why she has adopted him. They say he is a very pushing and a very designing young man, and that he twists poor Susan round his little finger. I know she sent him to Cambridge and spent an enormous sum on him there—two or three hundred a year at the very least—and now he has returned and lives with her and is to take the management of her estates. She has been buying a lot of fresh property—but I am sick of the subject. Florence, you ought to have been in the position which young Mr. Trevor occupies."

"I am glad I am not," replied Florence. "I'm twice the girl for being independent. Mother, Kitty and I want to go out and have a walk by the seashore."

"Do, my dear, do. I have a great deal to contrive and manage, and Sukey's temper is not what it was. Oh, don't breathe it too loud. I wouldn't part with her for the world, but really she does rule me. She'll be as cross as two sticks because we sat so long over supper. Do go. It's a lovely evening."

So the two girls put on their hats and went out. There was a silver moon shining that night on a silver sea, and the place looked calm and peaceful—as if no storms had ever ruffled those waters, as if no trouble had ever visited those shores.

Kitty, whose heart was full of song and her face of delight, almost danced as she walked. Florence's steps were also full of spring, but they were a little slower than her companion's.

"What are you thinking of, Flo?" asked the younger girl.

"All sorts of things," replied Florence. "About that man, Maurice Trevor, for instance. I don't envy him."

"Nor do I. I wonder why he submits to it," Kitty mused. "But don't let us think of him. He has nothing whatever to do with us."

"He has nothing in store," answered Florence, "but to eat the bread of dependence, to eat *her* bread! Oh, he must be a horror! I only trust I shall never meet him."

Kitty now linked her arm inside her companion's.

"You must often come and stay with me," she said. "It would be delightful. I will coax and beg Father to have a house where you can come; then you will have two homes, Florry—the little Mum's home, as you always call your mother, and my home. You will be equally welcome at both. Oh, dear, you are quite my very greatest friend—the greatest friend I have in all the world."

"You are wonderfully good to put up with me," said Florence. "But there, I have repented of that old sin, and it is not going to darken my life."

"There is only one thing I dislike about you, Florence," said Kitty. She frowned slightly as she spoke.

"What is that?"

"You always revert to the old times. Just do promise me that you won't speak of them again, at least to me."

"I will try not, darling, but you are good to forget."

The Little Mum's Arrangements

t was hard to say how many knew the facts—that Florence Aylmer left Cherry Court School under a cloud, that Kitty Sharston won the prize offered by Sir John Wallis and stayed on at the school, and that Bertha Keys, finding her game was up and her wickedness discovered, disappeared—it was hoped by Florence—never to show her face again.

In this old world of ours, however, bad people do not always receive their punishment. It came to pass that Bertha Keys, although she had failed in the case of Cherry Court School, did manage to feather her nest and to secure a very comfortable post for herself. So daring an adventuress was this young woman that she absolutely made up her mind to lay siege to no less a person than Mrs. Aylmer the great.

It was easy for her to do this. Mrs. Aylmer had not noticed her on that auspicious occasion when all the girls of the school were collected in Sir John Wallis' fine old house. The part that Bertha had played in the affair, which had lowered her niece in Mrs. Aylmer's eyes forever, was very slightly impressed on her memory. There was a pupil teacher who had not behaved right, but what the name of that pupil teacher was had never sunk into the good lady's memory.

She was terribly disappointed about her niece, Florence, although she pretended not to care, and a month or two afterward she advertised in a local paper for a companion.

The person who answered this advertisement was Bertha Keys. She managed to satisfy the good lady with regard to testimonials, taking care never to breathe the name of Cherry Court School. She secured the post and from that moment ruled Mrs. Aylmer, although Mrs. Aylmer supposed that she ruled her.

Florence had found a friend in Sir John Wallis, who put her on the foundation of an excellent school which he knew of. She was well educated, and had received a present of twenty pounds from Sir John Wallis on leaving school. Now at the age of twenty, with this slender provision, she meant to fight the world and find her own niche.

Kitty Sharston had fulfilled all her early promises of beauty and grace. Her father was now returning to England, and she was to go and live with him.

Mrs. Aylmer the less was just as determined and just as peculiar as in the days of old. She always spoke out what she thought, and the next morning at breakfast, as the two girls with rosy faces and bright eyes sat round the very tiny table, she expounded her views.

"Florence," she said, "I am nothing if I am not frank."

"We know that, Mum," replied her daughter with a twinkle in her bright eyes. "What is up now?"

"Only this, I have been thinking things in the night."

"Oh, do satisfy my curiosity, Mrs. Aylmer," exclaimed Kitty. "Where did you sleep last night? You don't know how uncomfortable Florry and I were, fearing we had taken your bed."

"Which you did, my dear. If it was a subject of fear, your fears were not realized," responded the little widow.

"I must and will pay you a pound a week for my board," said Kitty. "Why, it is cheap— so cheap that father will be more than astonished, and the place is so lovely, and I am enjoying it greatly. Can you put me up and give me what food I require for a pound a week, Mrs. Aylmer?"

"The very best possible way to have everything that was wrong put right, is for you, Florence, to secure the young man, Maurice Trevor, as your husband."

"It will be riches," said Mrs. Aylmer, with tears in her eyes. "The fact is, I can feed you both comfortably for ten shillings a piece, and the rest will be clear profit. Why, I won't know myself. I might be able to buy some new clothes. I declare, my dears, I am shabby, having turned and turned and contrived and contrived until my clothes are past wearing. Your aunt has not sent me a box of her cast-offs for over a year, and I think it is extremely unkind of her."

"But you have not told me yet where you slept last night, dear Mrs. Aylmer," said Kitty.

"Well, dear, if you must know, I slept here in this room. I slept on the dining table. I borrowed some extra pillows from a neighbor, or, rather, Sukey borrowed them for me, for it would never do for my friends to suppose that I have not got abundance of pillows in my own house. I have had quite a luxurious night, my dear girls, so pray don't trouble about me."

Kitty looked somewhat inclined to cry, but Florence burst out laughing. She jumped up, went to her mother, and put her arms round her neck. "You dear little Mum," she said. "You are too comical for anything."

"There is no doubt whatever," replied Mrs. Aylmer in answer to this caress, "that God Almighty makes us each in the most useful shape and form. Now, you are big, Florence, and could never manage on a table, but a little woman like me—why, it comes in most handy. Everything is arranged for the best, and so I always say." Here she glanced around her with her black eyes full of merriment, and certainly she looked as happy, notwithstanding her very uncomfortable bed, as any woman could look.

"Well, Mummy, and what was that thought you said you had in the back of your head?" continued Florence.

"Oh, that," said Mrs. Aylmer. She looked at both girls. "I wonder, Kitty Sharston," she said, "if you can keep a secret?"

"Try me, Mrs. Aylmer," replied Kitty.

"Well, I was thinking things over in the night, and it struck me that the very best possible way to have everything that was wrong put right is for you, Florence, to secure the young man, Maurice Trevor, as your husband."

"Oh, Mother, how can you talk such nonsense?" said Florence. "As if I would," she added, jumping to her feet and shaking the crumbs from her dress.

"There," said Mrs. Aylmer, "that's just like you. I have been planning it all. You have but to show the fascinations which all women ought to possess, and you will soon twist him round your little finger."

"I could never, never think of it, Mother, and I am distressed that you should say it, and more particularly before Kitty," was Florence's answer.

Mrs. Aylmer laughed.

"Girls always say that," she remarked, "but in the end they yield to the inevitable. It would be splendid. She would be forced to have you living with her after all. I am told she has made the young man the heir of all she possesses and—but what is the matter, my dear?"

"I really won't listen to another word," cried Florence, and she jumped up and ran out of the room.

Mrs. Aylmer's eyes now filled with tears. She looked full at Kitty.

"I don't know what is the matter with Florence," she said. "I had hoped that the dreadful thing which happened years ago had subdued her spirit and tamed her a trifle, but she seems just as stubborn as ever. It was such a beautiful idea, and it came over me in the night. I thought I would tell Florence at once, and we might put our heads together and contrive a means by which the young folks could meet. But if she takes it up in that dreadful spirit, what is to be done?"

"But, of course, Mrs. Aylmer, it would never do," said Kitty. "How can you think of such a thing for a single moment?"

A Startling Meeting

itty went out soon afterward and joined Florence on the beach. They walked up and down, chatting eagerly. For a time nothing whatever was said about Mrs. Aylmer's queer suggestion, then suddenly Florence spoke of it.

"There is one thing I ought to say, Kitty."

"What is that?" asked Kitty.

"You must never mind the little Mum's oddities. She has lived alone on extremely circumscribed means for many years, and when she gets an idea into her head she broods on it."

"You mean, of course, what she said with regard to Mr. Trevor," said Kitty, flushing as she spoke.

"Yes, it wasn't nice of her," said Florence with a sigh. "And we won't either of us think of it again, Kitty. I have made up my mind not to marry."

"Why so?"

"For a great many reasons. One of them is that I vastly prefer my independence. Another is that I do not think a rich man is likely to come my way, and I do not want to have anything to do with a poor man whether he is nice or nasty. I have seen too

The two girls sat down on the beach then, and Florence rested her head on her friend's lap. "I will never scheme again, Kitty. I will never do anything underhand, and I will not marry the man my mother has singled out for me," she declared.

much of poverty. I have had it close to me all my days. I mean to do well in the world and to be indebted to no one. In a fortnight's time I am going to London. I have in my trunk half a dozen introductions to different people. I mean to use them; I mean to get something to do; I mean to be a success—to prove to the world that a girl can fight her own battles, live her own life, secure her reward, and be, in short, a success."

"Why, Florence," said her companion, "how well you speak, how excited you look!"

"I have not gone through all I have gone through in my life for nothing," was Florence's reply. The two girls sat down on the beach then, and Florence rested her head on her friend's lap. "I will never scheme again, I will never do anything underhand, and I will not marry the man my mother has singled out for me."

She had scarcely said the words before the attention of both girls was arrested by the sound of a merry laugh not ten yards away. They both looked around, and Florence's cheeks first of all grew vivid and then turned white. A gracefully dressed woman, or rather girl, was crossing the sands accompanied by a young man in a gray suit.

The man had broad shoulders, closely cropped, rather fair hair. He had a nice, open sort of face. He was tall, nearly six feet in height, and was bending toward the girl and talking to her. The girl continued to laugh, and once she glanced with a quick darting movement in the direction where Kitty and Florence were sitting. Then, touching her companion on the arm, she said, "I am tired; will you take me back to the hotel?"

Neither Kitty nor Florence said a word until the pair—the good-looking young man and the girl in her pretty summer dress—disappeared from view. Then Florence turned to Kitty.

"It is?" questioned Florence.

Kitty nodded.

"Who would have believed it?" continued Florence. She started up in her excitement.

"I do not think I can quite stand this," she said.

"But where has she come from?" asked Kitty.

"How can I tell? I never want to see her wicked face again."

"She looks just as young as she did six years ago," said Kitty. Then she added impulsively, "I am sorry I have seen her again; I never could bear her face. Do you think her eyes are set in her head straight, Flo?"

"I don't know anything about that," answered Florence recklessly. "Long ago she did me a great deal of harm. There came a time when I almost hated her. Whether her eyes are straight or not, her mind at least is crooked. Who is that man she is with?"

"He is good-looking and seems nice also," said Kitty.

Florence made no reply. The girls paced up and down together, but somehow the edge of the day's enjoyment seemed gone. They went in to their midday meal between twelve and one, and afterward Kitty, who said she felt a little tired, went to lie down. Florence, however, was still restless and perturbed. She hated the thought of Bertha Keys, and yet she had a curious longing to know something about her.

"I am not going to fight shy of her or show her that I am in the least afraid of her," thought Florence. "I can make myself much more disagreeable to her and much more dangerous than she can ever make herself to me. I wonder where she is staying?"

Mrs. Aylmer proposed that she and her daughter should spend the afternoon on the sands.

"Let us visit the shrimp-woman and get some fresh shrimp and perhaps a crab or a lobster for supper," said the little Mum, holding out a bait which would have quite won the day in the old times. But Florence had outgrown her taste for these special dainties.

"I want to go out alone, Little Mum," she said. "You and I and Kitty can have a walk after tea, but just for the present I must be alone." She pinned on her hat, put on her gloves, and left the cottage.

Mrs. Aylmer stood on the porch and watched her.

"A good girl, a fairly good-looking girl too," she said to herself, "but obstinate, obstinate as a mule. Even that trouble of long ago has not tamed her. She is the image of her poor dear father; he always was a man with a desperate will of his own."

Mrs. Aylmer watched Florence until she disappeared in the direction of the pier. There was a bench there, and a girl was seated on it. She wore a pink dress of some washing material and a large black shady hat. Florence came nearer and nearer. The girl, who was reading a book, dropped it and gazed in her direction. Presently Florence found herself within less than two hundred yards from the place where the other girl was seated. At this moment the girl flung down her book, uttered a hasty exclamation, and came forward.

"Is it or is it not Florence Aylmer?" she said. She held out both her hands, uttering a little cry of apparent pleasure.

Florence did not notice the outstretched hands. She came up to her.

"I have come on purpose," she said. "I knew you were here. What are you doing here?"

"Why should I tell you what I am doing?" replied Bertha. Her eyes slightly contracted, she pushed her hair away from her forehead, then she looked full at Florence and uttered a laugh. "What is the good of quarreling?" she said. "We have met. I am in the running. You are out of it. I am up and you are down. My prospects are first-rate, yours—"

"What do you mean? How can you tell anything about my prospects? Why do you trouble me? Why did you come to meet me just now?"

"Speak the truth," said Miss Keys, "were you not coming on purpose to see me?"

Florence was silent for a moment.

"I recognized you this morning," she said, "and I was restless to know why you were here."

"You always were queer and rude, Bertha, and time has not improved you."

"Ah, curiosity, you are Eve's own daughter," said Bertha Keys with a laugh. "Well, now that we have met, we may as well talk the thing out. Can you deny that you are down and I am up?"

"I neither deny nor affirm your statement," replied Florence. "I have never heard of you—I have never mentioned your name since that dreadful day at Cherry Court six years ago."

"Six years this autumn—not quite six years yet," replied Bertha, correcting her. "Yes, I too remember that day," she said thoughtfully. "It seemed a bad day for me, and yet it was a good one. I have feathered my nest. You stepped out of it and I stepped in. Do you understand?"

"I don't."

"You have grown a good deal, Florence Aylmer," Bertha commented, looking her all over. "You are what would be called a fine young woman. If you had had the advantages of a refined life, of very good dress, you might, now that you are grown up, command almost any future. As it is . . ." she shrugged her shoulders.

"What is the matter with my dress?" asked Florence. "You always were queer and rude, Bertha, and time has not improved you."

"You cannot say that I am badly dressed," said Bertha Keys, and she glanced at her exquisitely cut pink zephyr skirt, her pretty blouse, and her neat shoes.

Florence also eyed her all over.

"You are well dressed up," she said. "But what of that? Your face never changes."

"Thank you for the compliment," replied Bertha. "I cannot say that you are well got up, and your face, if it has changed, is not more beautiful than it promised to be."

"Pray leave my face alone. It belongs to me, not to you," retorted Florence.

"Do you want to know what I am doing now? How I am managing to live?" asked Bertha.

"You can tell me if you please. If you prefer not to say anything, it does not matter in the least."

"But it does matter. It matters a good deal," replied Bertha. "You did something very silly long ago. You thought to succeed, but you failed. It was not my fault. I did what I could for you. I have a gift for writing, but I need not wear my brain out thinking of curious essays and well-devised stories and clever plots. I am working at my own story, and I think it will come off well."

"But what do you mean? Where are you?"

"We are staying at the Crown and Garter for the present."

"We?" questioned Florence in a questioning tone.

"Yes. Have not you guessed? Mrs. Aylmer, Mr. Trevor, and I."

"You don't mean it?" said Florence, springing to her feet. "Aunt Susan! Are you staying with her?"

"Yes, and I fancy I am indispensable to her. I have lived with her for nearly six years. I manage her affairs; I write her letters; I attend to her business; she consults me about everything. She goes where I like; she does what I want. The nest is comfortable. It was meant for you, but it fits me. Now perhaps you know."

"And Mr.—Mr. Trevor?" said Florence, in a trembling voice.

"Oh, he fits me too. He is a very good fellow, very nice indeed. He thinks I am quite an angel. He admires my talent, as he calls it. I believe he would be very sad if I were not there. Yes, Florence, you did well for me when you lost that scholarship. I thought I would tell you."

"Oh! oh!" said Florence, trembling and turning pale. "But if Aunt Susan knew! If she knew!"

"Yes, if she knew," said Bertha, "but she does not know, and of course you won't tell her."

"You think I won't. But—but Mum will."

"I don't think so. It would be much worse for yourselves if you did. I can hoodwink her—I can turn her against your mother; I can make her more bitterly opposed to you. Now you have to understand. I have long felt that I must come to an understanding with you. You must keep silent. If you speak you will do very little good, but it is possible you may give me an uncomfortable half-hour. Now, I don't care to have an uncomfortable half-hour, and above all things, I don't want Mr. Trevor set against me."

"Do you—do you mean to marry him?" asked Florence abruptly.

Bertha Keys colored very faintly.

"You are impertinent," she said. "I refuse to answer. I am comfortable where I am, and I mean to stay there. If you put Mr. Trevor against me, if you put Mrs. Aylmer against me, it will be all the worse for yourself. But if, on the other hand, you respect my secret, I can make things perhaps a shade more comfortable for you."

"Oh, oh, Bertha, no," said poor Florence. She covered her face—her cheeks were crimson. "I hate you! I can never be your friend. Why did you come here?"

"I came on purpose. I have not lost sight of you. You know something about me which I do not want the world to know. You could make things uncomfortable for me. I guessed that you would be coming here about now, and Mrs. Aylmer, Mr. Trevor, and I came to the Crown and Garter at my suggestion. We will leave again the day after tomorrow. But not—not until you have made me a promise."

An
Evil Genius

fter Bertha said the last words, Florence was quite
silent. Bertha turned and looked at her and she said to
herself, "She will protect me for her own sake. The girl
who could stoop to deceit, who could use my assistance to gain
her own ends six years ago, is not immaculate now. She will be
extremely useful in many ways, and my secret is absolutely safe."

So Bertha leaned back against the bench, crossed one prettily
shod foot over the other, and looked out across the summer sea.
Presently Florence spoke in a low tone.

"Goodbye," she said. She rose as she uttered the word.

"Why do you say that? Sit down again. We have come to no
terms."

"We cannot come to any," answered Florence, still in that low,
almost heartbroken voice. Then all of a sudden, without the
least warning, she burst into tears.

"You bring the hateful past back to me, Bertha," she said.

"It is very silly of you indeed to cry," said Bertha. "And as to
the past, goodness knows it is dead and buried deep enough
unless you choose to dig it out of its grave. Leave it alone,

Florence, and come to terms with me. Now, for goodness' sake stop crying!"

"I won't tell of you just at present," said Florence. "That is the only thing I can say now." Once more she rose.

"You had Kitty Shars-ton with you this morn-ing," continued Bertha. "She recognized me too, did she not?"

"Yes, we both recognized you."

"I never did anything particular to injure her; I mean, everything came right for her," continued Bertha. "She could

She did not want to injure Bertha, and yet she disliked her as much as it was possible for her to dislike anyone.

scarcely interfere. It is you and your mother who can do me harm. Even if you try, I may not be deprived of my present comfortable home and my delightful future. But I do not choose to run the risk, so you must promise that you won't betray me."

"Does mother know that Mrs. Aylmer—that Aunt Susan is staying at Dawlish?" continued Florence.

"She probably knows it by this time. Mrs. Aylmer has written her a note asking her to call to see her. She won't see you, so don't imagine it."

"I don't want to see her."

"Before your mother accepts that invitation, I want you to secure her silence," continued Bertha briskly, "or I will see her myself." She thought for a moment over a new idea that had come to her. Her lips then broke into a smile.

"How stupid of me!" she said. "I never thought of your mother before; she is the very person. I will meet you tomorrow morning here, Florence, and then you can tell me what you decide. It will be all the better for you if you are wise; all the worse for you if you are silly."

Florence turned away from her companion without even bidding her goodbye. Her heart was in a tumult. She did not want to injure Bertha, and yet she disliked her as much as it was possible for her to dislike anyone. "She makes me feel so terrible!" thought Florence. "She brings back the dreadful past. Oh, I was a wicked girl. But she helped to make me so!"

By the time she had reached her mother's cottage, she resolved to tell her exactly what had transpired and to ask her advice. "The little Mum will tell me what is right to do," thought the girl.

But when she entered the house Mrs. Aylmer was nowhere to be seen.

Sukey came forward instead. "Well, Miss Flo," she said, "that aunt of yours has put in an appearance. Your mother has had a note from her. She is staying at the Crown and Garter, and Mrs. Aylmer has gone up there to tea. No, you are not invited, Miss Flo, and sorry I am that you are not."

"It doesn't matter, Sukey," replied Florence. She sighed as she spoke.

"Have you a bit of a headache, my dear?" asked the old servant.

"Yes, I think I have," answered the girl.

"I'll get you your tea, and the tea for the other pretty young lady too. You can have it on the porch. It's a lovely evening. It doesn't do for girls to have headaches, but there's nothing to set you right like a cup of tea."

Sukey bustled off to prepare the simple meal, and presently Kitty came downstairs. She was refreshed by her sleep and inclined to be merry with Florence. Florence, however, felt too anxious to talk much.

"What is the matter with you, Florry? Are you worried about anything?" asked her companion. "Oh, I suppose it is about that wretched Bertha Keys. What can she be doing here?"

Afternoon Tea

The good hostess knows, as a rule, both how to buy and how to make tea. It pays to buy the best; the best costs considerably more than the ordinary quality, but goes farther.

The assistance of the maid is not required for the simple five-o'clock tea service, even when guests are present. After she has placed the tray before her mistress she may retire. The hostess, or a daughter or friend of the house, pours the tea, and the guests help themselves and each other. There is no formality about it. The keynote of the afternoon tea should be sociability.

The only necessary accompaniment in the way of solid refreshment is bread and butter—the bread cut very thin—dainty wafers, or delicate cakes of some kind. This, of course, is "afternoon tea," in its simplest form.

—The Modern Hostess, 1904

"You'll be amazed when I tell you that I saw Bertha this afternoon," Florence offered. "Where do you think she is staying? What post do you think she has secured?"

"How can I tell?" answered Kitty, raising her brows. "I am afraid I don't greatly care. All you and I want is that she should not come into our lives."

"But she has come into my life once more," said poor Florence, clasping and unclasping her strong white hands as she spoke. "I believe she is an evil genius. Do you know where she is staying?"

"No."

"She is living with Aunt Susan Aylmer as her companion."

Kitty was so much startled by the news that she sprang to her feet.

"Never!" she cried.

"It is the case. She has been with Aunt Susan for years."

"But how did she get the post? From the little I have seen of your aunt, she is one of the most particular, fastidious women in the world."

"Trust Bertha to manage that," replied Florence in a bitter tone. "But anyhow, she is very much afraid of me. She does not want me to see Aunt Susan nor tell her what I know."

"And what will you do, Flo?"

"I am undecided at the present moment."

"I think you ought to tell her," said Kitty quite gravely.

"She won't see me, and I do dread making Bertha a greater enemy than she is at present."

"All the same, I think you ought to tell her," replied Kitty. She looked serious and earnest as she spoke.

"If I were you, I would" replied Florence with some bitterness. "But she frightens me. And she threatened to make it go harder for Mum."

"Well, take your tea," said Kitty with a frown, "and let us go out for a walk."

~V~

Maurice Trevor

he girls had just finished their tea when Mrs. Aylmer, with flushed cheeks, and wearing her very best turned-for-the-twentieth-time dress, entered the little room where they were seated.

"Well, well, girls," she said, "where do you think I have been?"

"I know, Mummy," said Florence.

"You know!" replied Mrs. Aylmer. "Who told you?"

"Sukey."

"Really that woman can keep nothing to herself. Your aunt is going to send me a trunk full of old clothes. I dare say some of them may be made to fit you, Flo."

"I don't think so, Mother," answered Florence.

"What is the use of being proud? She's a very fine figure of a woman still. And she has a most charming secretary, a sort of companion, a delightful girl. She and I walked down together almost to this door. She is in your shoes, my poor Florence. But she is really a *very* nice girl."

"I have seen her today, Mother; I know who she is," said Florence gravely. "Her name is Bertha Keys."

"Bertha Keys," replied Mrs. Aylmer. "Bertha Keys?"

"You know who Bertha Keys is, Mother. She is the girl, the pupil teacher, who behaved so badly at Cherry Court School six years ago."

"Oh, we won't mention that affair. It is dead and buried. We are not going to dig it out of its grave," replied Mrs. Aylmer.

Florence looked full at her mother. Then she got up hastily. "The fact is, Mother, I do not care to talk of it," she said. "The whole thing has upset me very much."

"Well, darling, I cannot think that it is your affair. It is bitterly disappointing that you should have lost your Aunt Susan's patronage. But your aunt was most agreeable today. We had quite a nice little tea, and that young man I told you of, Mr. Trevor, he came in. He is a charming person, my dear. Quite fascinating. I was much taken with him. I longed to ask him to call, but I saw Susan would allow no liberties."

"We are going for a walk now, Mother," said Florence.

"Well, dear, do. You both look pale. I want you to have a right good time. Yes, I am quite pleased with my visit. There is no use in quarreling with your relations. Oh, and the moment Susan looked at my poor turned skirt—it is shiny, is it not, Miss Sharston?—she spoke about that trunk of clothes which is to arrive next week. She turned to the charming Miss Keys and asked her to collect them."

"And you stood it, Mother? You really stood it?" asked Florence, the color coming and going on her face.

"My dear, good girl, beggars cannot be choosers. I have been absolutely at my wit's end for clothes. I not only stood it, but on the way home I gave Miss Keys a hint as to the sort of things I wanted. I told her to try and smuggle into the trunk one of your aunt's rich black silks. She said she thought she could manage it, as she has at least four or five at the present moment, and never can tell herself how many she has. I told Miss Keys to let it be four in the future, and send the fifth one to me, and she laughed. She is a very clever, agreeable girl and said she thought it could be done. I am made. I'll astonish the neighbors this winter."

"Come out, Kitty," said poor Florence, turning to her companion. She felt that, fond as she was of the little Mum, she could not endure any more of her society for the present.

The moment the girls had departed, Mrs. Aylmer turned abruptly, went to the door of the little sitting room and locked it. She then put her hand into her pocket and brought out four sovereigns. "Is it true? She says she can give me more by-and-by. Have I the evidence of my own senses?" she thought. "I never met a nicer girl than Miss Keys. Of course, she did wrong years ago. But so, for that matter, did my own poor Florence. That she is setting her cap at that handsome Mr. Trevor there is no doubt, but perhaps Florence can win him over her head. We will see about that. Anyhow, I am not going to injure the poor, dear girl, and I shall tell Florence so."

Mrs. Aylmer felt far too excited to sit down. From the depths of poverty she suddenly felt herself raised almost to a pinnacle of wealth, as she estimated it.

As she considered the possibility of a very definite line of action, she still continued to stand by the tiny window of the sitting room, and from this vantage point she saw a young man in a gray tweed suit strolling slowly in the direction of the beach.

"Mr. Trevor!" she said to herself. "Mr. Maurice Trevor, as gentlemanly looking a young fellow as I have seen for many a day. He reminds me of poor dear Florence's father. He had just that downright sort of air, and he was fond of sticking his hands into his pockets too—yes, and he used to whistle, as I see that young fellow is whistling. I am always told that whistling shows a generous disposition. Now, if I could only introduce them! Florence and Kitty Sharston are on the beach—Mr. Trevor is going down to the beach. I'll go and take a walk. It is a fine evening and it will do me good."

She could walk quickly enough when she chose, and she knew every yard of the ground. Soon she was on the beach. Mr. Trevor was walking slowly in front of her. His straw hat was pushed slightly forward over his blue eyes, his hands were still in his pockets, he was looking straight ahead. His thoughts were evidently not quite to his taste, for he frowned now and then and looked over the wide expanse of sands. Occasionally he stood quite still. Thus Mrs. Aylmer found it easy to catch up.

"Good evening, Mr. Trevor," she said in her cheerful tone.

He started when she spoke to him, turned to look at her, and then took off his hat.

"Good evening," he said. "I did not recognize you at first."

"No wonder, as you only saw me for the first time today. I am taking a stroll. It is very pleasant here in the evenings, is it not?"

"Very pleasant! It is a charming place," said Trevor.

Mrs. Aylmer considered for a moment whether she should proceed on her walk alone, or whether she should try to induce the young man to accompany her.

"I am looking for my girls," she said. "They went down on the beach half an hour ago. Did you happen to see them, Mr. Trevor, as you were walking?"

"I have only just come out. I have not seen anyone," was his answer.

"Are you quite sure? I *know* they were going on the sands, my two girls, my daughter and her friend. I should like to introduce you to my daughter, Mr. Trevor."

36

"I should be pleased to know her," he answered, still speaking in that vague sort of way which showed that he was thinking of something else.

Mrs. Aylmer held both her hands before her eyes. Thus shaded from the evening sun, she was able to look long and steadily across the beach.

Florence was gazing with a frown between her dark brows at her mother and the man who was by her mother's side. If she could have fled, she would have. . ."

"I do declare I believe those two are the very girls we are looking for," she cried. "If you will come with me now—if you don't have anything special to do—I'll introduce you."

Trevor had, of course, no excuse to make.

"It was the greatest possible pleasure to me to meet you today," continued the little widow. "I am so glad that my poor sister-in-law has a bright young fellow like you to look thoroughly after her affairs."

"But I don't look after them," he said. "Mrs. Aylmer has been extremely good to me, but the person who manages her business affairs is that very clever young lady Miss Keys."

"Oh, what a genius she is!" said Mrs. Aylmer. "A wonderful girl, quite charming."

"Do you think so?" answered Trevor. He looked at the little widow, and the faintest dawn of an amused smile stole into his eyes.

"Do I think so? I am immensely taken with her," said Mrs. Aylmer. "She is, I know, the greatest comfort to my dear sister-in-law. How splendidly considerate Susan is! I don't know what I should do without her, Mr. Trevor. I will say it, you are a very lucky person to be such a favorite."

"Mrs. Aylmer has done a great deal for me," said the young man. "She has, after a fashion, adopted me."

"And you are very glad, are you not?"

"Yes, I am glad," he replied. "Is that your daughter?" he continued, as if he wished to turn the conversation.

"That is my dear daughter, Florence," Mrs. Aylmer said excitedly.

Florence and Kitty Sharston were seated on the edge of a rock. Kitty was poking with her parasol at some sea anemones which were clinging to the rock just under the water. Florence was gazing with a frown between her dark brows at her mother and the man who was by her mother's side. If she could have fled, she would have, but Mrs. Aylmer, who knew Florence's ways to perfection, now raised her voice in a shrill scream.

"Stay where you are, Florence. I am coming to sit with you. So is Mr. Trevor. Don't stir until we come up."

Poor Florence's blush was so vivid that it was good it was too far off to be noticed. There was nothing to do, however, but to obey. Mrs. Aylmer came up in high good humor and made the necessary introductions.

~VI~

Mrs. Aylmer's Strategy

ow, this is cozy," said the widow. "Quite what I call friendly. I love these impromptu little meetings. Look at those great rolling waves, Mr. Trevor, and tell me if you ever saw anything finer."

"Oh, Mother, don't be a goose," said Florence. Try as she would she couldn't help laughing. Trevor looked into her dancing eyes, noticed how white her teeth were and, moving a step nearer, sat down by her side.

"Do you know this place well?" he asked.

"It has been my home for the greater part of my life," was Florence's reply.

She felt inclined to be rude to Mr. Trevor, the man who was adopted by Aunt Susan, who was doubtless the chosen and confidential friend of Bertha Keys. But Trevor had a gentle and very polite manner. It never occurred to him that this somewhat showy-looking girl could dislike his company. He was accustomed to being made much of and petted a good deal by women, and before many minutes had passed Florence, in spite of herself, was chatting gaily with him.

39

She forgot that her mother had maneuvered in the most open and brazen way to secure this introduction; she forgot everything but the pleasure of talking to a fellow-creature who seemed to understand her sentiments—and also to approve of them. When a young man approves of a girl's ideas, when he likes to look into her face and watch the sparkle of her eyes, she must be one in a thousand if she does not find him agreeable, sympathetic, and all the rest.

Presently Trevor suggested that he and Florence should go down on the beach and find a certain pool, which at low water contained the most lovely of sea anemones to be found anywhere round the coast.

"Oh, come too, Mother; come too, Kitty," said Florence, as she jumped to her feet.

"No, my dear, I am much too tired," said Mrs. Aylmer. She clutched at Kitty's skirt as the young girl was about to rise and pulled her back.

"Stay by me, Miss Sharston. I have much to say to you," remarked the widow.

Accordingly, Florence and Trevor, Florence well-knowing that Kitty had not been allowed to come with her, started on their tour of investigation alone. They found the sea anemones and chatted about them. Trevor asked Florence if she would like to begin to make a collection. Florence began by saying, "Yes," but finally refused the tempting offer which Trevor made to help her.

"I am going to London in a few days," she said.

"To London?" he asked. "Now? In this broiling weather?"

"Yes, why not? Don't you like London in August?"

"I never care for London at any time—in August it is particularly detestable," was his reply. "We are going to stay here for a day or two. I think you know Miss Keys. She told me that you were an old friend."

"She was at the same school with me years ago," said Florence, flushing as she spoke. "Oh, do look at that beauty in the corner—a kind of dark electric-blue. What a wonderful creature! Oh, and that rose-colored one near it! Sea anemones are like great tropical flowers."

Meanwhile Mrs. Aylmer was consulting with Kitty.

"Shall we or shall we not ask him to supper?" she said. "What do you think?"

"I am sure I don't know," said Kitty. She looked at her companion with those innocent, wide-open gray eyes, which were her greatest charm.

"He has quite taken to Florence; don't you see for yourself?"

"Oh, yes. Everyone takes to her," replied Kitty with enthusiasm. "She is so nice and honest and downright."

Mrs. Aylmer sighed.

"She has had her troubles, poor child, but in the end things may come round in a most wonderful way. Do you know, I like him very much?"

"Like who?" asked Kitty.

"Really, Miss Sharston, you are a little silly—Mr. Trevor, Mr. Maurice Trevor, the adopted son of my wealthy sister-in-law Susan Aylmer."

"Oh, yes," said Kitty. "I forgot that you were talking about him."

"I was asking you, my dear, if you thought we might invite him to join us at supper."

"Why not?" said Kitty.

"Well, Sukey's temper grows worse and worse. We were going to have a very small supper, not what you could put a man down to. But if he were coming you and I might just whip round to the shrimp shop and get a lobster. Lobster with a nice salad is what young men delight in. It is an enormous expense to go to, but if in the end—"

"Oh, dear," said Kitty, rising. She looked at Mrs. Aylmer, and the color rose in a delicate wave all over her pretty face. "Oh, I would not," she said. "I don't think Florence would like it—I am certain she would not. Oh, you know her. She will be rude; don't do it, please don't."

But if there was one person more determined than another to have her own way, it was the little Mum. She had only vaguely considered the possibility of asking Mr. Trevor to partake of their humble meal when she first spoke of it; now that Kitty opposed it she made up her mind that by hook or by crook she would convey him to their house. "What a victory it would be! Susan Aylmer, her rich sister-in-law, would be waiting and wondering why her handsome and fascinating young protégé did not appear. And all the time he'd be in the tiny cottage, partaking of the humble fare of Mrs. Aylmer the less, with Florence close to his side. Oh, it was worth a struggle!"

Mrs. Aylmer rose to her feet. A good stiff wind was beginning to blow, and she staggered for a moment as it caught her stout little person. Then she raised her voice, "Florence!"

"Yes, Mother," called Florence, turning. She was a hundred yards away now, and Trevor was talking in a more fascinating way than ever about sea anemones and their beauties.

"If Mr. Trevor would come back to supper with us, we should be much pleased to see him. I will expect you, dear, to bring him in when you have done your little stroll. So pleased if you will join us, Mr. Trevor."

All these words were shrieked on the sea breeze. Florence made a reply which did not quite reach her mother's ears. Mrs.

Aylmer shouted once more and then, seizing Kitty's hand, turned in the direction of the little town.

"Now for the shrimp woman," she said. "We must be as quick as possible. Sukey will be in a flurry. But never mind. It is worth the effort."

Poor Kitty had never felt more uncomfortable. Really, there were times when the little Mum was almost unendurable. The lobster was chosen—quite a nice expensive one. Kitty was sent to the nearest greengrocer's shop in order to secure the crispest lettuce and half-a-pound of tomatoes. Laden with these spoils, the girl and the elder lady reentered the tiny cottage.

"They say he is a very pushing and a very designing young man, and that he twists poor Susan round his little finger."

"Now then, Sukey," called out Mrs. Aylmer, "brisk is the word. I have caught the most charming young man you ever heard of, and he is coming to supper with us."

Sukey stared at her mistress.

"What folly are you up to now, ma'am?" she asked.

"No folly at all, my dear Sukey. Here's sixpence for you; don't say anything about it. Make the salad as only you know how and trim the lobster. I was considerate, Sukey, and I got things that will not give you trouble. Kitty, my dear sweet little girl, help me to arrange the table. It will be quite romantic. The young man will enjoy it; I am certain he will. Dear Flo! What fortune to have a mother like me to look after her and see that she does not waste her opportunities."

"But," said Kitty, changing color as she spoke, "do you really mean—"

THE FRUGAL DINNER

For the small dinner to which guests have been invited informally, the menu is prepared with the same care that would be given to a more elaborate menu, and the order of the courses is the same. Where there is but one maid to do both cooking and serving, everything that can be done in advance to facilitate matters should be attended to.

Place upon the table all of the knives and forks that will be needed. See that during dinner such articles as will be required from time to time are in their place upon the sideboard or the side table.

Have a clean table-cloth; it is a great moral factor, and so, too, are flowers on the table, however simple the bunch. In other words, serve what there is to serve, even the frugalest meal, as daintily as possible, and it will add incalculably to the attractiveness of the home

—The Modern Hostess, 1904

"I mean that mum's the word at present," was Mrs. Aylmer's mysterious remark. "Help me, Kitty Sharston, like a good girl, and for goodness' sake don't make yourself look too pretty tonight. I don't want him to turn his attention to you, I may as well say frankly."

Kitty earnestly longed for the moment when she should leave Mrs. Aylmer's cottage.

The supper was prepared; everything was arranged. And then the two ladies stood by the window watching for the return of the truants, as Mrs. Aylmer was now pleased to call Florence and Mr. Trevor.

Presently she saw her daughter coming up the somewhat steep path alone.

"Flo, Flo, child, where is he? Is he coming?" she called out.

"Oh no, Mother," said Florence.

"Did you give him my invitation?"

"I told him he was not to accept it," said Florence. "Oh dear me, Mother, don't be silly. But I say, what a nice lobster, and I am so hungry."

≈ VII ≈
Straining Against Silken Chains

eanwhile Trevor went slowly back to the hotel. He had enjoyed his talk with Florence. He liked her brusque way. She didn't flatter him, and she was, he considered, a particularly attractive girl. In Mrs. Aylmer's society he was made a great deal of and fussed over, and when that happens to a young man he always enjoys the sort of girl who snubs him by way of contrast. As he liked Florence, and was in the mood for a bit of adventure, he would gladly have accepted her mother's invitation to supper if she had not tabooed it.

"You are not to come," said Florence, looking at him with her wide-open, frank, dark eyes. "Mother is the soul of hospitality, but we are very poor. We have nothing proper to give you for supper, and I for one would much rather you did not come."

"I do not in the least mind what I eat," he said in a somewhat pleading tone, and he looked full at Florence with his blue eyes.

"Nevertheless, you are not to come. It is only my mother's way. She always goes on like that with strangers. I never allow people to accept her invitations."

After this there was nothing more to be said, and Florence and Trevor bade each other a very friendly goodbye.

When Trevor reached the Crown and Garter he found that Mrs. Aylmer and Miss Keys were already at dinner. They had both wondered where he was, and Bertha Keys had been a little anxious and a little uneasy. When he came in, the faces of both ladies brightened.

"What makes you so late?" said Mrs. Aylmer, looking up at him.

"I had a bit of an adventure," he said. He drew his chair to the table. "There was a slight chance of my not coming in to supper at all," he continued. "I met that charming little lady who visited you today, Mrs. Aylmer."

"What?" said Mrs. Aylmer, dropping her knife and fork.

"I met her again and she introduced me to her daughter and to another young lady who is staying with them. By the way, they are your relations, so the little lady told me. She was very hospitable and invited me to supper. I should have been very glad to go if the young lady had not told me that I must not accept her mother's invitation."

Now, these remarks were anything but agreeable to Mrs. Aylmer, and still less did they suit Bertha Keys. Neither lady said anything, however, at the present moment, but each glanced at the other. After a time, Mrs. Aylmer stretched out her hand and touched Trevor on his sleeve.

"I am sorry you have made the acquaintance of Miss Florence Aylmer," she said.

"Sorry? Why?" he asked. "I consider her a remarkably nice girl."

"I regret to have to inform you that she is anything but a nice girl. I will tell you about her another time. It is quite contrary to my wishes that you should have anything to do with her. Do you understand?"

Trevor flushed. He had a way of looking annoyed at times, and he looked annoyed now. His silken chains sometimes vexed him a great deal. He often wondered whether he had done right in allowing himself to become Mrs. Aylmer's adopted son. Bertha, however, gave him a warning glance, and he said nothing.

Presently dinner was over, and Bertha beckoned him to join her on the balcony.

"Shall we go out on the sands?" she said. "I have something I want to say to you."

"But Mrs. Aylmer has something to say to me also—something about that particularly nice girl, Miss Florence Aylmer."

"She will not say it to you tonight. She has a headache, and I persuaded her to go early to bed. I quite sympathize with you, too, about Florence. She is one of my greatest friends."

Trevor gave Bertha a grateful glance.

"I am so glad you like her," he said. "I was never yet mistaken about anyone, and I took to her frank ways. She looks like the sort of girl who will never deceive you."

Bertha gave a peculiar smile, which vanished almost as soon as it visited her face.

"Shall we meet, say, in twenty minutes," she said, "just by the pier? I must see Mrs. Aylmer to bed."

"Very well," he answered.

Bertha left the balcony, and Trevor tried to soothe his somewhat ruffled feelings. He had never liked Mrs. Aylmer less than he did at that moment.

"It is horrid when a woman runs down a girl," he said to himself. "Such bad form, and, as to this girl, it is impossible Mrs. Aylmer can know anything against her."

Presently he looked at his watch and prepared to keep his appointment with Bertha. He liked Bertha Keys very much. She was always jolly and good-tempered, and she often tried to smooth over matters when there was any little difference between himself and Mrs. Aylmer. When he reached the pier he found her waiting for him. It was a moonlit night and the young couple began to pace up and down.

"What is it?" he asked at last. "Have you anything special to say?"

"I know you are in a bad humor, and I am not surprised," she said.

"Listen, Miss Keys," said Trevor. He turned and faced her. "I often feel that I cannot stand this sort of thing much longer. It is like being in chains. I would much rather talk the matter out with Mrs. Aylmer—tell her I am very much obliged to her for her kind intentions with regard to me, but that I would sooner carve out my own career in life and be indebted to no one."

"And how silly that would be!" said Bertha. "But what do you want Mrs. Aylmer to do?"

"To let me go. I feel like a captive in her train. It is not manly. I never felt more annoyed than when she spoke to me as she did this evening. It is horrid when a woman abuses a girl—such bad taste."

"You know how peculiar she is," said Bertha. "But you suit her better than anyone I know. You want her to give you money to allow you to live in town. I am sure I can manage it. I quite understand that you must hate being tied to her apron trings."

"It is detestable," said the young man, "and if it were not for my own mother, who seems so happy about me and so grateful to Mrs. Aylmer, I should break with her tomorrow."

"I quite sympathize with you," remarked Bertha. "You must have money, and you must go to town. You want to read for the law exam. I will see that it is arranged. Mrs. Aylmer is rich, but not rich enough for you to live your life in idleness. It would break her heart now if you deserted her. She has gone through so much."

"What do you mean?"

"I cannot tell you."

"Why does she dislike Miss Florence Aylmer?"

"I would rather not say."

"But she will tell me herself."

"I shall beg of her not to do so."

"If there is a frank, openhearted, nice-looking girl, she is the one . . . I defy you to throw a stone at her."

"By the way," said Trevor, after a pause, "is this girl Mrs. Aylmer's niece?"

"She is her niece by marriage. Mrs. Aylmer's husband was Florence Aylmer's uncle."

"Then in the name of all that is just," cried Trevor impetuously, "why should I have the fortune that is really meant for Florence Aylmer? Oh, this is unendurable," he declared. "I cannot stand it. I will tell Mrs. Aylmer tomorrow that I am obliged to her, but that I will not occupy a false position."

"You will do fearful harm if you make such a remark," said Bertha. "Something which I cannot tell you, but—" Bertha's lips quivered and her face was very pale.

"What is it? Having told me so much, you must go on."

Bertha was silent for a moment.

"What has Miss Aylmer done? If there is a frank, openhearted, nice-looking girl, she is the one. I do not care so much for her mother, but Miss Aylmer herself—I defy you to throw a stone at her."

"I own that she is a nice girl, a very nice girl. But once, once—well, anyhow, she managed to offend Mrs. Aylmer. You must not ask me for particulars. I want you to be most careful to avoid the subject with Mrs. Aylmer. Florence offended her, and she has resolved to never see her and never speak to her again. She is annoyed at your having made her acquaintance, and I doubt not we shall leave Dawlish tomorrow on that account. Be satisfied that Florence only did what perhaps another girl equally tempted would have done, but it was—"

"It was what? The worst thing you can do is to throw out innuendoes about a girl. What did she do?"

"She was not quite straight, if you must know—not quite straight about a prize which was offered in the school where she was being educated."

"She told me that you were a teacher in the same school."

"Did she?" said Bertha. Her face turned pale, but her companion was not looking at her at that moment. "Ah, yes, poor girl. That is how I happen to know all about it. It was hushed up at the time, and of course Florence has quite retrieved her character. But if you do not wish to bring fresh trouble upon the niece you will avoid the subject with her aunt. That is what I wished to say to you."

"How can I avoid it? It is quite impossible for me to be long with Mrs. Aylmer and prevent her speaking her mind to me."

"I have been thinking of that," said Bertha. "The very best thing you can do is to go up to London tomorrow morning."

"I go to London tomorrow?"

"Yes. Go away for the present. I will tell her that you have had sudden news of your mother."

"But it wouldn't be true." Trevor darted a keen glance at his companion.

Bertha colored again.

She said, after a pause, "I want you to keep away for your own sake. If what I have suggested does not please you, think of something else."

"I will tell her that I wish for a change. That is true enough," he answered. "But how will that help me? When I come back, she will tell me the thing you do not wish me to hear about Miss Aylmer."

"Oh, I never said I did not wish you to hear it. I think it would be better for your peace of mind not to hear it."

Trevor stamped his foot impatiently. "I will *not* go away tomorrow," he said after a pause. "I should like to see Miss Florence Aylmer again. I will ask her to tell me frankly what occurred some years ago."

"You will?" cried Bertha, and her face looked frightened.

"Yes," he answered, looking full into her eyes, "I will. She is perfectly honest. She can excuse herself if necessary. Anyhow, she shall have the chance of telling her own story in her own way."

~VIII~

Bertha's Quandary

t was by no means the first time that Bertha Keys had found herself in a quandary. She was very clever at getting out of these tight corners. But never had she been more absolutely nonplused than at the present moment.

When she and Florence had both left Cherry Court School her prospects had been dark. She had been dismissed without any hope of a character reference, and had, as it were, to begin the world over again. Then chance put Mrs. Aylmer the great in her way.

Mrs. Aylmer was very sore and angry just then. She disliked Florence immensely for having disgraced her, and she was looking around anxiously for an heir. With Bertha Keys she felt soothed, sympathized with, restored to a good deal of her former calm. By slow degrees she told Bertha almost all of her history. In particular, she consulted with Bertha on the subject of an heir.

"I must leave my money to someone," she said. "I hate the idea of giving it to charities. Charity, in my opinion, begins at home."

"That it does, truly," answered Bertha, her queer green-gray eyes fixed on her employer's face.

"And Florence Aylmer being completely out of the question," continued Mrs. Aylmer, "and Florence's mother being about the biggest fool that ever breathed, I must look in another direction for my heir."

"Why not adopt a boy?" said Bertha on one of these occasions.

"Adopt a boy? A boy?"

"Well, a young man," said Bertha, coloring.

Mrs. Aylmer gave Bertha a withering look for response, and this young lady found herself more or less in disgrace for the next few days. Nevertheless, the idea took root. Mrs. Aylmer, having found girls failures, began to think that all that was desirable might be encompassed in the person of a boy.

So Mrs. Aylmer began to look around for a suitable boy to adopt and leave her money to. No sooner did she seriously contemplate this idea than the opportunity to adopt a very special boy occurred to her. She had an old friend, a great friend, a woman whom as a girl she had really loved. This woman was now a widow. Mrs. Trevor had married an army man who had died gloriously in battle. He had won his Victoria Cross medal before he departed to a better world. His widow had a small pension and one son. Mrs. Trevor happened just about this very time to write to Mrs. Aylmer. She told her of her great and abiding sorrow and spoke with the deepest delight and admiration of her boy.

"Send Maurice to spend a week with me," was Mrs. Aylmer's reply via telegraph.

In some astonishment, Mrs. Trevor packed up her boy's things—he was a lad of eighteen at this time—and sent him off to visit Mrs. Aylmer in her beautiful country place.

Maurice Trevor was frank, innocent, open as the day. He pleased the widow because he did not try to please her in the least. He spent a week, a fortnight, a month with the widow, and went back to his mother, having secured a great deal more than he bargained for in the course of his visit.

Mrs. Aylmer now wrote to Mrs. Trevor and said that she liked Maurice very much, that she had no heir to leave her money to, and that if Maurice really turned out quite to her satisfaction she would make him her future heir. He must live with her during the holidays. He must give up his mother's society, except for a very short time in the year. He must be thoroughly well educated. He must, on no account, enter the army. He must have a university education.

These terms, generous in themselves, were eagerly accepted by the all-but-penniless widow. She had some difficulty, however, in persuading young Trevor to, as he expressed it, sell his independence. In the end her wishes prevailed. He went to Trinity College, Cambridge, took honors there, and now at twenty-four years of age was to a certain extent his own master. And yet, he was more tied and fettered than almost any other young man he knew. To tell the truth, he hated his own position. Mrs. Aylmer considered that he owed her undying gratitude. And lately he felt he could scarcely stand his silken fetters any longer.

❧ ❧ ❧

Bertha, as she stood now in the moonlit window of her little room at the Crown and Garter, thought over Maurice Trevor—his future prospects and his past life. She also thought about Florence.

"From the way he spoke tonight," she thought, "very, very little would make him fall in love with Florence. Now that is quite the very last thing to be desired. They must not meet again. I mean to inherit Mrs. Aylmer's property, either as the heiress in my own person or as the wife of Maurice Trevor. It is true that I am older than he, but I have three times his sense. I can manage him if another girl does not interfere. He must leave here immediately. I must make some excuse. His mother is not quite so impractical as he is; I must manage things through her. One thing, at least, I am resolved on: He must not hear the story of Florence—at least not through Florence herself. And Mrs. Aylmer must not tell him the story of what occurred at Cherry Court School."

"It is true that I am older than he, but I have three times his sense. I can manage him if another girl does not interfere."

Bertha thought a very long time.

"If he really falls in love with Florence, then he must no longer be Mrs. Aylmer's heir," she said to herself. "But he shall not meet her. I want him for myself, and when the time comes, I will marry him. He shall not marry another woman and inherit all Mrs. Aylmer's property."

Bertha stayed up for some time. It was between two and three in the morning when at last she laid her head on her pillow. She had gone through an exciting and even a dangerous day, but that did not prevent her sleeping soundly. Early in the morning, however, she rose. She was dressed before seven o'clock, and waited anxiously for eight o'clock, the time when she might send off a telegram. She procured a telegraph form and carefully filled it in.

These were the words she wrote: "Make some excuse to summon Maurice to London at once. Must go. Will explain to you when writing. Do not let Maurice know that I have telegraphed. Bertha Keys."

This telegram was addressed to Mrs. Trevor, Rose View, 10 St. Martin's Terrace, Hampstead, England. Punctually as the clock struck eight, Bertha sent off her telegram and returned with a good appetite for breakfast.

At about ten o'clock a telegram arrived for Trevor. He was eating his breakfast in his usual lazy fashion and was inwardly wondering if he could see Florence again—and if he could lead up to the subject of the school where she had suffered disgrace. He was hoping she herself would explain to him that which was making him far more uncomfortable than the occasion warranted.

"A telegram for you," announced Bertha, handing him the little yellow envelope. He opened it, and his face turned pale.

"How queer!" he said. "This is from Mother. She wants me to come up today. She says it is urgent."

"Why," said Bertha, "here is Mrs. Aylmer. Mrs. Aylmer, Mr. Trevor has had an urgent telegram from his mother. She wants to see him."

Mrs. Aylmer looked annoyed. "I wanted you to come with me this morning, Maurice," she said, "on an expedition to Warren's Cove. I thought you might drive me in a pony carriage."

"I can do that," said Bertha in her brisk way.

"Of course you can, my dear, if Maurice feels that he really must go . . . When can you be back again?"

"I will try and return tomorrow," said Trevor, "but, of course, it depends on what really ails Mother. From the tone of her telegram I should say she was ill."

"And I should say nothing of the kind," answered Mrs. Aylmer shortly. "She is one of those faddists who are always imagining that they require—"

"Hush!" said Trevor in a stern voice.

"What do you mean by 'hush'?"

"I would rather you did not say anything against my mother, please."

He spoke with such harshness and such determination that Bertha trembled in her shoes, but Mrs. Aylmer gave him a glance of admiration.

"You are a good boy to stand up for her," she said. "Yes, go, by all means. Only return to me, your second mother, as soon as you can."

"Thanks," he answered, softening a little, but the gloomy look did not leave his face.

"I will walk with you to the station, Mr. Trevor," offered Bertha, who thought that he required soothing and felt that she was quite capable of administering consolation.

"Thanks," he replied.

Bertha's Offer

y the next train Bertha saw Maurice Trevor off to London. When she had done so, she went slowly in the direction of the sands. She had induced Mrs. Aylmer to put off the drive until the afternoon. Bertha was now very anxious to see Florence.

In all probability Florence would be on the beach. She would know that Bertha was coming to get the answer which Florence had not given her the day before. She walked slowly, holding her parasol up to shade her face from the sun.

Her thoughts turned to a little account which was weekly swelling in the Post Office Savings Bank. She was intensely fond of money, but she knew that the time had come when it might be necessary to sacrifice some of her savings.

Presently she said, "Hullo, Flo, is that you?" and went to meet Florence Aylmer.

Florence's face was quite pale, and her eyes were red as if she had been crying.

"Goodness!" said Bertha. "What does this mean? Have you had any calamity since I saw you last?"

"No, not any except what you are making," replied Florence. "I wish you would go away, Bertha. Leave me in peace."

"Well, darling, we return to Aylmer's Court tomorrow, so you will not be long worried by us. I have just been seeing that nice fellow, Maurice Trevor, off to town."

"Indeed," answered Florence.

"Don't you like him extremely?" continued Bertha, giving her companion a quick glance.

"I scarcely know him," replied Florence.

"But you do just know him. How did you become acquainted with him?"

"My mother introduced him."

"Ah! Just like the little widow," said Bertha in a thoughtful voice. "Well, Flo, you and I have a good deal to say to each other. Let us walk to the other end of the sands, where we shall be alone."

Florence hesitated. For a moment she looked as if she were going to refuse, but then she said in an almost sulky tone, "Very well." They turned in that direction and walked slowly. At last they neared the spot where Mrs. Aylmer had discovered Kitty and Florence the day before.

"It was there I first saw him," thought Florence Aylmer to herself. "What a true, good expression he had in his blue eyes. How upright he looked! How different from Bertha! Oh, what a miserable, wretched girl I am! Why do I not tell Bertha that I do not fear her? Why should I put myself in her power?"

At last they reached the rocks.

"It is nice here, and quite romantic," said Bertha. "We can come to our little arrangement. You have made up your mind, of course, that you will not speak to Mrs. Aylmer of what you know about me?"

"I do not see why I should keep your secret for you," said Florence. "I do not particularly want to injure you, much as you injured me in the past. But at the same time, why should I make a promise about it? The time may come when it will be to my benefit to tell Mrs. Aylmer what I know."

"At the present moment she would not speak to you. She hates you as she hates no one else in the world. Your very name is as a red rag to her. If I want to rouse her worst passions, I have but to allude to you. Even if you told her, she would not believe a word against me."

"I am not so sure of that."

"But you will not," said Bertha. "You want money badly. You would like to be independent?"

"That is quite true."

"You have had a fairly good education and you want to earn your own living?"

"I mean to earn it."

"But you will require a little money until you do. Now, look here, Florence. I don't want to injure you. I know I did long ago. But I have now managed to get into a comfortable nest. It suits me, and I do not mean to go out of it. But I pity you, and I should like to help you. Will you borrow a little money from me?"

"Borrow money from you? No, no," said Florence.

"I can quite conveniently lend you fifty pounds," continued Bertha, gazing across the summer sea. "It is not much, but it is something. With fifty pounds in your pocket you can go to London or to any other large town and advertise what you are worth. You have, I presume, something to sell. Some knowledge, for instance, or perhaps you have a talent for writing. Don't you remember our wonderful essay?"

"Don't!" said Florence. "Don't!" She covered her face with her hands.

Bertha gave a queer smile.

"Now, I could earn money by writing essays," she said, "and suppose I could earn money by writing stories. Suppose, I write stories and send them to you, and you publish them as your own—how would that do? I will furnish you with a short story, say, once a fortnight, or once a month. I can do it in the evenings, and you shall have it. Don't you think that I am paying you well to keep silence? I am offering you an honorable livelihood, and in the meantime there is the fifty pounds. You may as well have it; it will keep you until the money for the stories comes in, and you can pay me back when you like. Now what do you say? It seems to me to be a very good offer, indeed."

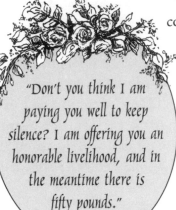

"Don't you think I am paying you well to keep silence? I am offering you an honorable livelihood, and in the meantime there is fifty pounds."

"I have absolutely no taste for it," said Florence.

"Well, think it over," said Bertha, rising as she spoke, "and in the meantime I will send you the money this evening."

"Oh, I cannot take it. Please don't!"

"I will send it to you," said Bertha in a gay voice. "It is quite arranged. Goodbye, dear. I wish you success. When you are a great writer we can cast up accounts and see on which side the balance lies. You quite understand? I have a gift in that way which I think can be turned to account. You will agree to do what I wish, will you not, Florence?"

"It is all horrible!" answered Florence.

"I see in your eyes that you mean to accept; you cannot help yourself. You cannot possibly starve, and you will find when you go to London that the posts of teachers and secretaries are overful. But the writer of clever short stories can always find a market for his or her wares."

Florence rose to her feet. "I don't like it," she said.

"Well, try for yourself before you think of the story part. But, anyhow, you must take the fifty pounds—you really must."

Bertha rose, touched Florence lightly on her cheek, and before the other girl could say a word turned and left her. She walked across the beach now with a dancing step.

❧ ❧ ❧

Florence didn't return to the cottage until past the usual dinner hour. When she did so, her mother, who appeared to be very much excited, met her in the porch.

"There has come a little parcel for you," she said, "from the Crown and Garter Hotel. The messenger did not want to leave it when I told him that you were out. He said it had been given him by Miss Keys to bring to you, and that he was to give it into your hands. I wonder what it can be?"

"Oh, it is nothing of importance," said Florence, turning quite pale. "Give it to me, please, Mother."

"Nothing of importance, indeed!" said the little widow, tossing her head. "It seemed to me very much of importance. The messenger was quite fussed when he found you were not here. He said perhaps he had better take it back, but I assured him that I did not lose things when they were addressed to my daughter, and that he might safely trust me to put the parcel into your hands. He was one of the waiters from the hotel—a very stylish-looking person indeed. What riches and what luck follow some people! Why should Miss Keys have everything and my poor girl be left out in the cold?"

"Oh, Mother, I would not change with Bertha Keys for anything," said Florence, "but give me the parcel, please."

"Here it is. You'll open it and assuage my curiosity."

"It is only a letter from Bertha. I quite know what it contains," said Florence. She got red first and then pale. Her mother's bright beady black eyes were fixed on her face.

"What's in the letter, Flo? If you are too tired to read it just now, I will open it for you."

"No, thank you, Mother; I know what it contains. It is a message from Miss Keys. I met her on the sands this morning and—and she said she would write."

With a wild fluttering of her heart, Florence popped the sealed packet into her pocket and sat down near the door.

"I am thoroughly tired," she said, "and my head aches."

Mrs. Aylmer appeared to be annoyed and disappointed.

"Mother," Florence spoke up suddenly, "I shall be leaving you shortly. I shall probably be going to London tomorrow or next day."

"So soon, after arranging to spend the holidays with me?"

"I have changed my mind about that now," said Florence restlessly. "I must work and begin to earn money."

"I have not a penny to give you to start with, you understand that."

"I have a little money," said Florence, and her face colored and then turned white. "I think I can manage."

The little widow glanced at Florence but did not speak. A shrewd expression came into her eyes, and she pursed up her lips.

"I will go and coax Sukey to make a cup of coffee for you," she said. "There is nothing like really strong coffee as a cure for a headache, and you can have some bread and butter. I am sorry to say I can afford nothing else for your dinner today."

"Oh, coffee and bread and butter will do splendidly," said Florence.

Her mother left the room. A moment later Kitty came down.

"Flo," she said, "I have just received a letter from father. He will reach Southampton tomorrow, and I am to go and meet him there. Won't you come too?"

"Oh, may I go with you?" asked Florence, sensibly brightening.

"May you? Of course you may. It will be so splendid to see him again, and you must constantly stay with me—constantly, Flo dear. Oh, I am so happy, so happy!"

Florence's
Good Angel

hat is the matter, Flo?" asked Kitty. The two girls were in their tiny bedroom. They were to leave Dawlish the next morning in order to be present when Kitty's father, Colonel Sharston, once more set foot on his native land.

Kitty was very much excited, but she was too gentle and noble a girl, too absolutely unselfish, not to notice that her companion was distraught and anxious. No one could be much more worried than poor Florence was that evening.

All during the long day which had followed she kept saying to herself, "Shall I or shall I not? Shall I take the fifty pounds from Bertha and put myself in her power forever, or shall I return her money, fight my way to fortune with the weapons which God has given me, and not descend to her temptations?"

One moment Florence had almost made up her mind to choose the right path, but the next instant the thought of the struggle which lay before her, and the terrible adventures which any girl must meet who fights the world without any money, rose to weaken her resolve. It would be so easy to accept that fifty pounds, and Bertha would scarcely dare to ask her to repay it. She would at least have plenty of time to collect the money bit by bit, and so return it to Bertha.

So she wavered all day long, the pendulum of her mind now swinging to one side, now to another. The result was that she felt quite worn out when night came.

"What is it?" questioned Kitty. "What is worrying you?"

"Oh, never mind," answered Florence. The tears rose to her eyes, she pressed her hands for a moment to her face, then she said abruptly, "Don't ask me."

"I will ask you. I have seen all day that you are feeling wretched. You must tell me what has gone wrong with you."

"I am tempted, that is all," said Florence.

"Then do not yield to temptation," was Kitty's answer. "If it is something you would rather not say to me—"

"No, Kitty, I must not tell you, but I am tempted strongly," Florence responded.

"The only thing to do, however hard the temptation, is not to yield to it," said Kitty.

Florence looked for a moment at her companion. Kitty, too, had known what it was to want for money. Kitty had been poor. It is true that, since the day she took the prize which Florence through deceit had lost, her kind friend, Sir John Wallis, had never ceased to shower small benefits upon her. She was not only his pet, but almost his idol. In his heart of hearts he felt that he would like to adopt her, but he did not dare even to suggest such a thing, knowing how passionately she was attached to her father.

Now Colonel Sharston was returning to England, having been appointed to an excellent home post, and so Kitty's money troubles were quite at an end.

"She will want for nothing in the future," thought Florence to herself as she looked at the graceful figure and bright, beautiful face of the young girl who was standing a short distance away. "She will want for nothing; she will never know the real heartache of those who have to earn their daily bread. How can she understand?"

"Why are you looking at me like that, Flo?" said Kitty.

"Oh, I don't know. I . . . sometimes envy you. You have rich and powerful friends."

"Then it is money. I thought as much," said Kitty. "Listen to me, Florence. I am sure I can guess what is troubling you. That dreadful Bertha wants to bribe you to be silent. She has offered you money."

Florence's face turned quite pale.

"Give it back to her. You shall—you must. I know Father will help you when he comes back. I will speak to him. You must not yield, Flo. You must not!"

Florence stood irresolute.

"It is not too late," said Kitty. "We are both leaving here early in the morning. Has she sent you any money now?"

"Yes," said Florence. Her voice scarcely rose to a whisper. The word trembled on her lips.

"Then we will return it to her. You must not take it."

"It is too late. I have taken it."

"It is not too late. What is the time? It is only half-past ten. I am quite certain that Miss Keys is not in bed yet. Come, Flo, put on your hat. Your mother won't mind. We will take the latchkey and let ourselves in. We will go to the hotel and return the money."

"Oh, I dare not."

"Then I dare," said Kitty. "You have told me nothing, remember. But I will not let you sink or yield to this temptation."

Florence colored crimson.

"You have a great power over me," she said. "I feel as if you are my good angel."

"Then for heaven's sake, Florence, yield to the entreaties of your good angel. Come, come. The hotel won't be shut up. Where is the money?"

"In my pocket."

Florence was inspired by Kitty, whose voice was strong and her face brave and bright, as befitted one who lived for the right and rejected the wrong.

Florence was inspired by Kitty, whose voice was strong and her face brave and bright, as befitted one who lived for the right and rejected the wrong.

A moment later the two girls left the cottage. They walked quickly in the direction of the big hotel. There were lights in many rooms, servants walking about, and the hall door was open. They walked up the steps, and Kitty entered the hall. Florence followed her, pale and trembling.

"Can I see Miss Keys?" asked Kitty of the porter.

"I will enquire if Miss Keys is up still," replied the man. "What name shall I say?"

"Miss Sharston. I want to see her for a moment about something important."

"Will you come in?"

"No. Perhaps she would see me here. Say also that Miss Florence Aylmer is with me."

The man withdrew. A moment later, Bertha, in her evening dress, looking pretty and excited, ran downstairs.

"What is it? What is the matter?" she said. "Is that you, Florence? Kitty, what is the matter?"

"We don't want to stay. We don't want to get you into trouble of any sort," said Kitty, speaking rapidly and drawing Bertha aside as she spoke. "But we want to give this back and to let you know that what you suggested is impossible—quite impossible."

As she spoke, she thrust the little packet which contained the fifty pounds into Bertha's hand, and then took Florence's.

"Come, Flo. I think that is all," she said.

Bertha was too stunned to say a word. Before she had recovered from her astonishment, the two girls had walked down the steps and gone right out into the night.

"What does this mean?" said Bertha to herself. "I don't like it at all, but thank goodness we are leaving here tomorrow. I don't suppose Florence will really tell on me. I must discover some other way to get her into my power."

She went slowly back to the sitting room. Mrs. Aylmer looked up discontentedly.

"Who called to see you? I didn't know you had any friends in the town, Bertha." she said.

"Nor have I, but a couple of young girls who are staying here called to return a little packet which I dropped on the beach today and lost. They found it. My name was on it, and they brought it back to me."

"Oh, indeed. I thought I heard the waiter say that Miss Florence Aylmer had called."

"You were mistaken, Mrs. Aylmer," replied Bertha in her calm voice. She fixed her gray-green eyes on the widow's face, then took up the book that she had been reading.

"Shall we go on with this, or shall we have a game of two-handed patience?" she asked quietly.

"I will go to bed," said Mrs. Aylmer. "I am tired and cross. After all, my life is very dull. You didn't manage to amuse me today, Bertha; you were not like your old self. And then I miss Maurice. He has become almost indispensable to me. I hope he will return tomorrow."

"We shall probably find him before us at Aylmer's Court."

"I shall send him a telegram the first thing tomorrow to ask him to hurry home," said Mrs. Aylmer. "He is such a pleasant, bright fellow. You used to be much more amusing than you are now, Bertha. Is there anything the matter?"

"Nothing, my dear friend," Bertha said. She looked full at Mrs. Aylmer and tears rose slowly to her eyes. Now, no one could possess a more pathetic face than Bertha when she pleased. Mrs. Aylmer was not a good-natured woman, she was not kindhearted, she was not in any sense of the word amiable, but she had certain sentiments, and Bertha managed to arouse them. When she saw tears in her young companion's eyes, she laid her arm on Bertha's.

"What is the matter, dear? I should be sorry to be cross with you. You are a very good girl and suit me admirably."

"It was just the fear that I was not quite suiting you that was troubling me," replied Bertha. "Say that again, kind, dear bene-factress, and you will make me the happiest girl in the world."

"No one has ever suited me so well. You are surely not jealous of my affection for dear Maurice?"

"Oh, no. I love him myself," said Bertha.

Mrs. Aylmer looked grave. She rose slowly.

"Ring for my maid, will you, Bertha? I shall go to bed. I am tired," said the great lady.

The maid appeared a moment later, and the two left the room together. As Mrs. Aylmer slowly undressed, she thought of Bertha's last words, "I love him myself."

"Nonsense!" said Mrs. Aylmer to herself. "She is ten years his senior if she's a day. Nevertheless, I must be careful."

Downstairs Bertha slowly unfastened the little parcel and looked at the five ten-pound notes which were rolled up within.

"After all, it's just as well that I should have this money by me as that I should give it to Florence Aylmer," she said to herself. "I must think of some other way to tempt her, and the money will be useful for that. I shall put it back into the Post Office Savings Bank and wait. She is certain to go to London, and equally certain to fail. I can tempt her with some of my stories. I will manage to get her address. Yes, clever as you think yourself, Florence, you will be in my power before many weeks are over."

Alone
in London

lorence and Kitty left Dawlish the next day and went to Southampton. There they met Colonel Sharston, and Florence had the great bliss of seeing Kitty's intense happiness with her father. They stayed at a hotel at Southampton for the better part of the week, and then the three went to London. Kitty and her father were going to Switzerland for a month's holiday. They begged Florence to go with them, but nothing would induce her to accept the invitation.

"I know well that Colonel Sharston even now is far from rich," she said to herself. "I will not let Kitty feel that I have put myself upon her."

So very firmly she declined the invitation, and one short week after she had bidden her mother goodbye at Dawlish she found herself alone in London. She had seen Kitty and Colonel Sharston off by the night train to Dover, then left the great railway station slowly and sadly.

She had taken a bedroom in a large house which was let out in small rooms. It was one of the first houses that had been let out in flats for women in London, and Florence considered herself very fortunate in being able to take up her quarters there. There was a large restaurant downstairs where the girls who lived in the house could have their meals provided at low prices.

Florence's bedroom was fairly neat, but very small and sparsely furnished. It was an attic room, of course, for she could only afford the cheapest apartment. She had exactly twenty pounds with which to support herself until fortune's ball rolled her way. She felt confident enough. She had been well educated; she had taken certain diplomas which ought to enable her to get a good situation as a teacher. But if there was one thing which poor Florence disliked it was the thought of imparting knowledge to others. If she could obtain a secretaryship or any other post she would certainly not devote her life to teaching.

That evening, after the departure of Kitty and her father, she retired to her bedroom. She had bought a little tea, sugar, bread, and butter, and she made herself a small meal. The prices at the restaurant were very moderate, but Florence made a calculation that she could live for a little less by buying her own food.

"I will take dinner at the restaurant," she thought, "and make my own breakfast and get my own supper. I must make this twenty pounds go as far as possible, as I do not mean to take the first thing that offers."

That evening she wrote a long letter to her mother and another to Sir John Wallis. She told Sir John that she was preparing to fight the battle in London and gave him her address.

"I am determined," she said in her letter, "not to eat the bread of dependence. I am firmly resolved to fight my own way, and the money you have given me is, I consider, a steppingstone to my fortunes."

The Family Letter

First, and most important of all, comes the family letter. Women always write these best. They know how to pick up those little items of interest which are, after all, nearly the sum-total of home life, and which, by being carefully nar-rated, transport, for the time being, the recipient. These letters should give little gossipy items about neighbors and acquaintances. They may even descend to trifles about dress.

Having furnished all the news, they should make kind and careful inquiries concerning the feelings and doing of the recipient; and if this recipient is not adept in the art of letter-writing, they may furnish questions enough to be answered to make the reply an easy task. They should con-clude with sincere expressions of affection from all for the absent one, a desire for his best welfare, and a request for an early answer.

There really is no set model for a family let-ter. But it should be written as an agreeable and intelligent woman would chat.

—Etiquette for Ladies and Gentlemen, 1877

She wrote frankly and gratefully, and when Sir John read the letter he determined to keep her in mind, but not to give her any further help for the present.

Mrs. Aylmer the less also received a long letter from Florence. It was written in a very different vein from the one she had sent to Sir John. Mrs. Aylmer delighted in small news, and Florence tried to satisfy her . She told her about Kitty's dresses and Kitty's handsome bonnets and all the different things she was taking for her foreign tour.

She described her own life with the Sharstons during the few days she had spent with them at a London hotel, and finally she spoke of her little attic up in the clouds, how far she would make her money go, and how confident she was that in the future she could help her mother. Finally she sent the little Mum her warmest love.

That letter brought great delight to Mrs. Aylmer. By parcel post that very same day there also came a large packet for her from Bertha Keys, sent straight from Aylmer's Court. This packet contained a wardrobe which set the little widow's ears tingling, flushed her cheeks, brightened her eyes, and caused her heart, as she expressed it, to bound with joy.

Among the clothes, lying by itself, was a thick envelope. Mrs. Aylmer tore it open. There tumbled out of it two golden sovereigns.

"Dear, dear!" thought the widow. "My sister-in-law Susan must be changing her mind to send me all these lovely clothes and this money. But the writing is not in Susan's hand—it is doubtless the hand of that charming young creature, Miss Keys."

Bertha's letter ran as follows:

Dear Mrs. Aylmer—

I have collected a few things which I think may prove
useful, especially the silk dress which you seemed so
much to covet. I also send two sovereigns, as I think you
would like to have the funds to pay the dressmaker for
cutting it down to your figure. Please use the sovereigns
in any way you think best.

I have a little request to make of you, dear Mrs. Aylmer.
I am not likely to come to Dawlish again, but I am much
interested in your dear daughter Florence. I would be
greatly obliged if you would favor me with her address in
London. Will you send it to me by return post, and will
you put it into the addressed envelope which I enclose,
as I do not want my benefactress, Mrs. Aylmer, to know
anything about this matter? If I can help you at any time
pray command me.

Yours sincerely, Bertha Keys

Mrs. Aylmer was so excited by this letter, and by the fact that
she possessed two sovereigns more than she had when she
awoke that morning, that she could scarcely drink the cocoa
when Sukey appeared with it.

"Sukey," she exclaimed to that worthy woman, "it never rains
but it pours. We will have a tea party. Such a tea party it shall
be—done in style, I can assure you. All the neighbors who have
ever shown any kindness to me shall be invited. I will go to
Crook's, in the High Street, and order the cakes and the pastry
and the sandwiches, and we will hire enough cups and saucers
and teaspoons and all the other things which will be necessary."

"You had better begin by hiring an increased apartment,
ma'am," said Sukey in a dubious voice. "I don't say nothing
against this parlor, but it ain't large. How will you crowd in all
the visitors?"

"It is fashionable to have a crowded room," said Mrs. Aylmer, pausing for a moment to consider this difficulty. "People can stand and sit on the stairs—"

"How will you pay for it, ma'am?"

"I tell you I have the money. What do you say to these?"

As Mrs. Aylmer spoke, she held a sovereign between the finger and thumb of each hand.

Sukey opened her eyes.

"Is it your sister-in-law, ma'am," she said, "that is changing her mind?"

"No, it is not. I wish it were. I can tell you no more. But when both our silk dresses are made to fit us we will have the party."

Sukey went softly out of the room.

"There's something brewing that I don't quite like," she said to herself. "I wish Miss Florence was at home! I wish the missus hadn't those queer ways! But there, when all's said and done, I have learned to be fond of her."

That evening Mrs. Aylmer wrote to Bertha Keys thanking her effusively for the parcel, telling her that she felt that she owed her lovely silk dress to her, and further thanking her for the sovereigns. The letter ran as follows:

> I am not proud, my dear. And a little extra money comes in extremely handy. I mean to give a party and show my neighbors that I am as good as any of them. It will be a return for many little kindnesses on their part and will ensure me a comfortable winter. I shall have so many invitations to tea when they see me in that silk dress and eat the excellent cakes, muffins, and crumpets, which I shall provide for them, that they won't dare to cut me in the future.
>
> If you want dear Florence's address, here it is—12, Prince's Mansions, Westminster. She has taken a room

in a sort of common lodging house, and I understand from the way she has written to me that she is in one of the attics. It seems a sad pity that the dear child should pinch herself as she does, and if you, Miss Keys, could add to your other virtues that of effecting a reconciliation between Florence and her aunt by marriage, you would indeed fill my cup of gratitude to the brim.

Yours sincerely, Mabel Aylmer

P.S. If by any chance that most charming young man, Mr. Maurice Trevor, should be coming to Dawlish, I shall always be pleased to give him a welcome. You might mention to him where Florence is staying in London. He seemed to have taken quite a fancy to her, but mum's the word, my dear. Mothers will have dreams, you know.

XII

A Chance Encounter

lorence settled down in her attic and made herself as comfortable as circumstances would permit. She made her little attic look as neat and cheery as she could and set to work at once trying to obtain employment.

Now, Florence honestly hated the idea of teaching. She was a fairly clever girl, but no more. She had certain aptitudes and certain talents, but they did not lie in the teacher's direction. For instance, she was no musician, and her knowledge of foreign languages was extremely small. She could read French fairly well, but could not speak it; and she was not an artist. Her special forte was English history and literature, and she also had a fair idea of some of the sciences.

With only these weapons in hand, and the sum of twenty pounds in her pocket, she was about to fight the world. She herself knew well, none better, that her weapons were small and her chance of success not particularly brilliant.

With a good heart, however, she started out from her lodgings on the morning after her arrival in town. She went to a registry office for employment and entered her name there. From this office she went to two or three more in the West End. Having put down her name in each office and answered the questions of the clerk, she returned home.

She had been assured in four different quarters that it was only a matter of time. As soon as the schools began she would get employment.

"There is no difficulty," one and all said to her. "If you want to get a teacher's post, you are quite sure to succeed. There will be plenty of people requiring assistance of all sorts at the schools when the holidays are over."

"What shall I do in the meantime?" said Florence, who knew that several weeks of the holidays had yet to run.

"In the meantime," said all these people, "there is nothing to do but wait."

Florence wondered if she had left her mother too soon.

"It would have been cheaper to stay on with the little Mum," she said to herself. "But August is nearly through, and the schools will open again about the twentieth of September. By then I shall surely hear of something. Oh, it is hateful to teach, but there is no help for it."

She wrote and told her mother what she had done and resolved to spend her time studying at the British Museum.

There were not many people yet in London, and she felt strange and lonely. Her money seemed to her to be already melting away in a remarkably rapid manner. She wanted new boots and a new dress and thought she might as well get these necessary articles of apparel now as later. But, although she bought boots at the very cheapest place she could find, her funds melted still further, and before September was half through she had spent between five and six pounds of her small stock of money.

It was already time for different mistresses at schools to be applying to her for her valuable services. But although she listened with a beating heart as she heard the postman run up the stairs and deposit letters in the different hall doors of the various flats, very seldom indeed did the good man come up as far as her attic, and then it was with a letter from her mother.

She turned quickly and was much astonished to see the bright face and keen blue eyes of Maurice Trevor . . .

She decided to go again to the offices where she had entered her name and inquire if there were any post likely to suit her which she could apply for. She was now received in a totally different spirit.

"It is extremely unlikely, miss," said one and all of the clerks, who had been so positive on the occasion of her first visit, "that we can get you anything to do. You are not a governess, you know, in the ordinary sense. You cannot teach music, not languages, nor drawing. What can you expect, madam?"

"But you told me," began poor Florence, "you told me when I paid my fee on the previous occasion of calling that you could get me a post without the slightest difficulty."

"We will do our utmost, of course, madam. But with your want of experience, we can make no definite promise. We certainly made none in the past."

"If you cannot get me anything to do as a teacher, is there nothing else you can think of to suit me? Secretaries are sometimes employed, are they not?"

"Secretaryships are not in our line," said the clerk. "At least not for ladies.

"People prefer men for the post—clever men who understand shorthand. You, of course, know nothing of that?"

"Certainly not! Girls never learn shorthand," said Florence.

She left one office after the other, feeling sadder and sadder.

Florence was returning slowly home by way of Trafalgar Square when she heard a voice in her ear. She turned quickly and was much astonished to see the bright face and keen blue eyes of Maurice Trevor.

"I thought it must be you," exclaimed the young man. "I am glad to see you. You passed me in a hurry just now and never noticed me, so I took the liberty of following you. How do you do? I didn't know you were in town."

"I have been in town for over a fortnight," replied Florence. She found herself coloring, then turning pale.

"Is anything the matter? You don't look well."

"I am tired, that is all."

"May I walk part of the way home with you? It is nice to meet an old friend."

"Just as you please," replied Florence.

"Where do you live?"

"I am in a house in Westminster—12, Prince's Mansions, it is called. It is a curious sort of place, with rooms let out to girls like myself. There is a restaurant downstairs. It is a nice, convenient place, and it is not expensive. I think myself very lucky to have a room there."

"I suppose you are," assented Trevor, "but do you like living alone in London?"

"I have no choice," replied Florence.

"I was sorry not to have seen you again before we left Dawlish. We had a good deal in common, don't you think? That was a pleasant afternoon that we spent together looking at the sea anemones."

"Very pleasant," she answered.

"And how is your mother, Miss Aylmer, and that nice young friend—I forget her name."

"Mother is quite well. I heard from her a few days ago. Kitty Sharston is abroad."

"Kitty Sharston. That is a pretty name."

"And Kitty is so pretty herself," continued Florence, forgetting her anxieties. "She is one of the nicest girls I have ever met. Her father has just returned from India, and he and she are enjoying a holiday together. But now, may I ask you some questions? Why are you not with Mrs. Aylmer and Bertha Keys?"

"I have not been at Aylmer's Court for some days. My mother has not been quite well, and I have been paying her a visit. But do tell me more about yourself. Are you going to live long in London?"

"I hope so."

"What a pity I didn't know it before! Mother would so like to know you, Miss Aylmer. I have told her something about you. Won't you come and see her some day? She would call on you, but she is quite an old lady."

"Of course. I should be delighted to see your mother," said Florence, brightening. "I have been very lonely," she added.

"When I go home tonight I will tell mother that I have met you, and she will write to you. Will you spend Sunday with us?"

"Shall you be at home?"

"Yes. I am not going back to Aylmer's Court until Tuesday. I will ask mother to invite you. I could meet you and bring you to Hampstead. We have a cottage in a terrace, and you will enjoy the air on Hampstead Heath. It is nearly as good as being in the country."

"I am sure it must be lovely. I am glad I met you," said Florence.

"You look better now," he answered. "But please give me your address over again."

As Trevor spoke he took a small, gold-mounted notebook from his pocket, and when Florence gave him the address he entered it in a neat hand.

"Thank you," he said. "You look more rested now. I am very sorry for Londoners. I should not care to live in London. . . ."

"Nor should I. But all the same, I expect I shall have to. Perhaps I ought to tell you, Mr. Trevor, quite frankly, that I am a very poor girl and have to earn my own living—that is why I am staying in a place like Prince's Mansions. I have an attic in No. 12, a tiny room up in the roof, and I am looking for employment."

"What sort of employment? What do you want to do?" said Trevor.

"I suppose I shall have to teach, but I should like to be a secretary."

"A secretary—that is rather a wide remark. What sort of secretary?"

"Oh, I don't know. But anything is better than teaching. It is just because a secretaryship sounds vague that I think I should like it."

Trevor was thinking to himself. After a moment he spoke. "Do you mind my asking you a very blunt question?"

Florence gave him a puzzled glance. "What sort of question? What do you mean?"

"Are you not Mrs. Aylmer's niece?"

"Yes. I am her niece by marriage. Her husband was my father's brother."

"I understand. But how is it she never asks you to Aylmer's Court nor takes any notice of you?"

"I am afraid I cannot tell you."

"Cannot? Does that mean that you will not?"

"I will not, then."

Trevor flushed slightly. They had now nearly reached Westminster.

"Here is a tea shop," he said, "will you come in and have tea with me?"

Florence hesitated. "Thank you. I may as well," she said slowly.

They entered a pretty shop with little round tables covered with white cloths. That sort of shop was a novelty at the time.

Trevor and Florence secured a table to themselves. Florence was very hungry, but she restrained her appetite, fearing that he would notice. She longed to ask for another bun and pat of butter.

"Oh, dear," she was saying to herself as she drank her tea and ate her thin bread-and-butter, "I could devour half the things in the shop. And this tea must take the place of another meal."

A few moments later Trevor had bidden her goodbye. "My mother will be sure to write to you," he said.

She would not let him walk with her as far as her lodgings, but shook hands with him with some pleasure in her face.

"I am so glad I met you," she repeated, and he echoed the sentiment.

As soon as he got home that day he went straight to his mother.

"You are better, are you not?" he said to her.

Mrs. Trevor was a middle-aged woman, who was more or less an invalid. She was devoted to her son, Maurice, and, although she delighted in feeling that he was provided for for life, owing to Mrs. Aylmer's generosity, she missed him morning, noon, and night.

"Ah, darling, it is good to see you back again," she said. "But you look hot and tired. What a long time you have been in town!"

"I have had quite an adventure," he said. "Mother, I want to know if you will do something for me."

"You have but to ask, Maurice."

"There is a girl"—he hesitated, and a very slight color came into his bronzed cheeks. "There is a girl I have taken rather a fancy to. Oh, no, I am not the least bit in love with her, so don't imagine it, little mother. But I pity her and like her also exceedingly. I met her down at Dawlish. I want to know if you will be good to her. I came across her today while walking in town, and she was looking oh so tired! I said you would write and invite her to come and see us here, and I promised that you would ask her to spend next Sunday with us."

"Oh, my dear Maurice, your last Sunday with me for who only knows for how long!"

"But you don't mind, do you, Mother?"

She looked at him very earnestly. She was a wise woman in her way.

"No, I don't mind," she said. "I will ask her, of course."

"Her name is Miss Florence Aylmer, and this is her address."

"Aylmer! How strange!"

"It is all very strange, Mother. I cannot understand it, and it troubles me a good deal. She is Florence Aylmer, and she is my Mrs. Aylmer's niece by marriage."

"Very queer," said Mrs. Trevor. "I never thought Mrs. Aylmer had any relations. What sort of girl did you say she was?"

"Not exactly handsome, but with a taking face and a good deal of pluck about her—and, oh, Mother, I believe she is starvingly poor. She has to earn her own living. I made her have a cup of tea and some bread-and-butter tonight, and she ate as if she were famished. It's awfully distressing. I really don't know what ought to be done."

Edith Franks

hen Florence reached home she sat down for a long time in her attic and did not move. She was thoroughly tired, and the slight meal she had taken at the restaurant had by no means satisfied her appetite. After about half an hour of anxious thought, she took off her hat, and, going to her tiny chest of drawers, unlocked one of them and took her purse out. She carefully counted its contents. There were twelve unbroken sovereigns in the purse, and about two pounds worth of silver—nearly fourteen pounds in all.

"How fast it is going!" thought the girl. "At this rate it will not see me through the winter, and, if those terrible people at the different registry offices are right, I may not get any work during the whole winter. What shall I do? I will not go back to the little Mum, to live upon her and prove myself a failure. I shall not ask anybody to help me. Oh, this hunger! What would I not give for a good dinner!"

She took up one of the shillings and looked at it longingly. With this in her hand, she could go down to the restaurant and

Florence was so hungry that she determined to be, as she expressed it, greedy for once.

have as much food as she required. Suddenly she made up her mind.

Hastily putting back the rest of her money and locking her drawer, she went downstairs to the restaurant. She went to a table where she had sat before and ordered her meal. She looked at the menu and ordered her dinner with extreme care. She could have anything she fancied for a shilling. A good many girls had really excellent and nourishing meals for a sixpence, but Florence was so hungry she determined to be, as she expressed it, greedy for once. So she made her selection, and then sat back to wait as best she could for the first of the dishes to arrive.

A girl with a rosy face and bright, dark eyes presently came and took the seat opposite her. She was a stranger to Florence. The waitress came up and asked what the girl would like to have for dinner.

"Soup, please, and a chop afterward," was the hasty reply.

The waitress went away and the girl, taking a German book out of her bag, opened it and began to read eagerly. She did not notice Florence, who had no book and was becoming feverishly anxious for her dinner. Presently Florence accidentally dropped her napkin ring, making a little clatter as she did so. The girl seated opposite started, stooped, and picked it up for her.

"Thank you," said Florence.

There was something in her tone which caused the strange girl to drop her German book and look at her attentively.

"Are you very tired?" she said.

"Tired, yes, but it does not matter," answered Florence.

"It is the hot weather," said the girl. "It is horrid being in town now. I should not be, only—" She paused and looked full at Florence, then she said impulsively. "You will be somewhat surprised. I am going to be a doctor—a lady doctor. You are horrified, no doubt. Before ten years are out there will be women doctors in England. They are much wanted."

"But can you, do they allow you to study in the men's schools?"

"Do they?" said the girl. "Of course they don't. I have to go to America to get my degree. I am working here, and I shall go to New York early in the spring. Oh, I am very busy and deeply interested. The whole thing is profoundly interesting. I am reading medical books, not only in English, but also in French and German. Do you mind if I go on reading until dinner arrives?"

"Of course not. Why should you stop your studies on my account?" said Florence.

The girl again favored her with a keen glance, and then, to Florence's surprise, instead of continuing her reading, she immediately closed her book and looked full across at her companion.

"Why don't you read?" asked Florence in a voice that was almost cross.

"Well, you interest me. You are fearfully anemic. You ought to take iron."

"Thank you," said Florence. "I don't want anything which would make me more hungry than I am at present. Iron is supposed to promote appetite."

"Yes. Do you live in this house?"

"I do," answered Florence.

"I have taken a room on the third floor, No. 17. What is your number?"

"The number of my room is 32."

"May I come and see you?"

"No, thank you."

"What a rude girl! You certainly are *fearfully* neurotic. Ah! here comes—no, it's not my dinner, it is yours."

The soup Florence had ordered was placed before her. How she wished this bright-eyed girl with the rude manner would resume her German.

"Would you like me to go on reading?" said the girl.

"You can please yourself, of course," answered Florence.

"I won't look at you, if that is what you mean. But I do wish, if I may not come to see you, that you will come to see me. There are so few girls at present in the house, and those who are there ought to make friends, ought they not? See, this is my card—Edith Franks."

"And you really mean to be a doctor—a doctor?" questioned Florence, not glancing at the card which her companion pushed toward her.

"It is the dearest dream of my life. I want to follow in the steps of Mrs. Garrett Anderson. Is she not noble? I thought you would be pleased."

"I don't know that I am. It does not sound feminine," replied Florence. She was devouring her soup and hating Edith Franks for staring at her.

Presently Edith's own dinner arrived, and she began to eat. She ate in a leisurely fashion, sipping her soup, and breaking her bread into small portions. She was not very hungry; in fact, she was scarcely hungry at all.

As Florence's own quite large meal proceeded, she began to consider herself the greediest of the greedy.

Miss Franks sat on and chatted. She talked very well, and she had plenty of tact, and soon Florence began to consider her rather agreeable than the reverse. Florence had ordered five distinct dishes for her dinner, and she ate each dish right through.

"There is no doubt the poor soul was starving," Miss Franks said to herself.

At last Florence's meal was over. The two girls left the table together.

"Come to my room, won't you, tonight? It is not seven o'clock yet. I always have cocoa between nine and ten. Come and have a cup of cocoa with me."

"Thank you," said Florence, "you are very kind. My name is Florence Aylmer."

"And you are studying? What are you doing?"

"I am not studying."

"Aren't you? Then—"

"You are full of curiosity, and you want to know why I am here," said Florence. "I am here because I want to earn my bread. I hope to get a situation soon. I am a girl out of a situation— you know the kind." She gave a laugh and ran up the winding stairs to her own attic at the top of the house without glancing back at Edith Franks.

"Shy, poor, and half-starved," said the medical student to herself. "I thought my work would come to me if I waited long enough. I must look after her a little bit."

Meanwhile, the very first thing Florence found when she entered her room was a letter, or, rather, a packet, lying on her table. She pounced upon it, as the hungry pounce on food. Her appetite was thoroughly satisfied at last, and her mind was just in the humor to require some diversion. She flung herself into the first chair and tore it open. She glanced, a puzzled expression on her face, at pages of closely written matter, and then she picked up a single sheet, which had fallen from the packet. The letter was from Bertha Keys and ran as follows:

My dear, good, brave Flo—

I have obtained your address, no matter how, no matter why, and I write to you. How are you getting on? You did a daring thing when you returned you know what. I respect you all the more for endeavoring to be independent. I think, however, it is quite possible that you may have considered my other suggestion.

Now, Flo, I should like to see myself in print—not myself as I am, but my words, the ideas which come through my brain. I long to see them before the world, to hear remarks upon them. Will you, dear Flo, read the tale which I enclose, and if you think it any good at all, take it to a publisher and see if he will use it? You had better find an editor of a magazine, and offer it to him. It is not more than four thousand words in length, and it is, I think, exciting. And will you put your name to it and publish it as your own? I don't want the world to know Bertha Keys writes stories, but I should like the world to know the thoughts which come into her head, and if we make a deal between us there can be nothing wrong in it. Do, dear Flo, make use of this story. I do not require any money for it. Make what use of it you can, and let me know if I am to send you more.

Your aunt, Mrs. Aylmer, is a little more snappish than usual. I have a hard time, I assure you, with her. My great friend Maurice Trevor returns, I think, in a day or two. Ah, Florence, you little know what a great, great friend he is!

Yours affectionately,

Bertha Keys

On the Brink
of an Abyss

lorence sat for a long time with the manuscript of
Bertha's story on her lap. Having read the letter once, she
did not trouble herself to read it again. It was the sort of
letter Bertha always wrote—the letter which meant temptation,
the letter which seemed to drag its victim to the edge of an abyss.

She had not read the title of the manuscript, but presently
she took it in her hand and felt its weight. Then she turned the
pages one by one and glanced at them for a moment. She saw
that they were all written out very neatly, in a sort of copper-
plate writing which was not the least like Bertha's. Bertha had a
bold, dashing sort of hand, but this hand might be the work of
anyone. Then, with a sudden quick movement, she dashed the
manuscript away from her to the other side of the room, and
walked over and stood by the open window looking across
London. The view scarcely appealed to her.

"It all looks worldly and sordid," thought the girl to herself. "I
suppose it is very nice that I should see those tops of houses,

tier upon tier, faraway as the skyline, but I am sick of them. They all look sordid. They all look cruel. London is a place to crush a girl. But I—I *won't* be crushed."

She paced up and down her room. Bertha's letter was the one object of her thoughts. Suddenly she came to a resolution. "I know what I'll do," she said to herself. "I won't read that manuscript, but I'll get Miss Edith Franks to read it. She shall be the judge of its merits, but I won't decide yet whether I shall use it or not—only she shall tell me whether it is worth using. She looks as if she could give one a very downright, honest opinion, and she is literary and cultivated and would know if the thing is worth anything."

So Florence washed her face and hands, made her hair tidy, and put on a fresh white linen collar. Soon after nine o'clock, with the manuscript in her hand, she ran downstairs and presently knocked at the door of No. 17. The brisk voice of Miss Franks called, "Come in!" and Florence entered.

"I am right glad to see you," said Edith Franks. "What do you think of my diggings—nice, eh?"

"Oh, you are comfortable here," said Florence, with the ghost of a sigh. Truly the room, as compared with her own, looked absolutely luxurious. There was a comfortable sofa, which Miss Franks told her afterward she had contrived out of a number of old packing cases, and there was a deep, straw armchair lined with chintz and abundantly cushioned. And on a table pushed against the wall were jars full of lovely flowers—roses, verbena, sweetbriar, and quantities of pinks. The room was fragrant with these flowers, and Florence gave a great sigh as she smelled them.

"Oh, how sweet!" she said.

"Yes, I put this verbena on the little round table near the sofa. You are to lie on the sofa. Come and put up your feet this minute."

"But I really don't want to," said Florence, protesting and beginning to laugh.

"But I want you to. You can do as you please in the restaurant, and you can do as you please in your own diggings, but in mine you are to do as I wish. Now, then, up go your feet. I am making the most delicious cocoa by a new recipe. I bought a spirit-lamp this morning. You cannot think how clever I am over all sorts of cooking."

"I tell you, you are anemic and troubled; indeed, at the present moment you are in quite a dilemma, and do not know what to do."

"But what are those things on that table?" asked Florence.

"Oh, some of my medical tools. I do a tiny bit of dissecting now and then—nothing very dreadful. I have nothing tonight of the least importance, so you need not shudder. I want to devote myself to you."

Florence could not but own that it was nice to be waited on. The sofa made out of packing cases was extremely soft and comfortable. Miss Franks put pillows for her guest's comfort, and laid a light couvre-pied, or blanket, over her feet.

"Now then," she said, "a little gentle breeze is coming in at the window and the roses and pinks and mignonette smell more sweetly as the night advances. I will not light the lamp yet, for there is splendid moonlight. I can make the cocoa beautifully by moonlight. It will be quite romantic, and then afterwards I will show you my charming reading lamp. I have a lamp with a green shade lined with white, the best possible thing for the eyes. I will make you a shade when I have time. Now, then, look out of the window and let the moon soothe your ruffled feelings."

"You are very kind, and I don't know how to thank you," said Florence. "But how can you possibly tell that I have ruffled feelings?"

"I see them in your brow, my dear, and I observe them in your face. I am not a medical student for nothing. I tell you, you are anemic and troubled; indeed, at the present moment you are in quite a dilemma, and do not know what to do. Oh, I can read people through and through, but I like you, my dear. You are vastly interesting to me. Now, then, look at your dear lady moon and let me make the cocoa in peace."

"What an extraordinary girl!" thought Florence to herself.

Miss Franks darted here and there, busy with her cooking. After a time, with a little sigh of excitement, Florence saw her put the extinguisher on the spirit-lamp. She then hastily lit the lamp with the green shade, placing it on the table where the verbena and the sweetbriar and mignonette gave forth such intoxicating odors. Then she laid a cup of steaming, frothy cocoa by Florence's side and a plate of biscuits not far off.

"Now then, eat, drink, and be thankful," said Miss Franks. "I love cocoa at this hour. Yours is made entirely of milk, so it will be vastly nourishing. I am going to enjoy my cup also."

She flung herself into the straw chair lined with cushions, and took her own supper daintily and slowly. While she ate, her bright eyes kept fastening themselves with the keenest penetration on Florence's flushed face.

Florence felt that never in the whole course of her life had she enjoyed anything more than that cup of cocoa.

When the meal was finished Miss Franks jumped up and began to wash the cups and saucers.

"You must let me help you," asked Florence. She sprang very determinedly to her feet.

"You shall wipe, and I will wash," said Miss Franks. "I don't at all mind being helped. Division of labor lightens toil, does it not? There, take that tea towel. It is a beauty, is it not? It is Russian."

It was embroidered at each edge with wonderful stitches in red and was also trimmed with heavy lace.

"I have a sister in Russia, and she sent me a lot of these things when I told her I meant to take up housekeeping," said Miss Franks. "Now that we have washed up and put everything into apple-pie order, what about that manuscript?"

"What manuscript?" asked Florence, starting and coloring.

"The one you brought into the room. You don't suppose I didn't see? You have hidden it just under that pillow on the sofa. Lie down once more and let me run my eye over it."

"Would you?" asked Florence. She colored very deeply. "Would you greatly mind reading it aloud?"

"You have written it, I presume?" said Miss Franks.

Florence did not say anything. She shut up her mouth into rather a hard line. Edith Franks proceeded to read the manuscript. She had a perfectly well-trained voice without a great amount of expression in it. She read on at first slowly and smoothly. At the end of the first page she paused for a moment, then looked full up at her companion.

"How well you have been taught English!" she said.

Still Florence did not utter a word.

At the end of the second page Miss Franks again made a remark.

"You writing is so good that I have never to pause to find out the meaning of a word, and you have a very pure Saxon style."

"Oh, I wish you would go on and make your comments at the end," said Florence.

Edith Franks proceeded with the manuscript. Her even voice flowed on without pause or interruption. She turned the pages now rapidly, and about the middle of the story her voice changed its tone. It was no longer even or smooth. It became broken as though something oppressed her, then it rose triumphant and excited. She had finished. She flung the manuscript back almost at Florence's head with a gay laugh.

"And you pretend, you pretend," she said, "that you are a starving girl—a girl out of a job? You are a sham, Miss Aylmer—you are a sham."

"What do you mean?" said Florence.

"Why, this," said Edith Franks. She took up the manuscript again.

"What about it? I mean do you—do you—like it?"

"Like it? It is not that exactly. I admire it, of course. Have you written much? Have you ever published anything?"

"Never a line."

"But you must have written a great deal to have achieved that style."

"No, I have written very little."

"Then you are a genius."

"I do not know why you say that."

"Because you have written that story, that queer, weird, extraordinary tale. It is not the plot alone. It is the way you have grasped the situation and made all those characters live. They move backward and forward. They are human beings. I am so glad that Johanna won the victory. She was so brave, and it was such a cruel temptation. Oh, I shall dream of that story, and yet you say you have written very little."

"You jump to conclusions," said Florence. She spoke in a queer voice. "I never told you that I had written that story."

"But you have, my dear, I see it in your face. Oh, I congratulate you."

"Would it be possible to—to publish it?" was Florence's next remark, made after a long pause.

"Publish it? I know half a dozen editors in London who would jump at it. My brother is a journalist, and he has talked to me about those things. He is a very clever journalist. Editors are only too thankful to get the real stuff, but they seldom do get it. You will be paid well for this. Of course, you will make up your mind to be an author, a writer of short stories, a second Bret Harte. Oh, this is splendid, superb!"

Florence got up from her sofa. She felt a little giddy. "Do you—do you know any publishers personally?"

"Not personally, but I can give you a list of half a dozen at least. I shall watch your career with intense interest, and I can advise you, too. On Sunday I will go and see my brother Tom, and I will tell him about you, and ask him what he would recommend. You must not give yourself away. You have a great career before you. Of course, you will lead the life of a writer and nothing else?"

"Good night," said Florence, "I am very tired, but I am awfully obliged to you."

"But, I say, you are leaving your darling, precious manuscript behind you." Miss Franks darted after Florence and thrust the manuscript into her hand.

"Take care of it," she said. "It is the work of a genius. Now, good night."

Florence went upstairs. Slowly she entered her dismal little attic. She lit a candle and locked her door. She laid the manuscript on the chest of drawers. Then with a hasty movement she unlocked the drawer where she kept her purse and thrust the manuscript in. She locked the drawer again and put the key into her writing desk. Then she undressed and got into bed and covered her head so that she could not see the moon shining into her room. She said under her breath, "O please, let me sleep as soon as possible, for I cannot, I dare not think."

Nearer
and Nearer

lorence had lived without letters for some time, but now they seemed to pour in. The next morning, as she was preparing her extremely frugal breakfast, she heard the postman climbing all the way up to her attic door, and a letter was dropped in. It was from her mother. Mrs. Aylmer wrote in some distress:

My Darling Child—

The queerest thing has happened. I cannot possibly account for it. I have been robbed of five pounds. I was on the sands yesterday talking to a very pleasant, jolly, fat little man, who interested me by telling me that he knew London, and that he considered I had done extremely wrong in allowing you to go there without a chaperone. He described the dangers to which young girls were subjected in such terrible and fearful language that I very nearly screamed.

I thanked him for his advice and told him that I would write to you immediately and ask you to come home. My darling, it would be better for us both to starve at home than for you to run the risks which he has hinted at.

But to come to the real object of this letter. I am five pounds short, my dear Florry—I had five pounds in my pocket, two which I had received unexpectedly, and three from my very, very tiny income. Sukey and I were going to have quite a nice tea party, but, fortunately, providence prevented my ordering the buns and cakes or sending out the invitations.

Somebody robbed the widow. Oh, what a judgment will yet fall upon his head!

Dear Flo, will you lend me five pounds, darling, and send it at once? Do not hesitate, my love. It shall be returned to you when I get my next allowance. I will write to you later on with regard to your coming back to Dawlish. In the meantime think of your poor mother's distress, and do your utmost for her.

Florence let the letter drop from her hands. She slowly and listlessly raised her cup of tea to her lips. "I seem to be pushed gradually nearer and nearer to the edge," she said to herself. "What possessed Mother to lose that money? Of course the man was a thief. Mother is so silly, and she really gets worse as she grows older. Dear little Mum, I love her with all my heart. But how she does try me sometimes."

The day was going to be a particularly hot one. There was a mist all over the horizon, and the breeze was barely moving. Florence had her window wide open and was wondering how she could live through the day. Today was Saturday. Tomorrow she would have a pleasant time. She looked forward to meeting Maurice Trevor more than she dared to admit to herself. She wondered what sort of woman his mother was.

These thoughts had scarcely come into her head before there came a knock at the door. Florence went to open it. Edith Franks stood on the threshold, very neatly dressed and looking businesslike and purposeful.

"How do you do?" she said. "I am just off to my work. I am about to have a very hard day, but I thought I would refresh myself with a sight of you. May I come in?"

"Please do," said Florence, but she didn't look altogether happy as she gave the invitation. Her bed was unmade, her dressing things were lying about, her breakfast was just the sort which she did not wish the keen-eyed medical student to see. There was no help for it, however. Edith Franks had come up for the purpose of spying, and spy she did. She looked quickly round her in that darting birdlike manner which characterized all her movements. She saw the untidy room, she noticed the humble, insufficient meal.

Edith Franks had the kindest heart in the world, but she was sometimes a little, just a very little, lacking of tact.

"My dear," she said, "may I sit down? Your stairs really take one's breath away. What I especially came for is to tell you that Tom has promised to call for me this morning."

"Who is Tom?" asked Florence.

"Don't you know? What a short memory you have! I told you something about him last night—my clever journalist brother. He is on the staff of the *Daily Tidings* and the new sixpenny magazine that people talk so much about, the *Argonaut*. If you will entrust your manuscript to me, I will let Tom see it. He is the best of judges. If he says it is worth anything, your fortune is made. If, on the other hand—"

"Oh, but he won't like it, and I think I would rather not," said Florence. She turned very pale as she spoke. Edith gave her another glance.

"Let me have it," she said. "Tom's seeing it means nothing. I will get him to run his eye over it while we are lunching together."

Florence rose. Her feet seemed weighted with lead. She unlocked her drawer, took out the manuscript, and had the urge to fling it at Edith's head. She restrained herself, however, and stood with it in her hand looking as undecided as a girl could look.

"You tempt me mightily," she said.

"I am glad I tempt you, for you want money, you poor, proud, queer girl. I like you—I like you much, but you must let me help you over the crisis. Give it to me, my dear."

She nearly snatched the manuscript from Florence, then thrust it into a small leather bag which she wore at her side.

"Tom shall tell you what he thinks of it, and now ta ta!"

Miss Franks was heard tripping downstairs as fast as her feet could carry her, and Florence covered her face with her hands.

"I have yielded," she said to herself. "What is to be done?" She got up desperately. She could not take any more breakfast. She was too tired, too stunned, too unnerved. She dressed herself slowly and determined, after posting the necessary money to her mother, to go the round of the different registry offices where she had entered her name.

"If there is any chance, any chance at all, I will tell Edith Franks the truth tonight," she said to herself. "If there is no chance of my earning money—why, this sum that Mother has demanded of me means I shall be penniless before many weeks are over."

Florence wrote a short letter to her mother. She made no allusions whatever to the little woman's comments with regard to the dangers in which she herself was placed. "Oh, Mum, do be careful," she said in the postscript, "it has been rather hard to spare you this, though, of course, I do it with a heart and a half."

Afterward poor Florence went the dreary round—from Harley Street to Bond Street, from Bond Street to Regent Street, from Regent Street to the Strand she wandered, and in each registry office she received the same reply: "There is nothing at all likely to suit you."

At last, in a little office on Fleet Street, she was handed the address of a lady who kept a school, and who might be inclined to give Florence a small post.

"The lady came in late last night," said the young woman who spoke to her across a crowded counter, "and she said she wanted someone to come and live in the house and look after a lot of girls. You might look her up. I know the salary will be very small, but I think she is willing to give board and lodging."

Slightly cheered by this vestige of hope, Florence mounted an omnibus and presently found herself at South Kensington. She found the right street and stopped before a door of somewhat humble dimensions. She rang the bell. A charwoman opened the door after some delay, told her Mrs. Fleming was within, and asked her what her message was.

Florence said she had come after the post which Mrs. Fleming was offering.

The charwoman looked dubious.

"I wouldn't if I were you," she said in a low voice, hiding both her hands under her apron as she spoke.

Florence simply said, "Will you tell your mistress that I am here?"

"Willful lass," muttered the old woman. She crossed a dirty passage and opened a door at the farther end. A moment later Florence found herself in the presence of a tall woman with a very much powdered face and untidy hair. She was dressed in rusty black, wore a dirty collar and cuffs, and had hands evidently long strangers to soap and water. She invited Florence to seat herself and then looked her over.

"Hmm! You've come after the situation. Your name, please."

"Florence Aylmer."

"Your age?"

"I am twenty-one."

"Very young. Have you had experience in controlling the follies of youth?"

"Have you had experience in controlling the follies of youth?"

"I have been pupil teacher at my last school for over a year," said Florence.

"Ah, and where was your school?"

Florence mentioned it.

"Have you ever got into any scrape of any sort, been a naughty girl, or anything of that kind? I have to make the most searching enquiries."

"Why do you ask?" said Florence. She colored first and then turned very pale.

Mrs. Fleming gazed at her with hawklike eyes.

"Why don't you answer?"

"Because I cannot see," replied Florence with some spirit, "that you have any right to ask me the question. I can give you excellent testimonials from the mistress of the school where I was living."

"That will not do. I find that nothing so influences youth as that the instructress should be able plainly to show how *she* has conquered temptation, and risen even above the *appearance* of evil. If there is a flaw in the governess, there will also be a flaw in the pupils—understand, eh?"

"Yes, madam," said Florence. "I am afraid your post won't suit me. I have certainly a great deal of flaws. I never supposed you wanted a perfect governess."

"I have certainly a great deal of flaws. I never supposed you wanted a perfect governess."

"Impertinent," said Mrs. Fleming. "Here am I ready to offer you the shelter of my roof, the excellent food which always prevails in this establishment, and fifteen pounds a year, and yet you talk in that lofty tone. You are a very silly young woman. I am quite sure you won't suit me."

"It is a foregone conclusion," said Florence, indulging in a little pertness as she saw that the situation would no more suit her than she it. She walked toward the door.

"I will wish you good morning," she said.

"Stay one moment. What can you teach?"

"Nothing that will suit you."

"I must certainly remove my name from that registry office. I stipulated that I should see godly maidens of spotless character. You, who evidently have a shady past, dare to come to me to offer your polluted services! I will wish you good morning."

"I have already wished you good morning," said Florence. She turned without another word and left the house.

When she got to the street she was trembling.

"It is hard for girls like me to earn their own bread," she said to herself. "What is to be done? Nearer and nearer am I getting to the edge of the cliff."

She returned home and spent the rest of the day in a state of intense depression. Her attic was so suffocating that she could not stay in it. There was a sitting room downstairs, so she went there and picked up a well-thumbed novel which another girl had left behind on a previous evening.

A certain Miss Mitford, the head of this part of the establishment, wandered in, saw that Florence was quite alone, noticed how ill and miserable she looked, and sat down next to her.

"Your name is, I think, Aylmer," said this good woman.

"Yes. Florence Aylmer," replied Florence, and she scarcely raised her eyes from her book.

"You don't look very well. I am going for a little drive. A friend of mine is lending me her carriage. I have plenty of room for you. Will you come with me?"

"Do you mean it?" asked Florence, raising her eyes.

"I certainly do. My friend has a most comfortable carriage. We will drive to Richmond Park. What do you say?"

"That I thank you very much, and I—"

"Of course you'll come."

"Yes, I'll come," said Florence. She ran upstairs more briskly than she had done yet. The thought of being alone with a woman who knew absolutely nothing about her was soothing. The carriage arrived and Miss Mitford and Florence got in. They drove for a quarter of a mile without either of them uttering a word. Then the coachman drew up at a shabby house. Miss Mitford got out, ran up the steps, and rang the bell. In a moment or two three little girls with very pasty faces and lackluster eyes appeared.

"I am sorry I was late, dears," said Miss Mitford. "But jump in. There is room for us all."

Florence felt now almost happy. There was no chance of Miss Mitford discovering her secret. Indeed, the superintendent of No. 12, Prince's Mansions, had not the faintest idea of enquiring into Florence's affairs. She could bestow a passing kindness on a sad-looking girl, but it was not her habit to enquire further. She chatted to the children, and Florence joined in. Presently she found herself laughing.

When they reached the park, they all sat under the trees. Miss Mitford produced a mysterious little basket, out of which she took milk and sponge cakes. Florence enjoyed her feast just as much as the children did. It was seven o'clock when she arrived home again, and Edith Franks was waiting for her in the downstairs hall.

~XVI~

Rose View

he moment Edith saw Florence, she went up to her, seizing her by the arm. She said in an imperious voice, "You must come with me to my room immediately."

"But why?" asked Florence, trying to release herself from the firm grip in which Edith Franks held her.

"Because I have something most important to tell you."

Florence did not reply. She had been cheered and comforted by her drive, and she found that Edith Franks, with all her kindness, had a most irritating effect upon her. There was nothing to do, however, but to comply. The two went upstairs as far as the third story together. There they entered Edith's sitting room. She gently pushed Florence down on the sofa and, still keeping a hand on each of her shoulders, said emphatically, "Tom read it."

"What do you mean?" was Florence's almost inane answer.

"How silly you are!" Edith gave her a little shake. "When I am excited—I, to whom it means practically nothing, why should you not be? Tom read it, and he means to show it to his chief. You are made, and I have made you. You will starve no longer.

111

What is more, you will have fame. You will have an honorable future in front of you. Look up! Lose that lackluster expression in your eyes. Oh, good gracious! The girl is ill." For Florence had turned ghastly white.

"This is a case for a doctor," said Edith Franks. "Lie down— that is better."

Edith rushed across the room, took the necessary bottle from her medical shelf, prepared a dose, and brought it to the half-fainting girl.

Florence sipped it slowly. The color came back into her cheeks, and her eyes looked less dazed.

"Now you are more yourself. What was the matter with you?"

"But you—you have not given it. He—he has not shown it—"

"You really are most provoking," said Miss Franks. "I don't know why I take so much trouble for you—a stranger. I have given you what would have taken you months to secure for yourself—the most valuable introduction into the very best quarter for the disposal of your wares. Oh, you are a lucky girl. But there, you shall dine with me tonight."

"I cannot."

"Too proud, eh?"

"Oh, you don't know my position," cried poor Florence.

"Nonsense! Go up to your room and have a rest. I will come for you in a quarter of an hour. I have ordered dinner for two already. If you don't eat it, it will be thrown away."

"I am afraid it will have to be thrown away! I—I don't feel well."

"You are a goose; but if you are ill you shall stay here and I will nurse you."

"No. I think I'll go upstairs. I want to be alone."

Florence staggered across the room as she spoke. Edith Franks looked at her for a moment in a puzzled way.

"I shall expect you down to dinner," she said. "Dinner will be ready in a quarter of an hour. Mind, I shall expect you."

Florence made no answer. She slowly left the room, closing the door after her.

Edith Franks clasped both her hands to her head. "Well, really," she thought, "why should I put myself out about an ungrateful girl of that sort? But there, she is deeply interesting. Poor girl, she has great genius! When that story is published all the world will know. I never saw Tom so excited about anything. He is the most critical of men. He distrusts everything until it has proved itself good, and yet he accepted the talent of that story without a hesitation."

Miss Franks hurriedly moved about the room, changed her dress, smoothed her hair. She looked at her little metal watch and then tripped downstairs to the dining room. She looked eagerly into the great room with its small tables covered with white cloths. There were seats in the dining room for one hundred and fifty people.

Edith Franks, however, looked over to a certain corner. There, at one of the tables, quietly waiting for her, and also neatly dressed, sat Florence Aylmer.

"That is right," said Miss Franks. "You are coming to your senses.

"Yes," answered Florence, "I am coming to my senses."

There was a bright flush on each of her cheeks and her eyes were brilliant.

Edith gazed at her with admiration. "So you are drinking in the delicious flattery and preparing for the fame which awaits you," said the medical student.

113

"I want to say one thing, Miss Franks," remarked Florence, bending forward.

"What is that?"

"When you came up this morning to my room I did not wish to give you the manuscript. You promised that your brother's seeing it would mean nothing. You did not keep your word. Your brother has seen it, and from what you tell me, he approves of it. From what you tell me further, he is going to show it in a certain quarter where its success will be more or less assured. Of course, you and he may be both mistaken, and the story which you think so highly of may be worth nothing."

"It is worth a great deal. The world will talk about it," said Edith Franks.

"But I don't want the world to talk of it," said Florence. "I didn't wish to be pushed and hurried as I have been. I did wrong to consult you, and yet I know you meant to be kind. When your brother receives news I shall be glad to know, but even then I want to hear the fate of the manuscript without comment from you. If you will promise me that, I will accept your dinner and be grateful to you—only will you promise not to talk of the manuscript anymore?"

"Certainly, my dear," answered Edith Franks. "Have a potato, won't you?"

As Edith helped Florence to a floury potato, she exclaimed under her breath, "A little mad, poor girl—a most interesting psychological study."

❦ ❦ ❦

It was a most glorious Sunday, and Florence felt cheered as she dressed for her visit to Hampstead. She resolved to put all disagreeable things out of her mind.

"I fell before," she said to herself, "and I am falling again. I am afraid there is nothing good in me. I have put myself again into the power of an unscrupulous woman. But for today, at least, I will be happy."

So she made herself look as bright and pretty as she could in a white washing dress. On her way downstairs she met Edith Franks.

"Where are you going?" asked that young lady.

"I am going to Hampstead to spend the day with friends."

"That is very nice. I know Hampstead well. What part are you going to?"

"Close to the heath, to people of the name of Trevor."

"Not surely to Mrs. Trevor of Rose View?" exclaimed Edith Franks, starting back a step and raising her brows as she spoke.

"Yes."

"And do you know her son, that most charming fellow, Maurice Trevor?"

"I know him slightly."

"Oh, but this is really delightful. We have been friends with the Trevors, Tom and I, ever since we were children. This seems to be quite a new turn to our friendship, does it not?"

Florence felt herself stiffen. She longed to be friendly with Edith, who was all that was kind. Nevertheless, a strange sensation of depression and of coming trouble was over her.

"I don't know the Trevors well," she answered. "I have met Mr. Trevor once or twice, but I have never even seen his mother. His mother has been kind enough to ask me to spend today with her. I will say goodbye now."

"Be sure you give my love to dear Mrs. Trevor, and remember me to Maurice. Tell him, with my kind regards, that I am sorry for him."

"Why so?" asked Florence.

"Because he has had the bad luck to be adopted by a rich, eccentric old lady, and he will lose all his personality. Tell him I wouldn't be in his shoes for anything. And now ta ta! I see you are dying to be off."

Florence ran downstairs and entered an omnibus which would convey her the greater part of the way to Hampstead. She arrived there a little before ten o'clock. As she was walking up the little path to the Trevor's cottage, Maurice Trevor came down to meet her.

"How do you do?" he said, shaking hands with her, and taking her immediately into the house.

Mrs. Trevor was standing in the porch.

"This is Miss Alymer, Mother," said the young man.

Mrs. Trevor held out her hand, looked earnestly into Florence's face, then drew her toward her and kissed her.

"I am glad to see you, my dear," she said. "My son has told me about you. Welcome to Rose View. I hope you like the place."

Florence looked around her and gave an exclamation of surprise and delight. The house was a very small one, but it stood in a perfect bower of roses; they were climbing all over the house and blooming in the garden. There were standard roses, yellow, white, and pink, moss roses, the old-fashioned cabbage rose, and the Scotch roses, little white and red ones.

"I never saw anything like it," said Florence, forgetting herself in her astonishment and delight.

Mrs. Trevor watched her face.

"We will go round the garden," Mrs. Trevor said. "It is not time for church yet. I am not able to go this morning, but Maurice will take you presently. You have just to cross the heath and you can go to a dear little church, quite in the depths of the country. I never need change of air here in my rose bower. But come. What roses shall I pick for you?"

"I must give Miss Aylmer her flowers, as she is practically my guest," said Trevor, coming forward at that moment. He picked a few Scotch roses, made them into a posy, and gave them to Florence. She placed the flowers in her belt. Her cheeks were already bright with color, her eyes dewy with happiness. She bent down several times to sniff the fragrance of the flowers. Mrs. Trevor drew her out to talk, and soon she was chatting and laughing and looking like a girl who had not a care in the world.

He picked a moss rose bud and a few Scotch roses, made them into a posy, and gave them to Florence.

"I never saw anything so sweet," she said. "How have you managed to make all these roses bloom at once?"

"They are my specialty. I think roses are the great joy of my life," said Mrs. Trevor. But as she spoke she glanced at her sturdy, handsome son, and Florence guessed that he was his mother's idol. She wondered how Mrs. Trevor could part with him to Mrs. Aylmer.

"The church bells are beginning to ring," he said suddenly. "Would you like to go to church, or would you rather just wander about the heath?"

"I think I would rather stay on the heath this morning," answered Florence. She colored as she spoke.

"All right. We'll have our service out of doors then. We'll be back, Mother, in time for lunch."

An Awkward Position

revor raised the latch of the gate as he spoke, and Florence and he went out into what the girl afterward called an enchanted world. During the walk Florence was lighthearted as a lark and forgot all her cares.

Trevor made himself a very agreeable companion. He had from the first felt a great sympathy for Florence. He was not at that time in love with her, but he did think her an especially attractive girl. He noticed, however, that she was sorrowful, and feeling that he himself was doing her an injury by being Mrs. Aylmer's heir, he was more attentive to her and more sympathetic in his manner than he would otherwise have been.

They found a shady dell on the heath where they sat and talked of many things. It was not until it was nearly time to return home that Trevor looked at his companion and said abruptly, "I do wish you and my mother could live together. Do you think it could be managed?"

"I don't know," said Florence, starting. "For some reasons I should like it."

"I cannot tell you," he continued, flushing slightly as he spoke, "what a great satisfaction it would be to me. I must be frank with you. I always feel that I have done you a great injury."

"You certainly have not done me an injury; you have added to the pleasure of my life," said Florence.

"If I am to be Mrs. Aylmer's heir, I shall have to spend most of my life with her. But so long as you are in the world, I ought not to hold that position."

"Oh, never mind about that," said Florence.

"She is your aunt?"

"She is my aunt by marriage. It does not matter. We don't get on together. She—she never wishes to see me nor to hear of me."

"But I wonder why. It seems very hard on you. You and your mother are poor, while I am no relation. Why should I usurp your place?"

"You are not. If I did not have the money, someone else would. I should never be my aunt's heiress."

"And yet she knows you?"

"She did know me."

"Did you ever do anything to offend her?"

"I am afraid I did."

Trevor was on the point of asking, "What?" But there was an expression in Florence's face which kept the word on his lips. She had turned white again, and the tired, drawn expression had come to her eyes.

"You must come home now and have lunch," he said. "Afterward I will take you for another walk and show you some fresh beauties."

They rose slowly and went back to the house. Lunch was waiting for them, and during the meal Mrs. Trevor and Maurice talked on many things which delighted and interested Florence immensely. They were both highly intelligent and had a passionate love for horticulture. Florence found some of her school knowledge now standing her in good stead.

In the course of the meal she mentioned Edith Franks.

Both mother and son laughed when her name was spoken of.

"What! That enthusiastic, silly girl who actually wants to be a doctor?" cried Mrs. Trevor. "She is a first-rate girl herself, but her ideas are—"

"You must not say anything against Edith Franks, Mother," exclaimed her son. "For my part, I think she is very plucky. I have no doubt," he added, "that women doctors can do very good work."

"She is much too learned for me, that is all," replied Mrs. Trevor. "But I hear she is to undergo her examinations in America. I trust the day will never come when it will be easy for a woman to obtain her medical degree in this country. It is horrible to think of anything so unfeminine."

"I do not think Edith Franks is unfeminine," said Florence. "She has been awfully kind to me. I think she is experimenting on me now."

"And that you don't like, my dear?"

"She is very good to me," repeated Florence, "but I do not like it."

Mrs. Trevor smiled, and Maurice gave Florence a puzzled, earnest glance.

"I do wish, Mother," he said suddenly, "that you could arrange to have Miss Aylmer living with you."

"Oh, my dear, it would be much too far, and I know she would not like it. If she has to work for her living, she must be nearer town."

"I am afraid it would not do," said Florence with a sigh. "But, of course, I—I should love it."

"You have not anything to do yet, have you?" asked Trevor.

"Not exactly." She colored and looked uncomfortable.

He gave her a keen glance and the thought flashed through Mrs. Trevor's mind: "The girl has a sorrow. I wish I could draw her secret from her."

The meal over, Trevor and Florence once more wandered on the heath. The day, which had been so sunny and bright in the morning, was now slightly overcast. They had not walked half a mile before rain overtook them. They had quite forgotten to provide themselves with umbrellas, and Florence's thin dress was in danger of becoming wet through.

As they walked quickly back they were overtaken by a man who said to Florence, "I beg your pardon, but may I offer you this umbrella?"

Before she could reply, the stranger looked at Trevor and uttered an exclamation.

"Why, Tom!" cried Trevor. He shook hands heartily with him, and introduced him to Florence. "Mr. Franks—Miss Aylmer."

"Aylmer!" said the young man. "Are you called Florence Aylmer?" He looked full at the girl.

"Yes, and you have a sister called Edith Franks," she answered.

All the color had left her face. Her eyes were full of a sort of dumb entreaty. Trevor gazed at her in astonishment.

"You must come back and see my mother, Franks," he continued, turning again to the young man. "It is very kind of you to offer your umbrella to Miss Aylmer, but I think you must share it with her."

There was no help for it. Florence had to walk under Mr. Franks' umbrella.

"Of course," she thought, "he will speak of the manuscript."

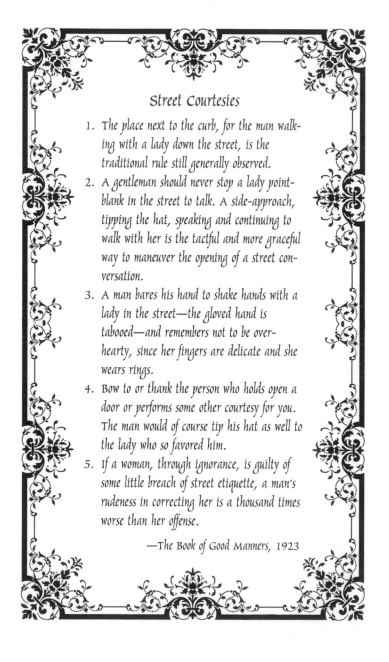

Street Courtesies

1. The place next to the curb, for the man walking with a lady down the street, is the traditional rule still generally observed.

2. A gentleman should never stop a lady point-blank in the street to talk. A side-approach, tipping the hat, speaking and continuing to walk with her is the tactful and more graceful way to maneuver the opening of a street conversation.

3. A man bares his hand to shake hands with a lady in the street—the gloved hand is tabooed—and remembers not to be over-hearty, since her fingers are delicate and she wears rings.

4. Bow to or thank the person who holds open a door or performs some other courtesy for you. The man would of course tip his hat as well to the lady who so favored him.

5. If a woman, through ignorance, is guilty of some little breach of street etiquette, a man's rudeness in correcting her is a thousand times worse than her offense.

—The Book of Good Manners, 1923

She rushed recklessly into conversation in order to avoid this, but in vain. During the first pause Mr. Franks said, "I have good news for you, Miss Aylmer. I showed your story to my chief, Anderson, last night. I begged of him to read it at once. He did so to oblige me. He will take it for the *Argonaut*. I thought you would be glad. He wants you to call his office tomorrow, when he will arrange terms with you. Forgive us, won't you, Trevor, for talking business, but it was such a chance, coming across Miss Aylmer like this.

Trevor glanced at Florence in some astonishment.

"Does this mean that you write?" he asked. "And that you have had an article accepted?"

"A very promising article accepted extremely willingly," said Franks. "Miss Aylmer deserves your hearty congratulations, Trevor. She is a very fortunate young lady indeed."

"I know I am, and I am grateful," said Florence.

Trevor again looked at her. "She is not happy. What can be wrong?" he wondered to himself.

"Have you ever published anything before?" continued Franks.

"Never."

"Well, you are lucky. Your style—I do not want to flatter you, but your style is quite formed. You must have been a very successful essay-writer at school."

"No, I never wrote much," said poor Florence. "I—I hate writing," she said the next moment. The words burst impetuously from her lips.

"What do you mean by that? Surely it would be absolutely impossible for anyone who hated writing to do so with your ease and fluency!"

"We are nearly home now, and Miss Aylmer seems very tired," said Trevor. "Will you come in, Franks?"

"No, thanks. I must be getting home. You will call at our office tomorrow, Miss Aylmer?"

"Thank you," said Florence. "At what hour?"

"I shall be in and will introduce you to my chief if you can come at twelve o'clock. Well, goodbye for the present."

Her hand, which had been trembling, lay still in his palm. He clasped his own strong, firm hand over it. "I wish I could help you," he said in a low voice.

"I must congratulate you," said Trevor, as the young man and the girl walked up the little path to the house.

"What for?" she asked. She raised eyes full of dumb misery to his face.

"For having won a success—and a very honorable one."

"Oh, don't ask me any more," she said. "Please, please don't speak of it. I thought I should be so happy today."

"But does not this make you happy? I do not understand."

"It makes me terribly miserable. I cannot explain. Please don't ask me."

"I won't. Only just let me say that whatever it is, I am sorry for you."

He held out his hand. The next moment he had taken hers. Her hand, which had been trembling, lay still in his palm. He clasped his own strong, firm hand over it.

"I wish I could help you," he said in a low voice. Then they both entered the house.

Mrs. Trevor, through the little latticed window in the tiny drawing room, had witnessed this scene. "What?" she said to herself. "Is my boy really falling in love with that nice, interesting, but unhappy girl? Of course, I shall not oppose him."

≈ XVIII ≈

The Story Accepted

ea was prepared. The sun came out after the heavy shower, and Florence found the Trevors even more kind and agreeable than they had been at lunch. When the meal was over, Trevor called his mother out of the room. He spoke to her for a few moments alone, and then she reentered the little drawing room.

Florence was seated by the open window, looking out across the rose garden. At that moment Trevor went quietly by. He stopped to pick one or two roses, then he turned and looked at Florence. Florence smiled very faintly, and a rush of color came into Trevor's face. Mrs. Trevor then came up to Florence and spoke.

"My son has told me of your great success in the literary market. You, young and inexperienced, have had an article accepted by so great a magazine as the *Argonaut*. You scarcely know what an immense success you have won. I did not, of course, understand what your occupation in London was likely to be; but if you are to be a writer, why not come and live with me

Florence was seated by the open window, looking out across the rose garden. At that moment Trevor went quietly by. He stopped to pick one or two roses, then turned and looked at Florence. Florence smiled very faintly . . .

here? I have a nice little room which I can offer you, and this drawing room will always be at your disposal, for I sit as a rule in my dining room. You can go into town when you want to, and you will make me happy, and—and I think Maurice would like it."

As Mrs. Trevor spoke she looked full at the girl, and Florence found herself trembling and even coloring as Trevor's name was mentioned.

"Will you think it over, my dear," said Mrs. Trevor, "and let me know?"

"I will. You are very kind to me. I scarcely know how to thank you enough," replied Florence.

"As to the terms," continued Mrs. Trevor, "they would be very moderate. My cottage is my own, and I have few expenses. I could take you in and make you comfortable for fifteen shillings a week."

"Oh!" said Florence. She thought of that money which was getting daily less. She looked into the lovely garden and her heart swelled within her. Her first impulse was to throw her arms round Mrs. Trevor's neck and say it would be peace, comfort, and happiness to live with her. She would save money and her worst anxieties would be removed. But she restrained herself.

"I will let you know. You are more than kind," she said.

A moment afterward she had said goodbye to Mrs. Trevor, and Maurice and she were hurrying down the hill to meet the omnibus which was to convey the girl back to Prince's Mansions.

"My mother has told you what we both wish?" he asked. "To be honest with you, I feel that we owe you something. I am usurping your place; I can never get over that fact."

"I wish you wouldn't think of it, for it is not the truth," said Florence. "I have told you already that even if you did not exist I should never inherit a farthing of my aunt's money. And what is more," she added, crimson tinting her cheeks, "I wouldn't take it if she offered it to me."

"You are a strange girl," he said.

He bade her goodbye as she entered the omnibus, and then he turned to walk up Hampstead Hill once again.

The next day at twelve o'clock Florence Aylmer, neatly dressed and looking bright and purposeful, appeared at Mr. Anderson's office. She was received with the politeness which is ever accorded to the successful. The very clerks in the outer office seemed to know that she was not to be confused with the ordinary young person who appears daily and hourly offering unsalable wares. Florence's wares were salable—more than salable. She was ushered into a room to wait for a moment, and then very soon Franks appeared.

"How do you do, Miss Aylmer?" he said, shaking hands with her. "I am very pleased to see you. Will you come with me now, as I should like to introduce you to Mr. Anderson?"

They left the waiting room together, went up some broad stairs, and entered a very spacious apartment on the first floor. Here an elderly man with gray hair and a hooked nose was waiting to receive them. He stood up when Florence appeared, bowed to her, and then held out his hand.

"Will you seat yourself, Miss Aylmer?" he said.

Florence did so. Mr. Anderson stood on the hearth and looked her over. He had a keen, hawklike glance, and his scrutiny was very penetrating. Florence found herself coloring under his gaze. Once again that terrible, overpowering sense of guilt was visiting her.

Mr. Anderson was a Scotchman to the backbone—a man of very few words.

"I read your story," he said. "It is sharp and to the point. You have a nice style and an original way of putting things. I accepted your story for the *Argonaut*. It may not appear for some months, but it will certainly be published before the end of the year. We had better now arrange terms. What do you think your manuscript worth?"

"Nothing at all," was Florence's unguarded answer.

This was so unexpected that both Franks and the editor smiled.

"You are a very young writer, indeed," said Mr. Anderson. "You will soon learn to appraise your wares at their true value. As this is your first effort I will pay you two guineas for every thousand words. There are from five to six thousand words in the manuscript. You will receive a cheque, therefore, say, for twelve guineas on the day of publication."

Florence gave a short gasp.

"It really is not worth it," she said again.

Franks felt inclined to say, "Don't make such a fool of yourself," but he restrained himself.

Mr. Anderson now drew his own chair forward and looked at Florence.

"I should be glad," he said, "to receive further contributions. You have doubtless many ideas, and you have at present the great and inestimable charm of novelty. You write in a fresh way. We are always looking for work of the sort you have given us. I should be sorry if you took your stories to anyone else. Would it be possible to make an arrangement for us to receive all your contributions, say, for twelve months?"

"I assure you," here interrupted Franks, "that this is so unusual an offer that you would be very silly indeed, Miss Aylmer, to reject it."

Florence gazed from one to the other in growing alarm.

"What I mean is this," said Anderson, pitying her supposed innocence. "When your story appears it will attract the attention of the critics. It will receive, beyond doubt, some very favorable comments. Other editors who are looking out for what is fresh and novel, will write to you and ask you to work for them. I do not wish to injure your future prospects, but I think you would do better for yourself, and eventually increase the value of your contributions, by giving us your work during the first year. When can we find room for this story of Miss Aylmer's, Franks?"

Franks thought for a moment.

"There is no reason why it should not appear in November," he said. "We could dispense with illustrations—at least, one illustration will be sufficient."

"Very well. You will soon receive proofs, Miss Aylmer. And can you let me have another small story of about the same length a month from now? You will think over my proposal. I do not want you to hurry nor to appear to coerce you in any way, but we shall be proud to be the publishers who introduced you to a very large audience."

Florence, seeing that the interview was at an end, bowed and went away. Franks accompanied her downstairs.

"You will, of course, accept Mr. Anderson's offer?" he questioned.

"Of course I shall," replied Florence. "Why should I not?"

She returned home, avoided Edith Franks, and stayed for the remainder of that day in her own attic.

"Soon my monetary difficulties will be at an end," she said to herself. "I shall soon get over my remorse; my conscience will soon cease to prick me. If I receive twelve guineas for each story I shall earn a considerable sum. I can then live easily myself, and I shall be able to send a great amount to the little Mum."

She walked across the room and looked out. The expression on her face had changed. It had grown hard and defiant. She took up her pen, drew a sheet of notepaper before her, and began to write:

The expression on her face had changed. It had grown hard and defiant.

Dear Bertha,

The story is accepted by that new sixpenny magazine, the *Argonaut*, and they want more. Please send me something else. I have succumbed to temptation. I am once again, as you so earnestly desire, in your power.

Yours, Florence Aylmer

Having written this letter, Florence proceeded to write another:

Dear Mrs. Trevor,

I have thought of your kind offer of yesterday. Indeed, I have scarcely ceased to think of it since I left you. It is with great, great sorrow that I must decline it. You and your kind son had better think no more about me. I am not what I seem. I am not a good girl, nor a nice girl in any way. If I were straight and simple and honest I could be the happiest of the happy in your house. But I am not, and I can never tell you what I really am. Please forget that you ever knew me.

Yours with gratitude, Florence Aylmer

Bertha
and Trevor

ertha Keys found herself in a state of pleasurable excitement. She was in the highest spirits.

Mrs. Aylmer watched her flit about the room and listened to her gay conversation. She said to herself, "A more charming companion could not fall to the lot of any woman."

"Now what is it, Bertha?" she asked. "Your face quite amuses me. You burst out into little ripples of laughter at the smallest provocation. It is a pleasure to see you. What is it, my dear? Have you heard any specially good news?"

"I have heard this news, and I think we ought both to be very happy," said Bertha. "Mr. Trevor comes home this evening, and he will be with us to dinner."

Mrs. Aylmer gave her companion a keen glance. "Miss Keys," she said slowly.

"Yes," Bertha answered, pausing and laying her hand lightly on a little table near. "Do you want me to do anything?"

"Nothing special. You are always doing things for me. You are a good girl and a valuable secretary to me. You suit me to perfection. Now, my dear, I have no wish to part with you."

"To part with me?" questioned Bertha. She looked startled and raised her curious gray-green eyes with a new expression in them.

"To part with you, Bertha. If you set your heart on Mr. Maurice Trevor you and I must part."

"What does that mean? Do you want to insult me?"

"No, my dear, by no means. But girls will be girls. How old are you, Miss Keys?"

"I am seven-and-twenty."

"And Maurice is four-and-twenty," said Mrs. Aylmer. "He is three years your junior. But in affairs of the heart, I am afraid, that does not matter much. You like him, I can see. My dear Miss Keys, the moment I see my adopted son paying you the slightest attention you must leave here. I daresay he never will pay you that kind of attention, and probably it is all right. But a word to the wise is enough, eh?"

"Quite enough," said Bertha. "You are a little unkind, my dear friend, to speak to me in that tone. Believe me, I have not the slightest intention of marrying anyone. I have seen too much trouble in married life to cast in my lot with married folks. I shall live with you as your companion as long as you want me. May I not like Mr. Trevor and be a sort of sister to him?"

"Certainly, only don't be too sisterly or too friendly. Do not ask for his confidence; do not think too much about him. He is a charming fellow, but he is not intended for you. My heir must marry as I please, and I am already looking out for a wife for him."

"Indeed. How very interesting."

"There is a young girl I happen to know who lives not far from here. She is extremely handsome and will have a great deal of money. I mean to invite her to Aylmer's Court next week. Now you, Miss Keys, can do a great deal to promote a friendly feeling between the young people, but I will tell you more of this tomorrow."

"Thank you," replied Bertha. "I wonder," she continued, "who the girl is."

"At present you are to know nothing about it."

The sound of wheels was now heard on the gravel. Bertha ran downstairs.

Trevor had entered the hall, and Bertha went to meet him.

"How do you do?" she said in her gayest voice. She was dressed in the most becoming way and looking wonderfully attractive. Her dark auburn hair was always a striking feature; her complexion was of the palest cream and dazzlingly fair; her eyes looked big, and as she raised them to Trevor's face they wore a pathetic expression.

He wrung her hand heartily, asked for Mrs. Aylmer, and ran upstairs three steps at a time.

"How nice he looks!" thought the girl. "It would be possible for me to like him even as much as Mrs. Aylmer fears, but I will not show my hand at present. What does this fresh combination mean? I wonder who the girl is to be brought to Aylmer's Court on purpose to be wooed by Maurice Trevor."

The dinner gong sounded, and soon Mrs. Aylmer, Trevor, and Bertha sat round the table. He chatted gaily, telling both the ladies some amusing adventures and causing Mrs. Aylmer to laugh heartily several times.

"You are a very bad boy to stay away from me so long," she said. "But now you are not to stir. Your work is cut out for you. I mean you to take complete control of the estate. Tomorrow you and I will have a long conversation on the subject."

"But I am not at all a businessman," he answered, frowning slightly and glancing from Bertha to Mrs. Aylmer.

"Never mind. You can learn. You surely ought to know something of what is to be your own eventually!"

"I thought that your steward and Miss Keys managed everything."

"Miss Keys manages a good deal, perhaps too much," said Mrs. Aylmer, frowning and glancing in a somewhat suspicious way at her companion. "You and I will have a talk after breakfast tomorrow, Maurice."

"Yes. I shall be glad to have a talk with you," he answered. He looked at her gravely.

Bertha wondered what was passing in his mind.

That same evening, when Mrs. Aylmer had retired to bed and Bertha was about to go to her own room, she met Trevor on the stairs.

"Are you disengaged?" he asked. "I should like to speak to you for a mo-ment or two."

"I am certainly disengaged to you," she replied. "What can I do for you?"

"Come back to the drawing room. I won't keep you many minutes."

They both reentered the beautiful room. The night was so warm that the windows were open. The footman appeared and prepared to close them, but Trevor motioned him back.

"I will shut up the room," he said. "You need not wait up."

The man withdrew, closing the door softly behind him.

Bertha found herself standing close to Trevor. She looked into his face and noted with approval how handsome and manly and clear-eyed he was. An ideal young Englishman,

"Bertha found herself standing close to Trevor. She looked into his face and noted with approval how handsome and manly and clear-eyed he was."

without guile or reproach. He was looking back at her, and once more that peculiar expression in his honest blue eyes appeared.

"I want to consult with you," he said. "Something is giving me a good deal of uneasiness."

"What is that, Mr. Trevor?"

"When I was in town I met Miss Florence Aylmer."

"Did you really? How interesting!" Bertha dropped lightly into the nearest chair. "Well, and how was the dear Florence? Is she very busy? She is terribly poor, you know."

"She is disgracefully, shamefully poor," was his answer. He spoke with indignation, color flaming over his face.

Bertha didn't say anything, but she looked full at him. After a moment's pause, she uttered softly, "Yes."

"She is disgracefully poor!" he repeated. "Miss Keys, that ought not to be the case."

"I do not understand you," said Bertha.

"May I explain?" He dropped into a chair near her and bent forward. His hands were within a couple of inches of hers as they lay in her lap.

"My benefactress, the lady who has adopted me, is aunt by marriage to the girl who is now struggling hard to earn a living in London. Between that girl and starvation there is but a very thin wall. I am in a false position. I ought to have nothing to do with Mrs. Aylmer. Florence Aylmer is her rightful heiress; I am in the wrong place. I thought I would speak to you. What do you advise?"

"How chivalrous you are!" said Bertha, and her queer big eyes were full of a soft light, a dangerous light of admiration.

"You see how manifestly unfair the whole thing is," continued the young man. "I am no relation whatever to Mrs. Aylmer. Yet she has promised that I am to inherit her wealth. Have you the least idea what her income is, or what wealth I am in the future likely to possess?"

"You will be a very rich man," said Bertha slowly.

"How do you know?"

"Because Mrs. Aylmer has a large yearly income. Her estates are considerable, and she has enough money besides to give you a considerable yearly income. Think what that means. This money you can realize at a moment's notice. Her own income I cannot exactly tell you. But this I do know, that she does not spend half of it. Thus she is accumulating money, and she means to give it all to you."

"But it is unfair. It cannot be right. I will not accept it."

"Is that kind to your mother? You left off your professional studies in order to take your present position. You thought of your mother at the time. You have often spoken to me about your great love for her."

"Because I love her I cannot accept the present state of things."

"Why did you accept them in the beginning?"

"I knew nothing of Florence Aylmer. She is the rightful heiress."

"Do you think if you refuse all this wealth that she will inherit it?"

"Why not? She ought to inherit it. But there, I have but little more to say. My mind is made up. No objections you can urge will make me alter what I have firmly resolved to do. I shall talk to Mrs. Aylmer about her niece tomorrow. I will show her how wrong she is. I will ask her to put that wrong right."

Bertha gave a low laugh. The fear which had risen again in her breast was not allowed to appear. She knew that she must be very careful or she would betray herself. She thought for a moment, then she said softly, "You must do as you please. After all, this is scarcely my affair. But I will tell you what I know."

"What is that?"

"You cannot force Mrs. Aylmer to leave her money except where she pleases. She dislikes Miss Aylmer. She will have nothing to do with her, and she will be very angry with you. If you refuse the money, you do not make things any better for Miss Aylmer. Mrs. Aylmer can leave her money to charities. It is easily disposed of."

Trevor sat quite still gazing out into the summer night. After a pause he walked toward the window and closed it. He fastened the bolts and drew down the blinds. Then he turned to Bertha and held out his hand.

"I thought you could have counseled me, but I see you are not on my side," he said. "Goodnight."

"There is only one thing I must add," said Bertha.

"What is that?"

"If you deliberately choose to injure yourself, you must not injure me."

"What do you mean by that? How can I possibly injure you?"

"You can say what you like with regard to Florence Aylmer, but you must not mention one fact."

"What is that?"

"That I happen to know her."

"What do you mean?"

"I do not choose to say what I mean. I trust to your honor not to injure a woman quite as dependent and quite as penniless as Florence Aylmer. I have secured this place, and I wish to stay here. I ask you not to mention to Mrs. Aylmer that I know Florence."

"I will, of course, respect your confidence, but I do not understand you."

"Someday you will—and also what a great fool you are making of yourself," was Bertha's next remark.

She sailed past him out of the room and up to her own bedroom.

⚓ XX ⚓

Trevor's Resolve

revor rose early and went for a long ride before breakfast. He did not return until he knew Bertha would be busy over household matters and Mrs. Aylmer would be alone in her private sitting room.

He tapped at her door between eleven and twelve o'clock, and at her summons entered and closed it behind him.

"Ah, Maurice, that is good," said the lady. "Come and sit near me. I am quite prepared to have a long chat with you."

"And I want to have a long chat with you, Mrs. Aylmer," was his answer. He drew a chair forward and sat where he could see right out over the landscape.

"It is a beautiful day," said the lady.

"Yes," he replied.

"Maurice," she said after a pause, "you must know that I am very much attached to you."

"You have always been extremely good to me."

"It is easy to be good to those one loves. I have never had a child of my own. You stand to me in the place of a son."

"But in reality I am not related to you," he answered.

She frowned slightly.

"There are relations of the heart," she said then. "You have touched my heart. There is nothing I would not do for you."

Again he said, "You are very kind."

She was silent for half a minute, then she proceeded. "You are my heir."

He fidgeted.

"Do not speak until I have finished. I do not like to be interrupted. You are my heir and I mean to settle upon you immediately one thousand pounds a year for your own expenses. You can do what you please with that money."

"It is a great deal too much," he said.

"It is not. It is what you ought to have. You can give some of it to your mother—not a great deal, but a little—and the rest you can spend on yourself, or you can hoard it if you like."

"I shall not hoard it," he answered, and his face flushed.

"It will be yours from next month. I am expecting my lawyer, Mr. Wiltshire, to call here this afternoon. Several matters have to be arranged. Maurice, you will live with me for the present. That is, until you marry."

"I do not mean to marry," he answered.

"All young men say that," she replied. "You will marry as others do. You will fall in love and you will marry. I shall be very glad indeed to welcome your wife. She shall have the best and most affectionate welcome from me, and I will treat her as though she were my daughter— just as I treat you as though you were my real son."

"But I cannot forget that I am not your son," he answered. "Mrs. Aylmer, there is something I must say."

His words disturbed her. "If you have something disagreeable to tell me, at least hear my point of view first. I am particularly anxious that you should marry. As my heir, you are already comparatively rich and your expectations excellent. You will have at my death a very large income. You will also be the owner of this fine property. Now, I should like you to marry, and I should like you to marry wealth."

"Why so? How unfair!" said the young man.

"It is a wish of mine. Wealth attracts wealth. There is a girl whom I have some years ago seen—a very sweet, very graceful, very pretty girl. Her name is Miss Sharston. She was poor, but I have lately heard that Sir John Wallis, the owner of Cherry Court Park in Buckinghamshire, is going to make her his heiress. She is coming on a visit here. I cannot, of course, force your inclination, Maurice. But if by any chance you and Catherine Sharston should take a fancy to each other, it would be a union after my own heart."

"Thank you," he answered. He rose immediately to his feet. "You have always been most generous. I am the son of a widow with very small means. My father was strictly a man of honor. He was a soldier, and he fell in his country's cause. I hope that, although he could not leave me gold, he could and did leave me honor. I cannot afford to have my honor tarnished."

"Maurice! I tarnish your honor! You really make very extraordinary insinuations. What does this mean?"

"You didn't think about it, dear friend. It has not occurred to you to look at it in this light, but such is the case."

"Maurice!"

"I only knew of it lately," he continued, "and by an accident. You want to give me a great deal of money now. You want to leave me a large sum of money in the future. You propose that I shall, if possible, marry a girl who is also to be rich. That is a subject which cannot even be discussed. I do not think, whatever happens, that I could marry any girl I did not love. If this girl comes here, I shall, of course, be glad to make her acquaintance. But to proceed to other matters. If I were to accept your offer just as you have made it, I should no longer feel happy when my brave father's name was mentioned, nor should I feel happy when I looked into the eyes of my real mother."

"Go on, Maurice; this is very disturbing and, let me add, very fatiguing," said Mrs. Aylmer.

"I will come to the point at once. You ought not to leave your money to me. You ought to leave it to Miss Aylmer."

"Miss Aylmer! What Miss Aylmer?"

"Her name is Florence. I met her in London. I met her also at Dawlish. She is very poor. She is a brave girl, independent, with courage and ability. She is about to make a striking success in the world of literature. But she is poor—poor almost to the point of starvation. Why should she be so struggling, and why should I, who am no relative of yours, inherit all this wealth? It won't do, Mrs. Aylmer, and I won't have it."

Mrs. Aylmer was so absolutely astonished that she did not speak at all for a moment.

"You are mad," she said then, slowly.

"No I am not mad. I am sane. I shall be very glad to receive a little help from you. I shall be your devoted son in all but name, but I do not want your money. I mean, I don't want any longer to be your heir. Give your wealth to Florence Aylmer. Believe me, you will be happy if you do so."

"Are you in love with this girl?" Mrs. Aylmer asked slowly.

"You have no right to ask the question, but I will answer it. I do not think I am in love with her. I want you to do justice to this girl, and I want to give you in return my undying gratitude and undying respect."

"Now, my dear Maurice, you have just gone a step too far. As you have spoken of Florence Aylmer, I will tell you something about her. There was a time when I intended to leave her my money. I intended to adopt her, to educate her, to bring her out as my niece and heiress. She herself, by her own unworthy conduct, prevented my doing so. She acted in a most dishonorable way. I will not tell you what she did, but if you wish to know more, go and see Sir John Wallis of Cherry Court Park, and ask him what he thinks of this Miss Florence Aylmer."

"Then you refuse to do what I ask?"

"I utterly and absolutely refuse to leave Florence Aylmer one halfpenny of my money. And what is more, the thousand a year which I intend to settle on you will be only given on condition that you do not help Florence Aylmer with one penny of it. Do not answer me now. You are young and impulsive. I will ask Mr. Wiltshire to postpone his visit for three months. During that time you can consider matters. I expect everything to go on just as usual. During part of that time Miss Sharston and her father, and also Sir John Wallis, will be my guests. At the end of that time I will again have an interview with you. But unless you promise to give up your present mad ideas and let Miss Aylmer pursue her own career, unhelped by you, I shall find another heir or heiress for my property."

"I don't want the time to consider," said Maurice, whose face was white with suppressed rage. "My mind is made up."

"I will not take your decision now, you foolish boy. You are bound, because of my kindness in the past, to take three months to consider this matter. But leave me now, as I am tired."

At Aylmer's Court

ylmer's Court was in the full perfection of its autumn beauty when Sir John Wallis, accompanied by Kitty Sharston and her father, drove up the winding avenue. A private omnibus from Aylmer's Court was sent to the railway station to meet them, and their luggage was now piled up high on the roof.

Kitty was seated beside her father and opposite her old friend. She looked sweet and bright, with that gentle, high-bred, intelligent expression which she always wore. Kitty's heart was light. Her beloved father had come back to live with her, and her old friend, Sir John Wallis, had only recently declared her his heiress. And although Kitty would never leave her father for anything that mere money could offer, she was glad to feel that he was no longer anxious about her future.

As to Kitty herself, however rich she might be, she would always be simple-hearted and think of wealth in terms of what it could do to promote the happiness of others, and not merely as a means of increasing her own splendor or pleasure.

"You have two fathers, you know, Kitty," said Sir John, as they drove up the avenue. "You are bound to be a very prudent young lady, as you are under such strict surveillance."

"You need not suppose for a single moment that I am the least afraid of either of you," was her answer, and she gave her head a little toss which was not in the least saucy, but was very pretty to see.

Colonel Sharston smiled and turned to his friend. "How is it that we have accepted this invitation?" he said. "I do not know Mrs. Aylmer. What sort of woman is she?"

"I have known her for many years. I felt that we could not do less than give her a few days of our company, and Aylmer's Court is a beautiful place."

So it truly was—the park rising away to the edge of the landscape, and acres and acres of forest land visible in every direction. A little lake came into view left of the house, on which a small pleasure boat was now being rowed. In that boat sat a girl dressed in dark blue with a sailor hat on her head. Kitty bent forward. Then she glanced at Sir John Wallis and suddenly squeezed his hand.

"Do you know who is rowing on the lake?" she said.

"Who, my dear? Why, Kitty, you have turned quite white."

"I met her before, but do you know, I had absolutely forgotten it. She is Mrs. Aylmer's companion."

"But who is she, dear? What is the matter? You look quite ill."

"Don't you remember Bertha Keys?"

"Miss Keys. Why, that was the girl who behaved so badly at the time when I offered my scholarship, was it not?"

"The very same girl," said Kitty.

"And what do you want me to do regarding her, Kitty?"

"I don't know. I don't want to do her any injury. Don't be surprised when you meet her, that is all, and—"

"Kitty, your heart is a great deal too tender. You ought not to belong to this evil world at all," said Sir John.

Her father looked at Kitty and asked for an explanation.

"Another time, Father. All Sir John has to do is to treat Miss Keys as if he had never met her before."

"Well, I daresay I can manage more than that for your sake, Kitty."

It was a good face, eyes of the sweetest gray, an intelligent forehead, lips true and pure.

Mrs. Aylmer and Maurice Trevor were standing on the steps to meet their guests. The moment she saw Trevor, Kitty smiled and took an eager step forward to meet him. He held out his hand.

"This is a real pleasure," she said. "I had forgotten all about your being here. Do you remember Dawlish?"

"Of course I do," he answered. "I do not easily forget pleasant occasions."

Mrs. Aylmer now turned to Kitty, took her hand in hers, and turning her gently round, looked into her face. It was a good face, eyes of the sweetest gray, an intelligent forehead, lips true and pure. Mrs. Aylmer scarcely knew why she sighed, and why a sensation rose up in her heart that she never felt before. Just for the moment she forgot all about Kitty's future riches, and she welcomed her for herself.

"Would you like to go for a walk before dinner?" asked Trevor. "Miss Keys is rowing on the lake. We will go to meet her."

"I should be delighted. May I go, Father?"

"Certainly my love."

"Then will you two gentlemen come into the house?" said Mrs. Aylmer. She nodded to Trevor, who walked off immediately with Kitty. As soon as they got out of earshot, Kitty faced her companion.

"I never knew that I should meet you here. I am so glad. I heard from Florence a few days ago. She said you were so good and kind to her when you were in London. I must thank you now in her name."

"I should like to be kind to her, but I was able to do only very little for her," said Trevor. "Does she write to you? How is she getting on?"

"She seems to me to be getting on in the most wonderful way. She has quite a considerable amount of literary work to do. Two of her stories have already been accepted, and she is asked to do a third, and I have no doubt that other work also will fall in her way. She will now be able to support herself comfortably. I cannot tell you what a relief it is to me."

Trevor smiled.

"She is wonderfully clever and interesting," he said. "I am glad she is your friend. She has talked to me about you and—"

Just at that moment Bertha Keys, having moored her little boat, came to meet them.

She came straight up to Kitty and spoke in a defiant voice, and as if she were talking to a perfect stranger.

"How do you do?" she said. "I suppose I must introduce myself. My name is Miss Keys. I am Mrs. Aylmer's companion. I shall be pleased to do everything I can to promote your comfort while at Aylmer's Court. Have you been here very long?"

"Only a few moments," answered Kitty, taking her cue, "and Mr. Trevor has most kindly offered to show me around the place. I am so tired of sitting still that it is delightful to move about again."

"Then I won't keep you. Dinner is at half-past seven, and the dressing gong sounds at seven. Mrs. Aylmer's maid will help you to dress, Miss Sharston—that is, unless you have brought your own."

"Oh, I don't keep a maid," said Kitty merrily. "I don't care to keep maids, and in any case I am not rich enough to afford one."

Miss Keys raised her brows.

Kitty went up to her own room and managed to dress before Mrs. Aylmer's maid appeared. Then she proceeded to the drawing room where she found Bertha alone. She went straight up to her.

"Do you wish it known?" she said.

"Wish what known? I do not understand," replied Bertha.

Bertha was looking her very best in a black lace dress with some Gloire de Dijon roses in her belt. She raised her eyes and fixed them insolently on Kitty.

"Do I wish what known?" she repeated.

"Why, that I met you, that I knew you, you understand. You must understand."

Bertha suddenly took hold of Kitty's hands and drew her into the recess by the window.

"Keep it a secret," she said. "Pretend you never knew me. Don't tell your father or Sir John."

"But Sir John remembers you—he must remember you. You know what happened at Cherry Court School. How can he possibly forget?"

"I shall be ruined if it is known. Mrs. Aylmer must not know. Get Sir John to keep it a secret. You must—you shall."

"I have asked him not to speak of it. But I must understand how you came to be here. I will say nothing tonight. Tomorrow I will speak to you," said Kitty.

Just then other people entered the drawing room, and the two girls immediately separated.

Sir John, having taken his cue from Kitty, treated Miss Keys as a stranger. She was very daring and determined, and she looked better than she had ever looked before. Her eyes were shining and no dress became her like black lace, so dazzling fair were her neck and arms, so brilliant her plentiful hair.

Sir John and Colonel Sharston looked at her more than once—Sir John with the knowledge in his eyes which Bertha knew quite well he possessed, and Colonel Sharston with undisguised admiration.

The next day after breakfast, Kitty found herself alone with Bertha. Bertha was feeding some pigeons in a dovecote not far from the house. Kitty ran up to her and touched her on the arm.

"Yes?" answered Bertha.

There was a fresh note in Kitty's voice—a note of resolve. "I have spoken to Sir John and also to my father. They know—they cannot help knowing—that I knew you, and that my dear friend, Sir John Wallis, knew you some years ago. But we do not want to injure you, so we will not say a word about it. You can rest quite content. We will not talk of your past."

"In particular you will not talk of my past to Mr. Trevor?"

"No, not even to Mr. Trevor. In short," continued Kitty, "we have made up our minds to respect your secret, but on a condition."

"Yes?" said Bertha. She spoke in a questioning tone.

"As long as you behave in a perfectly straightforward way, as long as I have no reason to feel that you are doing anything underhand to anybody's name, we will respect your secret. I think," continued Kitty, "that I partly understand matters. You have come here without telling Mrs. Aylmer what occurred at Cherry Court School and at Cherry Court Park. You don't want her to know how terribly you injured my great friend, Florence Aylmer. If you will leave Florence alone now, I and those I belong to will respect your secret. But if I find that you are tampering with Florence's happiness, then my duty will be plain."

"What will your duty be?" asked Bertha. As she spoke she held out a lump of sugar to a pretty white fantail that came flying to receive it. She raised her eyes as she spoke and looked full at Kitty.

"I shall tell what I know," said Kitty. "I think that is all." She turned on her heel and walked away.

XXII

A Smiling World

hings were going well now with Florence Aylmer. She was earning money, and it was unnecessary for her to live any longer in the top attic of Prince's Mansions. She had gotten over her first discomfort. She knew that she was losing a good deal, and that the worth and stability of her character were being slowly undermined. But she was winning success. The world was smiling at her just because she was successful, and she resolved to go on now, defying fate.

She wrote often to her mother and to Kitty Sharston, and told both her mother and Kitty of her successes. She never wrote to Bertha except about business. Bertha, as a rule, enclosed directed envelopes to herself, so that Florence's writing should not be seen by Mrs. Aylmer or Trevor. Bertha was very wise in her ways, and when she did a wrong thing she knew how to do that wrong thing cleverly.

Florence was now quite friendly with Edith Franks. Edith took an interest in her. She still believed that there was something behind the scenes—something which she could not quite fathom—but at the same time she fully and with an undivided heart believed in Florence's great genius, as did her brother Tom.

By Edith's advice, Florence secured the room next to hers, and the girls were now constantly together. Tom often dropped in during the evenings and took them to plays.

Florence began to own that life could be enjoyable even with a heavy conscience and tarnished honor. She was shocked with herself for feeling so. She knew that she had fallen a good many steps lower than she had fallen long ago at Cherry Court School. Nevertheless, there seemed no hope or chance of going back. She had to go forward and trust to her secret never being discovered.

Early in November, or, rather, the latter end of October, her first story was published in the *Argonaut*. It was sufficiently striking, terse, and original to receive more than one good review. She was spoken of as a young writer of great promise, and a well-known critic took the trouble to write a short paper on her story. This mention gave her, as Tom assured her, a complete success. Hers was the first story of any promise which had appeared in the English magazines for some time. The next from her pen was eagerly awaited, and it was decided that it was to be published in the December number.

Bertha having provided the story, Florence carefully rewrote it in her own hand and sent it to the editor. It was a better story than the first, but more critical. There was a cruel note about it. It was harrowing. It seemed to go right down into the heart and to pierce it with a note of pain. It was a wonderful story for a girl of Florence's age to have written. The editor was charmed.

"I don't like the tone of the story," he said to Franks, "I don't think that I should particularly care to have its author for my wife or daughter, but its genius is undoubted. That girl will make a very big mark. We have been looking for someone like her for a long time. She may do anything if she goes on as well as she has begun."

"And yet she does not look especially clever," said Franks in a contemplative voice. "Her speech is nothing at all remarkable. In fact, in conversation I think her rather dull than otherwise."

"We must make much of her, Franks," replied the editor. "I don't want her to be snapped up by others. We must raise her terms. I will give her three guineas a thousand words for this new story."

> She received Franks with a coolness which was newborn within her.

Franks called upon his sister and Florence Aylmer on the evening of the day when the editor of the *Argonaut* made this remark. He found them both in his sister's comfortable room. Florence was reclining on the sofa, and Edith was busily engaged over some of her biological specimens.

"Oh, dear!" said Franks, as he entered the room. "Why do you bring those horrors home, Edith?"

"Don't interrupt me. Go and talk to Florence. She is in a bad humor this evening."

"In a bad humor, are you?" questioned Franks. He drew a chair up and sat at the foot of Florence's sofa.

She was nicely dressed, her hair was fashionably arranged, and she had lost that look of hunger that had made her face almost painful to see. She received Franks with a coolness which was newborn within her.

"I don't know why you should be depressed," he said. "Anyhow, I hope to have the great pleasure of driving the evil spirits away. I have come with good news."

"Indeed!" answered Florence.

"Yes. My editor, Mr. Anderson, is so pleased with your second story, 'The Judas Tree,' that he is going to raise his terms. You are to receive three guineas a thousand words for your manuscript. It is, I think, exactly six thousand words in length. He has asked me to hand you a cheque tonight. Will you accept it?"

As Franks spoke, he took out of his pocketbook and handed Florence a cheque for eighteen guineas.

"You will be a rich girl before long," he said.

"It seems like it," she answered. She glanced at the cheque and laid it quietly on a little table by her side.

"And now, Miss Aylmer, there is something I specially want you to do for me. I hope you will not refuse it."

"I will certainly do what I can," she answered.

"It is this. The *Argonaut* is, of course, our monthly magazine. It holds the very first position among the sixpennies and has, as you doubtless know, an enormous circulation. You will very soon be the fashion. We are about to issue a weekly paper, a sort of review. We trust it will eclipse even the *Spectator* and the *Saturday*, and we want a paper from your pen. We want it to be on a special subject—a subject which is likely to cause attention. Can you and will you do it? Anderson begged of me to put the question to you, and I do so also on my own account."

"But what subject do you want me to write upon?" asked Florence, feeling sick and faint.

"The subject is to be about women as they are. They are coming to the front, and I want you to talk about them just as you please. You may be satirical or not, as it strikes your fancy. I want you in particular to attack them with regard to the aesthetic craze which is so much in fashion now. If you'd like to, show them that they look absolutely foolish in their greenery-yallery gowns, their hair done up in a wisp, and all the rest of the thing. Then you can throw in a note about a girl like my sister."

"Oh, come!" exclaimed Edith from her distant table, "that would be horribly unfair."

"Anyhow, I want you to write about women in their improved aspects. That is the main thing," said Franks. "Will you do it or will you not?"

Florence thought for a wild moment. It would be impossible for Bertha to help her with this paper. She could not get information or subject matter in time.

Dare she do it?

"I would rather not," she said.

Franks' face fell.

"That is scarcely kind," he said. "You simply must do it."

"You will not refuse Tom," said Edith.

"It is for our new venture," Franks explained to his sister, welcoming her support. "Miss Aylmer is scarcely the fashion yet, but she soon will be. It is to be an article. 'Woman in Her Many Crazes' can be the title. No one can know more on the matter than she does."

"Oh, I'll prime you up with facts, if that is all," said Edith. "You must do it. It would be most ungenerous and unkind to refuse Tom after the way he has brought you to the front."

"But I must refuse," said Florence. She rose from the sofa. Her face looked pale with desperation.

Edith looked at Florence with what Tom called her scientific face. "Sit down," she said, "sit down. Why should you not do it?"

"Because I am no good at all with that kind of paper."

"But your style will be invaluable, and you need not say much," said Franks. "We want just the same simple, terse, purely Saxon style. We want one or two of your ideas. You need not make it three thousand words long. It does not really matter.

You will be well paid. I have the editor's permission to offer you twelve guineas. Surely you will not refuse such a valuable cheque."

Florence looked with almost vacant eyes at the cheque which was lying on the table near her.

"I suppose I must try," she said. "I have never written any prose worth reading in my life. You will be dreadfully disappointed. I know you will."

"I am quite certain we shall not be disappointed. Anyhow, I am going to risk it. You must not go back on your promise. Write your paper tomorrow morning when you are fresh. Then post it to me in the evening. Goodbye. I am awfully obliged to you."

The young journalist took his departure before Florence had time to realize what she had done. She heard his steps descending the stairs, and then turned with lackluster eyes to Edith.

"What have I done?" she cried.

"Done?" said Edith, in a tone of some impatience. "Why, your duty, of course. You could not refuse Tom after all his kindness to you. Where would you be but for him—but for me? Do you suppose that, just because you are clever, you would have reached the position you have if it had not been for my brother? You must do your very best for him."

"Oh, don't scold me, please Edith," said poor Florence.

"I don't mean to. But really your queer ways of accepting Tom's favors exasperate me now and then."

"Perhaps I had better go to my own room," said Florence. "I am in your way, am I not?"

"When you talk nonsense you are. When you are sensible I delight to have you here. Lie down on the sofa once more, and go on reading."

Edith returned once more to her task, lit a strong lamp which she had gotten for this special purpose, put on her magnifying glasses, adjusted her microscope, and set to work.

Florence took up her book and tried to read. Half an hour before this book had interested her, now she found it dry as sawdust. She could not follow the argument nor interest herself in the tale. She let it drop on her lap and stared straight before her. How was she to do it? Her crutch was no longer available. The ghost who supplied all her brilliant words and felicitous turns of speech and quaint ideas was not to be secured. What could she do?

She felt restless and uncomfortable.

"I did wrong ever to consent to it," she said to herself, and she took up the cheque for eighteen guineas. Starvation was indeed now far removed. But, nevertheless, at that moment she felt the strongest regret of all her life. And she longed for the old hungry days when she had been an honest, good girl, able with a clear conscience to look all people in the face.

"But to court discovery now would be madness," she said to herself. "I cannot. Come what may, I must write that article. How am I to do it—and in twenty-four hours? Oh, if I could only telegraph to Bertha!"

XXIII

Almost Betrayed

lorence spent a restless night. She rose early in the morning, avoided Edith, and went off as soon as she could to the British Museum.

She resolved to write her article in the reading room. She was soon supplied with books and pamphlets on the subject, and began to read them. Her brain felt dull and heavy. Try hard as she would, she could not think. She had never been an especially good writer. And tossed about as she had been in the world, she had not studied the thoughts of men and women on this subject. She could not, therefore, seize the salient points from the pamphlets and books which she glanced through.

The paper was at last produced—and was not so good as the ordinary schoolgirl's essay. It was feeble, without metaphor, without point, without illustration. She did not dare to read it over twice.

She directed her miserable manuscript to Thomas Franks at the office of the *Argonaut* and dropped the packet into the pillarbox. She then went home.

Edith Franks was waiting for her.

"Have you done the article?" she asked.

"Yes," replied Florence in a low voice.

"I am glad of it. I felt quite uneasy about you. You seemed so unwilling to do such a simple thing last night."

"It was not at all a simple thing to me. I am no good at anything except fiction."

Edith gave her foot an impatient stamp.

"Don't talk rubbish," she said. "You know perfectly well that your style must come to your aid in whatever you try to write. But never mind, my dear. I have good news for you. Tom has obtained tickets for us all three to see Irving in his great piece—'The Bells.'"

Florence certainly was cheered up by this news. She wanted to forget herself, to forget the miserable article which she vainly hoped that Tom Franks would not even read. She ate her dinner with appetite, then went upstairs to her room. Her means were sufficiently good to enable her to dress prettily. She, Edith, and Tom found themselves just before the curtain rose in comfortable stalls at the theater. Florence had never looked better. Franks gave her a glance of downright admiration from time to time. Suddenly he bent forward and whispered to her, "What about my article?"

"I posted it to you some hours ago," she answered.

"Ah! that is good." A smile of contentment played around his lips. "I look forward most eagerly to reading it in the morning," he said. "It will be at my office by the first post, of course."

"I suppose so," said Florence in a listless voice. Her gaiety and good humor suddenly deserted her.

The play proceeded. But between the acts the thought of her miserable schoolgirl essay came back to haunt her. Just before the curtain rose for the final act she touched Franks on his sleeve.

Theatre Conduct Rules
for Women

1. Do not take advantage of the semi-obscurity of the theatre or "movie house" to indulge in flirtation. It is very vulgar and even though you may not be seen you cannot, though you whisper, escape being heard.

2. Avoid all audible criticism or comment; the exclamation of delight as well as the sigh or groan of disgust.

3. Certain vulgar offenses include: chewing gum; giggling or sobbing; wearing a hat; extending any part of your body beyond your legitimate seating space; waving to acquaintances whom you may recognize in another aisle.

4. It is not good form—as some girls do—to carry small animal pets, guinea-pigs, lizards and the like, in the pocket of your cloak or wrap.

—The Book of Good Manners, 1923

"What is it?" he asked, looking at her.

"I wish you would make me a promise."

"What is it?"

"Don't read the stuff I have sent you. It is not good. If you don't like it, send it back to me."

"I cannot do that. I have advertised your name. But of course it will be good. You could not write anything poor."

"Oh, you don't know. Mine is a queer brain. Sometimes it won't act at all. I was not pleased with the article. Perhaps the public would overlook it, if you would only promise not to read it."

"My dear Miss Aylmer, I would do a great deal for you, but now you ask for the impossible. I must read what you have written. I have no doubt I shall be charmed with it."

Florence sat back in her seat. She could do nothing further.

The next day, when he arrived at his office, Tom Franks eagerly pounced upon Florence's envelope. He tore it open and began to read the silly stuff she had written. He had not gone halfway down the first page before the whole expression of his face altered. Bewilderment, astonishment, almost disgust, spread themselves over his features. He turned page after page, looked back at the beginning, glanced at the end, then set himself deliberately to digest Florence's poor attempt from the first word to the last.

Finally, he flung the paper from him with a gesture of despair. Had she done it to trick him? A third-form schoolgirl would have done better. There were even one or two mistakes in spelling, the grammar was slipshod, the different observations were so banal, so threadbare, so used-up. Where was that terse and vigorous style? Where was the pure Saxon which had delighted his scholarly mind in the stories which she had written?

He rang his office bell sharply. A clerk appeared.

"Bring me the last number of the *Argonaut*," he said.

It was brought immediately, and Franks opened it at Florence's last story. He read a sentence or two, compared the style of the story with the style of the article, and finally shut up the *Argonaut* and went into his chief's room.

"I have a disappointment for you, Mr. Anderson," he said.

"What is it, Franks?" asked the chief, raising his head from a pile of papers over which he was bending.

"Why, our new literary star has come to a complete collapse. Something has snuffed her out; she has written rubbish."

"What? You surely do not allude to Miss Aylmer?"

"I do. I asked her to do a paper for the *General Review*, thinking that her name would be a great catch in the first number. She consented, I must say with some unwillingness, and sent me *this*. Look it over and tell me what you think."

Mr. Anderson read the first one or two sentences.

"She must have done it to play a trick on us," he said. "It is absolutely impossible that this can be her writing."

"It cannot be printed," said Franks. "What is to be done?"

"You had better go and see her at once. Have you any explanation to offer?"

"None. It must be a trick. I will rush off at once and see if I can find her," he said.

"Offer her bigger terms to send us a paper tomorrow. We must overlook this very shabby trick she has played on us."

"Of course, the thing could not possibly be printed," said Franks. "I will go and see her."

He snatched up his hat and drove straight to Prince's Mansions. He arrived there just as Florence was going out. She turned pale when she saw him. One glance at his face made her fear the worst. He had found her out.

"What is it?" she said.

He glanced at her and said in a gruff voice, "Come up to my sister's room. I must speak to you."

They went upstairs together. As soon as they entered the room, Florence turned and faced Franks. "You—of course you won't use it?"

"How can I use it? It is nursery nonsense. Why did you send it to me? I didn't think that you would play me such a trick."

"I told you I could only write fiction."

"Nonsense, nonsense! I might have expected something poor compared to your fiction, but at least you did know how to spell. You have behaved very badly, and I feel certain that this is a trick. Come, have we not offered you enough? I will pay you a little more, but I must have another essay in twenty-four hours."

"And suppose I refuse?"

"In that case, Miss Aylmer, I shall be driven to conclude that your talent was but fictitious, and that—"

"I will write something," she said, "but give me two days instead of one."

"What do you mean by two days?"

"I cannot let you have it tomorrow evening; you shall have it the evening after. It shall be good; it shall be my best. Give me time."

"That's right," he said, grasping her hand. "Upon my word you gave me a horrid fright. Don't play that sort of trick again, that's all. We are to have that article, then, in two days?"

"Yes, yes."

He left her. The moment he had done so Florence snatched up the paper which he had brought back, tore it into a hundred fragments, thrust the fragments into the fire, and rushed downstairs. She was desperate now. She went to the nearest telegraph office and sent the following message to Bertha Keys: "Expect me at Aylmer's Court tomorrow at ten. Must see you. You can manage so that my aunt does not know."

XXIV

Desperate Actions

he Sharstons and Sir John Wallis were enjoying themselves very much at Aylmer's Court. Mrs. Aylmer took her guests to all sorts of places of local interest. She had neighbors join them to dine in the evenings, she had good music and games for the young folks, and dancing on more than one occasion in the great hall. The time passed on wings, and the three guests thoroughly enjoyed themselves.

Both Trevor and Bertha were greatly responsible for this happy state of things. Bertha, having quickly discovered that Kitty would not betray her secret, resumed that manner which had always made her popular. Bertha, in reality one of the most selfish women who ever lived—who had wrecked more lives than one in the course of her unscrupulous career—could be to all appearances the most absolutely unselfish. So day after day, by tact, by apparent kindness, by much cleverness, she led the conversation into the brightest channels. Kitty could not help owning that she was charming. Now and then, it is true, she sighed to herself and wished that she could forget the dark spot in Bertha's past.

Sir John Wallis looked often at the strange girl with a feeling of surprise struggling with a newborn respect. After all, was he to bring up the girl's past to her? She had conquered, no doubt. She had turned over a new leaf. Of course, he and Kitty and his old friend, Colonel Sharston, would never breathe a word to injure her. And Bertha, who was quick to read approval in the eye of those she wished to please, felt her heart grow light within her.

Trevor, too, was more or less off his guard. He knew what Mrs. Aylmer expected of him, but he resolved to shut away the knowledge. He liked Kitty most heartily for herself. She was one of the most amiable and one of the most sweetest girls he had ever met. But the sore feeling in his heart of hearts with regard to Florence never deserted him, and it was her image which rose before his eyes when he looked at Kitty, and it was about Florence he liked best to speak.

Kitty and Trevor often went away for long walks together, and during those walks they talked of Florence. Trevor gradually but surely began to tell her how bitterly he felt the position in which Mrs. Aylmer had placed her own niece.

"I cannot take her place," he said. "You would not if you were placed in the same position?"

"If I were you I would not," said Kitty in her gentle voice. But then she added with a sigh, "Although she is so kind to us, I am afraid Mrs. Aylmer will never forgive poor Flo."

Trevor was silent for a moment, then he said slowly, "This mystery of the past, am I never to know about it?"

Kitty looked at him, and her gentle gray eyes flashed. "You are never to know about it from me," she said.

He bowed, and immediately turned the conversation.

A fortnight had nearly gone by, and the guests now felt themselves thoroughly at home at Aylmer's Court. Late one afternoon, the telegraph boy was seen coming down the avenue. He met Trevor and asked him immediately if Miss Keys were at home. Trevor replied that he did not know where Miss Keys was. It turned out that she had been away for several hours. Trevor consented to take charge of the telegram. As no answer was possible, the boy departed on his way.

Bertha didn't come home until it was time to dress for dinner. It was quite late, for they dined at a fashionable hour. The telegram was lying on the hall table. She saw that it was addressed to herself, and started. She did not often receive telegrams. She tore it open. Its contents were the reverse of reassuring. If Florence appeared on the scene now, what incalculable mischief she might effect! How could she stop the headstrong girl? She glanced at the clock and stamped her foot with impatience. The little telegraph office in the nearest village had been closed for the last hour and a half. It would be impossible, except by going by train to the nearest town, to send off a telegram that night.

In spite of all her efforts, she could scarcely maintain conversation during the evening which followed. Part way through the evening, Trevor asked her privately if she had received her telegram. "It came two or three hours ago," he said. "The messenger wanted to wait for an answer, but I knew you would not be home until late. I hope you have had no bad news."

"Irritating news," she replied in a whisper. "Pray don't speak of it to others. I don't want it mentioned that I have had a telegram."

He glanced at her and slightly raised his brows. She saw that he was disturbed and that a sort of suspicion was stealing over him. She came nearer, and by way of looking over the illustrated paper which he was glancing through, said, in a very low voice, "It was from Florence Aylmer. She has got herself into a fresh scrape, I am afraid."

He threw back his head with an impatient movement.

"What do you mean?"

"Nothing, but if you wish to do her a good turn you will not mention the fact that I have received this telegram."

There was nothing more to be said, and Trevor walked across the room to the piano. He and Kitty both had good voices, and they sang some duets together.

During the night which followed Bertha slept but little. Again and again she took up Florence's telegram and looked at it. She would be at Hamslade, the nearest station to Aylmer's Court, between nine and ten o'clock. Bertha resolved to meet her at the station.

Bertha got up early the next morning. She ran downstairs and had a private interview with the cook. It was Mrs. Aylmer's custom, no matter what guests were present, to breakfast in her room. Immediately after breakfast Bertha, as a rule, waited on her to receive her orders for the day. These orders were then conveyed to the cook and the rest of the servants.

She had a chat with the cook and then wrote a brief note to Mrs. Aylmer. It ran as follows:

> I am going in the dogcart to Hamslade. Have just ascertained that the pheasants we intended to have for dinner today are not forthcoming. Will wire for some to town, and also for peaches. I will leave a line with Kitty Sharston to take head of the table at breakfast.

"She will be awfully cross about it all," thought Bertha, "and of course, it is a lie, for there is plenty of game in the larder, and we have an abundant supply of peaches and apricots, but cook will not betray me."

The dogcart was round at the door sharp at nine o'clock, and Bertha, having sent up a bit of paper to Kitty's bedroom asking her to pour out coffee, started on her way. She reached the station a little before the train came in, and sent the necessary telegrams to the shops in London with which they constantly dealt. A large party was expected to dine at Aylmer's Court that night, which was Bertha's excuse for ordering the fruit and game.

"What mad craze is this?" she cried. "You know you cannot possibly come to Aylmer's Court. I came here to prevent it. Now, what is it you want with me?"

The train was rather late, which added to her impatience. She paced up and down the platform. When at last Florence's anxious, perturbed face appeared, Bertha was by no means in the best of humors.

"What mad craze is this?" she cried. "You know you cannot possibly come to Aylmer's Court. I came here to prevent it. Now, what is it you want with me?"

"I must speak to you, and at once, Bertha," said Florence.

"Come into the waiting room for a moment. You must return by the next train, Florence. You don't know how terribly annoyed I am and what risks I run in coming here. The house is full of company, and there is to be a dinner party tonight. Mrs. Aylmer won't forgive me in a hurry."

While Bertha was talking Florence remained silent.

"We must find out the next train to town," continued Bertha.

"I am not going back until you do what I want," said Florence. "I dare not. If you do not choose to have me at Aylmer's Court, I will stay here. But you must do what I want."

"What is that?"

"I want you to write an essay for me immediately."

"Oh, my dear, what utter folly! Really, when I think of the way in which I have helped you, and the splendid productions which are being palmed off to the world as yours, you might treat me with a little more consideration. My head is addled with all I have to do, and now you come down to ask me to write an essay."

"Listen, Bertha, listen," said poor Florence. She then told her story in as few words as possible.

"I made such a fool of myself. I was very nearly betrayed, but fortunately Mr. Franks and Mr. Anderson took it as a practical joke. I have promised that they shall have an admirable essay by tomorrow evening. You must write it; you must let me have it to take back with me."

"What is the subject?" said Bertha, who was now listening attentively.

"The modern woman and her new crazes. You know you have all that sort of thing at your fingertips," said Florence.

"Oh, yes, I could write about the silly creatures if I had time. But how can I find time today? It is not even a story. I have to think the whole subject out and start my argument and—it cannot be done, Florence."

"But it must be done," replied Florence. "Bertha, I am desperate. I have gone wrong again, and you are the cause, and now I will not lose all. Oh, I am a miserable girl!"

"Don't talk such folly," said Bertha. "Do let me think."

They were now both seated in the waiting room, and Bertha covered her face for a moment with her hands. Florence felt hemmed in, and now that she was face to face with Bertha she found that she regarded her with loathing.

Presently Bertha raised her head and glanced at her.

"You must have it tonight?"

"Yes."

"Well, the best thing I can possibly do is to go straight home. I will leave you here. You must on no account let anyone see you. I will try to get to the station this evening and let you have it. I don't know that I can write anything worth reading in the time."

"But at least you will give style and pure English," said poor Florence, who was sore after the bitter words with which her own production had been received.

"Yes, I shall at least write like a woman of education," said Bertha. "Well, stay here now, and I will, by hook or by crook, come here in time for you to take the last train to town. I suppose it would not do if I posted it?"

"No, it would not. I dare not go back without it. You think I am altogether in your power. But I am desperate, and if you do not let me have that essay tonight I will come to the Court, whoever dines there, and see you. What does it matter to me? Aunt Susan cannot hate me more than she does."

"You shall have the essay, of course," said Bertha, who turned pale when Florence uttered this threat.

When Bertha entered the house she saw that Mrs. Aylmer was in just as bad a humor as Bertha had expected. Everything, she declared, was going wrong. She wished she had not asked those guests to dinner. If there was no game or proper fruit for dessert, she, Mrs. Aylmer, would be disgraced for life.

Bertha roused herself to be soothing and diplomatic. She brought all her fund of talent and ingenuity to the fore, and presently had arranged things so well that she was able to rush to her desk in Mrs. Aylmer's boudoir and begin to write Florence's essay.

Bertha was a quick writer and had a great deal of genius, but she was harassed and worried today. For a time the paper which she had promised to give to Florence did not go smoothly. She was in reality much interested in the struggles of the woman who was called "modern." She felt that she herself belonged to the class. Had she time she would have written with much power, upholding her, commending her, assuring her that by-and-by those who watched her struggles would sympathize with her more and more.

But she had not time to do this. It was much easier to be sarcastic, bitter, crushing. This was her real gift. She determined to write quickly and in her bitterest vein. The paper she was writing would make the modern woman sit up and would make the domestic woman rejoice. It was dead against all reform with regard to women's education. It was cruel in its pretended lack of knowledge of woman's modern needs.

If Bertha possessed one weapon which she used with greater power than another it was that of sarcasm. She could be sarcastic to the point of cruelty. Soon her cheeks glowed and her eyes shone. She was writing quickly, and she was writing well. But it was not a kind paper. It was the sort of paper to do harm, not good. She finished it just before the luncheon gong rang, and felt that she had done admirable work.

"After all," she said to herself, "why should I work through the channel of that little imp, Florence Aylmer? Why should she have the fame and glory, and I stay here as a poor companion? Why should I not throw up the thing and start myself as a writer and get praise and money? Why should I not do it?" Bertha thought. She held the paper in her hand. It was but to betray Florence and go herself to the editor of the *Argonaut* and explain everything, and the deed was done. But she could not do it. She knew better—she was trying for a bigger prize.

"Either I inherit Mrs. Aylmer's wealth or I marry Maurice Trevor and inherit it as his wife," she thought. "I think I see my way. He will never marry Kitty Sharston. He neither wants her nor she him. He is to be my husband, or he goes under completely and I secure Mrs. Aylmer's wealth. No amount of writing would give me what I shall get in that way. I can keep Florence quiet with this, and she is welcome, heartily welcome, to the cheap applause."

XXV

Trevor
and Florence

t was Bertha's intention to go back to the railway station in the dogcart in order to secure the pheasants and fruit for the coming party. But just as she was preparing to jump on the cart, Mrs. Aylmer herself appeared.

"My dear Bertha," she said, "where are you going?"

Bertha explained.

"That is quite unnecessary. You can send Thomas. I want you to come for a drive with me. I wish to see Mrs. Paton of Paton Manor. I have not yet returned her call. There are also other calls which I want to make. The young people are away enjoying themselves, and our elderly friends have gone shooting. You must come with me, as I cannot possibly go alone."

As Mrs. Aylmer spoke the jingle of bells was heard and Bertha, raising her eyes, saw the pretty ponies which drew Mrs. Aylmer's own special little carriage trotting down the avenue. Bertha had always driven Mrs. Aylmer in this little carriage, and much as she enjoyed doing so, it was by no means her wish to do so now. She looked at Mrs. Aylmer.

"The cook really does want the things from town."

"That does not matter, my dear. Thomas is driving the dog-cart and can call for the things. He had better go straight away at once."

Mrs. Aylmer gave directions to the man, who whipped up the horse and disappeared down the avenue.

Bertha felt a momentary sense of despair. Then her quick wit came to the rescue. "I quite forgot to give Thomas a message," she said. "He must have it. Excuse me one minute, Mrs. Aylmer."

Before Mrs. Aylmer could prevent her she was running after the dogcart as fast as she could go. She shouted to Thomas, who drew up.

"Yes, miss," he said. "What is it?"

"You must take this parcel. There is a young lady waiting for it at the station. See that she gets it. Get one of the porters to put it into her hand. There is no message; just have the parcel delivered to her."

"But what is the name of the young lady, miss?"

Bertha had not thought of that. She looked back again at the house. Mrs. Aylmer was getting impatient and was waving her hand to her to come back.

"Her name is Miss Florence Aylmer. See that the parcel is put into her hands."

Thomas, not greatly caring whom the message was for, promised to see it safely delivered.

"I do trust things will go right," thought Bertha to herself. "It is extremely dangerous. Florence certainly was mad when she came to this part of the country."

There was no help for it, however. Bertha was learning once more that the way of transgressors is hard. She had to stifle all her feelings of anxiety, help Mrs. Aylmer into her pretty pony carriage, and take the reins.

Meanwhile Thomas and the spirited mare went as fast as possible to the railway station. The mare did not like the trains, which were coming and going at this moment in considerable numbers. She did not like to stand still with so many huge and terrible monsters rushing by. Thomas did not care to leave her, so he called to a porter who stood near.

"I have come for some things from town. They must have arrived by the last train. Are there any packages for Mrs. Aylmer of Aylmer's Court?"

"I'll go and see," said the man.

He presently returned with the pheasants and fruit, which had arrived in due course. Thomas saw them deposited in the dogcart and was just turning the mare's head toward home when he suddenly remembered the parcel. He drew up the animal again almost on its haunches. It reared in a state of fright. The porter had already disappeared into the station, and Thomas knew better than to return home without obeying Bertha's orders. He looked around him, and just at that moment he saw Maurice Trevor crossing a field in a leisurely fashion. Maurice drew up when he saw Thomas.

"Hallo," he said. "What are you doing here, Thomas?"

"I came for some parcels from town, sir. I wonder, sir, if you would either hold the mare for a minute or do a commission for Miss Keys?"

"I will do the commission. What is it?"

"It is not much, sir. Just to deliver this parcel to a young lady who is waiting for it at the station."

"A young lady who is waiting for it at the station?" questioned Trevor.

"Yes, sir. Miss Florence Aylmer. There is no answer, sir."

Trevor received the little brown paper parcel in unbounded astonishment.

Thomas, relieved and feeling that his duty was well done, gave the mare her head and was soon out of sight. Trevor entered the station. He went to the ladies' waiting room and there saw Florence Aylmer. She came to the door the moment he appeared.

"What are you doing here?" was his exclamation.

"You may well wonder. But why are you here?"

"I came to give you this." As he spoke he placed the little parcel in Florence's hands.

"Thank you," she said. She had brought a small bag with her. She opened it and dropped the parcel into it. Her face had turned red when she saw Trevor; it was now very white.

He stood leaning up against the door of the waiting room and contemplated her in astonishment.

"What have you been doing here all day?" he repeated.

"That is my affair," she answered.

"Forgive me. I do not want to be unduly curious, but surely when you were so near you might have come on to the Court. We should all have been glad to see you."

"You must please remember, Mr. Trevor," said Florence, speaking in as stately a tone as she could assume, "that Mrs. Aylmer does not act as my aunt—she does not wish to have anything to do with me."

"But you have been here for hours in this dingy waiting room."

"No, I took a walk when I thought no one was looking."

"That means you do not wish it to be known that you are here?"

"I earnestly beg of you not to mention it. Did Miss Keys really give you the parcel to bring to me?"

"She really did nothing of the kind. She gave it to one of the grooms, who could not leave a spirited mare. He saw me and asked me to deliver it into your hands."

"Thank you," said Florence. She stood silent for a moment, then she looked at the clock.

"I must go," she said. "There is a train back to town immediately, and I want to cross to the other platform."

"I will see you into the train if you will allow me."

Florence could not refuse, but she heartily wished Trevor anywhere else in the world.

"You will be sure not to mention that you saw me here," she said.

"I may speak of it, I suppose, to Miss Keys?"

"I wish you would not."

"I won't promise, Miss Aylmer. I am very uncomfortable regarding the position you are in. It is hateful to me to feel that you should come here like a thief in the night and stay for hours at the railway station. What mystery is there between you and Miss Keys?"

Florence was silent.

"You admit that there is a mystery?"

"I admit that there is a secret between us which I am not going to tell you."

He reddened slightly, and then he looked at her. She was holding her head well back, her figure was very upright, and there was a proud indignation about her. His heart ached as he watched her.

"I think of you often," he said. "Your strange and inexplicable story is a great weight and trouble on my mind."

"I wish you would not think of me. I wish you would forget me."

Florence looked full at him, her angry dark eyes were full of misery.

"Suppose that is impossible?" he said, lowering his voice. There was something in his tone which made her heart give a sudden bound of absolute gladness. But what right had she to be glad? She hated herself for the sensation.

Trevor came closer to her side.

"I have very nearly made up my mind," he said. "When it is quite made up I shall come to see you in town. This is your train." He opened the door of a first-class carriage.

"I am going third," said Florence.

Without comment he walked down a few steps of the plat-form with her. An empty third-class carriage was soon found.

"Goodbye," he said. He took off his hat and watched the train move out of the station. Then he returned slowly—very slowly—to Aylmer's Court. He could not quite account for his own feelings. He had meant to go to meet Kitty and her father, who were both going to walk back by the river, but he did not care to see either of them just now.

He was puzzled and very angry with Bertha Keys—even more angry than he was with Mrs. Aylmer. And he had a sore sense of unrest and misery with regard to Florence.

"What can she want with Miss Keys? What can be the secret between them?" he said to himself over and over again. He was far from suspecting the truth.

Bertha returned from her drive in apparently excellent spirits. She entered the hall to find Trevor standing there alone.

"Why are you back so early?" she said.

He did not speak at all for a moment, then he came closer to her. Before he could utter a word she sprang to a small table and took up a copy of the *Argonaut*.

"You are interested in Miss Aylmer. Have you read her story—the first story she has ever published?" she asked.

"No," he replied. "Is it there?"

"It is. The reviews are praising it. She will do very well as a writer."

Kitty Sharston and her father appeared at that moment.

"Look, Miss Sharston," exclaimed Trevor. "You know Miss Aylmer. This is her story. Have you read it?"

"I have not," said Kitty. "How inter-esting. I did not know that the *Argonaut* had come. Florence told me she was writing in it." She took it up and turned the pages.

"You are one of those painfully priggish people, Mr. Trevor, who will never get on in the world. Have you not yet discovered that being extra good does not pay?"

"Oh!" she exclaimed once or twice.

Trevor stood near.

Bertha went and warmed herself by the fire.

"Oh!" said Kitty, "this is good." Then she began to laugh. "Only I wish she were not quite so bitter," she exclaimed a moment later. "It is wonderfully clever. Do read it, Mr. Trevor."

Trevor was impatient to do so. He took the magazine when Kitty handed it to him and began to read rapidly. Soon he was absorbed in the tale. As he proceeded with it an angry flush deepened on his cheeks.

"What is the matter?" said Bertha, who, for reasons of her own, was watching this little scene with interest.

"I don't like the tone of this," he said. "Of course, it is clever."

"It is very clever, and what does the tone matter?" said Bertha. "You are one of those painfully priggish people, Mr.

Trevor, who will never get on in the world. Have you not yet discovered that being extra good does not pay?"

"I am not extra good. But being good pays in the long run," he answered. He darted an indignant glance at Bertha Keys and left the hall. Scarcely knowing why he did so, he strode into Mrs. Aylmer's boudoir. Bertha's desk, covered with paper, attracted his attention. There was a book lying near which he was reading. He picked it up and was just turning away when a scrap of thin paper arrested his eye. It was scribbled over in Bertha's well-known hand. Before he meant to do so he found that he had read a sentence on this paper. There was a sharpness and subtlety in the wording of the sentence which puzzled him for a moment. And suddenly he was startled by the resemblance to the style of the story in the *Argonaut*, which he had just read.

He scarcely connected the two yet, but his heart sank lower in his breast. He thought for a moment, then opening his pocket-book, he placed the torn scrap of paper in it and went away to his room. It was nearly time to dress for dinner.

Mrs. Aylmer always expected her adopted son to help her to receive her guests, but Trevor made no attempt to get into his evening suit. His valet knocked at the door, but he dismissed him.

"I don't want your services tonight, Johnson," said the young man. Johnson withdrew.

"It is all horrible," thought Trevor. "All this wealth and luxury for me and all the roughnesses for her, poor girl! But why should I think so much about her as I do? Why do I hate that story, clever as it is? The story is not like her. It hurts me to think that she could have written it. Is it possible that I—" And here his heart beat more quickly than usual—"Is it possible," he repeated softly, under his breath, "that I am beginning to like her too much? Surely not too much! Suppose that is the way out of the difficulty?" He laughed aloud, and there was relief in the sound.

XXVI

Plotting
Hearts

itty Sharston, wearing the softest of white dresses, was playing Trevor's accompaniment at the grand piano. He had a beautiful voice—a very rich tenor. Kitty herself had a sweet and high soprano. The two now sang together. The music proceeded, broken now and then by snatches of conversation. No one was especially listening to the young pair, although some eyes were watching them.

In a distant part of the room Sir John Wallis and Mrs. Aylmer were having a discussion.

"I like him," said Sir John. "You are lucky in having secured so worthy an heir for your property."

"You don't like him better than I like your adopted child, Miss Sharston," was Mrs. Aylmer's low answer.

"Ay, she is a sweet girl—no one like her in the world," said Sir John. "I almost grudge her to her father, much as I love him. We were comrades on the battlefield, you know. Perhaps he has told you that story."

"I have heard it, but not from him," said Mrs. Aylmer with a smile. "Your friendship with each other is quite of the David and Jonathan order. And so, my good friend"—she laid her white hand for an instant on Sir John's arm—"you are going to leave your property to your favorite Kitty?"

Sir John frowned, then said shortly, "I see no reason for denying the fact. Kitty Sharston, when it pleases God to remove me, will inherit my wealth."

"She is a sweet, very sweet girl," replied Mrs. Aylmer. She glanced down the room.

Sir John followed her look. Kitty and Trevor had now stopped all music. Trevor was talking in a low tone to the girl. Kitty's head was slightly bent and she was pulling a white chrysanthemum to pieces.

"I wonder what he is saying to her?" thought Mrs. Aylmer. Then all of a sudden she made up her mind. "I should like it," she said aloud, "I should like it much."

Sir John started, and a slight flush of color came into his ruddy cheeks.

"What do you mean?" he said.

"Have you never thought of it? It is right for the young to marry. This would be a match after my own heart. Would it please you?"

"It would if it were God's will," said Sir John emphatically. He looked again at the pair by the piano, and then across the long room to Colonel Sharston. Colonel Sharston was absorbed in a game of chess with Bertha Keys. He was noticing nothing but the intricacies of the game.

"All the same," added Sir John, "her father and I are in no hurry to see Kitty settled in life. She is most precious to us both. We should scarcely know ourselves without her."

"Oh, come now, I call that selfish," said Mrs. Aylmer. "A pretty girl must find her true mate, and there is nothing so happy as happy married life."

"Granted, granted," said Sir John.

"You and I, Sir John, are not so young as we used to be. It would be nice for us to see those we love united, to feel that whatever storms life may bring they will bear them together. But say nothing to Colonel Sharston on the subject yet. I am glad to feel that when *my son*, as I always call Maurice, proposes to *your daughter*, as you doubtless think Kitty, there will be no objection on your part."

"None whatever, except that I shall be sorry to lose her. I have a great admiration for Trevor. He is a man quite after my own heart."

Soon afterward Sir John moved away.

Mrs. Aylmer, having sown the seed she desired to sow, was satisfied. From time to time the old man watched the pretty, bright-eyed girl. During the rest of the evening Trevor scarcely left her side. They had much to talk over, much in common. Mrs. Aylmer was in the highest spirits.

"Yes, I must bring things to an issue," she told herself. "The Sharstons and Sir John leave on Monday. Maurice must make up his mind to propose to Miss Sharston almost immediately afterward. He can follow them to Southsea, where they have taken a house for the winter. We will have a grand wedding in the spring, and Kitty shall come and live with me. I need not keep Bertha Keys when Kitty is always in the house. Kitty would suit me much better. I seldom saw a girl I liked more thoroughly."

Meanwhile Kitty Sharston and her companion, little guessing the thoughts which were passing through the minds of their elders, were busily talking over the one subject which now occupied all Trevor's thoughts. Like bees round a flower, these thoughts drew nearer and nearer every moment to the subject of Florence Aylmer. Incidents of Florence's life at school always

"Hush!" she whispered. "Be careful what you say. Remember you injure her. Mr. Trevor, I think I see Mrs. Alymer beckoning to you."

made him laugh. He was glad to hear of her small triumphs, which Kitty related to him with much enthusiasm.

That evening, while Mrs. Aylmer was quite certain that Maurice was saying something very tender and suitable, Trevor was asking, "Was Miss Aylmer ever remarkable for the excellence of her essays and themes?"

"Ever remarkable for the excellence of her essays or themes?" repeated Kitty.

Before she could reply, Bertha, whose game was over, and who had just given an emphatic checkmate to her enemy, strolled across the room. Kitty's eyes met hers, and Kitty's cheeks turned pale.

"I don't think she was especially remarkable for the excellence of her writing," said Kitty then, in a low voice.

"You surprise me. Such talent as she now possesses must have been more or less inherent in her even as a child."

"It does not always follow," said Bertha, suddenly joining in the conversation. "I presume you are both talking of your favorite heroine, Florence Aylmer. But you remember an occasion, however, Miss Sharston, when Florence Aylmer *did* receive much applause for an essay."

"I do," said Kitty. "How dare you speak of it?" She rose to her feet in ungovernable excitement. Her eyes blazed, her cheeks were full of color.

Another instant and she might have blurted out all the truth and ruined Bertha forever, had not that young lady laid her hand on her arm.

"Hush!" she whispered. "Be careful what you say. Remember you injure her. Mr. Trevor, I think I see Mrs. Aylmer beckoning to you."

Mrs. Aylmer was doing nothing of the kind, but Trevor was obliged to go to her. Kitty soon subsided on her seat.

"Why did you say that?" she said.

"Can you not guess? I wanted to save the situation. Why should poor Florence be suspected of having written badly when she was young? It is much more natural for you, who are her true friend, to uphold her and to allow people to think that the great talent which she now possesses was always in evidence. I spoke no less than the truth. That essay of hers was much commented on and loudly applauded."

"Oh, you know you have told a lie—the worst sort of lie," said Kitty. "Oh, what am I to say? Sometimes I hate you."

"I know you hate me, but you have no cause to. I am quite on your side."

"I don't understand you, and I will not talk to you any further." Kitty rose, crossed the room, and sat down by her father.

"She is a very nice girl. Far too good to be thrown away on him," thought Bertha to herself. "I admire her as I admire few people. She was always steadfast of purpose and pure of soul. She will be a charming wife for a man who loves her, someday. But she is not for Maurice Trevor. He does not care like *that* for her! Yes, I know the old folks are plotting and planning, but all their plots and plans will come to nothing. There will be a fine fracas soon, and I must see that whatever happens, my bread is well buttered."

XXVII

Trevor Rebels

n the morning of the day when the guests were to depart, Mrs. Aylmer sent for Trevor to come to her room. He entered unwillingly. He had begun to dislike his little talks with Mrs. Aylmer very much.

"Now, my dear boy, just sit down and let us have a cozy chat," said the old lady.

Trevor stood near the open window.

"The day is so mild," he said, "that it is almost summer. Who would suppose that we were close to December?"

"I have not sent for you, Maurice, to talk of the weather. I have something much more important to say."

"And what is that?" he asked.

"You remember our last conversation in this room?"

He knitted his brows.

"I remember it," he answered.

"I want to carry it on now. We have come to the second chapter."

"What do you mean by that?"

"Our last conversation was introductory. Now the story opens. You have behaved quite as well as I could have hoped during the time that the Sharstons and Sir John Wallis have stayed here."

"I am glad you are pleased with my behavior. But in reality I did not behave well, according to your meaning. I am just as much a rebel as ever."

"Maurice, my dear boy, try not to talk nonsense. Try to look a little ahead. How old are you?"

"I shall be six-and-twenty early in the year."

> "I intend to propose to Florence Aylmer. Whether she will accept me or not, I only know I love her."

"Quite a boy," said Mrs. Aylmer in a slightly contemptuous voice. "In ten years you will be six-and-thirty, in twenty six-and-forty. In twenty years from now you will much rejoice over what—what may not be quite to your taste at the present moment. Though it is impossible, absolutely impossible, that you should not love that sweet and beautiful girl."

"Which girl do you mean?" queried Trevor.

"You know perfectly well to whom I allude."

"Miss Sharston? She is far too good, far too sweet to have her name bandied between us. I decline to discuss her."

"You must discuss her. You can do so with all possible respect. Kitty Sharston is to be your wife, Maurice."

"She will never be my wife," he replied. His tone was so firm, he stood so upright as he spoke, his eyes were fixed so sternly, that just for a moment Mrs. Aylmer recognized that she had met her match.

"You refuse to do what I wish?" she said then slowly. "I, who have done all for you?"

"I refuse to do this. This is the final straw of all. No wealth is worth having at the price you offer. I will only marry the woman I love. I respect, I admire, I reverence Miss Sharston, but I do not love her, nor does she love me. It is sacrilege to talk of a marriage between us. If I offered she would refuse. Besides—"

"Why do you stop? Go on. What is your intention in the future?"

"Justice," he replied. "I cannot bear this. It troubles me more than I can say. If you will not reinstate the girl who ought to be your heiress in her right position, I will do what I can for her. I will offer her all I have."

"You! you!" Mrs. Aylmer now indeed turned pale. She rose from her seat and came nearer the young man.

"You are mad. You must be mad," she said. "What does this mean?"

"It means that I intend to propose to Florence Aylmer. Whether she will accept me or not, I only know I love her."

"You told me a short time ago that you were not in love with her."

"I had not then looked into my own heart. Now I find that I care for no one else. Her image fills my mind day and night. I am unhappy about her—too unhappy to endure this state of things any longer."

"Do you think she will take you, a penniless man? Do you think you are a good match for her or for any girl?"

"That has nothing to do with it. If she loves me she will accept all that I can give her, and I can work for my living."

"I will not listen to another word of this. You have pained me inexpressibly."

"You gave me time to decide, and I have decided. If you will forgive Miss Aylmer whatever she happened to do to displease you, if you will make her joint heiress with me in your estates, then we will both serve you and love you most faithfully and most truly. But if you will not give her back her true position, I will offer her all that a man can offer—his heart, his worship, and all the talent he possesses. I can work for my wife, and I shall be fifty times happier than in my present position."

Mrs. Aylmer pointed to the door.

"I will not speak to you anymore," she said. "This is disastrous, disgraceful! Go! Leave my presence!"

⁂

Thomas Franks was much relieved when, on the morning after her return to town, Florence sent him the paper which Bertha had written. Florence herself took the precaution to carefully copy it out. As she did so, she could scarcely read the words. There were burning spots on her cheeks, and her head ached terribly.

Having completed her task, she sent it off by post, and in good time Tom Franks received Bertha's work. He read it over at first with some slight trepidation, then with smiling eyes and a heart beating high with satisfaction. He took it immediately to his chief.

"Ah! this is all right," he said. "Read it. You will be pleased. It quite fulfills the early promise."

Mr. Anderson glanced rapidly over Bertha's paper.

"Miss Florence Aylmer has done good work," he said when he had finished. "And yet—" A thoughtful expression crossed his face. "It is difficult for me to believe that any girl could write in what I call so agnostic a spirit. There is a bitterness, a want of belief, an absence of all feeling in this production. I admit its cleverness, but I should be sorry to know much of the woman who has written it."

"I admire talent in any form," said Tom Franks. "It will run, of course. People who want smart things will like it. Believe me, it will do good, not harm."

"It may do good from a financial point of view," said Mr. Anderson, "but I wish the girl who has those great abilities would turn them to a higher form of expression. She might do great things then, and move the world in a right way."

"I grant you that the whole thing is pessimistic," said Franks. "But its cleverness redeems it. It will call attention, and the next story by Miss Aylmer which appears in the *Argonaut* will be more appreciated than her last."

"See that that story appears in the next issue," said his chief to Franks, and the young man left the room.

Florence received in due time a proof of her paper for correction. There was little alteration, however, needed in Bertha's masterly essay. But Florence was obliged to read it carefully, and her heart stood still once or twice as she read the expressions which she herself was supposed to have given birth to. She had just finished when Edith Franks came into the room.

"I have just seen Tom," she said. "He is delighted with your essay. Is that it? Have you corrected it? May I look through it?"

"I would much rather you did not read it, Edith."

"What nonsense! It is to be published, and I shall see it then."

"Well, read it when it is in the paper, only I would rather you didn't read it at all."

"What do you mean?"

"I don't like it."

"Why do you write what you don't like?" asked Edith, fixing her sharp eyes on her new friend's face. Edith went up to her and possessed herself of the long slip of proof she was holding in her hand.

"I am going to read it now," she said. "I always said you were neurotic. Oh, good gracious! What an extraordinary opening sentence! You are a queer girl!"

Edith read on to the end. She then handed the paper back to Florence.

"What do you think of it?" said Florence, noticing that she was silent.

"I hate it."

"I thought you would. Oh, Edith, I am glad!"

"What do you mean by that?"

"Because I so cordially hate it, too."

"I would not publish it if I were in your place," said Edith. "It may do harm. It is against the woman who is struggling so bravely. It turns her noblest feelings into ridicule. Why do you write such things, Florence?"

"One cannot help oneself," replied Florence.

"Rubbish! One can always help doing wrong. You have been queer all through. I cannot pretend to understand you. But as Tom admires it so much, I suppose it must go into the paper. Will you put it into an envelope, and I will post it?"

Florence did so. She directed the envelope to the editor, and Edith took it out with her.

As she was leaving the room, she turned to Florence and said, "Try and make your next thing more healthy. I hope to goodness very few people will read this."

She ran downstairs. Just as she was about to drop the little packet into the pillarbox, she glanced at her watch.

"I shall have time to go and see Tom. I don't like this thing," she said to herself. "Miss Aylmer ought not to write what will do direct harm. It ought not to be published. I will speak to

Tom about it. Some of the worst passages might at least be altered or expunged."

Edith arrived in her brother's own private room shortly before he was finishing for the day.

"Here is the work of your precious protégée," she said, flinging the manuscript on Tom's desk. He took it up.

"Has she corrected it? I want to send it to the printer. By the way, Edith, have you read it?"

"I grieve to say I have."

Tom Franks looked at her in a puzzled way.

"Why do you speak in that tone?"

"Because it is so horrible and so false, Tom. Why do you publish it? Don't send it to the printers like that. Poor Florence must be a little mad. Cut out some of the passages. Give it to me, and I'll show you. This one, for instance, and this."

Tom Franks took the paper from her. "It goes in entire, or it does not go in at all," he said. "Its cleverness will carry the day. I must speak to Miss Aylmer. She must not give vent to her true feelings. In the future she must put a check on them."

"She must have a terrible mind," said Edith. "If I had known it, I don't think I could have made her my friend."

"Oh, don't give her up now," said Tom, "poor girl, she is to be pitied."

"Of course she is. Great talent like hers often means a tendency to insanity. I must watch her."

"She is monstrously clever," said Tom Franks. "I admire her very much."

Edith, feeling that she had done no good, left the office.

XXVIII

Reprimands from Home

n due time the first issue of the new weekly paper appeared, and Florence's article was on the leading page. It created, as Tom Franks knew it would, a good deal of criticism. It met with a shower of abuse from one party, and warm notices of congratulation from another. It certainly increased the sale of the paper and made people look eagerly forward to the next work of the rising star.

Florence, who would not glance at the paper once it had appeared, and who did her utmost to forget Bertha's work, tried to believe that she was happy. She had now really as much money as she needed to spend and was able to send her mother cheques.

Mrs. Aylmer was in the seventh heaven of bliss. As to Sukey, she was perfectly sick of hearing of Miss Florence's talents and Miss Florence's success. Mrs. Aylmer the less thought it high time to write a congratulatory letter to her daughter.

> My dear Flo,
>
> You are the talk of the place. I never knew anything like it. I am invaded by visitors. I am leading quite a picnic life, hardly ever having a meal at home. And with your

cheques I am able to dress myself properly. Sukey also enjoys the change. But why, my dear love, don't you send copies of that wonderful magazine to your loving mother? I have just suggested to a whole number of your admirers to meet me at this house on Wednesday next, when I propose to read aloud to them either your article in the *General Review* or one of your stories in the *Argonaut*. Do send me the copies, dear.

At this point in her letter Mrs. Aylmer broke off abruptly. There had come a great blot of ink on the paper, as if her pen had suddenly fallen from her hand. Later on the letter was continued, but in a different tone.

Our clergyman, Mr. Walker, has just been to see me. What do you think he has come about? He brought your paper with him and read passages of it aloud. He said that it was my duty immediately to see you, and to do my utmost to get you into a better frame of mind.

He says your style—I am quoting his exact words—and your sentiments are bitterly wrong, and will do a lot of mischief. My dear girl, what does this mean? Just when your poor, doting old mother was so full of bliss and so proud of you, to give her a knock-down blow of this sort! I must request, my precious child, the next time you write for the *General Review* to do a paper which will not cause such remarks. You might write a nice little essay on flowers, spring flowers?—I think that would be so sweet and poetic—or the sad sea waves? I really did not know that I had such a clever brain myself. You must have inherited your talent from me, darling.

Now, do write a paper on the sad sea waves. I know I shall cry over it. I feel it beforehand. Don't forget, my love, the lessons your poor mother has tried to teach you.

Your affectionate Mother

This letter was received by Florence on the following morning. She was seated at her desk, carefully copying the last production sent to her by Bertha Keys. It was not an essay this time, but a story, and was couched in rather milder terms than her two previous stories. Florence thrust it into a drawer, read her mother's letter from end to end, and then, covering her face with her hands, sat for a long time motionless.

"It seems to me I am casting away my own soul," she said to herself. "Nothing gives me pleasure. Even last night, at that party which the Frankses took me to, when people came up and congratulated me, I felt stupid and heavy. I could not answer when I was spoken to, nor carry on arguments. I felt like a fool, and I know I acted as one. If Mr. Franks had not been so kind, I should have openly disgraced myself. Oh, dear! The way of transgressors is *very* hard."

Florence was interrupted by a tap at the door. She was now able to have two rooms at her command in Prince's Mansions, and Franks, who had come to see her, was ushered into a neatly furnished but simple sitting room.

Florence rose to meet him.

"Are you well?" he said, staring at her.

"Why do you ask? I am perfectly well," she replied in a tone of some annoyance.

"I beg your pardon. You look so black under the eyes. Do you work too hard at night?"

"I never work too hard, Mr. Franks. You are absolutely mistaken."

"I am glad to hear it. Is your next story ready?" asked Franks.

"I am finishing it."

"May I see it?"

"No, I cannot show it to you. You shall have it by tomorrow or next day at latest."

"Do you feel inclined to do some more essays for our paper?"

"I would rather not," said Florence.

"But why so?"

"You didn't like my last paper, you know."

"Oh, I admired it for its cleverness. I didn't care for the tone."

"I have just had a letter from mother," said Florence. "I will show you her comments. You will see that, although she was proud of me, it was the pride of ignorance. This is what our clergyman, Mr. Walker, says, and he is right."

Franks read the few words.

"I suppose he is right," he answered. He looked full at the girl and half smiled.

"It would be extremely successful if you would do a paper in a *totally* different tone," he said. "Could you not try?"

"I cannot give what is not in me."

"Well, have a good try. Choose your own subject. Let me have the very best you can. I must not stay any longer now. The story at least will reach me in good time?"

"Yes, and I think you will like it rather better than the last. Goodbye," said Florence.

He held her hand lingeringly for a moment and looked into her face. As he went downstairs he thought a good deal about her. She interested him. If he married, he would as soon have clever and original Florence Aylmer for his wife as any other woman he had ever met.

He was just leaving the house when he came face to face with Trevor. Maurice was hurrying into the house as Franks was going out. He started when he saw Trevor.

"Hallo," he said. "Who would have thought to see you here? How are you?"

"Quite well, thank you."

"I imagined you to be in the country safe with that kind old lady who is feathering your nest."

"I don't think that will come off, Franks. But I do not feel inclined to discuss it. I have come up to town to see Miss Aylmer. How is she?"

"I don't think she is very well. I have just seen her. What a wonderfully clever girl she is!"

"So it seems," said Trevor in a somewhat impatient tone. "Is she in?"

"Yes, I have just come from her."

"Then I won't detain you now." Trevor ran upstairs, and Franks went quickly back to his office.

XXIX

Trevor Proposes
to Florence

revor's vigorous knock came upon Florence's door. She crossed the room and opened the door wide. When she saw Trevor she uttered an exclamation and her eyes shone.

"Is it possible that you have come?" she said. "How are you? Won't you come in?"

He took her hand.

"Yes, I have come," he answered. "Can you give me a little time, or are you too busy?"

"I am never busy," said Florence.

He looked at her in some surprise when she said that, but resolved to take no notice. He had quick eyes and a keen intuition, and he saw at a glance that Florence was uneasy and suffering. She asked him to seat himself and took a chair near.

"How are they all at Aylmer's Court?" she asked.

"When I left yesterday morning they were well," he replied. "Did you know that your friend, Miss Sharston, was on a visit there?"

"Yes, I heard of it. Kitty wrote to me. Do you like Kitty, Mr. Trevor?"

"Of course I like her," he replied, and, remembering what was expected of him by Mrs. Aylmer with regard to Kitty, the bronze on his cheeks deepened.

Florence noticed the increase in color, and her heart beat rapidly.

"I wonder if he does like her and if she likes him. I should not be surprised. I ought to be glad," she thought. But she knew very well that she was not glad.

"I have come with a message from my mother," said Trevor, who was watching her while her eyes were traveling toward the fire. He was thinking how ill and worn she looked, and his heart was full of pity as well as love, but he would not speak yet. He must wait. He must be sure of her feelings before he committed himself.

"I have come with a message from my mother," he repeated. "I want you to come back with me now. You enjoyed your last day at the cottage. It was summer then. It is early winter now, but the heath is still beautiful. Shall we go together and after lunch have a walk on the heath?"

"I am very sorry, but I cannot go," replied Florence. She looked longingly out of the window as she spoke. "No," she repeated, "I cannot."

"But why not? You say you are not busy."

"In one sense I am not busy. But I have some work to do."

"Some of your literary work?"

Florence nodded, but did not speak.

"I have to copy something," she said, after a pause. "I have to send it to the editor of the *Argonaut*."

"Do you know, I have only read one of your stories, the first which appeared in the *Argonaut*? It was clever."

"I wish it had been idiotic," replied Florence. "Everyone says to me, 'Your story is clever.' I hate that story."

"I am delighted to hear you say so. I did not admire it myself. Of course I saw that it was—"

"Don't say again that it was clever. I don't wish to hear anything about it. I cannot come with you today. I have to do some copying."

"Why do you say copying?"

"Because I always copy the manuscripts faithfully before Mr. Franks has them for the *Argonaut*. He is waiting, and I am a slow writer."

"Shall I copy the story for you?"

"Not for all the world," replied Florence.

Trevor rose, a look of annoyance on his face.

"I am sorry you should think of my offer of help in that spirit," he said. "You don't quite understand. Perhaps some day I may be able to make things plain to you. I take a very great interest in you. You have brought—"

"What?" said Florence.

"You have brought a great anxiety and trouble into my life, as well as a very great absorbing interest. But I can say no more now."

"If you will go away," said Florence, "I will begin to work. I have a headache, and I am confused. Go away and come back again, if you like. I shall be better the next time you come."

"Why don't you tell me what is troubling you?"

"How do you know anything troubles me?"

"How do I know?" said Trevor. "I have eyes—eyes and a certain amount of intuition," he added.

"I cannot go today," said Florence, who took no notice of his words. "But perhaps on Sunday I may go to see your mother. Will you be there then?"

"Yes, did you not hear? I have broken with Mrs. Aylmer."

"What!" said Florence. She forgot herself in her excitement. She came two or three steps forward.

"Yes, I cannot stand the life. Mrs. Aylmer is very kind to me and means well. But so long as she is so cruel to you I cannot endure it. I have told her so, and I am going to earn my own living in the future. I am no longer a rich man—indeed, I am a very poor one. But I have brains and I think I have pluck, and someday I am certain I shall succeed."

Trevor held himself erect. His eyes, full of suppressed fire, were fixed on Florence's face. He wanted her to say she was glad; he wanted to get a word of sympathy from her. On the contrary, she turned very white and said in a low, almost broken voice, "Oh, I am terribly sorry! Why have you done this?"

"You are *sorry?*"

"Yes, I am."

"I have done it for you. I cannot stand injustice."

"I could never under any circumstances accept Mrs. Aylmer's money," said Florence. "You do me no good and yourself harm. And your mother was so happy about you. Oh, do go back to Mrs. Aylmer. I know she must be very fond of you. It makes me so miserable to think you should have done this for me. Oh, do go back! She will be so glad to receive you. I know she will receive you with rejoicing."

"Do you know what she wants me to do?" he said. He was very white now. He had thrown prudence to the winds.

"Do you hear me? I love you! I have come today to tell you that I give my life to you. I put it into your hands."

"What?"

" I am obliged to be frank."

"Say what you please. I am willing to listen."

Trevor dropped once more into a chair.

"When I last saw her she made a proposal to me. It was not the first time. It was the second. She wanted me to marry—"

"I know," said Florence. "She wants you to marry Kitty. But why not? She is so sweet. She is the dearest girl in all the world."

"Hush!" said Trevor. "I do not love her, nor does she love me. I can scarcely bear to tell you all this. It is sacrilegious to think of marriage under such circumstances, and above all things to mention it in connection with a girl like Miss Sharston."

Florence found tears springing to her eyes.

"You are very good," she said. "Too good, to sit here and talk to me. Of course, if you don't love Kitty, there is an end of it. Are you quite sure?"

"Positive. I know my own heart too well. I love another."

"Another?"

Florence had a wild fear for a moment that he was alluding to Bertha Keys. A desperate thought came into her brain.

"At any cost, I will open his eyes," she thought. "I will tell him the truth."

Trevor had come nearer and was bending forward and trying to take her hand.

"You are the one I love," he said. "How can I, who love you with all my heart and soul and strength, who would give my life for you, how can I think of anyone else? It does not matter whether you are the most amiable or the most unamiable woman in the world, Florence. You are the one woman on God's earth for me. Do you hear me, Florence? Do you hear me? I love you! I have come today to tell you that I give my life to you. I put it into your hands. I didn't mean to speak, but the truth has been wrung from me. Do you hear me, Florence?"

Florence certainly did hear, but she did not speak. Trevor had taken her hand, and she did not withdraw it. She was stunned for a moment. The next instant there came over her, sweeping round her, entering her heart, filling her whole being, a delicious and marvelous ecstasy. The pain and the trouble vanished. The treachery, the deceit, and the fall she had undergone were forgotten. She only knew that, if Trevor loved her, she loved him. She was about to speak when her eyes fell for a moment on a page of the manuscript she had just written. Like a flash, memory came back.

It stung her cruelly as a serpent might sting. She sprang to her feet and flung down his hand. "You don't know whom you are talking to! If you knew me just as I am, you would unsay all those words. And, Mr. Trevor, you can never know me as I am, and I can never marry you."

"But do you love me? That is the point," Trevor said.

"I—do not ask me. No—if you must know. How can I love anybody? I am incapable of love. Oh, go, go! Do go! I don't love you, of course I don't! Don't think of me again. I am not for you. Try and love Kitty and make Mrs. Aylmer happy. Do leave me! I am unworthy of you, absolutely, utterly."

"But if I think differently?" asked Trevor. He was very much troubled by her words. She alluded to such strange and impossible things that he failed to understand her. Then he said slowly, "You are stunned and surprised. But darling, I am willing to wait, and my heart is yours. A man cannot take back his heart after he has given it, even though a woman does scorn it. But you won't be cruel to me. I cannot believe it, Florence. I will come again tomorrow and see you."

He turned without speaking to her again and left the room.

Florence never knew how she spent the rest of that day. She was to go out that evening with the Frankses. She was now, although the London season had by no means begun, a little bit in request in certain literary circles. And Tom Franks, who had taken her in tow, was anxious to bring her as much forward as possible.

"A man cannot take back his heart after he has given it, even though a woman does scorn it."

Edith and Tom were going to drive to a certain house in the suburbs where a literary lady, a Mrs. Simpson, lived. Florence was to be the lioness of the evening, and Edith came in early from her medical work to apprise her of the fact.

"You had better wear that pretty black lace dress, and here are some crimson roses for you," she said. "They will suit you very well. But I wish you would not lose all your color. You certainly look quite worn out."

"On the contrary, I am not the least bit tired," said Florence. "I am glad I am going. I have finished the story for your brother and can post it first. I have had a hard day's work, Edith, and deserve a little bit of fun tonight."

"Now that I look at you, you don't seem as tired as usual," said Edith. "Tom was vexed last night. He says you work so hard that you are quite stupid in society. Try and allow people to draw you out. If you make even one or two of those pretty little speeches with which your writing is full, you will get yourself talked of more than ever. I presume, writing the sort of things you do, that you are going in for fame, and fame alone.

Well, my dear, at least so live that you may obtain that for which you are selling yourself."

"I am not selling myself. How dare you!" said Florence.

Edith left her, and Florence went into her bedroom and carefully made her toilet. Her eyes were soft as well as bright. The dress she wore suited her well; there was a flush of becoming color in her cheeks.

She joined Edith just as Tom drove up. He ran upstairs and was pleased to see that the two girls were ready.

"Come, that is nice," he said, gazing at Florence with an increased beating of his heart. He said to himself, "She is absolutely handsome. She would suit me admirably as a wife. I may propose to her tonight if I have the chance."

He gave his arm to Florence with a certain chivalry which was by no means habitual to him, and the two girls and Franks went downstairs.

"There is to be a bit of a crush," he said, looking at Florence, "and by the way, did I tell you who was to be present? You saw him today—Maurice Trevor. He is a great friend of Mrs. Simpson, and he and his mother have been invited."

Florence's hand was still on Franks' arm when he spoke, and as he uttered the words "Maurice Trevor" she gave that arm an involuntary grip. He felt the grip, and a queer sensation went through him. He could not look into her face, but his suspicions were aroused. Why had she been so startled when Trevor's name was mentioned? He would watch the pair tonight. Trevor was not going to take Florence from him.

XXX

At the Party

he guests were all interesting, and the room sufficiently large not to be overcrowded. Franks seemed to watch Florence, guarding her against too much intrusion, but at the same time he himself kept her amused. He told her who the people were. As he did so, he watched her face. She had lost that heavy, apathetic air which had angered Franks more than once. He noticed, however, that she watched the door, and as fresh arrivals were announced her eyes brightened for an instant. He knew she was watching for Trevor, and he condemned Trevor in his heart.

"She is in love with him. What fools women are!" muttered Franks to himself. "If she married a man like that—a rich man with all that money could give—her literary career would be ended. I have had the pleasure of introducing her to the public. She is my treasure-trove, my one bright particular star. I will not give her up. I love her just because she is clever, because she is a genius. If she had not that divine fire, she would be as nothing and worse than nothing to me. As it is, the world shall talk of her yet."

Presently Trevor and his mother arrived, and it seemed to Florence that some kind of wave of sympathy immediately caused his eyes to light upon her in her distant corner. He said a few words to his hostess, watched his mother as she greeted a chance acquaintance, and elbowed his way to her side.

"This is good luck," he said. "I did not expect to see you here tonight." He sat down by her, and Franks was forced to seek entertainment elsewhere.

Now his voice dropped. If he could, he would have taken her hand. They were as much alone in that crowd as though they had been the only people in the room.

Florence expected that after the way she had treated Trevor early that day he would be cold and distant. But this was not the case. He seemed to have read her agitation for what it was worth. Something in her eyes must have given him a hint of the truth. He certainly was not angry now. He was sympathetic, and, the girl thought with a great wave of comfort, "he does not like me because I am supposed to be clever. He likes me just for myself. But why didn't he tell me so before—before I fell a second time? It is all hopeless now, of course. And yet is it hopeless? Perhaps Maurice Trevor is the kind of man who would forgive. I wonder!"

She looked up at him as the thought came to her, and his eyes met hers.

"What are you thinking about?" he asked. They had been talking a lot of commonplaces. Now his voice dropped. If he could, he would have taken her hand. They were as much alone in that crowd as though they had been the only people in the room.

"What are you thinking of?" he repeated.

"Of you," said Florence.

"Perhaps you are sorry for some of the things you said this morning?"

"I am sorry," she answered gravely, "that I was obliged to say them."

"But why were you obliged?"

"I have a secret. It was because of that secret I was obliged."

"You will tell it to me, won't you?"

"I cannot."

Trevor turned aside. He did not speak at all for a moment.

"I must understand you somehow," he said then. "You are surrounded by mystery, you puzzle me, you pique my curiosity. I am not curious about small things as a rule, but this is not a small thing. I have a great curiosity as to the state of your heart, as to the state of your—"

"My morals," said Florence, slowly. "Of my moral nature—you are not sure of me, are you?"

"I am sure that, bad or good—and I know you are not bad—you are the only woman that I care for. May I come and see you tomorrow?"

"Don't talk any more now. You upset me," said Florence.

"May I come and see you tomorrow?"

"Yes."

"If I come, I shall expect you to tell me everything?"

"Yes."

"You will?"

"I am not certain. I can let you know when you do come."

"Thank you! You have lifted a great weight from my heart."

A moment later Tom Franks appeared with a very learned lady, a Miss Melchister, who asked to be introduced to Florence.

"I have a crow to pluck with you, Miss Aylmer," she said.

"What is that?" asked Florence.

"How dare you give yourself and your sisters away? Do you know that you were very cruel when you wrote that extremely clever paper in the *General Review?*"

"I don't see it," replied Florence. Her answers were lame. Miss Melchister prepared herself for the fray.

"We will discuss the point," she said. "Now, why did you say—"

Trevor lingered near for a minute. He observed that Florence's cheeks had turned pale, and he thought that for such a clever girl she spoke in a rather ignorant way.

"How queer she is!" he said to himself. "But never mind, she will tell me all tomorrow. I shall win her. It will be my delight to guard her, to help her, and if necessary to save her. She is under someone's thumb, but I will find out whose."

His thoughts traveled to Bertha Keys. He remembered that strange time when he met Florence at the railway station at Hamslade. Why had she spent the day there? Why had Bertha sent her a parcel? He felt disturbed, and he wandered into another room. This was the library of the house. Some papers were lying about. Among others was the first number of the *General Review*. With a start Trevor took it up. He would look through Florence's article.

He sank into a chair and read it slowly over. As he did so, his heart beat at first loud, then with heavy throbs. A look of pain, perplexity, and weariness came into his eyes. One sentence in particular he read not only once, but twice, three times. It was a strange sentence; it contained in it the germ of a very poisonous thought. It puzzled him. He had the queer feeling that he had read it before. He repeated it to himself until he knew it by heart. Then he put the paper down, and soon afterward he went to his mother and told her he was going home.

"I am not very well," he said.

She looked into his face and was distressed at the expression she saw in his eyes.

"All right, Maurice, dear. I shall be ready in an hour. I just want to meet a certain old friend, and to talk to that pretty girl, Miss Aylmer. I will find out why she does not come to see us."

"Don't worry her. I would rather you didn't," said Trevor.

His mother looked at him again and her heart sank.

"Is it possible he has proposed, and she will not accept him?" thought the mother. And then she drew her proud little head up and a feeling of indignation filled her heart. If Florence was going to treat her boy, the very light of her eyes, cruelly, she certainly need expect no mercy from his mother.

XXXI

Franks'
Proposal

revor took his departure, and the gay throng at Mrs. Simpson's laughed and joked and made merry.

Florence had now worked herself into apparent high spirits. She ceased to care whether she talked rubbish or not. She was no longer silent. Many people asked to be introduced to the rising star, and many people congratulated her. Instead of being modest, and a little stupid and retiring, she now answered back with flippant words of her own. Her cleverness was such an established fact that her utter nonsense was received as wit, and she soon had throngs of men and women round her laughing at her words and privately taking note of them.

Franks all the while stood as a sort of bodyguard. He listened, and his cool judgment never wavered for a moment. He came up to her gravely, in a pause in the conversation, and asked her if she would like to go in to supper. She laid her hand on his arm, and they threaded their way through the throng. They did not approach the supper room, however. Franks led her into a small alcove just beside the greenhouse.

"Ah," he said, "I have been watching this place. Couples have been in it the whole evening, and now this couple, you and I, find ourselves here. We are as alone as if we were on the top of Mont Blanc."

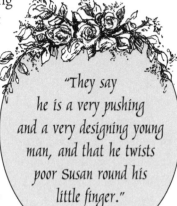

"They say he is a very pushing and a very designing young man, and that he twists poor Susan round his little finger."

"What a funny simile!" said Florence. She laughed a little uneasily. "I thought," she continued, "you were going to take me in to supper."

"I will presently. I want first to ask you a question, and to say something to you."

"I am all attention," replied Florence.

"There is no use in beating about the bush," said Franks after a pause. "Miss Aylmer, I take a great interest in you."

"Oh, don't, please," cried Florence.

"But I do. I believe I can help you. I believe that you and I together can have a most brilliant career. Shall we work in harness? Shall we become husband and wife? Don't say no at first. Think it over. It would be an admirable arrangement."

"So it would," said Florence. Her answer came out quietly. She looked full into Franks' cold gray eyes and burst into a mirthless laugh.

"Why do you look at me like that? Are you in earnest when you admit that it would be an admirable arrangement?"

"I am absolutely in earnest. Nothing could be more—more—"

"Let me speak. You are not in earnest. It is your good pleasure to take a great many things in life in a joking spirit. Now, for instance, when you sent me that bald, disgraceful, girlish essay, you played a practical joke which a less patient man would never have forgiven. Tonight, when you talked that rubbish to that crowd of really clever men and women, you played another practical joke, equally unseemly."

"I am not a society person, Mr. Franks. I cannot talk well in company. You told me to talk, and I did the best I could."

"Your chatter was nearly brainless. The people who listened to you tonight won't put up with that sort of thing much longer. It is impossible with a mind of your order that you should really wish to talk nonsense. But I am not going to scold you. I want to know if you will marry me."

"If I will be your wife?" asked Florence. "Why do you wish it?"

"I think it would be a suitable match."

"But do you love me?"

Franks paused when Florence asked him that direct question.

"I admire you very much," he said.

"That has nothing to do with it. Admiration is not enough to marry. Do you love me?"

"I believe I shall love you."

"May I ask you a very plain question?"

"What is that?"

"If I were not very clever, if I did not write those smart stories and those clever papers, would you, just for myself—just for my face and for my heart and my nature—desire me as your wife?"

"That is scarcely a fair thing to ask, for I should never have met you had you not been just what you are."

"Well, do you love me?" Florence questioned again.

"You are a very strange girl. I think on the whole I do love you. I fully expect to love you very much when you are my wife."

"Did you ever love anybody else better than you love me?"

"I didn't expect, Miss Aylmer, to be subjected to this sort of cross-questioning. There was once a girl—" A new note came into Franks' voice, and for the first time those eyes of his were softened.

"She died," he said softly. "You can never be jealous of her. She is in her grave. Had she lived we would have been married long ago. Don't let us talk of her tonight. You and I can have a brilliant career. Will you say 'yes'?"

"I cannot answer you tonight. You must give me time."

"Thank you. That is all I require. I am glad you will think it over. We can be married soon, for I have a good income. I want you to clearly understand that as my wife you will continue writing. I want to lead you forth as one of the most brilliant women before the world. Will you submit to my training?"

Florence shivered slightly.

"I will let you know tomorrow," she said.

"Come, let us go and have some supper," said Franks. He jumped up abruptly, offered Florence his arm, and took her into the supper room.

The party broke up soon afterward. Mrs. Trevor had no opportunity of seeing Florence, or rather, she would not give herself an opportunity.

Mrs. Simpson shook hands with the young literary *debutante* with marked favor. Florence looked prettier than anyone had ever seen her look before. Franks took his sister and Florence home to their flats. As he parted from the latter, he ventured to give her hand a slight squeeze.

"I will call tomorrow morning," he said. "Can I see you before I go to my work?"

"Yes," said Florence. "I shall be at home at"—she paused a moment—"nine o'clock."

"What! A rendezvous so early?" exclaimed Edith with a laugh. Franks laughed also.

"Quite so, Edith," he said. "We are all busy people and have no time to waste. This is merely a business arrangement between Miss Aylmer and myself."

"All right, Tom. I am sure I'm not going to interfere," said Edith. "Goodnight. Come in, Miss Aylmer. It is very cold standing out in the street."

The girls entered the house and went up to their respective rooms. Fires were burning brightly in each, and the doors stood open.

"You will come into my room and have cocoa, will you not?" Edith said to Florence.

"No, thank you, not tonight."

Edith looked full at her.

"Has Tom proposed to you?" she said suddenly.

"I don't know why you should ask me that question."

"Your face answers me. You will be a fool if you accept him. He is not the man to make any woman happy. Don't tell him that I said it, but he is cold through and through. Only one woman, poor Lucy Leigh, who died before she was twenty, ever touched his heart. What heart he had is in her grave. You will never kindle it into life. Take him if you wish for success, but do not say that I never warned you."

Edith went into her room and slammed the door somewhat noisily behind her. Florence entered hers. The late post had brought a letter—one letter. She started when she saw the postmark, and a premonition of fresh trouble came over her. Then standing by the fire, she slowly opened the envelope.

Aylmer's Court, Dec. 3rd.

My Dear Florence,

I would come to see you, but am kept here by Mrs. Aylmer's indisposition. She has been seriously unwell and in the doctor's hands since Maurice Trevor left her in the disgraceful fashion he has done. He has nearly broken her heart, but I hope to have the solace of mending it.

I wish to say now that from words dropped to Mrs. Aylmer, it is highly probably that he has gone to town for the purpose of proposing to you. Accept him, of course, if you wish. It is likely, very likely, that you will return his affection, for he is an attractive man and has a warm heart, and also a good one. I have nothing whatever to do with that, but clearly understand, the moment the news reaches me that you are betrothed to Maurice Trevor, on that very day I shall tell Mrs. Aylmer the whole truth with regard to the stories which are running in the *Argonaut* and the paper which has already appeared in the *General Review*. I do not mind whether I go under or not. But you shall be seen in your true colors before you ever become the wife of Maurice Trevor.

Yours faithfully—and faithful I shall be in that particular,

Bertha Keys

XXXII

Is it "Yes" or "No"?

lorence sat up a long while with that letter lying in her lap. The fire burned low and finally went out. Still she sat by the cold hearth, and once or twice she touched the letter.

"It burns into me. It is written in my heart in letters of fire," she said to herself finally. And then she rose slowly, and stretched her arms, crossed the room, and looked out at the sky. From the top of her lofty flat she could see just a little sky above the London roofs. It was a clear, cold night with a touch of frost, and the stars were all brilliant. Florence gazed up at them.

"There is a lofty and pure and grand world somewhere," she said to herself. "But it is not for me. Goodbye, Maurice. I could have loved you well. With you I might have been good, very good. With you I might have climbed up. Goodbye, Maurice."

She took Bertha's letter, put it on the cold hearth, set fire to it, and saw it consumed to ashes. Then she undressed and went to bed. And though she slept little, she rose in good time in the morning. She had a considerable amount to do. She was to see Franks at nine o'clock. She was to see Trevor later on.

She had to copy a whole, very brilliant story of Bertha's. She was a slow writer, and there was nothing of talent in her handwriting.

"I am a very stupid girl when all is said and done," she said to herself. "I have been years studying, but somehow I think I must have a frivolous sort of brain. Perhaps I have taken after the little Mum. The little Mum never was clever. She is a dear mother when all is said and done, and very comforting when one is in trouble. If I saw her now I might break down and fling my arms round her neck and confess to her. With all her silliness she would comfort me, but I must not tell."

She dressed, prepared her breakfast as usual, and had just put her little sittingroom in order when Franks' knock was heard at her door. He entered in that brisk, businesslike, utterly cool way which always characterized him. He looked immaculate and fresh. He was always extremely particular about his appearance. His collars were invariably as white as the driven snow, and his clothes well cut. He had straight black eyebrows, a neat little black mustache, and straight features. His skin was of an olive tint. Those well-cut, classical features gave to his face a certain cold sameness of outline. It was almost impossible to surprise him or to cause emotion to visit his countenance. He looked now as composed as though he had merely come to give Florence a fresh order for work.

"Ah," he said, "there you are. One minute past nine. Sorry I'm late. Accept my apologies."

Florence pushed forward a chair. She could scarcely bring herself to speak. Even her lips were white. Franks came a step nearer.

"I have exactly ten minutes," he said. "This is a purely business arrangement. Is it to be 'yes' or 'no'?"

"If you will faithfully assure me that—" began Florence, and then she stopped and wetted her lips. Her mouth was so dry she could scarcely proceed.

Franks gave an impatient start. He took out his watch and glanced at it.

"Yes," he said, "I am awfully sorry. If it is no, it won't be necessary to keep me now."

"I must speak. You cannot hurry me," said Florence calmly.

"Oh, all right. Take your own time," said Franks. His face beamed all over for a moment. He looked at the girl with a certain covetousness. After all, there was something about her which might develop into strength and even beauty. She had been pretty last night. She would assuredly be his stepping-stone to great fame. He was a very clever man himself, but he was not a genius. With Florence, with their two forces combined, might they not rise to any position?

"Yes, my dear, yes?" he said. "Sit down, Florence, sit down."

She shivered when he called her by her Christian name, but she did not drop into a chair. He drew his own close to her.

"I only want to ask you to repeat something which you said last night," said Florence.

"What is that?"

"Can you assuredly tell me that you are only marrying me because you think that you and I together can be famous?"

"You would not like me to say that sort of thing, would you?"

"On the contrary, if I firmly know, firmly and truly from your own lips, that you do *not* love me, that there is no love in the matter, that it is a mere business arrangement—"

"Well, what?"

"It would be, I think *possible*."

"Then that means 'Yes.'"

"I want it clearly to be understood," said Florence, "that I do not love you at all, and I don't want you to love me. . . . But if we can, as you say, work in harness, perhaps it would be best. Anyhow, I—"

"You say 'yes,' my dear girl. That is all I need. We can talk over these curious ideas of yours later on. You are engaged to me, Florence,—come."

He went quickly up to her, put his arm round her waist, drew her close to him, and kissed her on the forehead.

"I am not repugnant to you, am I?" he asked as she shrank away.

"I don't know," she replied. "I am selling myself, and you are buying me. I hope I shall prove a good bargain. I don't want you to imagine for a moment that I care for you, but I am selling myself."

"You must drop all that kind of nonsense when once you are my wife," he said. "As it is, I bear with it. We shall be married before Christmas. We will take a flat in a fashionable part of town and see literary people. Now goodbye. I will call again tonight. By the way, how is the story getting on?"

"I don't know that I can quite finish it all today, but you shall have it by the time I promised."

"Thank you, Florence. I believe you and I are acting wisely. I hope we shall be kind to each other. We have a great deal in common. Without my aid, you could not step up as high as I shall place you, and you are useful to me. It is an admirable arrangement. Goodbye, dear."

She shrank so far away that he did not venture to repeat his cold caress. He again looked at his watch.

"How late I shall be!" he said. "Anderson will be astonished. He will forgive me, however, when I tell him that I am engaged to my rising star. Goodbye, Florence."

"Thank goodness!" she muttered when the door closed behind him. She had scarcely time, however, for reflection before it was opened again. And this time without knocking. Edith Franks, wearing her hat and coat and buttoning on her gloves, entered briskly.

"I thought I heard Tom going downstairs. So he has been?" she enquired.

"Yes, Edith, he has been."

Edith came nearer and looked at Florence's face.

"So you are to be my new sister-in-law," she said.

"Don't scold me, please, Edith."

"Good gracious, no, dear. Now I am all congratulations. You will make a nice little sister-in-law, and we are proud of your ability. Go on and prosper. You have chosen ambition. Some women would prefer love, but everyone to their taste. I'm off. Goodbye, Florence. I see you would much rather not be kissed. Tom has been doing that, doubtless. I will see you again this evening."

Edith went out of the room in her brisk way. She shut the door quickly.

Florence went straight to the window. She stood there for a minute or two looking out. Then she dropped into a chair and, taking a sheet of notepaper, began to write. She was writing to Bertha.

> My Dear Bertha,
>
> The letter I received from you last night requires no comment. You may perhaps be glad to hear that I have just engaged myself to Mr. Franks, an editor of the *Argonaut*, and a very distinguished man. We are to be married before Christmas. It is his particular wish that I should go on writing, and it is one of the conditions that we shall both pursue our own careers independently of

the other, and yet each helped by the other. You will, I am sure, fulfill your part of the bargain. I shall want another story of about five thousand words next week, as terse, and brilliant, and clever as you can make it. I shall also want an article for the *General Review*. Make it smart, but avoid the woman question. I have been bullied on the subject and did not know how to answer.

Yours truly,

Florence Aylmer

This letter written, Florence did not even wait to reread it. She put it into an envelope and ran out with it to the nearest pillarbox. She dropped it in and returned to the house. It was not yet eleven o'clock. How tired she was! It was nearly two hours since Franks and she had ratified their contract. She was engaged now—engaged to a man who did not profess to love her, for whom she did not feel the faintest glimmering of affection. She was engaged and safe. Yes, of course, she was safe. No fear now of her ghastly secret being discovered! As long as Bertha lived, the stories could be conveyed to her, and the stories would mean fame and Franks would be rich. He would manage her financial affairs in the future. He would not allow her to sell her talent for less than it was worth. He would instruct her how to dress and how to speak when she was in public.

She could not think even for a moment of what she was throwing away—such was her feeling that she had chosen the wrong and refused the right. Great temptation had come, and she had not been able to resist it. And now the only way was to go straight on. Franks had made that way plain. It was the broad road which led to destruction. She was pricked by many thorns, and she saw dizzily how steep the hill would grow by-and-by, and how fast the descent would be. But never mind, she at least was safe for the present.

She panted and felt herself turning slightly cold as this last thought came to her. Then there was a tap at the door. Trevor, his face white, his blue eyes anxious, an expression of earnestness and love beaming all over his features, came in.

He was in every way the opposite of Tom Franks.

Florence looked wildly at him. She must go through the dreadful half-hour which was before her. She hoped he would not stay long, and that he would take his dismissal quietly. She dared not think too hard, in fact, she did her utmost to drive thought out.

"Well," said Trevor, "have I come too early?"

"Oh, no," said Florence. "It is past eleven," and she looked listlessly at the clock.

He tried to take her hand. She put it immediately behind her.

"You have come to ask me a question, have you not?" she said.

"I have. You promised me your confidence last night."

"I did not promise. I said I might give it."

"Am I to expect it?"

"What do you want to know?"

"I want to know this," said Trevor. He took out of his pocket a copy of the *General Review*. He opened it at the page where Florence's article appeared. He then also produced from his pocketbook a tiny slip of paper, a torn slip on which, in Bertha Keys' handwriting, was the identical sentence which had attracted so much attention in the *Review*.

"Look," he said.

Florence did look. Her frightened eyes were fixed upon the scrap of paper.

"Where—where did you get that?" she said.

"It is remarkable," he said. "I thought perhaps *you* would explain. I have read your paper—I am not going to say whether I like it or not. Do you remember that day when I saw you and gave you a packet at Hamslade Station?"

"Quite well."

"I think you would not be likely to forget. I was naturally puzzled to find you so near Mrs. Aylmer's house and yet not there. The packet I gave you was from Miss Keys, was it not?"

"There can be no harm in admitting that fact," replied Florence in a guarded tone.

He looked at her and shook himself impatiently.

"I was perplexed and amazed at seeing you at the station."

"You ought to try and curb your curiosity, Mr. Trevor," said Florence. She tried to speak lightly and in a bantering tone. He was too much in earnest to take any notice of her tone.

"I was curious. I had reason to be," he replied. "I went home. Miss Keys, Miss Sharston, and others were in the hall. They were talking of you, and Miss Sharston showed me one of your stories. I read it. We both read it with keen curiosity."

"Was it the first or the second?" said Florence.

"The first story. It was clever. It was not a bit the sort of story I thought you would have written."

Florence lowered her eyes.

"The style was remarkable and distinctive," he continued. "It was not the style of a girl so young as you are. I went upstairs to Mrs. Aylmer's boudoir because I wanted to fetch a book. I don't think I was anxious to read, but I was restless. The book lay on Miss Keys' desk. On the desk also were some torn sheets of paper. I picked up one automatically."

"You read what was not meant for you to read!" cried Florence, her eyes flashing.

Trevor gave her a steady glance.

225

"I admit that I read a sentence—the sentence I have just shown you. I will frankly tell you that I was surprised at it. I was puzzled by a resemblance between the style of the story and the style of the sentence. I put the torn sheet of paper into my pocketbook. I don't exactly know why I did it at the time, but I felt desperate. I was taking a great interest in you. It seemed to me that if you did wrong, I was doing wrong, myself. It seemed to me that if by chance your soul was smirched, or made unhappy, or blackened, or any of its loftiness removed, my own soul was smirched, too, my own nature lowered. And that night I learned for the first time that I was interested in you because I loved you, because you were the first of all women to me, and I—"

"I won't ask you too much. Only tell me, sweetest, with your own lips that you love me."

"Oh, don't," said Florence, "don't say any more." She turned away from him, flung herself on the sofa, and sobbed as if her heart would break.

Trevor stood near for a little while in much bewilderment. Presently she raised her eyes. He sat down on the sofa by her.

"Why don't you tell me everything, Florence?" he said with great tenderness in his tone.

"I cannot. It is too late. Think what you like of me! Suspect me as you will! I do not think you would voluntarily injure me. I cannot give you my confidence, for I—"

"There, dear. Don't tremble so. Poor little girl, you will be better afterward. I won't ask you too much. Only tell me, sweetest, with your own lips that you love me."

"I am not sweet, I am not dear, I am not darling. I am a bad girl, bad in every way," said Florence. "Think of me as you like. I dare not be near you. I dare not speak to you. Oh, yes, perhaps I *could* have loved you. I won't think of that now. I am engaged to another man."

"You're engaged!" said Trevor. He sprang to his feet as if someone had shot him. He trembled a little, then he pulled himself together. "Say it again."

"I am engaged to Mr. Franks."

"But you were not engaged last night!"

"No."

"When did this take place?"

"Two hours ago. He came at nine—a minute past, I think. We became engaged. It is all settled. Goodbye, Maurice. Forget me."

Florence still kept her hands behind her. She rose. Her miserable tear-stained face and her eyes full of agony were raised for a moment to Trevor's.

"Do go," she said. "It is all over. I have accepted the part that is not good, and you must forget me."

XXXIII

Bertha Keys
Defeated

here is little doubt that Mrs. Aylmer was very ill. Step by step an attack, which was apparently at first of little moment, became serious and then dangerous. The cold became pneumonia, the pneumonia became double pneumonia, and now there was a hard fight for life. Nurses were summoned, doctors were requisitioned, everything that wealth could do was employed for the relief and the recovery of the sick woman.

But there are times when Death laughs at wealth, with all its contrivances and all its hopes. Death has his own duty to perform, and now it entered that sick-chamber and stood by that woman's pillow and whispered to her that her hour had come. Mrs. Aylmer, propped up in her bed so that she might breathe better, called Bertha to her side. She could scarcely speak, but she managed to convey her meaning to the girl.

"I am very bad. I know I shall not recover."

"You have to make your will over again," said Bertha, who was as cool as cool could be in this emergency. Not one of the nurses could be more collected or calm than Bertha. She herself would have made a splendid nurse, for she had tact and sympathy, and the sort of voice which never grated on the ear. The doctors were almost in love with her. They thought they had never seen so capable a girl, so grave, so quiet, so suitably dressed, so invaluable in all emergencies.

The doctor said that Mrs. Aylmer might live for two or three days more, but that he did not think it likely. The disease was spreading, and soon it would be impossible for her to breathe. She was frightened. She had not spent an especially good life. She had given large sums to charity, but she had not really ever helped the poor, and had not brought a smile to the lip or a tear of thankfulness to the eye. For the first time, all the importance of money faded from her mind. No matter how rich she was and how great, she would have to leave the world with a naked, unclothed soul.

"Bertha," she said to her young companion. "Come here, Bertha."

Bertha bent over her.

"Is it true that I am not going to get better?"

"You are very ill," said Bertha. "You ought to make your will."

"But I have made it. What do you mean?"

"I thought," said Bertha, "that . . ." She paused, then she said gravely, "You have not altered it since Maurice Trevor went away. I thought that you had made up your mind that he and Florence Aylmer were not to inherit your property."

"Of course I have," said the sick woman, a frightened, anxious look coming into her eyes. "Not that it much matters," she added after a pause. "Florence is as good as another, and if Maurice really cares for her—"

"Oh, impossible," said Bertha. "You know you do *not* wish all your estates, your lands, your money to pass into the hands of that wicked, deceitful girl."

229

"I have heard," said Mrs. Aylmer, "that Florence is doing great things for herself in London."

"What do you mean?"

"She is considered clever. She is writing very brilliantly. After all, there is such a thing as literary fame, and if at the eleventh hour she achieves it, she as well as another may inherit my wealth. And I am too tired, Bertha, too tired to worry now."

"You know she must *not* have your property!" said Bertha. "I will send for Mr. Wiltshire. You said you would alter the will. You need only to add a codicil to the last one, and the deed is done."

"As you please," said Mrs. Aylmer.

Bertha hurried away.

Mr. Wiltshire, Mrs. Aylmer's lawyer, lived five miles distant. Bertha wrote him a letter and sent a man on horseback to his house. The lawyer arrived about nine o'clock that evening.

"You must see her at once. She may not live till morning," said Bertha. There was a pink spot on each of her cheeks.

"I made my client's will six months ago. All her affairs are in perfect order. What does this mean?" Mr. Wiltshire asked.

"Mrs. Aylmer and I have had a long conversation lately, and I know Mrs. Aylmer wants to alter her will," said Bertha. "Mr. Trevor has offended her seriously."

"Dear, dear!" said the lawyer. "How sad."

"How ungrateful, you mean!" said Bertha.

"That is quite true. How different from your conduct, my dear young lady."

As the lawyer spoke, he looked full into Bertha's excited face.

"Ah!" said Miss Keys with a sigh, "if I had that wealth I should know what to do with it. For instance, you, Mr. Wiltshire, should not suffer."

Now, Mr. Wiltshire was not immaculate. He had often admired Bertha, and he had thought her an extremely taking girl. It had even occurred to him that, under certain conditions, she might be a very suitable wife for him. He was a widower of ten years standing.

"I will see my client now that I have come," he said, rising. "Perhaps you had better prepare her for my visit."

"She knows you are coming. I will take you up at once."

"But it may be too great a shock."

"Not at all. She is past all that sort of thing. Come this way."

Bertha and the lawyer entered the heavily curtained, softly carpeted room. Their footsteps made no sound as they crossed the floor. The nurses withdrew, and they approached the bedside. Bertha had ink and paper ready. The lawyer held out his hand to Mrs. Aylmer.

"My dear, dear friend," he said in that solemn voice which he thought befitting a deathbed. "This is a most trying moment. But if I can do anything to relieve your mind and to help you to a just disposition of the great wealth with which providence has endowed you, it may ease your last moments."

"Yes," said Mrs. Aylmer in a choking voice, "they are my last moments. But I think all my affairs are settled."

Bertha looked at him and withdrew. Her eyes seemed to say, "Take my part, and you will not repent it."

Mr. Wiltshire immediately took his cue.

"I am given to understand that Mr. Trevor has offended you," he said. "Is that so?"

"He has, mortally. But I am too ill to worry now."

"It will be easy to put a codicil to your will if you have any fresh desires with regard to your property," said Mr. Wiltshire.

"I am dying, Mr. Wiltshire. When you come to face death, you don't care much about money. It cannot go with you, you know."

"But it can stay behind you, my dear madam, and do good to others."

"True, true."

"I greatly fear that Mr. Trevor may squander it," said Mr. Wiltshire slowly.

"I have no one else to leave it to."

"There is that charming and excellent girl. But dare I suggest it?"

"Which charming and excellent girl?"

"Your secretary and companion, Miss Bertha Keys."

"Ay," said Mrs. Aylmer, "but I should be extremely sorry that she should inherit my money."

"Indeed, and why? No one has been more faithful to you. I know she does not expect a farthing. It would be a grateful surprise. She has one of the best heads for business I have ever come across. She is an excellent girl."

"Write a codicil and put her name into it," said Mrs. Aylmer fretfully. "I will leave her something."

Pleased even with this assent, somewhat ungraciously given, the lawyer now sat down and wrote some sentences rapidly.

"The sum you will leave to her," he said, "ten, twenty, thirty, forty, shall we say *fifty* thousand pounds, my dear Mrs. Aylmer?"

"Forty—fifty if you like—*anything!* Oh, I am choking—I shall die!" cried Mrs. Aylmer.

Mr. Wiltshire hastily inserted the words "fifty thousand pounds" in the codicil. He then took a pen, and called two of the nurses into the room.

"You must witness this," he said. "Please support the patient with pillows. Now, my dear Mrs. Aylmer, just put your name there."

The pen was put into the trembling hand.

"I am giving my money back to—but what does this mean?" Mrs. Aylmer hastily pushed the paper away.

"Sign, sign," said the lawyer. "It is according to your instructions. It is all right. Sign it."

"Poor lady! It is a shame to worry her on the very confines of the grave," said one of the nurses angrily.

"Just write here, my dear. You know you have the strength. Here is the pen."

The lawyer put the pen in Mrs. Aylmer's hand. She held it limply for a minute and began to sign. The first letter of her Christian name appeared in a jagged form, the next letter was about to begin when the hand fell and the pen was no longer grasped in the feeble fingers.

"I am about to meet my Maker," she said with a great sob. "Send for the clergyman. Take that away."

"I shall not allow the lady to be worried any longer," said one of the nurses with flashing eyes.

Mr. Wiltshire was defeated. So was Bertha Keys. The clergyman came and sat for a long time with the sick woman. She listened to what he had to say and then put a question to him.

"I am stronger than I was earlier in the day. I can do what I could not do a few hours back. Oh, I know well that I shall never recover, but before I go I want to give back what was entrusted to me."

"What do you mean by that?" he asked.

"I mean my money, my wealth. I wish to return it to God."

"Have you not made your will? It is always right that we should leave our affairs in perfect order."

"I wish to make a fresh will, and at once. My lawyer, Mr. Wiltshire, has come and gone. He wanted me to sign a codicil which would have been wicked. God did not wish it, so He took my strength away. I could not sign the codicil, but now I can sign any fresh will which may be made. If I dictate a fresh will to you, and I put my proper signature, and two nurses sign it, will it be legal?"

"Quite legal," replied the clergyman.

"I will tell you my wishes. Get paper."

> "I give all that I possess back to God. He gave me my wealth, and He shall have it back again."

The minister crossed the room, took a sheet of paper from a table which stood in the window, and prepared to write.

Mrs. Aylmer's eyes were bright, her voice no longer trembling, and she spoke quickly.

> I, Susan Aylmer, of Aylmer's Court, Shropshire, being quite in my right mind, leave, with the exception of a small legacy of fifty pounds a year to my sister-in-law, Mrs. Aylmer, of Dawlish, all the money I possess to two London hospitals to be chosen by my executor.

"Have you put *all* the money I possess?" she enquired.

"Yes, but is your will fit?" he said. "Have you no other relations to whom you ought to leave some of your wealth?"

"I give all that I possess back to God. He gave me my wealth, and He shall have it back again," repeated Mrs. Aylmer.

This brief will was signed without any difficulty by the dying woman and attested by the two nurses. Two hours later, the rich woman left her wealth behind her and went to meet her God.

XXXIV

Mrs. Aylmer's Will

lorence stayed up late that night reading a letter from her mother that disturbed her greatly. At last she went to visit Edith in her room.

"You don't look well," said Edith. "What is the matter?"

"I don't exactly know what is the matter," said Florence. "I am worried by my mother's letter. My aunt, Mrs. Aylmer, is dying. She is a very rich woman. Mother is under the impression that, if she and I went to Aylmer's Court, Mrs. Aylmer might leave me her property. I don't want it. I should hate to have it. I have learned in the last few months that money is not everything. I don't want to have Aunt Susan's money."

"Well," replied Edith, staring her full in the face, "that is the most sensible speech you have made for a long time. It is my opinion, Florence, that the more we live *outside* money, and the smaller place money takes in the pleasures of our lives, the happier we are. For, after all, money can do so little, and I don't think any other people can be so miserable as the vastly rich ones."

"I agree with you," said Florence.

"It is more than Tom does," replied Edith, looking fixedly at her. "After all, Florence, are you not in some ways too good for my brother?"

"In some ways too good for him?" repeated Florence. She turned very white. "You don't know me," she added.

"I don't believe I do. And it occurs to me, the more I am with you the less I know you."

"Tom marries me for a certain purpose," said Florence flatly. "He gets what he wants. I do not feel that I am doing wrong in giving myself to him. But wrong or right, the thing is arranged."

"You are a strange girl. I am sorry you are going to marry my brother. I do not believe you will be at all happy."

"The marriage is to take place quite quietly three weeks from now," said Florence. "We have arranged everything. We are not going to have an ordinary wedding. I shall be married in my traveling dress. Tom says he can barely spend a week away from his editorial work, and he wants me to live in a flat with him at first."

"Oh, those flats are so detestable," said Edith. "No air, and you are crushed into such a tiny space, but I suppose Tom will sacrifice everything to the sitting rooms."

"He wants to get all the great and witty and wise around us. It ought to be an interesting future," said Florence in a dreary tone.

Edith gazed at her again.

"Well, I will say good night now, Edith. I am tired."

Florence went into her own flat and, lying down, tried to sleep. But she was excited and nervous, and no repose would come to her.

Up to the present, since her engagement, she had managed to keep thought at bay. But now the most terrible, the most dreary thoughts came in like a flood and banished sleep. Toward morning she found herself silently crying.

"Oh, why cannot I break off my engagement with Tom Franks? Why cannot I tell Maurice Trevor the truth?" she asked herself.

Early the next day Mrs. Aylmer the less received a telegram from Bertha Keys. This was to announce the death of the owner of Aylmer's Court. Mrs. Aylmer the less immediately became almost frantic with excitement. "There is little doubt," she said, "that we are both handsomely remembered. I have my fifty pounds a year—that was settled on me many years ago—but I shall have far more than that now."

⸎ ⸎ ⸎

The next few days passed without anything special occurring for Florence, aside from increasing apprehension and misery. Then the news of Mrs. Aylmer's extraordinary will was given to Florence in her mother's graphic language.

> Although she is dead, poor thing, she certainly always was a monster. I cannot explain to you what I feel. I have begged of Mr. Trevor to dispute the will. But would you believe it?—unnatural man that he is, he seems more pleased than otherwise.
>
> My little money is still to come, but no one else seems to have been remembered. As to that poor dear Bertha Keys, she has not been left a penny. If she had not saved two or three hundred pounds during the time of her companionship to that heathenish woman, she would now be penniless. It is a fearful blow, and the way Maurice Trevor takes it is the worst of all.

When Florence read this letter, she could not help clapping her hands.

"I cannot understand it," she said to herself. "But a great load seems to have rolled away from me. Of course, I never expected Aunt Susan's money, but mother has been harping upon it as long as I can remember. I don't think Maurice wanted it greatly. It seemed to me that that money brought a curse with it. I wonder if things are going to be happier now. Oh, dear, I am glad—yes, I am glad that it has not been left to any of us."

Florence's feelings of rapture, however, were likely soon to be mitigated. Her wedding day was approaching.

Mrs. Aylmer the less, who had at first told Florence that she could not on any account marry for three or four months, owing to the sad death in the family, wrote now to say that the sooner she secured Tom Franks the better.

"Maurice Trevor is a pauper," she said, "not worth any girl's serious consideration. Marry Mr. Franks, my dear Florence. He is not up to much, but doubtless he is the best you can get."

Neither Flo nor Tom intended to postpone the wedding. Mrs. Aylmer had not been loved by Florence, and as the couple were to be married quietly, there was not the least occasion why the ceremony should be delayed—only Florence had not a trousseau, in the ordinary sense of the word.

"I have no money," she said, looking full at Edith.

Tom Franks happened to come into the room at the time.

"What are you talking about?" he said. "By the way, here is a letter for you."

As he spoke, he laid the letter on the table near Florence's side. She glanced at it, saw that it was in the handwriting of Bertha Keys, and did not give it a further thought.

"Flo is thinking about her trousseau. All brides require trousseaux," said Edith.

"But why should we worry about a trousseau?" replied Tom. "I take Florence for what she is, not for her dress. I can give you things in Paris," he added, looking at her. "I have some peculiar ideas and my own notions with regard to your future dress. You want a good deal of rich color, and rich stuffs, and nothing too girlish. We will get your evening dress in Paris. I'm not a rich man, but I have saved up money for the purpose."

"I don't really care about clothes," said Florence.

"I know that, but you will change your mind. With your particular style, you must be careful how you dress. I will manage it. Don't waste your money on anything now. I want you to come to me as you are."

Tom then sat down near Florence, and began to give her particulars with regard to several flats which he had looked over. He was a keen man of business and talked until the girl was tired of the subject.

"I shall take the flat in Fortescue Mansions tomorrow morning," he said finally. "It will just suit us. There is a very fine reception room, and what is still better, all the reception rooms open one into the other."

"Surely you will wait until people call on Florence?" interrupted Edith. "You are too quick, Tom, for anything. You must not transgress all the ordinary rules of society."

Tom looked at his sister, shut his firm lips, and turned away.

A moment later he left the room. It was his custom when he met Florence to kiss her coldly on her forehead, and to repeat this ceremony when he left her. He did not neglect this little attention on the present occasion. As his steps were heard descending the stairs, Edith saw Florence raise her handkerchief to her forehead and rub the spot which Tom's lips had touched.

"How heartily you dislike him!" said Edith. "I would not marry him if I were you."

Florence made no reply. She took up her letter and prepared to leave the room.

"Why do you go? There is a good fire here, and there is none in your room. Sit by the fire, and make yourself comfy. I am going out for a little."

Edith pinned on her hat as she spoke, and a moment later left the flat.

Bertha
Changes Her Tone

lorence looked around her. She sank into an easy-chair and opened the letter. It was, as she already knew, from Bertha. She began to read it casually, but soon its contents caused her to start. Her eyes grew bright with a strange mixture of fear, relief, and apprehension. Bertha had written as follows:

My Dear Florence,

You will doubtless have been told of the fearful blow which the late Mrs. Aylmer of Aylmer's Court has inflicted on us all. Kind as we have been to her, and faith-fully as we have served her—I allude especially here to myself—we have been cut off without a farthing, whereas two monstrous establishments have been left the benefit of her wealth. The clergyman, Mr. Edwards, is responsible for this act of what I call sacrilege.

However, my dear Florence, to come to the point. I have not even had a ten-pound note left to me for my pains. It is true that I shall receive my salary, which happens to be a very good one, up to the end of the present quarter. After that, as far as I am concerned, I might as well never have known Aylmer's Court nor its mistress. Fortunately I was able to feather my nest to a very small extent while with her and have a few hundred pounds with which to face the world.

Now, Florence, I shall be obliged in the future to use my talent for my own aggrandizement. I find that it is a very marketable commodity. A few months' use of it has placed you in great comfort. It has also brought you fame. But you must face the fact that I can no longer supply you with stories or essays. I, *myself*, will write my own stories, and send them *myself* to the different papers, and the golden sovereigns, my dear, will roll into *my* pocket, and not into *yours*. You will naturally say, 'How will you do this, and face the shame of your actions in the past?' But the fact is, I am not at all ashamed, nor do I mind confessing exactly what I have done. I take the part of leading lady once for all *myself*. I am coming up to London tomorrow, and will call to see you, as I think that fourth story which you are preparing for the *Argonaut* might as well appear with my name to it.

Yours very sincerely,

Bertha Keys

Florence put the letter into her pocket and entered her bedroom. She didn't quite know what she was doing. She felt a little giddy, but there was a queer, unaccountable sense of relief all over her. On her desk lay her own neat copy of the story which she was preparing for the *Argonaut*. By the side of the desk also was quite a pile of letters from different publishers offering her work and good pay. These letters Tom Franks insisted on her either taking no notice of or merely writing to decline the advantageous offers. She looked at them all wistfully. It is true she had not yet lighted a fire in her room, but she put a match to it now, in order to burn the publishers' letters. The story she was copying was about half done. She had meant to finish it from Bertha's manuscript before she went out.

"I need never finish it now," she thought.

Just as this thought came to her she heard a tap at the door. It was a messenger with a note. She told him to wait, and opened it. It was from Franks.

> I quite forgot when I saw you an hour ago to ask you to let me have manuscript of the next story without fail this evening. Can you send it now by messenger, or shall he call again for it within a couple of hours? This is urgent.
>
> Thomas Franks

Florence sat down and wrote a brief reply.

> I am very sorry, but you cannot have manuscript tonight.
>
> Florence Aylmer

The messenger departed with this note and Florence, giving a wistful and yet pleased glance at the paper, left the room. She had dressed herself to go out, and she went quickly downstairs. As soon as she arrived in the street, she walked until she saw the special omnibus which she was looking for. She was taken straight to Hampstead, and she walked up the steep hill until she found the little cottage which she had visited months ago. Florence went to the door, and a neat servant with an apple-blossom face opened it.

"Is Mrs. Trevor in?" asked Florence.

"Yes, miss. What name shall I say?" She had been away on the Sunday when Florence had dined with Mrs. Trevor and had not an idea who the visitor was.

Florence gave her name. She was immediately ushered into the snug drawing room, bright with firelight. How cozy it looked, and although the rose-trees in the garden were now covered with snow, Florence seemed to see once more, as in a vision, the beauty of the different blossoms in their summer glory. She shut her eyes and a feeling of pain went through her heart.

"The way of transgressors is very, very hard," she thought. "Shall I ever keep straight? What a miserable character I must be."

Just then Mrs. Trevor entered the room. She had not been pleased with Florence. She had not been pleased with her manner to her son. Mothers guess things quickly, and she had guessed Maurice's secret many months ago. Florence had been apparently willing to accept his attentions, and yet she had engaged herself to another. She was the cause of all her son's trouble. But for Florence, he would now be a rich man. He was a very poor one, his career spoiled, his future apparently nowhere. Mrs. Trevor was in arms for her son, and on account of him she was cold to Florence.

Florence held out her hand wistfully and looked full at the little widow.

"I have come to speak to you," she said. "I want to know if you will," her lips trembled, "advise me."

"Sit down, my dear," said Mrs. Trevor. She motioned Florence to a seat, but the girl did not take it.

"I have come to you as the only one in all the world who can help me," continued Florence. "I have something very terrible to say, and I thought perhaps you would advise. May I speak to you just because I am a very lonely girl and you are a woman?"

"If you put it that way, of course you may speak," said Mrs. Trevor. "To tell you the truth, I have been displeased with you. I have thought that you have not been fair."

"To whom?" asked Florence.

"To my son, Maurice."

Florence colored. Then she put her hand to her heart.

"You must not judge me until you know all," she said. "Do you remember a letter I wrote to you some time ago?"

"You wrote to me once," said Mrs. Trevor very gravely. "I do remember that letter."

"In it I told you that I was not a good girl. That I was unworthy to come and live with you."

"You did."

"You never replied to my letter, Mrs. Trevor."

"What was there to say?"

"Will you tell me now what you thought of it?"

Mrs. Trevor had seated herself by the fire. She held out her small hands to the grateful blaze as she looked at the girl.

"Sit down, child," she said. "Take off your hat. If you wish to know what I really thought, I imagined that you were a little hysterical and that you had overstated things. Girls of your age are apt to do so. I was very sorry, for Maurice's sake, that you did not accept my offer."

"I see. Well, I must tell you now that I did not exaggerate. I have been bad through and through—quite unworthy of your attention and care, and quite unworthy of Mr. Maurice's regard."

"That is extremely likely," said the mother of Mr. Maurice, drawing herself up in a stately fashion.

Florence looked at her. For a moment she felt herself trembling all over. The next, she had dropped on her knees, taken one of Mrs. Trevor's hands and raised it to her lips. "Oh, don't be unkind to me. Do bear with me while I tell you. Afterward I shall go away somewhere, but I must relieve my soul. Oh, it is so sinful."

"Speak, child, speak. Who am I that I should turn away from you?"

"Years ago," began Florence, speaking in a dreary tone, "I was at a school called Cherry Court School. While there I was assailed by a very great temptation. The patron of the school, Sir John Wallis, offered a prize on certain conditions to the girls. The prize meant a great deal and covered a wide curriculum. In especial it was to depend on the merits of a certain essay. It was most important that I should win the prize, for if I did so, my aunt by marriage, Mrs. Alymer of Alymer's Court, would adopt me. She said she would take me as her own child, do all that was necessary for my education, and afterward leave me her money. I was very poor. My mother was, and is, very poor. It was a great opportunity, and I struggled hard to win. But Sir John Wallis, although he offered the prize to the school, in reality wanted a girl called Kitty Sharston, who was the daughter of his old friend, to get it. And it seemed very likely that she would, for she had more originality than I have."

"Oh, no, my dear, you are original," here interrupted Mrs. Trevor.

"Wait until you hear. Kitty Sharston was supposed to be most likely to win the prize, and she did win it in the end. But let me tell you how. In the school was a girl as pupil teacher, whose name was Bertha Keys."

"What!" cried Mrs. Trevor. "The girl who has been companion to Mrs. Aylmer, whom my son has so often mentioned?"

"The very same girl. Oh, I don't want to abuse her too much, and yet I cannot tell my terrible story without mentioning her. She was very clever, and she tempted me mightily. She wrote the essay for me, the prize essay which was hers, not mine. Oh, I know you are shocked, I feel your hand trembling. But don't draw it away. She wrote the essay, and it was read aloud before all the guests and all the other girls as mine, and I won the scholarship."

"That was very terrible, my dear. How could you bear it? How could you?"

"There is more to follow, and you must listen. I was miserable that night, and I could not stand it. I made a full confession and went away. Mrs. Aylmer of Aylmer's Court never forgave me, but she did not know anything about Bertha Keys. I was taken on the foundation of another school, and I got my education after a fashion, and I heard nothing more of Mrs. Aylmer until early this summer. I went with Kitty Sharston, who, notwithstanding everything, was still my friend, to Dawlish. There I found that Bertha Keys was installed as Mrs. Aylmer's companion. Bertha was very much frightened when she saw me. She spoke to me, and she asked me on no account to tell Mrs. Aylmer the story of the prize essay. I wanted to forget all that dreadful time. And then I met your son, and he was nice, and he could not understand why he should be heir to Mrs. Aylmer and I should be cut out of everything. I could not tell him. I could not bear to mention that time. It was like a blister on my mind. I went to London. You remember how I came to see you. I had very little money, just twenty pounds, and mother, who had only fifty pounds a year, could not help me. I went from one place to another offering myself as teacher, although I hated teaching and I could not teach well. But no one wanted me, and I was in despair. Then I had a letter from Bertha, and she made me a proposal. She sent with the letter a manuscript. Ah! I feel you start now."

"This is terrible!" said Mrs. Trevor. She stood up in her excitement. She backed a little away from Florence.

"You guess all, but I must go on telling you," continued the poor girl. "She sent this manuscript, and she asked me to use it as my own. She said she did not want any of the money, and I was tempted. But I struggled, I did struggle. It was Miss Franks who really was the innocent cause of pushing me over the gulf, for she read the manuscript and said it was very clever and she showed it to her brother, the man I am now engaged to. He said it was clever, and it was accepted for the *Argonaut* almost before I knew what I was doing . . .

"And that was the beginning of everything. I was famous. Bertha was the person who wrote the stories and the essays. I was wearing borrowed plumes, and I was not a bit clever. And, oh, Mrs. Trevor, the end has come now, for Mrs. Aylmer has died and has left all her great wealth to the hospitals. I have had a letter from Bertha. You may read it, Mrs. Trevor. This is what Bertha says."

As Florence spoke, she thrust Bertha's letter into Mrs. Trevor's hand.

"I will ring for a light," said the widow. She approached the bell, rang it, and the little rosy-faced servant appeared.

"Tea, Mary, and some hot cakes, and bring a lamp, please."

Florence continued to kneel. Mrs. Trevor softly pushed her into the nearest chair.

"I am glad and I am sorry you have told me," she said. "I will read the letter when the lamp comes. Now warm yourself."

"But can you speak to me again?"

"Who am I that I should judge you?" said the widow. "It is a terrible story, but who am I that I should judge?"

Then she said softly to herself. "This explains much."

The lamp was brought, and the tea, and still Mrs. Trevor did not read Bertha's letter. But she helped Florence to warm tea, and gave her some buttered cake, and made her eat.

"You poor girl," she said. "I will not touch this letter until I see you looking better."

And Florence, in spite of herself, drank the tea and ate a little of the cake, and the load lifted from her heart made her feel better and better. Then Mrs. Trevor took up the letter.

"I will read this in another room," she said. "You would like to be alone for a little."

She left the room softly with Bertha's letter, and Florence still sat by the fire. She sat so for some time, and, presently, soothed by the warmth and weary from all the agony she had undergone, the tired-out girl dropped asleep.

XXXVI

"All the Roses
Are Dead"

hen she awoke she heard someone moving in the room. There was the rustling of paper and the creak of a chair. At first she could not imagine where she was. Then she opened her eyes, saw the bright little room with its shaded lamp and its flickering firelight, and memory came back to her. She sprang to her feet, the color suffusing her cheeks and her eyes growing bright.

Then Florence did indeed color painfully, for Maurice Trevor stood before the excited girl.

"My mother has told me the whole story," he said.

He looked perturbed, his voice shook with emotion. His face was pale, and there was an angry scowl in his eyes. He took Florence's hand and pushed her into a chair.

"Sit down," he said.

She looked up at him drearily.

"All the roses are dead," she said softly, and she glanced out into the garden. The blinds were not drawn down, and the white light of the snow was reflected dimly into the room.

"All the roses are dead," she repeated. "The time of roses is over."

"No, it is not over. It will come back again at the proper season," said Trevor, "and don't think that I—"

"But do you know—"

"I know," he answered gravely. He bowed his head, then drew a chair forward.

"I must speak to you," he said.

She felt the comfort of his presence. It was as if she were leaning against a rock. She no longer had a queer, giddy sensation. The ground seemed to have become steady beneath her feet. However angry Maurice Trevor was, he would not cast her out into the cold.

"I am glad you came to Mother and told her. It is true I suspected much. You know that passage in Miss Keys' handwriting which I told you about some time ago, and the identically same passage in the newspaper article which was supposed to be yours? To a great extent my eyes were opened at that time, but not completely."

"You look very, very angry," she said.

"I am angry," he answered. "But I think I can say, with truth, not with you."

"With Bertha?"

"Please do not mention her name."

"But I have been to blame. I have been terribly weak."

"You have been terribly weak, you have been worse. You have done wrong, great wrong. But, Florence—may I call you by your Christian name?—winter comes in every year, but it is followed by spring, and spring is followed by summer, and in summer the roses bloom again, and the time of roses comes back, Florence, and it will come back even to you."

"No, no," she said, and she began to sob piteously.

He did not speak at all until her tears were partly over. Then he said softly, "I am very sorry, and I am not angry with you."

"You have been so good, so more than good to me," she said. "If you had known you would have despised me."

"And you will be worthy," he added, passion in his voice as he spoke, "because God, though He has not given you this special talent, has given you much."

"If I had known I should have gone straight to Miss Keys and put a stop to this disgraceful thing," was the young man's answer. "I suppose, Florence," he added after a pause, "if you have time to think of me at all, you pity me now because I am a penniless man?"

"Oh, no, no," she replied. "It is not good for people to be too rich. I have quite come to be of that opinion."

"Thank goodness. We are both of one way of thinking. As to Bertha Keys, her punishment awaits her, and we must leave her in the hands of the God whom she has offended. But as to you, Florence, you have to turn straight round and go into another path—the path of honesty—one worthy of you. And you will be worthy," he added, passion in his voice as he spoke, "because God, though He has not given you this special talent, has given you much."

"Much," she repeated, vaguely.

"Yes," he repeated, speaking earnestly. "He has given you attractiveness, great earnestness of purpose, and a thousand other things. He has at least done this for you, Florence. He has made you so that in all the wide world you are the only woman for me. I can love no one but you, Florence—no one else, even though you did fall."

"You cannot. It is impossible," answered Florence. "You cannot love me now."

"I have loved you all through, and this thing does not alter my love. You see, Florence," he added, "it was not the girl who was famous that I cared for. I never did care a bit about the wonderful writing which was supposed to be yours. Far from liking it, I hated it. I never wanted a wife who would be either famous or clever."

"And Tom Franks," continued Florence, "only wants me because he thinks me clever. But he will not wish to marry me now."

"I only wanted you for yourself. Will you wait for me and let me try to make a home for you, and when I have done that, will you come to me? I am going away to Australia. I have heard of a good post there, and I am going out almost at once. And if things succeed, you and my mother can come to me, and in the meantime will you stay with her and comfort her?"

"Oh, you are too good," said poor Florence. She clasped her hands and gazed straight into the fire. Then she looked up at Trevor with awe.

"God must have forgiven me when He sent you to me," she said simply.

The next moment he had clasped her in his arms.

"Remember, whatever you have done, I love you for yourself, and we have both plenty of faults, but I think we shall be happy together," was his answer.

Bertha Reclaims
Her Writing

om Franks was seated before his desk in his office. He did not look at all like a happy bridegroom.

"It is a case of jilting," he said to himself, and he took up a letter which he had received from Florence that morning. It was very short and ran as follows:

> I cannot marry you, and you will know why soon. When you know the reason you won't want me. I am terribly sorry, but sorrow won't alter matters. Please do not expect the manuscript.
>
> Yours truly, Florence Aylmer

"What does the girl mean?" he asked himself. "Really, at the present moment, the most annoying part of all is the fact that I have not received the manuscript. The printers are waiting for it. The new issue of the *Argonaut* will be nothing without it."

A clerk came in at that moment.

"Has Miss Aylmer's manuscript come, sir?" he asked. "The printers are waiting for it."

"The printers must wait, Dawson. I shall be going to see Miss Aylmer and will bring the manuscript back. Here, hand me a telegram form. I want to send a wire in a hurry."

The clerk did so. Franks dictated a few words aloud: "Will call to see you at twelve o'clock. Please remain in."

He gave the man Florence's address, and he departed with the telegram. Franks looked up at the clock.

"I must glance through some manuscripts and prepare one in case Florence is quite immovable," he said to himself. "She is a very strange girl. I doubt if I do well to try to marry her."

He thought for a little longer. Anderson opened the door of his room and called to him. "Is that you, Franks?"

"Yes, sir."

"May I speak to you for a moment?"

"Certainly," replied Franks. He went into his chief's room and shut the door.

"I have been thinking, Franks," said Mr. Anderson, "whether we do well to encourage that extremely pessimistic writing which Miss Florence Aylmer supplies us with."

"Do well to encourage it?" said Franks, opening his eyes very wide.

"I have hesitated to speak to you," continued Mr. Anderson, "because you are engaged to the young lady. But the manner in which she addresses her public is beginning to be noticed, and although her talent attracts, her morbidity will in the end work against the *Argonaut*, and even still more against the *General Review*. I wish you would have a serious talk with her, Franks, and tell her that unless she alters the tone of her writings—really I cannot accept them."

Franks uttered a bitter laugh.

"You are very likely to have your wish, sir," he said. "I am even now waiting for the manuscript of the fourth story which you know was advertised in the last *Argonaut*."

"Ah, yes, and of course *it* must appear; but you must cut it, you really must, Franks. Look, these letters came this morning. They express very strong views. I cannot have it said that our papers are advocating advanced views. It won't do, Franks, and you must let your clever young friend know the truth as soon as possible."

"I believe she will always write according to her convictions."

"And that is what pains me so much," continued Mr. Anderson. "I have myself looked over her proofs and have endeavored to infuse a cheerful note into them. But cutting won't do it, nor will removing certain passages. The same miserable, unnatural outlook pervades every word she says. I believe her mind is made that way."

"You are not very complimentary," said Franks, almost losing his temper. He was quiet for a moment, then he said slowly, "We are very likely to have to do without Miss Aylmer. I begin to think that she is a very strange girl. She has offered to release me from my engagement. In fact, she has declared she will not go on with it, and she says that she cannot furnish us with any more manuscripts."

"Then what are we to do for the next issue?" cried Mr. Anderson. "Look through all available manuscripts at once, my dear fellow."

"I'll do better than that," replied Franks. "Our public expects a story by Miss Aylmer in the next number, and if possible they must have it. I have already wired to say that I will call upon her, and with your permission, as the time is nearly up, I will go to Prince's Mansions now."

"It may be best," said Mr. Anderson. He looked gloomy and anxious. "You can cut the new story a bit, can't you, Franks?"

"I will do my best, sir."

The young man went out of the room. He was just crossing his own apartment when the door was opened and his clerk came in.

"A lady to see you, sir. She says her business is pressing."

"A lady to see me! Say I am going out. I cannot see anyone at present. Who is she? Has she come by appointment?"

"She has not come by appointment, sir. Her name is Miss Keys—Miss Bertha Keys."

"I never heard of her. Say that I am obliged to go out and cannot see her today. Ask her to call another time. Leave me now, Dawson. I want to keep my appointment with Miss Aylmer."

Dawson left the room.

Franks went to his desk and looked up one or two important documents. He then crossed the room to the peg where he kept his coat and hat and was preparing to put them on when once again Dawson appeared.

"Miss Keys says she has come about Miss Aylmer's business, and she thinks you will not lose any time if you see her, sir."

"Yes, you will not lose any time," said a strange voice.

Franks turned and looked intensely annoyed. Bertha Keys had quietly entered the apartment behind the clerk.

"I have come on the subject of Florence Aylmer and the manuscript you expect her to send you," said Bertha Keys. "Will you give me two or three moments of your valuable time?"

Dawson glanced at Franks. Franks nodded to him to withdraw, and the next moment Miss Keys and Mr. Franks found themselves alone.

Bertha was in deep black and looked her best. Her very fair complexion was shown up to advantage by her somber clothing. Her hat was slightly pushed away from her forehead; her big eyes were luminous with excitement. A great deal depended on this interview. Bertha was strung up to do her very best. Franks did not speak at all for a moment. Bertha in the meantime was taking his measure.

"May I sit down?" she said. "I am a little tired. I have come all the way from Shropshire this morning."

Franks pushed a chair toward her, but still did not speak. She looked at him, and a faint smile dawned around her lips.

"You are expecting Florence Aylmer's manuscript, are you not?" she said then.

He nodded, but his manner was as much as to say, "What business is it of yours?"

She nodded back at him, and the smile once again parted her lips, and he saw a flash of her white teeth. He was magnetized too by the curious expression in her eyes. He thought he had never seen such clever eyes before. He was beginning to be interested in her.

"I have come about Florence's manuscript, but all the same, you bitterly resent my intrusion. By the way, you are engaged to marry Florence Aylmer?"

"I was," replied Franks shortly. "But pardon me. I am extremely busy. If she has chosen you as her messenger to bring the manuscript, will you kindly give it to me and go?"

"How polite!" said Bertha with a smile. "I have not brought any manuscript from Florence Aylmer. But I have brought a manuscript from myself."

Franks uttered an angry exclamation.

"Have you forced your way into my room about that?" he said.

"I have. You have received and published three stories *purporting* to be by the pen of Florence Aylmer. You have also published one or two articles by the same person. You are waiting for the fourth story. The first three stories made a great sensation. You are impatient and disturbed because the fourth story has not come to hand. Here it is."

Bertha hastily opened a small packet which she held in her hand and produced the manuscript.

"Look at it," she said. "Read the opening sentence. I am not in the slightest hurry. Take your own time, but read the first page, if you will. If the style is not the style of the old stories, if the matter is not equal in merit to the stories already published, then I will own to you that I came here on a false errand and will ask you to forgive me."

Franks, with still that strange sense of being mesmerized, received the manuscript from Bertha's long slim hand. He sank into his office chair and listlessly turned the pages.

Of course this woman was an impostor. The story she was offering him was worthless. Nevertheless, he found himself doing her bidding. He read a sentence or two and then looked up at the clock.

"I have wired to Miss Aylmer to expect me at twelve. It is past that hour now. I really must ask you to pardon me."

"Miss Aylmer will not be in. Miss Aylmer has left Prince's Mansions. I happened to call there and know what I am saying. Will you go on reading? You want your story. I believe your printers are waiting for it even now."

Franks fidgeted impatiently. Once again his eyes lit upon the page. As he read, Bertha's own eyes devoured his face. She knew each word of that first page. She had taken special and extra pains with it. It represented her best, her very best. There was a note of passion and pathos, there was a deep undercurrent of feeling in her words. Franks read to the end.

If he turned the page Bertha felt that her victory would be won—if he closed the manuscript she had still to fight her battle. Her heart beat quickly.

Franks at last came to the final word. He hesitated, half looked up, then his fingers trembled. He turned the page. Bertha saw by the look on his face that he had absolutely forgotten her. She gave a brief sigh. The victory was won. She rose and approached him.

"I can take that to another house," she said. "The Throgmortons have, I understand, offered Miss Aylmer advantageous terms for her work. This can go into their magazine, *Society Bells*."

"No, no," said Franks. "There is great stuff in this. It is quite up to the usual mark. So Florence gave it to you to bring to me. Now, I do not quite like the tone nor does my chief, but the talent is unmistakable."

"You will publish it then?"

"Certainly. I see it is the usual length. If you will pardon me, as things are pressing, I will ring and give this to the printers."

"One moment first. You think that manuscript has been written by Florence Aylmer?"

"Why not? Of course it has!" He looked uneasily from the paper in his hand to the girl who stood before him. "What do you mean?"

"I have something to tell you. You may be angry with me, but I do not much care. *I* possess the genius, not Florence Aylmer. *I* am the writer of that story. Florence Aylmer wrote one thing for you, a schoolgirl essay, which you returned. I wrote the papers which the public devoured. I am the ghost behind Florence Aylmer. I am the real author come to you at last."

"You must be telling me an untruth," said Franks. He staggered back, his face became green, his eyes flashed angrily.

"I am telling you the truth. You have but to ask Florence herself. Has she not broken off her engagement with you?"

"She has, and a good thing, too," he muttered under his breath.

"Ah! I heard those words, though you said them so low, and it is a good thing for you. You would never have been happy with a girl like Florence. I know her well. I don't pretend that I played a very nice part, but still I am not ashamed. I want money now. I did not want money when I offered my productions to Florence. I hoped that I should be a very rich woman. My hopes have fallen to the ground; therefore, I take back that talent with which nature has endowed me. You can give *me* orders for the *Argonaut* in the future. You will kindly pay *me* for that story. Now I think I have said what I meant to say, and I wish you good morning."

"But you must stay a moment, Miss—I really forget your name."

"My name is Keys—Bertha Keys. I have taken the room which Florence has vacated in 12, Prince's Mansions. It will suit me admirably. I won't charge her anything for the stories which appeared in her name in the past. In the future I take my own winnings, and I wish to make fresh arrangements. You want my work—it does not matter in the least whether you want it or not. *Society Bells*, *The Chime of St. Paul's*, and other well-known magazines will pay me for all I can write for them. But I am willing to give you the *whole* of my writings, say for three months, if you are willing to pay me according to my own ideas."

"What are those?"

"You must double your pay to me. You can, if you like, publish this little story about Florence and myself in some of your society gossip—I do not mind at all—or you can keep it quiet. You have but to say in one of your issues that the pseudonym under which your talented author wrote is changed. You can give me a fresh title. The world will suspect mystery and run after me more than ever. I think that is the principal thing I have to say to you. Now, may I wish you good morning?"

"You astound me. I scarcely know whether I am on my head or my heels. Will you come again tomorrow?"

"That will be best. You will be calmer then. You can consult with your chief. Don't lose me, pray, for I am worth my weight in gold. You had the substitute. Now you have the reality. Consider yourself a most lucky man. Suppose, for instance, you had found all this out *after* the wedding ceremony?"

Bertha rose as she spoke, dropped a light mocking curtsey in Franks' direction, and let herself out of the room before he had time to realize that she was leaving.

XXXVIII

Redemption

y all the laws of morality, Bertha Keys ought to have come to punishment; she ought to have gone under; she ought to have disappeared from society; she ought to have been hooted and disliked wherever she showed her face.

These things were by no means the case, however. Bertha, playing a daring game, once more achieved success.

Franks and Anderson did not intend to allow this talented woman's productions to pass into the hands of their rivals. Bertha proved herself far more adaptable to their wishes than poor Florence had been during her brief moment of apparent success. When she saw she was going too far in a cynical spirit, she changed her tactics.

By means of threatening to take her work elsewhere, she secured admirable terms for her writing—quite double those which had been given to poor Florence. She lived in the best rooms in Prince's Mansions, and, before a year had expired, she was engaged to Tom Franks. He married her, and reports whisper that they are by no means a contented couple. It is known that Franks is cowed and, at home at least, obeys his wife.

263

Meanwhile, Florence, her conscience once more relieved from its burden of misery, bloomed out into happiness, greater faith in God's love, and also into success.

Meanwhile Florence, her conscience once more relieved from its burden of misery, bloomed out into happiness, greater faith in God's love, and also into success.

Of all people in the world, Mrs. Trevor was undoubtedly the best companion for the girl during her hours of humiliation. The little Mum, much as she cared for her, would have driven Florence nearly wild. But Mrs. Trevor, without alluding to the past, guided the girl's steps into the paths of honor and virtue.

Florence wrote weekly to Trevor, and Trevor wrote to her. His love for her grew as the days and weeks went by. The couple had to wait some time before they could really marry, but during that time Florence learned some of the best lessons in life. She was soon able to support herself, for she turned out to be, contrary to her expectations, a very excellent teacher. She avoided Tom Franks and his wife and could not bear to hear the name of the *Argonaut* mentioned. For a time, indeed, she took a dislike to all magazines and only read the special books which Mrs. Trevor indicated.

Kitty Sharston was also her best friend during this time. And when the hour at last arrived when Florence was to join Trevor, Kitty said to her father that she scarcely knew her old friend, so courageous was the light that shone in Florence's eyes, and so happy and beaming was her smile.

"I have gone down into the depths," she said to Kitty on the day when she sailed for Australia. "It is a very good thing sometimes to see oneself down to the very bottom."

As to Mrs. Trevor, she also had a last word with Kitty.

"There was a time, my dear," she said, "when knowing all that had happened in the past, I was rather nervous as to what kind of wife my dear son would have in Florence Aylmer. But she is indeed now a daughter after my own heart—brave, steadfast, earnest."

THE END

Victorian Bookshelf Series

DEAR THEODORA

A GIFT FOR ABIGAIL

PRISCILLA'S PROMISE

THE TIME OF ROSES

Sisters

Sisters

SUZANNE GOODWIN

cop. 2

St. Martin's Press
New York

Library of Congress Cataloging in Publication Data
Goodwin, Suzanne.
  Sisters.
  I. Title.
PR6057.0585S5   1985   823'.914   84-27559
ISBN 0-312-72748-8

First published in Great Britain by Severn House Publishers Ltd.

First U.S. Edition

10 9 8 7 6 5 4 3 2 1

Publisher's Note

This novel is a work of fiction. Names, characters, places and incidents are either the product of the author's imagination or are used fictitiously, and any resemblance to actual persons, living or dead, events, or locales is entirely coincidental.

Part I

Chapter One

The air raid warning came early, it was scarcely half past six, and the girl walking down the road quickened her step and muttered, 'Damn.' The siren rose and fell, rose and fell, wailing like the Irish banshee which people believe is a prophecy of death. The message moaned across the great lightless city, one district starting it, another picking it up and sending it onwards until the whole world seemed to echo. At last it groaned its way into silence.

Philippa walked fast but she did not run. The blitz had been on over London now for two months, and nobody ran during the raids. It was considered a sign of panic. The street lamp in the distance, shedding a ghostly glow round its base, faintly showed her that she was almost home.

As she stopped at the gate of the house, a figure in uniform emerged out of the dark. A thin ray of torchlight explored the painted name on the gatepost.

'Are you looking for St Helen's?' she asked.

'Why, yes I am.'

Overhead an ominous noise had started. It grew steadily louder, sounding like a swarm of giant bees. There was a distant muffled shudder of an explosion.

'If you want Doctor Tyrrell, I'm afraid he's at the hospital.'

'Oh, I'm not a patient. I just dropped by.'

'Well, whoever you are,' she replied curtly, 'don't you think we would be better indoors?'

'If you say so, Ma'am.'

Philippa led the way up the short gravel drive towards the dim shape of a large house. She unlocked the front door.

They plunged into a black cave. When the door was safely shut, she switched on the light. They were standing in an old-fashioned entrance hall. The visitor looked about curiously. There was a good deal of dark panelling, a heavy-looking staircase with carved banisters, a grandfather clock in a corner, its face showing the sun and moon. A Tudor chest against the

3

wall was large enough to hold two people. There were Persian rugs on the floor, which was tiled in patterns of black, white and brown stars.

While the stranger examined the house, Philippa looked at him and saw a tall olive-skinned young man, in very new RAF uniform. He had taken off his cap and he had thick dark hair. Catching her eye, he smiled.

'Barny Duval. Glad to know you. Dixon, he's the English Intelligence officer in our squadron, told me his father knows Doctor Tyrrell. They belong to the same club. When he knew I was coming to London he said what about calling around to say hello. He mentioned that the doctor had some daughters. Which are you, ma'am?'

'Philippa. The middle one. There are three of us.'

She thought him too friendly too soon.

He turned towards her and she saw a badge on his sleeve, of an eagle, one claw clasping arrows, the other an olive branch. Above the badge were the letters E.S.

'Eagle Squadron,' he said.

'I thought you were a Canadian.'

'We have some of them, but no. I'm a Yank.'

There was a deafening roar of gunfire.

'*About time!*' exclaimed Philippa suddenly.

'The guns, you mean?'

'I should think I do. There wasn't one when the blitz started in September. Not a single one. There we were, sitting ducks, while they flew over dropping their bombs wherever they liked. It made us sick. Now we're putting up a show. The bigger the guns, the more we like it.'

Another, nearer explosion made the house quake.

'Don't you prefer to shelter?' said the young man. 'Have you one of those what-do-you-call-its in the garden? Or we could go to the subway, I guess, but it's quite a way.'

'Oh, we don't shelter in the Underground! We've got one in the house. Let's go.'

She led the way into a room which, like the hall when they had first entered the house, was an extent of blackness, every window muffled by thick curtains pulled to exclude even a pinprick of light. Philippa's father had twice been fined for blackout infringements, both times it had been the fault of his daughters. Now he demanded blackout perfection.

4

'Wait a minute.'

She disappeared, appearing a moment later silhouetted in the open doorway of a further room. Barny Duval crossed what was apparently a drawing room filled with chairs, footstools and other traps for blundering strangers. He followed her into what turned out to be a large billiard room. She had lit a lamp which was on the floor under the billiard table.

'The family shelter,' she said, with a sort of flourish. 'My father fixed it up at the beginning of the war. Idiots that we were, we couldn't believe it would ever be used. It was quite a family joke. But my sister Trix and I did paint the double ceiling. It's made of corrugated iron.'

She pointed upwards, at a sheet of corrugated iron fixed to the ceiling and supported at each corner of the room by a stout wooden post. The iron was painted a glossy dark green.

Like the hall and the unlit drawing room, the billiard room was spacious. It was panelled from the floor to about five feet up the wall and above the panelling was a line of early nineteenth-century sporting cartoons, grotesque figures boxing or fencing. There was a rack of billiard cues, big leather chairs, a smell of cigars. The place was old-fashioned and prosperous.

Philippa crawled under the table and politely patted a cushion for her visitor. The floor was arranged as neatly as the interior of a tent, with mattresses and pillows, cushions and folded rugs. The lamp stood on a tray, with cups and saucers and a silver ashtray. There were books, copies of *Vogue*, and a pack of cards.

He crouched his six foot one and crawled in beside her.

She had decided that social conversation was necessary. After all this man was a stranger and an American. She remarked brightly that it was good, wasn't it, not to be shivering in an Anderson shelter at the bottom of the garden. A girl friend had found three inches of water in hers last week: she had been sharing the shelter with a family of toads.

He undid the button of his breast pocket and offered her an American cigarette. She refused.

'May I?'

'Of course,' she said, still the hostess.

Although she was the English girl making polite talk to set her visitor at ease in ludicrous circumstances, Philippa saw rather resentfully that there really was no need. She would have preferred him to be miserably shy, but he wasn't. Here she was,

5

in her own home, on the floor under a table with a strange man. But all he did was hunch up his long legs, lean back and look at her through the cigarette smoke.

The noise of the blitz went on, the giant bees droning, the explosions thumping. There went the guns again.

'Ah,' said Barny Duval, 'now that's a Bofors. And that – ' listening carefully, 'must be a 4.5.'

'My father says Londoners can recognize sixteen different noises in the blitz now. The various guns. Warden's whistles, warnings, different kinds of bombs. Falling shrapnel too. The other night when he was coming back from the hospital, a great lump of shrapnel fell on his head.'

'Was he badly hurt?'

'He had on his tin helmet. The only time he forgot it, he said it felt like being a crab without its shell. The shrapnel bounced off the tin hat and he found it in the gutter and brought it home. It was still warm.'

Barny looked at this matter-of-fact girl. She was pretty but not beautiful. Her eyes, wide apart, were grey and had a charming candid expression. Her mouth was large and when she smiled – but she hadn't done much of that – she looked very young. Her hair was brownish with copper lights, it was smooth and curled behind her ears. She looked so English. And yet there was something he couldn't exactly define which reminded him of the girls back home. She might be stiff and hostessy, but she had an independent carefree kind of look. But there the resemblance ended. In place of the frills and wide belts and glamorous gew-gaws worn by American girls, his blitz companion was in a brown sweater and skirt. At least she wore silk stockings; but her shoes were as heavy and low-heeled as a man's.

'My younger sister Trix is going to be furious when I tell her that somebody from Eagle Squadron called and she wasn't here,' remarked Philippa. 'She's out as usual. Dancing.'

'Is she a dancer?'

She burst out laughing.

'She's very good, but only on the dance floor at Grosvenor House.'

'But surely she comes home before the raids?'

'Not Trix. She has friends who live on the ground floor of nice solid blocks of flats. She rings them and goes there, and sleeps on the sofa of whoever-it-is.'

6

'Not in the subway?'
'You haven't met Trix.'
'Sounds as if I'd like to.'
They were silent for a moment. The blitz was in full swing.
'It was kind of you to ask me in. I feel very guilty at imposing on you like this.' Her social manner was very slightly wearing off, but he still felt it necessary to say that.
'We're always glad to meet friends of friends, Pilot Officer.'
'Oh, hell. Can't you manage Barny? Pilot Officer's such a mouthful and I haven't been in this uniform too long.'
'How long?'
'Well . . . four months. We landed in Southampton in August. Since then we've just been sitting around waiting to get trained. And becoming very frustrated.'
'I think it's wonderful, you coming here to England,' she said suddenly in a warmer voice.
'If we were in the States, I'd say "shucks".'
They looked at each other in a friendly way. They were huddled under the table, while an orchestra of destruction went on across the sprawling darkness of the city. Everywhere in London people were doing the same thing. They crouched in damp concrete shelters in the garden; they sat under the stairs or in cellars; on the crowded platforms in the Underground, or under the kitchen table, listening to the blitz which had been going on night after night for the last nine weeks. Doctor Tyrrell was right, people had become experts now at the different instruments of the orchestra. They knew the bark of the Bofors, the big-mouthed roar of the 4.5. They could tell when a bomb rushing earthwards was a thousand-pounder, they knew the light scattering noise of fire bombs, the rattle of machine-guns, the drone of enemy bombers. They listened and identified the sounds with a kind of stoic acceptance.

Philippa found herself grateful for this American's company. The family's old servant, Miggs, was down in the cellar of the house. She went there every night before the alert sounded, remarking that she liked her own company. Philippa never offered to join her and was often alone during the blitz, for her sister was always out and their father on duty at the hospital. She preferred a companion, even if he was a stranger. He also happened to be part of the thing she admired most in the world – the Royal Air Force.

7

From the start of the war she had fallen in love with flyers, as many English girls had done. This feeling had grown passionate now that the Battle of Britain was on. Philippa looked at pilots across the street, or in buses, or in restaurants, with eyes full of stars. She was like Desdemona, and loved them for the dangers they had passed.

She glanced at her companion. His face was thin and hawkish, his nose slightly aquiline, his dark hair fell in a lock on his forehead. There was something Latin about his looks. She had only known one American before in her life, a girl at her finishing school in Brussels. She, too, had seemed romantic to Philippa.

There was a louder burst of gunfire.

'Hotting up,' said Barny.

'Shall I make tea? I usually do.'

'Let me make it for you.'

'Gallant. But you'd never find anything in the kitchen. I sometimes can't either. Miggsy puts things in the oddest places. The tea is in the jar marked Rice, and the sugar in another marked Ginger. The biscuits, if we have any, are hidden. She does it to annoy because she knows it teases.'

'Is Miggsy another sister?'

'Gracious, no. She's our old nanny who has turned into an inefficient sort of housekeeper. She's been with the family forever.'

'Like a Mammy in Louisiana.'

'Oh, I know about them, I saw Gone With the Wind! But that was Georgia, wasn't it? Miggsy isn't a bit like a Southern Mammy. I wish she were. She was my grandfather's gardener's daughter, if you follow? She's quite old. She was my father's nurse and he inherited her. When the parents married and came here to Kensington, Miggsy came too. When we were born, she was our nanny. Now she has a stab at the housekeeping. She also calls herself the doctor's secretary. That's a laugh.'

He was looking at her with attention, and she saw with surprise that he was rather shocked, either by what she had said or her manner or both.

'Your family must love her, I guess,' he said, sounding very American.

'I'm afraid we don't. She can be very annoying. Specially when she deliberately lets the boiler go out before Trix and I have a bath. Miggsy doesn't approve of more than one bath a fortnight, she says it takes away the natural oils of the skin. But there she is. Miggs. Part of our lives. She's all we've got now. We used to have two maids as well before the war, but they vanished into the ATS.'

'Does the old lady live here?'

It was the first time in her life Philippa had heard Miggs so described.

'Oh, yes. She's in the cellar at present. It's quite snug and dry and my father had it whitewashed. She goes off there every night, taking the wireless and an enormous old rug and a thermos of tea.'

'Brave of her to stay in the blitz.'

'She's as tough as old boots.'

'I think,' he said, 'that *you* aren't as tough as you pretend.'

She raised her eyebrows. Were American girls really like Scarlett O'Hara's Southern girl friends, either ninnies or pretending to be? Did they pay lip-service to the obvious sanctimonious opinions, to match a man's idea of a tender, sensitive, vulnerable woman who must be protected?

She returned to the subject of tea.

'The bombs don't sound too close. I do long for tea – '

As she was speaking there was a terrifying scream, as a stick of bombs came hurtling through space. In that split second, expecting death, they fell into each other's arms. The explosion deafened them. The house seemed to jump in the air and then subside.

Silence.

She still grasped his shoulders. Then she relaxed.

'Well,' he drawled, 'that one didn't have our names on it after all.' He did not let her go, and with his arms still holding her she felt shy.

'I'm very glad you're here,' she suddenly said.

'Me too. You okay?'

'Perfectly.'

She was conscious of how close he was; she could see his dark eyelashes which curled like a girl's, and smell a faint scent of eau-de-cologne and clean skin. Her hair brushed his face. He let his arms drop at last, and she leaned back, tugging at a cushion.

'You're very beautiful.'

Philippa went scarlet.

9

'Hell, I've made you blush. You must know you're beautiful. A heap of guys have told you so before now . . . there are freckles on the bridge of your nose.'

She managed a laugh.

'Seven.'

'You counted them.'

'No, it was my sister Trix. She said that I must get rid of them. She bought some expensive stuff at Harrods before make-up disappeared from the shops. She used to rub it on my nose every day for a week. It didn't have the slightest effect. She was more disappointed than I was. She's the family's beauty expert.'

'You talk about her a lot.'

'So would you if you met her.'

'But isn't there another sister?'

'Yes, the married one. Elaine. She's with her husband at present. He's in the Royal Naval Voluntary Reserve, and he's got some leave.'

He nodded, indicating a kindly interest; he was very polite. He lit another cigarette and sat smoking and staring into space; unselfconscious, easy. It was odd to be here on the floor with this foreigner. It was rather fascinating to realise that she knew absolutely nothing about him; it gave him a kind of power in her thoughts. He came from the country she knew only from the cinema, and about which she had hazy ideas based on Hollywood. It was a land of the rich, the frivolous and the glamorous, where girls in white satin nightdresses were stranded in situations which could not offend the strictest Puritan. Everything American was foreign to Philippa. But this man wore English uniform.

'There isn't a moon tonight,' he said, after a pause. 'Moonlight helps.'

'The enemy?'

'No, no, the fighters. The idea of a bomber's moon is quite wrong, it ought to be called a hunter's moon, a fighter's moon.'

'Have you been in a fight, Barny?'

'Wish I could say yes. But no, we're still hanging around, supposed to be training. And God, there's one hell of a lot to learn.'

Suddenly he tensed. They both heard the sound outside the house, an extraordinary noise, plop, plop, plop, plop, as if somebody were dropping a thousand tennis balls. No explosions followed.

10

'What on earth – ' began Philippa, when there was a thunderous hammering at the front door. A voice yelled,

'Warden here! Warden here! Open up, your house is on fire!'

They threw themselves out from under the table and pelted to the front door. A man in blue uniform, wearing a tin hat, said quickly, 'Thank God you're here. There's a fire at the back. Look sharp.'

Not stopping to say more, he rushed back into the road. Out in the dark there was fire everywhere.

'I must get Miggs,' shouted Philippa, but just then a bent figure in a dressing-gown appeared at the top of the cellar steps.

The old woman said, 'I've seen it. It's the conservatory. You take the sand. I'll get water.'

She hurried to the kitchen.

Philippa grabbed a bucket of sand which had stood in the corner of the hall since the war began. She and Barny ran down the front steps. The blacked-out night was transformed. Small brilliant fires burned fiercely all down the road, and figures silhouetted in the dazzling orange flames were hurrying to quench them. An extraordinary sound broke out from road and gardens, as men and women put out the incendiaries with earth or water. It was laughter. The bombs fell like hail, weighing little, and burst into flames the moment they hit the ground. One girl contemptuously kicked a flaming bomb into the gutter.

Philippa and Barny ran round the corner of the house as a soldier appeared from nowhere, carrying a stirrup pump.

'Water?'

'We've got a tank.'

The conservatory, tinder-dry from the hot summer, was already burning with a roar, the sparks flying upwards like fireworks. Barny and the soldier began to pump, Philippa rushed forward to fling her sand into the flames.

'Hell!'

The sand was caked solid. Dashing to a flower bed, she dug the sand out with her nails, filled the bucket with earth and returned to throw it on the fire. Miggs came out of the kitchen door bent under the weight of an enormous iron kettle. Barny took it from her as if it were a feather. Protecting their faces, the men advanced into the smoke to seize deckchairs and mats which they threw on to the grass.

The leaping flames lit the garden as if it were Guy Fawkes'

11

night, throwing fantastic shadows. The smoke was choking. But after some minutes of pumping the water and dousing with earth, Miggs and Philippa hurrying to the kitchen and back over and over again and the tank providing a steady stream, the fire at last began to hiss.

'That's more like it,' grunted the soldier, wiping his face with a blackened hand. 'I'll go next door.'

He ran off towards the garden wall and a reddish gloom from a neighbouring house.

Miggs passed Barny a final kettle of water which he threw on smouldering windowsills. The old woman, hands on hips, looked at the smoking mess.

Barny said to Philippa, 'Shall we go too?'

A high wall separated St Helen's from the next house which had been empty since the war. Barny called, 'Let me give you a leg up,' but Philippa went over the wall like a bird.

The garden of the empty house shone with glittering fires on flower beds, lawns, and the steps by the French windows. There was a smash of glass as the soldier broke a window to go indoors – he'd seen a fire on the roof.

Earth quenched fires, as water did, but Philippa found a quicker way, she used a dustbin lid. She and Barny ran from fire to fire until there was nothing left but smoke and the smouldering ashes. The wardens' whistles had begun to blow again in the street – a fresh rain of incendiaries was falling, each bomb bursting into flames as it fell. The road was still crowded with helpers. Somebody shouted to Barny, as he pushed a ladder against the empty house.

At last it was over. The whistles were silent, the figures in dressing-gowns had melted away, every fire was out. Philippa put down her dustbin lid, and stood by the ladder, which Barny and the soldier were shinning down. The sky over towards the West End was stained dark red.

'We put up a good show, didn't we?' said the soldier, grinning. He loped away into the dark.

The front door of St Helen's was open.

'Where's the old lady?'

'Don't worry about her. She'll be back in her lair drinking tea. Tea! We need it!'

Slamming the front door, they went into the kitchen, and Philippa put on the light. The room was big and old-fashioned,

like the rest of the house, the floor tiled, and a coke boiler in the corner. The curtains were closely drawn, or they would have shown a first-rate view of the burnt conservatory.

Philippa made the tea and found about half a glass of brandy in a dusty bottle high up in the pantry. She divided it fairly, pouring it into the two cups. Then she sat on the table and looked at her legs. She sighed.

'Ruined.'

The precious, gleaming silk stockings were a mass of ladders through which her muddy legs showed. Her face was as black as a sweep's, her jersey filthy, her skirt, torn with jumping over the wall, was smeared with earth and smuts. Barny's uniform was as bad.

'Heroine.'

'Hero.'

'We make a fine pair.'

They drank the tea, refilling the pot and examined the brandy bottle for a few final drops. Carrying the tea tray to the billiard room, they crawled back under the table and settled down like birds in a nest. Guns still barked but the bombs were far off.

'Wish I could take you out for some champagne. And to dance.'

'I feel the same. I want to celebrate. But we'd never clean ourselves up, we need baths! And your uniform's really awful, Barny. We'd never get the muck off it.'

'Suppose you're right. Pity.'

He looked at her and added, 'My leave lasts until two o'clock tomorrow. What are you doing for lunch?'

'A sandwich and fund-raising. I write endless letters begging for cash for a children's hospital.'

'Could you stop begging long enough to eat lunch with me?'

'I don't know . . . yes, I think so.'

'That's nice. And what about breakfast before you go to work?'

'But we'll be having it here. You're staying, aren't you?'

'Somehow I feel I should scram. Your father – '

'He wouldn't mind.' Her voice said the opposite.

'I'd mind you spending the night with a strange man if you were mine. Come to think of it – I wish you *were* mine.'

He took her in his arms.

Philippa had wanted him to do that. She had kept thinking about it, imagining what it would be like if he kissed her. She

13

had found herself looking at his mouth, the lips firm and the bottom lip full. Now, as he closed his arms round her she gave a kind of sigh as she shut her eyes. She snuggled closer, giving and receiving passionate, exploring kisses. How beautiful he tasted, she thought. Her mind began to blur, she could no longer think, she could only feel. He shifted and lay on top of her, covering her with his weight and pushing her down into the cushions. He was heavy, and she was excited by the sensation of being crushed by the weight of a man. Between kisses he made choking sounds, half exclamations.

'Christ, you're so – oh, God!' He began to pull up her sweater, and putting his hands into her brassiere, he exposed one of her breasts. She came spinning back to earth.

'No. Please. No.'

When she gasped, 'No' he pushed her naked breast ridiculously back into the lace cup, resembling a man putting a peach into a paper bag. He pulled down her sweater. Philippa had never been half seduced before, and thought he would move away from her. But he did not. He still held her, looking down into her face.

'So you won't let me make love to you. You don't want us to.'

'But I do. Dreadfully. It's just that I never have.'

He rubbed his face against hers, scratching her skin.

'Then I guess you shouldn't.'

Her body throbbed, she felt giddy, she wanted to be kissed again.

'It's your fault I behave badly, you're such a luscious female.'

'I wish we *could*.' Her sorrowful look confused him. He ached for this brave foreign girl.

There was the sudden loud noise of a slammed door.

'Damn. That must be my father.'

Guilty as a schoolboy, Barny slicked back his hair and buttoned the filthy uniform jacket. Philippa pulled down her skirt. We might be in an old-fashioned French farce, she thought. They were sitting well apart when the billiard room door opened.

'Philippa?'

Her father's voice was hoarse.

'I'm here, Father. Trix hasn't come home but this is Pilot Officer Duval who came to help with the fire.'

Her father, in coat and tin hat and holding his doctor's bag,

14

stared down at them. Barny crawled out from under the table and politely introduced himself. Doctor Tyrrell did not reply. He went out, saying – which part of the house was burnt?

A moment later he put his face round the door again.

'Where in God's name is Miggs?'

'Safely back in the basement, sir. A wonderful old lady at helping put out a fire.'

Doctor Tyrrell grunted and disappeared.

Putting out his hand, Barny pulled Philippa to her feet. He thought how tired the pretty face looked under its smears and smuts.

'You could use some sleep. I must get weaving. Philippa - mind if I call you Flip?'

'My sisters do.'

'I'll join them. See you for lunch, then. The Ritz at one-fifteen okay?'

'Goodness, how extravagant.'

'You belong in places like that.'

He briefly kissed her, picked up his cap, turned to look at her for a moment, and left. She heard the front door close.

She crawled back under the table, covering herself with the rugs. Her father did not return – she heard him going up the stairs, and coming down again to his study. It, too, had an iron ceiling.

Lying open-eyed, she listened to the blitz. Was Barny safe in the dangerous streets? Where was he going, she had never asked him.

The All Clear did not sound until dawn.

15

Chapter Two

When Philippa came downstairs, bathed and dressed in neat working clothes, Miggs was in the morning room. The old nurse wore a hectic puce and green apron over her grey skirt and blouse, and stood with arms folded looking out of the window. She gestured in the direction of the conservatory.

In daylight the scene of last night's fiery drama had become a blackened mess against a background of leafless winter trees.

'The doctor's only just seen it properly. Stood starin' at it for ten minutes, then in he came and carried on somethin' shockin'.'

Miggs dropped her *g's* like a member of some aristocratic hunting set.

'I suppose it was shock, Miggs.'

The old woman snorted. 'He sees forty times worse every night. Some of the things he tells me, and he doesn't say much, mind, always reserved, your father, they make my hair curl. Anyway he was lucky last night; if you and that young chap hadn't looked sharp, the whole house would have burned up and me in it. I told him. He doesn't listen.'

Migg's manner of speaking about her employer was anything but respectful.

Her real name was Ada Margaret Higgins but nobody called her anything but Miggs. She had grown up in the gardener's cottage of the Sussex manor where Philippa's father was born. At seventeen she had been employed as nurse to the little Tyrrell boy. Theo had been Migg's only love affair. He had been good-looking, with sparkling blue eyes. He loved music and Miggs could play the piano. The little child in spotless white, or dressed like a sailor in imitation of the Royal children, would sit in a trance under the nursery piano while Miggs thumped away at *Floradora*. She read to him and he knew every old rhyme by heart. 'I saw three ships come sailing by, sailing by' Theo chanted, and Miggs put her arms round him and hugged him until he couldn't breathe. She waited on him like a slave, spoiled him dreadfully and never said a cross word to him. When he was a grown man and became engaged to be married, it did not occur either to Theo or to Miggs that she would not accompany him to his new home.

In her youth her back had been injured and she had something of a hump. She was as small as a child, stoutish, solid, and although in her seventies she moved niftily. She had a mole on one side of her cheek the size of a half-crown, and wicked little hazel eyes. When children first saw her she frightened them, she looked so like a witch. But after two minutes they were on her knee, giggling. So perhaps she was a white witch. Children and animals and Theo loved Miggs.

Her passion for Theo had altered, she no longer thought him perfect and often criticised him to his face – the only woman in his life who got away with that. She was possessive. She had been kind enough to Mary, Theo's wife and mother of the three girls, but Mary treated Miggs gingerly. She was not strong, and was glad of Miggs's sturdy presence while the children were young.

The three Tyrrell girls, Elaine, Philippa and finally Trix were all cared for by Miggs, but she never gave them her heart. She bossed them about and complained about them to their father. They enjoyed her when they were very small, but by the time they were old enough to go to school they were glad to be out of her way. There was no fun in having an old nanny if you weren't spoiled, and Miggs's reaction to a new frock was 'handsome is as handsome does', or to a good school report, 'think yourself clever now, do you?'. Elaine sometimes said that Miggs was jealous.

When the Tyrrell girls grew up, Miggs suddenly transformed herself. Theo's receptionist was leaving to be married. His Kensington practice was busy and he needed a girl at the desk in the hall, to answer the telephone, show the patients into the waiting room and send out the monthly bills. He was interviewing girls for the job and had not made up his mind who would suit him when Miggs appeared. She wore a white starched coat over her miniature humpy body. She'd bought it in the medical department of the Army and Navy stores. It had bone buttons and cufflinks, and she had had to take up the hem which had touched the ground.

Theo was staggered. If there was an argument about his old nurse's plan, the family never heard about it. He gave Miggs the

17

job. The two young housemaids working at St Helen's were delighted. Miggs would now have no time to order them about.

Since the war and the disappearance of the maids, Miggs transformed herself again. She remained receptionist, but was also housekeeper, cook and housemaid. Sketchy at all her duties, she was dead keen at answering the telephone.

'Sleep all right, Miss Philippa?' asked Miggs, leaving her scrutiny of the burnt conservatory with reluctance and going out of the room to fetch the tea.

'Yes, thank you, Miggs. Did you?'

The old woman returned with the teapot covered with a green knitted tea-cosy which she had made. It was hideous but the Tyrrells never dared to say so.

'Like a top. Never slept so well as I do in my shelter.' That was how she described the cellar. 'It's bone dry. I don't mind the noise either. Funny when I think in peacetime that gramophone in Mrs Next Door's garden on summer nights kept me awake till all hours. Just shows.'

She began to pour the tea, looked up and said, 'Ah, there you are.'

Doctor Tyrrell came in, carrying *The Times* and looking his usual spotless self. Nobody, thought Philippa, looked as clean as her father did. He wore old-fashioned checked tweeds, some of his suits were years old, but perfect in cut and of quality which never seemed to wear out. His cream-coloured silk shirts were washed and ironed by Miggs: he had a clean one every morning, blitz or no blitz. Philippa's mother used to say he was a dandy. But if his appearance was perfect, his expression was not. He looked very disagreeable.

The gas fire roared, as it did now since the blitz began, sending out a feeble warmth. Theo took his place with his back to what little comfort it gave.

In the winter of 1940, the second of the war, food was scarce, but he expected his breakfast formally served in the morning room where he and his family had breakfasted every day for the last twenty years.

'I suppose the damage is worse than you feared, Father,' said Philippa diplomatically. Miggs gave her a sardonic look, knowing what she was up to.

'No, it isn't. But the mess must be tidied up, it can't be left like that. It will be rebuilt eventually.'

18

'Eventually?' echoed Miggs.

'Yes. When the war is over. In the meantime, it must be cleared up.'

'Not much point, is there?'

Such a question from his daughters would have received a very cutting reply, but the doctor was reasonable when talking to his old nurse. He treated her as an equal.

'When it has rained and the dust has settled, it may be possible to get somebody to remove the worst,' he said.

Philippa was amused and faintly annoyed. Who but her father would suggest tidying up war damage in the middle of the blitz? Tomorrow St Helen's might be rubble.

'One of Trix's boyfriends might help when on leave,' she said unwisely, getting the inevitable.

'Where is your sister?'

He asked the question almost daily. Philippa wondered why he bothered. Trix was always out. During the day she met her friends, went shopping, and saw the latest Bing Crosby films. By six o'clock she was dancing in the big ballroom at Grosvenor House, which was packed with officers and their girls.

And, as Philippa had told Barny Duval, her young sister now had a network of useful London friends with safe ground floor flats where she could stay the night.

'She's probably with the Parkers at St Mary Abbott's Court. Their flat's facing the garden. They never go to a shelter.'

'Did she telephone?'

'Perhaps she couldn't get through.'

Looking down his nose, he returned to *The Times*. Trix's behaviour displeased him but he never bothered to quarrel with her.

Miggs, arms folded, regarded the newspaper behind which he had hidden.

'While you were out lookin' at the damage, I hope you remembered it was Miss Philippa who saved the house.'

She marched out, returning with a rack of symbolically burnt toast.

Miggs only said this to annoy; she knew he would never admit owing anything to one of his children. He groped for toast and marmalade, and when he was finally forced to put down the paper to pass his teacup, Miggs filled it in silence. She never sat with the family at meal times, but remained on her feet, a lumpy, aproned butler.

Philippa glanced anxiously at her father wondering if the fire had given him a shock. Perhaps, while on his way back from the hospital an air-raid warden had told him that St Helen's had been hit. He'd looked so alarmed when he burst into the billiard room last night. Had he thought she, Trix and Miggs had been killed? He was out in the blitz every night now. Bodies covered with sheets and laid out in gardens were a usual sight to him.

But Theo did not look shocked. His face was closed as it usually was, as if he had slammed it shut. He was a spare, shortish man, over sixty and aging well. His face resembled the famous head of Julius Caesar, he had the same strong bones, furrowed cheeks, determined jaw, and thin unrepentant lips. His hair had been fair but now it was sparse and white. He retained the fresh colour of fair-skinned people but his eyes, once blue and eloquent, were bloodshot. He had a certain air and Philippa had seen him being gallant with women. Her elder sister Elaine said he needed and despised them.

It was a year since Mary, Theo's wife for thirty years and mother of his daughters, had died. She was the only woman he ever loved and throughout his marriage he stayed faithful, although he was far more highly sexed than she. Sometimes he had been rude to her when his medical friends came to dine. He ignored her or frowned if she ventured an opinion. But he did the same with Philippa and Trix, although not with Elaine. Mary did not seem hurt by her husband's behaviour, but Elaine told her sisters that the way their father sometimes treated their mother made her sick.

'But he loves her!' protested Philippa.

'You really are,' declared Elaine, 'hopelessly sentimental.'

The family laughed over this trait. Philippa saw people in a rosy light. They forgot that this view of hers included themselves. In her girlhood Philippa accepted their verdict, but since her mother's death Philippa often asked herself if sentimental was another word for being right. Her father *had* loved her mother. He was an autocrat in the Victorian tradition but he had married for love.

The Tyrrells had lived at St Helen's, a large nineteenth-century house in d'Abernon Road, Kensington, since Theo and Mary were first married. It was near Addison Road and Holland Road, a leafy pleasant district. The houses had large gardens. Theo's father had bought him the practice before the Great War, and it had been a measure of Theo's taste for grandeur that he moved into St Helen's when he and Mary had no children and were not particularly well off. Theo had served in the Artillery during the war, was wounded and invalided out. He was one of the lucky ones.

Mary Tyrrell's parents were wealthy Quakers in the Midlands, she was accustomed to spacious houses and good living, but she always said St Helen's was too big. It had a study and a billiard room, a library which Theo used as his surgery, a dining room with French windows, a drawing room, a morning room and seven bedrooms. The kitchen quarters had been built for a large and comforting staff. It was a house which possessed its own authority – it required to be well run.

Like other massive rambling Kensington houses within walking distance of the gilded gates of Holland House, St Helen's had been built during the pre-Raphaelite period. Its owner, a Jeremiah Armstrong, had been a friend of the artists who settled in the district like flocks of peacocks during the 1860s. Lord Leighton made his house into a Persian paradise. G.F.Watts, bearded and nearly fifty, had a tall house with a vast studio. He married a ravishing seventeen-year-old Ellen Terry and brought her home there; the redheaded beauty didn't stay long.

Jeremiah had been a bad poet and a worse painter but he loved art and his artist friends and built a house to be near them. St Helen's was his creation. His taste had chosen the tiles patterned with yellow pansies round the drawing room fireplace, the carved mantelpiece of oak leaves and acorns. The handsome staircase was straight from a Victorian painting of *The Taming of the Shrew*. In the garden was a sundial which bore the motto *'Pereunt et Imputantur.'* 'The hours pass and are numbered against us,' translated Theo to his children. 'You should remember that.' A bronze Guinevere, none too well sculpted and covered in verdigris, still stood in her ivy-clad alcove. The garden was quite large, with pleasant high brick walls against which Mary had trained pears and peaches. The house needed its three servants.

But if St Helen's meant work, staff in the 1920s and 30s was cheap. The cleaning and coal carrying, grate polishing and cooking were done by two girls from St Ethelreda's orphanage. The girls came to the Tyrrells in two's for company. Every few years Theo and Mary drove to an orphanage in a distant London suburb, to be allotted two orphans who had reached the working age – about sixteen. The girls arrived at St Helen's with cardboard suitcases filled with stout uniforms. They were invariably so shy they were in a permanent blush. They stayed for three or four years, and then left for better wages, and back Theo and Mary would go on another orphan-foraging expedition.

Mary, with her Quaker upbringing, took her maids' welfare seriously. She saw that they joined the Girl Guides, which meant there was somewhere pleasant where they spent their half-day a week off. She chose their best uniforms, brown poplin, with coffee coloured lace collars and aprons. On the maids' birthdays the Tyrrell daughters gave them embroidered best aprons and caps threaded with velvet ribbon, and tins of Palm toffee. The girls liked their new aprons, but they loved the banana toffee.

Mary was a gentle soul. She was at home with her maids, and taught them to cook well. Sometimes when Philippa came into the kitchen, she heard her mother's slow voice, 'No, no, Alice, don't be so impatient. Cooking needs all the time in the world.' Mary laughed more with the maids than with her husband and children.

But despite Theo's impatient, authoritarian ways and distinct lack of generosity over money, Mary was serene. Her round face looked girlish, even in middle-age. Her nose was a little snub blob and her eyes were pretty. She wore her grey hair coiled in a knot on the top of her head.

Inherited money began to arrive, in slices of varying thickness, at St Helen's. Uncles died. So did a wealthy godfather of Mary's. On the death of her Quaker father, Mary actually became wealthy. She did not expect her money to be at her own disposal, but to do Theo justice he never suggested she should do what she did, which was to have the entire income paid into his bank.

Elaine was twenty at the time of her mother's inheritance. She was a girl of commonsense. She was small, the shortest and most valiant of the Tyrrell girls, with a straight nose, rather fixed blue eyes, a matter-of-fact voice, rather flat, never loud. She was as stylish as *Vogue*, where she worked.

'Mother, you are surely keeping some of Grandfather's money for yourself?'

'Oh no, dear, that is your father's business.'

'It is *not* Pa's business! The money is yours. Grandfather left it to you. Why not keep it? Or at least,' she finished severely, 'some of it.'

Her mother wore a smile which showed that nothing was going to move her. She prided herself on her strength of mind.

'Mother, can't you even write a cheque?'

'I've never done such a thing, why should I begin now? What matters is that my dear father left me his portrait and his books and the family Bible. And there's his gold watch, as well. Do you remember how you loved it when you were little?'

Elaine repeated the conversation to Philippa, who declared their mother was right and what mattered were the portraits and the watch. Elaine raised her eyebrows. Philippa was as hopeless as their mother.

Money had never been plentiful in the Tyrrell family when the girls were young; it hadn't been easy to afford the boarding school fees. Neither of the elder girls went to university, although they wanted to do so. Theo said he could not afford it, and since they were bound to marry, what was the point?

Both girls had jobs. Elaine managed to work at *Vogue*. She liked it very much, was fascinated by the photographers and models and journalists, and above all by the style. Philippa's job was dreary – she was a typist at Vickers Armstrong in Victoria Street, working in a huge room with sixty other girls. An elderly gorgon sat on a raised platform, dishing out the work and watching to see if anyone was wasting time.

'What is the point?' said Philippa to her family. 'There just isn't enough work to go round. I *asked* for some. And last week I read the whole of *Martin Chuzzlewit*, sitting at my desk.'

The girls – Elaine to begin with – had a number of boyfriends, the sons of friends. Men ran after Elaine but she did not fall in love. She was pretty and beautifully dressed, her connection with *Vogue* formed her tastes, she was bright and carefree. But Mary began to worry when her attractive eldest daughter did not find a husband by the time she was twenty-two. Mary believed that if girls did not marry when very young, they would land up on the shelf. Other girls, fresher and sweeter, were at their heels. 'I dislike,' said Mary, 'an old bride.' When she spoke anxiously of Elaine's single state to Theo, he said Elaine had a head on her shoulders. Mary could comfort herself with the certainty that Elaine would not do anything foolish. She'd be as sensible over getting married as she was about everything else.

He would not have said that about Philippa. Four years younger than Elaine she began to fall in love at sixteen, and continued to topple in and out of love like a child learning to walk, tottering a step, then collapsing, then scrambling to its feet again. She was hopelessly romantic.

Elaine introduced her to a number of young men and took her to dances. They drove out to the country to swim at newly opened road houses. They punted at Wargrave, or piled into open cars to go to the Aldershot Tattoo. In garden party clothes and white gloves, they accompanied their parents to Trix's Speech Day. Trix was now a leggy untidy teenager, outclassed in everything academic; she won the prize for gymnastics.

'Golly, what a relief,' hissed Trix to Philippa, 'I'm bottom at everything else.'

To celebrate the New Year, Elaine and Philippa went to the Chelsea Arts Ball. Elaine had a friend whose parents had a box, and she and Philippa had been invited.

The girls had a great deal of fun hiring their costumes at Nathans. They chose crinolines with enormous hoops sewn into linen petticoats, which swayed so much they were difficult to control. They carried fans, and Elaine wore a bonnet with a pale blue satin bow under her chin.

When they arrived inside the Albert Hall, they felt they were walking into an enormous jungle. Wherever they looked were hundreds of the strangest creatures; hectically coloured, feathered and crested, there were macaws and butterflies, parrots and orchids, walking orange trees, Rajahs and tigers. The girls were entranced. Clowns went by, and ballerinas. Black-clad Hamlets winked at them, and demons blew them kisses. At a corner they collided with a living Oxo cube. There was no need for introductions, everybody talked to everybody.

Just before midnight Elaine and Philippa were in their box watching the scene on the ballroom floor below. The students had built a series of huge cars, a different car for each College, and were dragging them in procession. There were towers of

24

flowers, palaces of cardboard, geometric creations, planets, ships. Girls in costume posed perilously high among rockets and fountains. Teams of boys pushed and pulled the cars to applause. At last the procession wobbled to a halt. Twelve o'clock had come, and balloons hidden in nets high up in the dome of the hall came floating down in thick multicoloured cascades. At the same moment everybody moved in a wave to the cars, and began to pull them to pieces. They wrenched down their own work which had taken them weeks to make, they pulled out chunks of painted cardboard and trampled on it. In a few moments the bright fantasies were gone, destroyed like houses swallowed up in hell.

As Elaine, half amused and half shocked by the mayhem, swayed out of the box she walked straight into her future.

'I'm most fearfully sorry! I'm a clumsy fool,' exclaimed a young man who had nearly knocked her over. 'Are you all right? What can I do? Shall I go down on my knees? Give me a task to prove my repentance, I beg!'

He was dressed as a sailor, with broad collar and trousers tight across the hips, a sailor's hat on the back of his head. He was tall and thin and dark and had a quick way of talking.

Elaine refused everything but the apology.

'Could we dance?' he asked. 'I saw you just now, you know. I was in all that scramble in the ballroom and I looked up and there you were in the box. I thought – I must find out who she is. Do you mind?'

When she knew him better she learned that was an expression of his. He would buy her flowers and say 'do you mind?' And he called girls lilies.

'You're the prettiest lily here,' he said.

He introduced himself. His name was Miles St Aird. They found they had a few – not many – mutual friends.

When he laughed, Miles St Aird seemed as if he really meant it and as if his laughter came from the heart. He was quick and casual, his narrow figure was graceful and his grey eyes were expressive and rather beautiful. He stayed with her all the evening, and when they parted he wrote her telephone number on his wrist in ink.

She thought she would never see him again. People said that sort of thing always happened at the Chelsea Arts. But he telephoned her the next day.

25

They began to meet a great deal. She thought him very attractive. She was stirred by his chaste goodnight kisses. When they parted late at night after dancing somewhere expensive – Miles never took her anywhere but to fashionable places – Elaine sat down at her dressing table, to cream her face and brush her hair. She wondered why she felt sad. She never saw him go without a feeling of loss.

He liked to give her things. A box came from Moyses Stevens containing three tiny white orchids. The scrawled card said, did she mind? Why did the flowers make her cry? She was being, she thought, as silly as Philippa.

The scare of war, strong, terrifying during the previous year, had faded. At least it did so for Elaine who forgot politics and fell in love. But Miles did not ask her to marry him, as all her other young men did. She had had, so far, six proposals. She always became very nervous when she knew a proposal was in the air. And was inevitably sick.

'But how do you manage?' asked Philippa with some curiosity.

Elaine laughed and made a face.

'When I know for certain that whoever it is is going to ask me, I begin to feel really queasy, exactly like on a Channel steamer when it's rough. Then, just before I absolutely *know* they're going to say it, I say will they forgive me for a second and I dash off to the ladies. Then I am really sick. It always gives me a colour, and when I get back I suppose I look fine. Then he pops the question and then I'm very nice and say, no.'

None of this happened to Miles. What was more, he had not done that other essential thing, introduced her to his family.

During the summer he stayed in London, in a cousin's flat in Sloane Street – his parents lived in the Cotswolds near Woodstock. Miles was working for his accountants' examinations, and at weekends he went sailing at Itchenor.

'You must learn to crew, Elaine, I'll begin by teaching you your knots.'

'Oh help!'

They were in Hyde Park. It was spring and they were sitting on a bench facing the Serpentine. Miles produced some string from his pocket and taught her the difference between a granny and a reef knot.

One of Elaine's elderly aunts lived at Bosham, so it was possible for her to go down at weekends, to sail with Miles in his

Sharpie in Chichester harbour. She spent her nights in blessed chastity in her aunt's spare bedroom.

Elaine liked doing things well, and soon became Miles' useful crew. They won two or three races in the Regatta.

Miles had joined the Royal Naval Voluntary Reserve, and after leaving the office on weekends he trained on HMS *President* moored near Blackfriars.

'There'll be a war this year,' he said briskly, 'So I shall be ahead when we're all called up.'

'There *won't* be a war. Don't let's talk about it.'

'But we must, sweetie. London will be bombed flat, you know, so you and your family will have to leave beforehand. They will send over bombers in five-minute waves until there's nothing left but smoking ruins.'

He was twenty-three and couldn't keep a note of Wellsian drama out of his voice.

'But Hitler's only threatening,' she said. Her voice quavered.

'Oh poppet, I've upset you, what a pig I am. But now that I've joined the RNVR and we do seem to be making plans I thought we ought to be engaged. Would you mind?'

That had been Miles' proposal.

Philippa never forgot Elaine's face when she told her the news. It had been ecstatic. It had been almost terrible, Philippa thought, to look at such happiness. When she thought of it, she remembered that while Elaine had stood there with her swimming eyes and heartbreaking bliss, Fats Waller had been singing 'Honeysuckle Rose'.

The past, the peaceful past, had been filled with music. The gramophone at St Helen's, sometimes muffled by a cushion so as not to disturb patients in the waiting room, was on at all hours. Fred Astaire. Bing Crosby. Fats Waller. And Miles' favourite, which was 'Plenty of money and you-hoo-hoo, Say baby what I wouldn't do-hoo-hoo.'

Philippa had a lot of admirers now. When she came home on hot summer nights, after dancing with some young man, they would jump into a taxi as closed and intimate as a hansom cab, the window at the back the size of a coffee saucer.

'Drive round the park, please.'

Accustomed to the order, the driver set off slowly into the dim and leafy park. And boy and girl fell into each other's arms to kiss until they were breathless. The boys never put their hands down

27

Philippa's low-cut evening dresses, or up her clinging satin skirts. It was never anything but lips-shut kisses. But their hearts thudded against each other.

Eventually the taxi stopped at the gate of St Helen's and the young man 'saw her to the door'. Standing in the porch they kissed again, pressing close their flushed youthful faces.

'Darling, darling, you're so sweet.'

They finally parted and Philippa yawned her way up the stairs. Moonlight slanted through a stained glass window and threw blue and yellow lozenges on the stairway.

In her room, her hair was untidy and the little wreath of gardenias was squashed and turning brown. Her lips were bruised. Philippa stripped off her white evening dress and left it on the floor. She and Elaine never wore any other colour but white in the evening. Their dresses were picked up and taken to the cleaners by Miggs on the following morning; no white evening dress was worn twice.

Summer was hot. People walked slowly in the parks under the elm trees, and sheep browsed there. It was a pastoral.

Those days were dead. They had resembled the elaborate cakes of icing sugar, confectioners' architecture created in the turreted shapes of the Houses of Parliament or the intricacies of the Eiffel Tower; elaborate, breakable, sweet. But the war had come like hammering rain and they had melted and vanished for ever.

Chapter Three

As Philippa left for work on the morning after the fire, the telephone rang.

'Flip?' said a metallic little voice, 'it's me.'

'Are you all right, Trix?'

'Of course I am. I'm with Jenny. I've told you, the flat's below ground. Could you ask Miggsy to rustle up something horrible for supper tonight? Unfortunately I've got to be home to finish making my dress. Oh, guess what. I picked up two Free Frenchmen on the bus. They're coming to lunch on Sunday.'

Philippa wasn't listening. She said that the house had been hit last night by fire bombs.

'Oh God! Is my room okay?'

'Aren't you going to ask if *we* are okay?'

'If you weren't, you wouldn't be answering the telephone, stoopid.'

Philippa grimaced, and briefly described the fire. When she rang off, picked up her handbag and leather gas-mask case and slung both over her shoulder, she was not even annoyed. It was always like that with Trix.

D'Abernon Road was a mess. Rain had worsened the quenched fires, the pavements and roadway were littered with heaped earth and the blackened remains of bombs, which also lay in the gutters. At the bus stop, a crowd of people waited. They were tired and pale, but there was a glitter in their faces, a leftover light from danger.

'Came down like rain in the docks, it did,' said a woman in a mackintosh, 'My hubby's in the brigade. The warehouses, tea and rum they were, burned something horrible. The barrels exploded like a second load of bombs. He said the tea burned as fierce as paint does, and the smell! Fair made him choke – all sweet and mucky and getting into your throat.'

Other people joined in with tales of destruction.

'Molotov cocktail on the roof.'

'Crater fifteen feet across.'

'Lamb and Flag pub's gone. Six people killed.'

'They say over three thousand incendiaries fell in ten minutes.'

When the bus lumbered up, everybody climbed on board and stood squeezed like sardines. Philippa looked out of the window at the panorama which each day changed for the worse. Houses were sliced through as if by a giant carving knife – one house standing, its neighbour collapsed in rubble of bricks and burned wood. Blast never had the same effect twice. One house had only the top rooms remaining, the rest a blackened hollow. In another, an attic bedroom was exposed, high up, untouched, with rose-patterned wallpaper and dresses and coats still hanging on a rail. In the next room a bath precariously hung from a half-destroyed wall.

Even in the bus the blitz smell was strong, a mixture of escaping gas, burning, and the bitter stink of high explosive. Pavements were covered with broken glass, and the workers on their way to offices picked a path through the glass, lifting their feet delicately like wading birds.

Rich houses or poor were identical after being bombed. Wealth and class had divided them but in their ruins they were the same. In the grey light of morning Philippa saw the remains of so many homes, the fireplaces round which people had gathered, mirrors which used to reflect happy faces, beds which had known love.

At Knightsbridge she edged her way out of the bus and went down the steps to the Underground, it was the quickest way to work. Closed streets, diversions, flaming gas jets and yawning craters made any bus journey hours long.

Swept down the escalator, she entered the Londoners' new catacombs.

The government had forbidden people to shelter in the Underground, but since the blitz began the usually docile English had ignored that. They simply moved into the Underground and took it over, it was their equivalent of the Tyrrells' billiard table. After two months of nightly bombing, the underworld kingdom was becoming organized. There were rows of neat bunks in many stations and the platforms smelled of antiseptic. Most of the shelterers were gone at six in the morning when the All Clear sounded; they were queuing in the evening for their places well before the siren went. They brought blankets and pillows. There was clean water, bucket lavatories in decent corners, a good deal of Jeyes Fluid. They settled down on the platforms, accustomed to the trains roaring by. They listened to the wireless when it was possible, made Cockney jokes and hot drinks. There were sing-songs and even a lending library. After nights in the Underground, people did find lice in their hair occasionally. But so did the well-born Wrens. One Wren whose father was an earl had stayed the night at St Helen's recently and had shouted at Philippa from the bathroom, 'I'm smearing my head with paraffin. Then I'll wrap it in a towel and leave the little things to die the death. Sorry if I stink.'

In Philippa's train compartment now there were a number of Scottish soldiers, their rugged faces full of wonder as they looked at London's underworld.

Her journey ended at Holborn. She came up the escalator among workers flowing like a river into Kingsway. There was so much glass in the street that it was hard to walk – scarcely a window remained in the office buildings, doors had burst off, and in one crater in the road was the remains of a burned-out car. As she made her slow progress, the morning was full of the noise of glass being swept from the pavements, and the sound of windows being knocked out for safety.

She no longer worked in the typing pool at Vickers Armstrong. After Elaine's wartime marriage, Mary Tyrrell became ill. She did not recover but faded slowly; Philippa gave up her job and helped Miggs to nurse her. Mary died early in 1940.

Theo took his wife's death very hard. He was stricken and lonely and often angry. Philippa wanted to join one of the women's services, all her friends were doing so, but felt she couldn't leave her father. He gave no sign that he needed her.

'He needs a bit of time. Later on, you can leave him to me. Dessay you want to get into uniform.'

'I suppose I do.'

'Quite right. Very edifyin'.'

'But even when Father feels better, Miggsy, what about my leaving Trix?'

'Do you think *she* needs any of us?'

During her mother's illness, Philippa had worked at home for a few hours each week on the thankless task of trying to raise money for a down-at-heel hospital. The lady who gave her the job was a Quaker friend of her mother's, Mrs Jane Alwynne.

31

After Mary's death, Mrs Alwynne took it for granted that Philippa would work for her full time. So Philippa agreed, still feeling out-of-date that she was not a Waaf or a Wren. It was as if by remaining a civilian she missed the essential heart of the war. Mrs Alwynne's offices were in Chicheley Buildings in a narrow street at the back of the Law Courts. The buildings, fifty years old, were a fantasy of orange-red brick, with turrets and a set of gargoyles for spitting out the rain. Every morning when she turned the corner, Philippa wondered whether Chicheley Buildings had survived. This morning they had – and there they were, rising out of a sea of broken glass, hideous as ever.

Before the war, prosperous insurance companies and small businesses had occupied Chicheley Buildings, but most of those were closed now. Mrs Alwynne, persuasive with landlords, had a set of rooms for which she paid almost nothing. Her rooms were lofty, with red Turkish carpets and bookcases and open fireplaces. When the blitz did not prevent her, a charwoman came from Hackney to light the fires, staggering up the stairs with buckets of coal.

This morning – no fire and no charwoman. Also no Mrs Alwynne, which meant peace. Philippa kept on her coat and sat down to work in the ice-cold room. Her desk was as old as the buildings, with a worn green leather top and brass-handled drawers patterned with swallows. She began to type letters to possible benefactors . . . but her thoughts were on Barny Duval. She kept remembering just how it had felt when he pressed her heavily down on the floor and kissed her.

At one o'clock she arrived, early, at the Ritz. She had only been to the hotel once, when her father gave a party for Elaine's twenty-first birthday. The place made Philippa feel shy. She was wearing her only winter coat, dark brown with a velvet collar, and a little hat with a blue feather. A woman in the entrance hall went by, swathed in fox furs. Philippa felt shyer still.

The Ritz was very Frenchified with its gilt and marble, and a little fountain playing in a basin. No wonder, thought Philippa, that Trix used Ritzy as an adjective.

Barny, also early, sat at a table which was too small for him, long legs stretched. He sprang up.

'On time. Few dames are.'

She couldn't help laughing.

He ordered champagne but the waiter sadly told him that

today there was only sherry; much Philippa cared. She would not have noticed if they'd drunk watery cocoa. But Barny was not in a trance as she was, and chatted to the waiter, saying he'd heard a rumour in the Squadron that the Ritz chef 'had gotten hold of some onions and lemons?' He must, he said, come and have a meal here soon while the supply lasted.

When the waiter had gone, Barny looked at her.

'Shall we eat here next leave? Seems like a nice idea. Do you know what, Flip. I've been thinking about our fire dousing. You sure went fast over that wall.'

'But my poor stockings! I had to throw them away. My second to last pair.'

'I thought of that too. I'll get my sister to send you some.'

It was the first time Philippa heard the authentic voice of American generosity. She did not know that was what it was; she thought her companion impulsive and kind, and didn't really believe he meant what he said. But that same voice, filled with the beautiful love of giving, was to speak in the years to come to English people, who would be as surprised and affected by it as she.

'How did your father react to you saving his house?'

'Oh, he didn't admit it. That's not his way.'

'I don't understand.'

'He'd hate to think a *woman* stopped the house from burning down. In any case, it wasn't me, it was you. After the war we'll put up a plaque. B.Duval, Eagle Squadron, saved this house during the London blitz, November 1940. We'll have your crest, the eagle and the E.S. What's Barny for?'

'Not for anything. I have one hell of a name. Jean Louis Desmond Duval, can you beat it? The first two are from some French ancestors my mother was proud of. I've been Barny since school. Not sure why.'

The waiter brought sandwiches on a silver salver, cut into mouthfuls inadequate for a big American.

Philippa said she had been thinking – they'd spent all those hours together, and she still knew almost nothing about him. Just that he came from Louisiana and had arrived last August. Could he begin at the beginning? She wanted to hear everything. About his home and his family and his childhood and being a pilot and coming to England. Everything.

'Sure you really want to hear all that?'

It was a rhetorical question because she looked at him so eagerly, and perhaps he just wanted her to repeat it all again. He described the country that he came from – a land of great heat, where the enormous live oaks grew, festooned with Spanish moss hanging in ghostly draperies. Louisiana had great swamps, and forests of huge cypresses, prairies of soggy grass from which hummocks of trees rose like islands. White herons lived in the swamps, and egrets, and snakes. The cane-brake rattler was the swamps' most dangerous creature, it could grow over eight feet long . . .

Both his parents were dead. She gave a little gasp when he said that. Yes, Barny agreed, it had been terrible but 'you get to bear things'. His family owned a timber business and three years ago his parents had been out in a motor boat, looking at the flooding river. The boat struck a submerged log and sank in minutes. Both were drowned.

'That isn't why I came over, Flip. I'd hate for you to think it was a kind of desperate getting away from it all.' He had been in love with flying since a child. Planes excited him. 'I must have read every darned book about the aces of the Great War before I was twelve. And the movies, I'd seen those over and over. *Hell's Angels* was the best.'

His father hoped he would work in the family business, but after he left college, Barny learned to fly. He joined a civilian air line flying freight from one State to another. When his parents died, his sister Mary Lou and her husband had taken over the firm.

'Then your war started, Flip. I thought – that's where I want to be. We aren't allowed to enlist for your war in the US, so I had to slip over the Canadian border. And here I am.'

He looked at his watch.

'Damnation. We've only gotten ten minutes left.'

Without thinking, she leaned forward and took his wrist to look at the time. His watch, wafer thin, was gold and on a crocodile strap. She pushed back his blue uniform cuff to glance at it, and his arm, covered with fine dark hair, was exposed. Barny put his other hand up and pressed hers very hard.

'I've got to see you next leave. Okay?'

'Okay.'

They walked in silence through the gilded rooms. At the doors he paused.

34

'Not allowed to kiss dames when I'm in uniform.'

He bent and kissed her.

'See you real soon.'

They parted in the cold dirty London afternoon.

Philippa returned to the Temple and climbed the stairs to her office: the lift had been out of order for months. The charwoman, hours late, had lit a smoky fire. Sitting down, Philippa looked vaguely at the work she had left an hour and a half ago. The afternoon rang with silence – no cars went by in the street. She shut her eyes. She felt as if she were at the top of a steep hill. It was a hill which had haunted her since girlhood although she did not know why; it had curved down from the gates of her boarding school in Devonshire, a steep incline in a road which dropped steadily until it reached the sea front. In her thoughts she had returned many times to the top of that hill, wondering what would happen if she began to run. Now her thoughts moved downwards, slowly, faster, until she could not stop. Her ghostly self, heart hammering, breath gasping, ran and ran, hurtling down faster and faster until she was thrown into the ocean of love.

After the night of the fire and her next day meeting with Barny, Philippa's life returned to its pattern of dull work by day and the nightly blitz. St Helen's shuddered as the bombs came down. London grew more and more chaotic. One crater in Piccadilly was so huge that ten people fell into it, with consequent broken limbs. Food grew ever scarcer. At night the streets were empty and the sky burned.

One person showing no sign of the strain was the youngest member of the Tyrrell family. Trix, just eighteen, was enjoying the arrival of foreign troops in London. She went to parties at night where, in the phrase of the day, 'we just ignored the blitz socially.' She went to lunches. She went to films. And her conversation had become international.

'Guess what, Flip, I danced with a Pole and he turned out to be a prince. He asked the band to play a mazurka. They didn't know how.'

'Two New Zealanders took me to lunch at Grosvenor House. The grill room's been re-named, it's the Shelter restaurant now. Wizard food.'

'If a boy rings called Ian, he's in the Black Watch and tell him I *need* to see him before he's posted.'

Philippa was amused by her young sister. She was also impressed for Trix had become a rare thing – she was a beauty.

Mary Tyrrell had been reading *Henry Esmond* when she was pregnant for the third time, and she decided if the child was another girl she would name her Beatrix. Trix detested her name from an early age. At school they called her Beaty and she loathed that too. Two years before the war, when she was an unremarkable fifteen, she had marched into the St Helen's garden one Sunday afternoon when the family were having tea.

'In future,' she announced, 'I shall be known as Trix.'

Everybody looked up. Her father said sarcastically, 'In future I shall be known as Horatio Bottomley.'

Elaine and Philippa giggled. Mary smiled.

Trix looked stony. 'You may as well all get used to it. I shan't answer to any other name.'

'No good speaking to me,' said Theo, 'if I am not addressed as Doctor Bottomley.'

Trix walked off.

Within a week the family had given in. It was too annoying to call her or speak to her and to get no reply.

In just the way that she made up her mind to change her name, Trix decided to be beautiful. She was sixteen when the transformation began. She was naturally slim, with long legs, but her shortish hair was mousy, her nails dirty and bitten, and the clothes her mother chose for her were simply dull. Trix washed her hair in camomile and touched it up with something else: it turned a silvery blonde. She grew it long in imitation of Hollywood stars. Nature had given her a thick-textured skin: somehow she made it look like the petals of a gardenia. She had the short straight Tyrrell nose and eyes the colour of black treacle. When she began to alter the way she looked, the men began to stare. Now, two years later, she was every serviceman's dream.

Pictures of girls looking like Trix were cut from magazines and pinned in army messes and steamy canteens. She was glued inside army lorries, in the cockpits of planes and the cabins of ships. She was painted on the whitewashed walls of army huts. A girl with Trix's face and figure and hair was the phantom goddess who travelled with the pilots and their impish gremlins in the upper air, and ploughed the Arctic seas, and wavered in desert heats. She stood in the dreams of the men fighting a war.

Philippa admired her young sister more than Elaine did. She thought it wonderful that Trix had turned herself from a leggy schoolgirl who sucked sweets and failed exams into a beauty. Trix had invented herself, a 1940 self. She not only made her hair into moonlight and painted her exquisite face, she also painted her legs, using dark sun-tan lotion and drawing a thick straight seam down the back with an eyebrow pencil. Her skin was smooth and silky, and her naked legs looked exactly as if they were clad in silk stockings.

It was Saturday morning. Theo had gone to the hospital early. Somewhere in the depth of the house was the familiar noise, a dull rattling thunder, which was Miggs filling the kitchen boiler. Philippa wandered into Trix's bedroom.

'Good, I can fit your dress,' said Trix.

The room, like its occupant, was much altered from its 1930s appearance. Trix had painted all the antique furniture white and covered her dressing table with stiff pink taffeta. There were some misty photographs of herself and a litter of large and small photographs, framed and unframed, of men in uniform. These were signed 'My love, darling, Peter'. 'Forever, Pat'. And 'Yours till hell freezes, Jack'. On the wall was a flat vase filled with ivy and yellow roses. Trix was always being given flowers.

She knelt down and began to pin Philippa into a dress made of Parma-violet wool which she'd found in her mother's trunk.

'You'll look lovely,' she said encouragingly.

The front door bell rang.

'Bother and blow, that's my two french A's, Quick, Flip. Get dressed. You know that I can't manage a word of French.'

Leaving Philippa still pinned, she skipped out and Philippa heard her at the top of the stairs calling, 'Bonjour!'

The gramophone began at once, and Fats Waller sang 'Honeysuckle Rose'. The music reminded Philippa of Elaine when she had first fallen in love. And love reminded Philippa of Barny. She was not sure why she had said nothing about him to Trix – she wanted to keep him a secret. When she heard the planes at night, the stutter of machine-gun fire, and thought of the fighter pilots up there in the dark, she had such a pain in her heart. *He* would soon be flying up there. She remembered a poem about an RAF pilot, 'keeping your station in the sky: solitary cunning star.'

'Here she is,' cried Trix, through the music, 'come and show your paces, Flip. In French.'

Philippa and the two A's smiled politely at each other.

Trix's nickname was apt, the French visitors shared the same first-name initial, they were Alain and Alexandre. But that was all they shared except their nationality. Alain was not in uniform but wore a shabby jersey and baggy old trousers. He was pasty-faced and spectacled. Alexandre was short, scarcely five foot eight, but he had drama. His black curling hair shone, his skin was swarthy, he burned with life, and when he laughed he had a mass of gold teeth. He wore navy blue French uniform, with a cape thrown over one shoulder and fastened with a gilt chain.

Philippa launched into her finishing-school French. Both men looked relieved and pleased.

'*C'est une perle!*' cried Alexandre.

'*C'est vrai*,' agreed Alain.

Trix re-wound the gramophone and put on a record she liked. 'Oh Johnnie, Oh Johnnie, How you can Love.'

'The two A's have brought us a pressie,' she said, 'Look, Flip.' She held up two beer bottles.

'How kind of them,' said Philippa, who detested beer.

'Stoopid,' said Trix, laughing, 'Wait and see.'

When Alexandre poured out, the bottles were full of burgundy.

'Nothing remarkable, from our canteen and alas, cold from being carried through the streets,' one of the visitors murmured in French.

'Tell him he is wonderful. Shall we save some for Pa? Perhaps not. It'll improve our horrible lunch. Miggs says all she can manage is veggie pie. Ugh.'

During the meal eaten by the Frenchmen without surprise, which Philippa thought particularly courteous, Trix bombarded the two men with questions. Philippa had to translate these, together with their replies. They were at present in what was called the Centre d'Acceuil in Kensington. When they mentioned the house, the sisters knew it. It was a big rambling old place in a large garden, where an elderly patient of their father's had lived until her death. Men arriving in England from Europe, the two A's explained, were brought to London and taken straight to the Centre for questioning. How did they come to England? asked Trix, fascinated. It seemed they had rowed across the Channel in an open boat.

'It was fortunate that I have the rudiments of navigation,' said Alain. 'With Alexandre in charge, we would have lost our way and rowed straight back to France. He knows nothing of the sea.'

'Do you?'

'Of course. I am a Breton.'

After freezing nights and danger from enemy planes, mercifully more intent on getting to London than on machine-gunning a small boat, they had beached at a seaside village in Kent.

'As we put foot on shore we were seized by English soldiers, sure we were spies. Then to the Centre for a litany of questions. And now – here we are.'

The girls looked at the men in awe. It was hard to grasp the fact that they had been so recently in the heart of darkness.

'Was the escape exciting?' asked Trix. Philippa translated.

They shrugged. .

'Explain to your sister, mademoiselle, that we are forbidden to speak. We may not tell of the weather or how many stones there were on the beach,' said Alexandre.

'Or the name of the rowing boat,' said Alain.

'Or how much Breton sugar Alain brought in a sack.'

'Or how we must throw it overboard for the weevils are eating it.'

'Or how they put me in this uniform of the French Air Force and never have I been in an aeroplane.'

They grinned as they described the many extraordinary questions they had had to answer at the Centre. Alain was made to describe his childhood, the name of his school and of the teachers ('some I forgot'), details of his village. In what square was the War Memorial? Was it the bronze figure of a poilu or the statue of a mourning woman? Or both? During the interrogation he became angry. He had not faced danger and the sea to answer questions of such idiocy. Was he a guide book?

The intelligence officer was soothing.

'Do not upset yourself. Last week we had two doctors here in the French Medical Corps. One was not a doctor. The other was not French.'

Alexandre, longing to burst in while Alain held the girls' attention, then described his questioning. It had lasted four hours longer than Alain's. He had been asked about his life in South America (he would tell them of this later!), and when he had obligingly launched into stories of Buenos Aires they

39

suddenly switched to his Burgundy childhood. Had he any family remaining there? He had visited the village early in 1940. By train or coach? When Alexandre said 'train' the officer gave a satisfied grunt. 'If you had said by coach, you would go to prison. There is no coach to that village.'

After the unappetising lunch, the four returned to the drawing room where Alexandre and Trix danced the rumba. 'Tell your sister she dances like the girls in Rio.' Alain sat with Philippa, and spoke of Brittany. He did not mention the Occupation.

As dusk fell, Alexandre gave a sigh.

'Soon will come the Alert and then we are commanded to run home like good little boys.'

Shortly afterwards the siren wailed. The two men kissed the girls' hands, thanked them, begged to be allowed to come again.

Trix showered invitations like confetti. They must come any time! All the time!

When they were gone, she looked at Philippa mischievously.

'If I told you what Alexandre hissed in my ear while we were dancing, you'd have a pink fit.'

For once, that night she was home and joined Philippa under the billiard table. The girls arranged their heavy coats and scarves, gas masks and handbags within reach in case the house was hit.

'If there is a bomb and we have time, or suppose it's an unexploded one, what'll you take with you? All I need is my biggest bottle of *Moment Suprême*.'

'I shall take an extra pair of outdoor shoes,' said Philippa perversely.

One night after an intensive blitz, when Theo returned he found Miggs in the hall. She was sitting wrapped in her voluminous old rug.

'All Clear's gone, Doctor, thought you'd like a cuppa.'

The sight of the bent figure huddled in a chair, like other old people dazed after being dug out of their homes, affected him. While she was making tea he said, 'If these bombardments continue –'

'They'll go on for months. The milkman says the government's preparin' for it. Cardboard coffins, thousands of 'em, and now they're opening up the old Plague pits for burial grounds.'

Miggs had not changed from the days when her favourite

40

story, read to him as a child, was one in which the old witch fattened up the children to eat them.

But he was not to be sidetracked and said seriously, 'I think you should be evacuated, Miggs, there is no need for you to remain in London. Nor, for that matter, Miss Philippa and Miss Beatrix. All three of you can go to our cousins in Devon.'

Miggs slowly began to saw off the top of a cottage loaf.

'You and the girls could leave today or tomorrow. The trains are pretty appalling, but at least they get there. You'll be comfortable on the farm. When Cousin Anny wrote to me she said there's no shortage of milk, eggs or poultry.'

He gave her a smile which very faintly reminded her of the child she used to love a long time ago.

'Well, Miggs?'

'Not a chance, Doctor. You're not goin' to get rid of me so easily. Miss Philippa won't go either. She wouldn't budge. As for young T – Miss Beatrix, can you see her on a farm? Bombs are better than bein' bored to death.'

Theo tried to persuade her, but he might as well have saved his breath. He mentioned the matter to his daughters – they were as adamant. It did not occur either to them, or to Miggs, that it would be a weight off his shoulders if they left London. Miggs said it was her duty to look after the doctor. She did not add that she hated the country, despite being born there. Philippa refused to leave her work; Trix just laughed.

The blitz provided something that suited Miggs. Drama. She read every column of the *Daily Mail* each morning, listened to the news bulletin on the wireless, and was up-to-the-minute in the triumphs of the RAF. 'We bagged forty last night,' she would announce, as if giving the cricket score, 'They only got three of ours.'

The growing food shortages also interested her. She enjoyed announcing that this or that had vanished from the shops. The family's four ration books were in her ancient leather handbag, and it was Miggs who queued for the minute weekly rations of bacon, sugar, butter and meat. The only ration she resented was tea, a measly two ounces each for a week. She cut open the tea packets with a pair of scissors as carefully as a surgeon performing an operation; it was to make sure not a single tea leaf was hidden in the folds of the paper. The Ministry of Food's

41

instructions: 'One spoon per person and none for the pot' annoyed her. She detested orders.

Theo was anxious about her; he was fond of her. He was too busy during the day at the hospital or attending his patients at home, and at night helping to care for the wounded and writing the pathetic certificates for the dead, to realize that he was blessed by Miggs remaining at St Helen's. Philippa knew it. 'What should we do without you, Miggsy?'

'Starve, I shouldn't wonder,' said Miggs, making a hideous grimace. She had just put a spoonful of golden syrup into her tea to replace sugar – the tea turned black and tasted disgusting.

Miggs went to Shepherds Bush for the family's food. She said the smart Kensington shopkeepers were bribed.

'Saw a woman in a skunk coat puttin' a pound note on the counter at John Buckle's. The man gave her a whole tin of salmon.'

But she had her triumphs. Rice had disappeared from the shops but a packet found its way into her shopping basket, and so did a tin of sardines. She queued for fish, the one unrationed food, and chatted to the women ahead and behind her. She waited two hours for a piece of salt cod. Once she'd tried whalemeat. After cooking it and gingerly forking herself a piece, she spat it out and threw the rest into the dustbin. It had tasted like cod-liver oil. After this experiment she said severely to Theo, 'Don't you be too proud, next time a patient offers you a chicken.'

Theo *had* been too proud, and wondered how the devil she knew. It did not occur to his honourable soul that she listened at doors.

Sidling through the big old house, moving fast to answer the telephone ahead of the girls, donning her white overall as Receptionist, her purple apron as cook, Miggs ran St Helen's. She was like the man at the ship's wheel. She steered, looked at the compass, saw her crew was fed if only on salt cod. Sometimes, standing on the bridge, she raised her eyes heavenwards and saw fire.

When Mary Tyrrell had been alive, Miggs' sense of what was proper kept her in check; she respectfully called her The Mistress while dodging the duties Mary tried to give her. But now that The Mistress was dead, and Elaine married and away, Miggs had the reins firmly in her gnarled old hands.

42

Philippa sometimes resented her but was too kind or too craven to do anything about it. Recently, though, Miggs had a new kind of charm for her – she had met Barny. Philippa had still not mentioned Barny at all to her sister. She felt she could not bear to listen to the old repetitious teasing, or hear the worn out word 'sentimental'. She had merely told Trix that a soldier had helped with the fire. Trix, her head full of conquests and clothes, had asked no questions.

Very early one morning Philippa came into the kitchen. Miggs, at present in her role of witch, was stirring the boiler with a misshapen poker.

'Dratted fire won't burn. Got it into its head to go out. Too early for breakfast, lady. The kettle doesn't boil for the askin'.'

'I don't mind, Miggs. I only got up because I was awake. I didn't sleep very well last night.'

'So we gather.'

Philippa sat down near the boiler; she was cold. She stared at the split through which the coke dimly glowed.

'How'd you meet that American chap, Miss Philippa?'

The girl gave a start.

'Nice lookin' fellow,' said Miggs. 'Friend of yours?'

'No, he called round by chance. Someone in his Squadron knows Pa and gave him the address, so round he came. You know how casual Americans are.'

'Can't say I do. Eagle Squadron, is he?'

'Yes. He came to England in August.'

'I've been readin' about them in the *Mail*. Young American chaps who say they don't feel neutral and come here to join the RAF. Very edifyin'.'

She stirred the boiler, and added, 'Tell you what, Miss Philippa. Just you keep that young chap to yourself.'

She looked straight at Philippa, hoping what she said would go home.

Nobody knew more about the family and its doings than Miggs. She watched the present with fascination and had an utter disinterest in the past. When Philippa had been young, it had seemed to the romantically-minded girl that somewhere in her old nurse's memory there must be a vision still, a living vision of a golden Victorian and Edwardian England. It was as if Miggs had a treasure hidden away in a kind of Monte Cristo's cave. But when she eagerly asked Miggs, all she was given was

43

an impatient laugh. Miggs couldn't remember a thing worth talking about. And in time Philippa saw that Miggs's sharp little eyes were fixed in her head so that they couldn't, and wouldn't, swivel backwards.

Just now, Miggs approved of Trix whom she saw as a goer and no mistake. The girl had been a trial when she was a child, and she never did a stroke of work at school. But now she certainly knew how to make the young chaps jump. In her youth, ugly though she had been, Miggs had had sex appeal. She had been a flirt. She had treated men as if they were the enemy to be vanquished, and that was what Trix did now.

But Philippa was another kettle of fish entirely. Miggs didn't use the old 'sentimental' cliché any more, but she still thought it was true. She had seen the girl falling in and out of love, eyes like stars one week and all red the next. She was just the sort, thought Miggs, to get herself hurt. Philippa had a silly look on her face when she mentioned that American chap. Miggs felt it only kind to warn her that with men, it was wise not to share.

At the start of December, one evening before the Alert began wailing, the telephone rang. Philippa answered it and Miggs, for once arriving too late, said, 'If it's a patient, let me have it.' She stood openly listening.

'May I speak to Philippa Tyrrell, if you please.'

'Barny!'

Feeling herself blushing, Philippa gestured crossly to Miggs to go away. Miggs raised her eyebrows and went back to the kitchen. They talked for a moment or two, and Philippa waited, tensed for an invitation. The Warning began just then.

'Better get under the billiard table, Flip. I can hear that clearly. Look, I can't stop, there's a goddammed lecture starting and we're working fit to bust. I called up to say I hope to hit town soon. When I do, can we meet?'

'That would be lovely.'

'I think so too.'

'Oh, Barny – ' anything for another word, 'how *are* you?'

'Missing you.'

She put down the receiver. The guns were barking like giant dogs and she heard the drone of planes. I suppose I must shelter under that beastly table, she thought. It was no good suggesting she should join Miggs in the cellar, for Miggs preferred it to herself and had turned it into a sort of private flat.

44

Alone during a blitz, Philippa was alternately frightened and bored. The stupid thing was that she had been asked out tonight by an ex-boyfriend of hers who had wanted to take her dancing to Hatchetts, one of Trix's favourite places, smart, and below ground. Why had she refused? She knew why. She had been hoping for that one meaningless telephone call.

She turned towards the drawing room in search of her book, like every other girl in London she was reading *Barchester Towers*, when her father's study door opened.

'I didn't know you were home, Pa.'

'How many times have I told you to call me Father.'

'Sorry,' she said automatically.

The lamplight behind him made a halo round his balding head. His face was in shadow. He was not standing as erect as he usually did.

'Would you like a glass of sherry? Only one. The bottle won't run to more.'

The invitation took her by surprise. As if in celebration the guns shook the house.

'Hope I'm not called out tonight,' he said, yawning. 'The Mobile Squad have my number, so I daresay I will be. Working is better than lying quaking in bed, I suppose.'

'Pooh. You never quake.'

'Of course I do and so does everybody else.'

Except Trix, thought Philippa.

He fetched the decanter and they went into the billiard room. Ignoring the shelter-table, he sat in a high-backed chair. She sat opposite him. He did look tired. The lines in his face were cut deep.

'It's Christmas in less than two weeks,' he said, handing her the glass. 'Miggs asked what I intend to do about it. Her old friend Stutfield who supplied us with poultry has finally shut up shop and left London.'

'That must be why she keeps giving us salt cod like dried flannel. Not too festive for Christmas.'

'A patient offered me a turkey.'

He looked pleased at her astonishment.

'By the by, your sister telephoned. Miles has been posted. She's been with him on leave in Oxfordshire and her in-laws asked her to remain. I said it was a good idea, but Elaine won't

hear of it. She is coming home. And bringing,' he said solemnly
'a Christmas pudding.'
Philippa murmured appreciation, looking at him gratefully.
People always looked at him like that when he decided to be
pleasant. He took it as his due.
They talked of the previous night's blitz, and Theo, approachable because he'd decided to be, said that two houses had been
hit in the North End Road.
'We managed to pull out an old couple. Poor things, they
looked like two bedraggled old birds, so thin and small and
covered with dust from head to foot. They were quite calm when
we pulled them out. Talked as if nothing had happened.'
'That sounds like a miracle.'
'No. Just shock. Reaction sets in later.'
He said how strange he found doctoring now, compared to the
last war. He couldn't get used to civilians being killed.
'Odd. I just can't,' he said and put down his glass. 'You must
get some sleep, Philippa. And so must I – until the telephone or
the front door bell rings.'
She lay among the cushions, scarcely conscious of the din
outside. She was thinking of love. On her way home from work
tonight London had seemed full of lovers. Couples whispering in
the bus. A sailor and his girl in the Underground staring at each
other. Even in d'Abernon Road in the blackout she hadn't been
able to get away from love. She had passed a couple locked in an
embrace. She thought of Barny. Her father was right. Reaction
set in later.

46

Chapter Four

When the train stopped at Oxford it was already so crammed that Elaine thought she would never manage to get in. But four soldiers had thrown open the door, stretched out their arms and laughingly dragged her into the corridor. When the train door was safely slammed and the train started, two of the soldiers squeezed themselves into the lavatory where they sat on the floor, so that Elaine could at least stand upright in the corridor. Despite the gallant gesture, she could scarcely breathe, squashed between their two companions, both made gigantic by back packs, bulging pouches, kitbags and rifles. The pair whistled in a melancholy way, and when they caught her eye, winked.

Elaine, like young wives all over England, was on her way home because her husband was going overseas.

She and Miles St Aird, engaged during the summer of 1939, had married the week after war was declared, by special licence in St Barnabas's church in Kensington. The marriage, a few months earlier, would have been an affair of white satin and four hundred guests. Now it was hurried, disorganised and in the dark. Miles had been at Devonport Barracks and was granted compassionate leave. He was five hours late for the ceremony, by which time daylight was gone and the blacked-out church lit by a few wavering candles. Most of the dozen guests, alarmed by the new blackout, had left. Miles' parents stayed. They were scarcely what Miggs called 'forthcomin'.' In their upper-class way, they made the occasion even more uncomfortable than it was. They did not approve of the match.

The St Airds had been quite hospitable when Miles first took Elaine to their Oxfordshire home; he did not introduce her to them until after he had proposed. The pleasant manner of her future in-laws had altered after she met them two or three times. Later she had the suspicion, turning into a certainty, that they had believed she was rich. They thought their son had wisely chosen to fall in love where there was money.

When they realised the truth they cooled. Miles did not seem to notice, and stayed his enchanting self both to his parents and to her. But Elaine knew she was being patronized.

Miles took his new life in the Navy with lively amusement. The spoiled only son of an aristocratic family, he learned to do his own washing, darn his socks, and cook the appalling greasy food which was served to the Lower Deck. With other enthusiastic beginners, he acquired the knack of scrubbing the collar of his uniform to make it look faded. This implied that he had been a sailor for years.

After months at sea, he was eventually picked out as what was called 'officer material'. He was sent home for the course which would turn him into a sub-lieutenant, at the officers' establishment called King Alfred, on the front at Brighton.

When Elaine was allowed to be near him, she went to stay at hotels, or took two-roomed flats. She lived for a while in Brighton and in Portsmouth. But when he was sent to places which were out of bounds to civilians, she returned home. Leaves were all spent at Shelton, the St Aird's family home. Elaine longed for his leaves, but when the precious time arrived she swung between joy and the nervous irritation of sharing him. On their last morning together they walked in the Shelton woods. He kissed her. Oh, how she loved him. He was everything she worshipped. Simply seeing his figure at a distance turned her bones to water. Even his faults allured her. He was restless and easily bored, and his standards particularly about women, were tiresomely high. He despised girls who looked tatty, as he called it. He admired style and a look of money, and had chosen a girl with much of the first and none of the second. His snobbery, which she detested in his parents, only made her smile.

'I wish you'd stay here at Shelton after I've gone. They want you to,' he said, pressing her close.

'Oh, darling. I can't cower in the country for the duration.'

'My mother would be delighted if you'd cower, sweetie. Not that she would call it that.'

'She's very kind,' lied Elaine, 'but I do miss the family. I'd like to be with them. You won't worry about me in the blitz, will you? We can't both worry, me about you at sea, and you about me in London.'

Miles grinned. He was young and adventurous, and he said

48

the blitz sounded exciting. When the talk was of the fighter pilots in the Battle of Britain, he said, 'If I wasn't in the Navy, I'd choose the RAF and fly.'

Now he was gone. And Elaine was on her way back to London. Thinking about Miles hurt her heart, so she made a mental effort not to long for him. She stared resolutely out of the train window. Since the danger of invasion, every name of every station and village, every signpost, had been removed in England. The stations which went by now had no names. It was a journey into nowhere.

When the train finally sighed itself to a stop, it was pitch dark.

'Waterloo? Must be, I suppose,' said one of the whistling soldiers.

The crowds poured out on to a platform, seeming to know their way by instinct. Everything was black and echoing and smelling of acrid train smoke. Gleams of torchlight bobbed here and there.

A disembodied voice rang round the station, 'An air raid has sounded. An air raid has sounded. Members of His Majesty's Forces must, repeat must, proceed at once to shelters. Passengers are advised to do the same.'

'We gotter go but *you* can take it or leave it, see?' said one of her soldier friends, clanking beside her.

Elaine decided to leave it. At last she made her way through the uniformed figures, tin hats, kit bags and suitcases, to the outside of the station. Torches showed the shapes of waiting taxis.

'Sure you want to have a go?' said a driver, 'You could go by Underground to High Street Ken.'

'I'll be quicker with you.'

'We live in hopes.'

As the cab set off into the obscurity he called over his shoulder, 'Sorry, miss, you must open the windows. Better to freeze than be cut with broken glass. Play for safety.'

The icy wind blew in as Elaine looked from the open window, at first seeing nothing. Then her eyes grew used to the dark and she realized there was a moon. Its bluish radiance shone down on the wounded face of London, the collapsed houses turned into rubble which resembled mountain shale. The blitz smell filled the taxi. Barriers had closed many streets and the rest were almost empty of traffic. But the driver stopped at every traffic

49

light, circles of black with a tiny green or red cross in the centre just like a hot cross bun.

At Hyde Park Corner she saw the dim shapes of buses and heard gunfire. Once the driver pulled the cab to a stop and she was poised, ready to throw herself on the floor.

'All right. False alarm. Thought I heard a bomb.'

The journey took a long time but at last they drew up at St Helen's and Elaine paid him and thanked him. He tipped his cap in a Cockney salute and drove away – to stop at every traffic light across the battlefield of London.

'Anybody home?' called Elaine, shutting the front door behind her.

The drawing room door opened, and her father's grim face broke into a smile. She allowed herself to be kissed, offering her cheek. She did that with everybody but Miles.

'Good to have you back, Elaine.'

They stood taking each other in, for she had been away for weeks. Both pairs of eyes, one bright, one bloodshot, examined the other. Theo thought his favourite child looked well, which was his way of describing the blossoming which came from Miles' lovemaking. Before her marriage she had merely been prettyish. Now her skin glowed, her eyes seemed to swim, her whole expression was relaxed, gentle and sweet. Miles had all her love, her absorbed love, and when she saw her father worn and tired, she felt guilty. It was as if that other violent sexual love were a kind of sin.

Asking her with abrupt courtesy about the journey, he took her into the drawing room. The wireless was on, the music growing loud, then soft, then loud again as it always did in a raid.

'The girls are out and Miggs is in the cellar. Would you like some tea? I could cut you a sandwich.'

Elaine would not allow him to do anything for her. She went into the kitchen to look for something to eat. All she found was bread, margarine and meat paste. She had brought her own packet of tea.

Returning to the drawing room she sat down with her tray. He looked at her, raising his eyebrows as if for news. Of what? thought Elaine. She could not tell him her heart was heavy because her husband had gone, that thinking of him reduced her to a jelly and that it took all her character not to cry. Nobody talked to her father about emotion, nobody in the family, that was. In St Helen's, such things were underground, powerful secret rivers which were deep and dangerous and must never be spoken of. Her parents had been like that about sex, and it had affected her in a way.

She could have told him how she disliked the St Airds, that would amuse him for he did not like them either. She decided not to. He looked so tired. She thought he missed their mother more instead of less. Apparently Philippa and Trix were no help.

Her calm presence had a relaxing effect on Theo, and to her he was approachable. He only rarely spoke to Philippa about his work, he sensed a tenseness in her and too much emotion. He certainly would not condescend to talk to Trix. But now he described his work with the hospital's Mobile Squad, whose job it was to go to a house which had been hit and in which wardens reported that people were trapped. The squad joined the police at the rescue. Last night a big old house had had a direct hit and was still smoking when the team arrived. The police had heard somebody's voice in the wreckage. The squad began to dig.

The house, near Addison Road, had been four storeys high, and digging in mountains of brick and smoking wood they had needed to shore up a wall before they could get closer to the eerie sound of a voice. It took hours to make a tunnel into the ruins; then two men wriggled down it inch by inch with Theo following them. The voice grew closer. It was a child sobbing. They reached her at last, a little girl scarcely seven years old. Theo gave her an injection. Her parents lay nearby, both dead. The child, mercifully now unconscious, was pulled to safety. She was not even bruised.

'Well,' he said, 'one child saved. Many of those we dig out die in our arms. Who was it who said that courage is the willingness to die quietly?'

In the days before Christmas, Elaine looked at her family with new eyes. Perhaps, she thought, one must go away to be able to do that. Her father was overstrained. Philippa seemed drawn and quiet, and Trix, lacking in any daughterly concern, was out the entire time. Miggs was at her most tiresome. Meals did not have to be quite so disgusting, but Miggs served them with an air bordering on triumph, as if it showed patriotism to eat food which choked you.

51

Elaine did not feel there was anything she could do for Theo. She turned her attention to Philippa. Their mother used to describe her second daughter as 'going about like a ship in full sail', but Philippa had lost that proud bearing. On the morning after Elaine's arrival, she came into her room with morning tea and sat on the bed.

She poured the tea and talked of this and that. Of Trix and the two Frenchmen, Trix and a New Zealand pilot. Trix refused to do any war work. 'She says,' said Philippa, dryly, 'she is not strong.' Philippa said nothing about herself. Her usually candid face, with the flicks of dark hair in two crescents on her cheeks, was closed. Was there a man in her sister's life, wondered Elaine, and was the romance going badly? Perhaps he did not want to marry her.

Elaine's ideas about love were formed in her teens in the 1930s. There were rigid rules. Going to bed with a man before he married you was wrong. It was (to quote Miles) second rate. There were labels for such girls, they were shop-worn, tarty and immoral. Elaine had known a few and disliked them. She thought there was something hectic and disturbing about them.

Well brought-up girls stayed virgins until the wedding day, and their pure white satin was both a symbol and a truth.

There was also a thing called honour. When Miles had fallen in love with her during the last peacetime summer, when they sailed at Itchenor, danced at Hurlingham, and kissed each other so passionately goodnight, she expected him to propose. When she had to wait for that, it worried her. But of course he asked her in the end. He behaved as young men of the educated classes had done for hundreds of years. They did not swear in front of girls whom they respected, they stood up when they entered a room, they always paid for everything. And there were no seductions. There were also accepted ways of behaving in smaller things. Girls were given chocolates and flowers. Never anything very expensive.

Less than twenty-four hours after arriving home, Elaine's rules were shattered.

'Hello, Sis,' cried Trix when she eventually arrived back. She gave Elaine a riotous welcome. 'I had a stroke of luck last night.'

Elaine was in the drawing room by a small coal fire, knitting a sweater for Miles. Her lap was full of navy blue wool. Trix, looking radiant in short skirts and a pale sweater with 'TT'

52

embroidered on the shoulder, waved something in a braceleted hand.

Elaine looked up vaguely and returned to her knitting.

'Did you win a raffle or something?'

'No, stoopid! Look properly.'

Trix rustled something in front of her – something which looked like two large pieces of tissue paper. Two £5 notes.

Elaine sat up as if scalded.

'Where on earth – '

'Andy, my New Zealander, gave them to me. I've got two New Zealanders, Bob and Andy, and Andy's going on ops now, so he said would I buy myself something special.'

She fanned herself with the notes.

'Do you mean you took *money* from this man?'

It was Trix's turn to be surprised.

'Of course. He's so generous, a real poppet. Last week he gave me the cash for my new nail varnish. It has a naughty name. It's called "The Night Afterwards".'

A desperate struggle was going on in Elaine. How long had her sister behaved in this disgusting way?

'I think it very unattractive for a man to give you money, and more for you to accept it,' she said, sounding cooler than she felt. 'Don't do it again. Wait until your friend is on leave, and then if he wants to, he can take you to choose a present.'

Trix giggled. Elaine, she said, must not be stuffy. Hadn't she heard there was a war on? She did hope and pray Elaine wasn't turning into one of the old folks already. Not waiting for an answer, she whisked out. She left the house soon afterwards, bound for Harrods, a shop Philippa called Trix's spiritual home.

When her sister had gone, the telephone rang and Elaine, with Miles always in her thoughts, ran out into the hall. But Miggs, who moved with the speed of lightning when she wished to, had already seized the telephone.

'Western 6468, Doctor Tyrrell's residence,' chanted Miggs, her voice retaining an echo of the old Sussex lilt. 'Ah yes, Mrs Renshawe. How is he?'

She listened and nodded. 'Just keep him warm and give him barley water and beef tea. No, no aspirins.'

Elaine returned to her knitting and her thoughts.

One way and another, St Helen's seemed to be running down, and Miggs was certainly one of the culprits. The rooms were none too clean. The only household enthusiasm the old nurse had shown recently was to damp down the boiler and prevent the girls from having a bath. And now she had the impertinence to dish out medical advice on the telephone. Mild though the advice was, it was quite wrong of her, and Theo would have a fit if he knew.

Miggs hobbled into the drawing room later, to announce that she had got hold of a Christmas tree. The greengrocer was sending a boy round with it. She waited for congratulations with a faint air of triumph. Miggs had a maddening trick of making it impossible for anyone to criticise her.

But in spite of her anxiety over the family, Elaine had an effect. She seemed to bring unity back to the house. Miggs did some cleaning and – when Elaine was about – gave no more doctorly advice to patients. Trix did not wave illicit money any more, but offered to make the mince pies. She did not say where she had obtained the mincemeat and Elaine preferred not to enquire. Philippa, two days before the Christmas holiday, climbed the ladder to the attic to fetch down the Christmas boxes.

She carried them into the drawing room, blowing the dust from them, and put them down on the floor in front of Elaine who was squatting on the hearthrug.

It was not yet blackout time and the curtains had not been pulled. Outside the windows was the December afternoon, misty and mysterious. Moisture hung on bare branches. It was almost like peacetime.

Elaine began to untie the strings round three large and ancient hat boxes which had once contained Mary's Ascot hats. For as long as the girls could remember, the boxes had been used to store the decorations for the Christmas tree.

'Nice to open them again – we haven't looked at them since war broke out, have we?' said Elaine, undoing the first tissue-papered packet. She glanced at her sister in a friendly way, and felt a stab of annoyance. What was the matter with Philippa? She herself had Miles away at sea, God knows where; what could Philippa have to worry over compared with that?

'Here's the glass teapot,' said Elaine, 'and the glass Father Christmas with the cotton Mother tied round his neck. And the lovely bluebird.'

54

'He's lost his beak.'

'You broke it. Quarrelling with Trix.'

'How many ages ago was that?' said Philippa sharply. The floor was beginning to be covered with purple and blue globes, with red bells and artificial holly wreaths, long strands of metallic-smelling tinsel, tiny Aladdin's lamps, paper chains, and a paper cherub glued to a circle of white spun glass.

'Old Mrs Hetreed gave *me* that,' said Philippa.

The door opened. It was Miggs.

'Miss Elaine. Telegraph boy.'

Philippa saw the colour drain from her sister's face.

At the door a boy in post office uniform was riffling through a sheaf of orange envelopes.

'Mrs St Aird?'

Elaine put out her hand.

Miggs stood and looked at Elaine, who stared back at her. Their eyes went to the envelope in Elaine's cold hand.

Everything she feared and dreaded, every terror which haunted her and which had to be fought before it tore her to pieces, came pressing and hovering about her. She could scarcely open the envelope.

> *Happy Happy Christmas, my darling,*
> *thinking of you non-stop will*
> *Chanel Five do love and kisses MILES.*

Trix had invited a small international gathering of troops for Christmas dinner. Her father usually disliked visitors, he called them 'strangers', but he seemed reconciled to the prospect of patriotic entertaining. Everybody in London had been in search of turkeys, and when the bird from the grateful patient arrived at St Helen's, there was general rejoicing. It was a handsome turkey and weighed eighteen pounds.

Elaine set up the tree in the drawing room and decorated it with every glittering bauble and tinsel strand from the Ascot hat boxes. The tree stood by the window and even when the blackout curtains were drawn, a slight draught made the tinsel shiver. Trix announced that there would be the two Frenchmen, a Polish officer called Jan Something and maybe her New Zealander.

55

'Why don't you ask somebody, too?' Elaine said to Philippa. Trix replied for her.

'Oh, Flip can't ask anyone of her own! She'll have her hands full coping with the two A's. Don't encourage her to skip her responsibilities. The Fighting French *need* her. She can speak French.'

'And why can't you, miss?' demanded her father, coming into the room at the end of the conversation.

'Pa! Sorry, Father. You know I didn't go to finishing school although I begged on bended knees.'

'War broke out.'

'Only the phoney war. Lots of girls got to Paris before the Occupation and then escaped in the nick of time,' said Trix, waving her hand, 'If I'd been in Paris singing for the troops I'd be able to speak French like a native by now.'

Theo did not deign to reply to a silly child talking nonsense, but Philippa laughed.

The dining room was to be used for Christmas dinner; it would be the first time a meal had been served there since Elaine had been away. Dining rooms, family silver, serving dishes (not food dumped on plates in the kitchen) were part of Elaine's civilizing effect. Miggs was now dusting the house every morning, Philippa cleaned the knives and forks, and Trix spent part of her ill-gotten ten pounds on a centrepiece for the table. It was made of tinsel and silver ribbon and miniature crackers. She also paid too much for a single branch of mistletoe which she tied to the lamp in the hall.

'Did you know that in France you must take a berry off every time you get kissed?'

Nobody answered that.

On Christmas morning Theo took his daughters to church, and Miggs was left in charge of the meal. She preferred Evensong. By the time the family returned, the house was filled with the unfamiliar smell of roasting turkey.

The two Frenchmen arrived first. Alain had at last been allowed his khaki, which was as thick as a blanket and so harsh and hairy to the touch that Trix, patting his arm, gave a scream. Alexandre was loth to take off his navy blue cloak which swung with Ruritanian gallantry. Both men had their arms full of beer bottles.

Nobody was better company than Theo when he wished to be,

56

and after some glasses of Centre d'Acceuil burgundy he was positively benign to the two A's, while all three talked of the progress of the war. But Trix put on the gramophone and dragged Alexandre away to dance. Later the front door bell rang again and Trix, abandoning him, dashed to answer it. She shared Miggs' passion for the telephone and the door.

Through the brown paper strips glued to the stained glass of the door, she saw another figure in uniform. It was a young man in RAF blue with a New Zealand flash on his shoulder.

'Merry Christmas, Bob!'

'These are for you, beautiful.'

He piled her arms with parcels, and then kissed her laughing face.

Trix hastily put down the parcels, stood on tiptoe, and pulled a berry off the mistletoe.

Like the majority of Trix's friends, the New Zealand pilot was conventionally handsome and not more than twenty-two. Theo was hospitable to him, but it was the Frenchmen who interested him more. He liked their politeness and their realism.

'Our companions bore us, *Monsieur le Docteur. Dieu,* how they bore us.'

'The forms we had to fill in, you would not believe.'

'Giving us these uniforms, imagine! Why is Alain in khaki and myself in Air Force blue? He cannot march a step and I have never entered a plane.'

'And how may we apologise for the quality of this wine?'

The meal was voted the best dinner that anyone could remember. When it was over everyone listened to the Empire Broadcast on the wireless, which followed the King's speech, and finished with the bells of Coventry Cathedral and Polish troops singing carols.

'That reminds me, where is Jan!' suddenly exclaimed Trix.

'Poles are so unreliable,' said New Zealand Bob, 'And *not* the favourites of our squadron.'

'We do not like them either,' said Alexandre.

'Have they not something of a reputation as lady killers?' said Theo, mellow with burgundy.

There were loud denials from the men, and Trix, appealed to, refused to give a verdict.

The party went on into the afternoon. Tea was served, with a dry eggless cake topped by a red candle, and for supper there were turkey sandwiches. Alain carved. When he, Trix and Elaine helped to get the supper, he took out an extraordinary knife which he wore in his belt. It had a horn handle, its blade was chased, it was short and heavy and very sharp. Theo came into the kitchen and remarked on it.

'That is a very unusual knife,' he said.

Alain lifted it by the blade and balanced it.

'Yes. It is a good knife. It throws well,' he said, and lunged as if to send it hurling through the air.

It grew dark, and the blackout curtains were pulled, but no wailing sounded over London. The Frenchmen could stay at ease by the fire, instead of grumbling back to headquarters.

'I reckon,' said Bob, 'it's a truce.'

It was. It lasted all that night, and the whole of the next day, and very strange it seemed. People spoke to each other in the street about it.

'Wasn't there a Christmas truce in the last war? Didn't the German soldiers and the Tommies meet in No Man's Land?'

'Think it'll last?'

When the second night of Christmas came, and there was still no sound of the banshees, no guns, no shuddering explosions, people in d'Abernon Road came out of their houses to look up at the sky.

'Where have they got to?' asked one of Theo's neighbours.

Theo was also looking up at the clear stars. Apart from being sickened at the death of civilians, his attitude to the blitz was one of intense curiosity.

'I daresay they are standing round their Christmas trees, singing *Stille Nacht*,' he said.

'Funny buggers.'

During the second night without bombs, the telephone rang. Trix was out and Miggs put her head round the door.

'Chap for you, Miss Philippa.'

Blushing scarlet, Philippa went out into the hall, closing the door behind her. Her heart was pounding. Weeks had gone by without a word, and she had thought of Barny and imagined he was dead.

'It's your pal in the Eagles,' said the American voice she had longed for. 'How are you fixed for tonight?'

'Do you mean now?'

'Sure. Have you eaten? Have you got a date? I just hit town, I'm at the Wings Club in Curzon Street.'

'I'd love to see you.'

'That's my girl. Grab a taxi.'

Still red-faced, Philippa returned to the drawing room.

'I've been asked out tonight.'

'How nice,' said Elaine mildly, 'anyone I know?'

Her manner was undemanding and kind. She always told the family whom she was meeting and where, rather like a man emptying his pocket of small change. Trix was the same. She reeled off the hotel or restaurant she was going to, and a litany of nicknames and countries, the two A's, Bob, my Canadian, my Pole.

'Only somebody in the RAF,' said Philippa. She did not know why it was that she couldn't bear to say.

It was cold and black and blessedly peaceful when Philippa left the house. The sky was thick with stars, and when she turned into Kensington High Street, the tiny crosses of the traffic lights were like smaller stars fallen to earth. She found a taxi which drove her to Curzon Street.

The Wings Club was in a very large old brick house overgrown with ivy, in a cobbled cul-de-sac. Before the war the house had only come alive during the London season. For four short months it echoed with dance music. Crimson carpets were unrolled across the cobbles, and girls in billowing tulle dresses arrived for debutantes' dances.

The door was answered by a smart RAF corporal who saluted her and said in an American voice, would she sign the visitors' book, if you please, ma'am?

The hall, which smelled of American cigarettes, was hung with dark over-varnished landscapes. It was also draped with the Stars and Stripes flag. There was a Christmas tree ten feet high hung with coloured parcels – for whom? Through an open door she heard the jingle of a jazz piano, and as she followed the corporal, some men in uniform came out of the room, talking and laughing boisterously. They were slightly drunk, and seemed oddly un-English in spite of the RAF blue with wings on the tunic.

In an overfurnished room with an open fire was Barny. He sprang up.

'I should have come to get you, I've been kicking myself. It's so good to see you, Flip. I'd like for you to meet Chuck.'

A man who had also stood up shook her hand. Chuck was younger than Barny and seemed scarcely more than a schoolboy. He had a fresh open face, a frank smile and hair much brilliantined. It sprang up on his forehead in a ridge. His accent was not as slow as Barny's.

'Proud to know you. Shall I get the drinks, Barny? Does Flip like rye?'

English girls did not drink whisky, but Philippa accepted it with a smile and left most of it.

They all sat down and the young men talked of the truce. It wouldn't last but it was welcome, wasn't it? He and Chuck were sure glad to get some leave. They felt they deserved a break.

'Boy. Do we,' said Chuck. 'We get so browned off, that's the English expression isn't it? To think how I imagined the moment I got here we'd be operational. Of course Barny has hundreds of hours in the air to his credit,' he went on admiringly, 'and I've only got thirty-five. I said I had fifty when I enlisted.'

He talked of how he and Barny had met on the ship coming to England, and of their disappointment at still being grounded. They'd come over to see action, hadn't they?

Like Trix's two Frenchmen, the young men had come from different worlds, sharing only their nationality. Chuck was from the smallest of the states, Rhode Island. He had been to Brown University, and to his family's disapproval had learned to fly . . . and left for Canada.

'If you knew Rhode Island you wouldn't be surprised,' drawled Barny. 'Rhode Island is the last place you'd go for a good time.'

Chuck disagreed. There were all kinds of pleasures there. The coast was fine for sailing, he'd managed a sixteen-footer when he was twelve years old. There was an English tradition in his home state, he told Philippa. It was a fine place. True, he'd left home. But that was because he couldn't resist what was going on over here. He'd always been in love with speed, had driven a motor cycle on a speedway before he joined the flying club, and – well – here he was rarin' to go.

'Barny and I both read all those books about flying in the Great War. Richthoven, Guynemer, all those guys. I guess I knew the air battles over France like other boys know the

60

gunbattles in the Wild West. So we came to England. The English seem glad to have us. Any man who can fly and wants to fight is welcome.'

'Except that we haven't done much of the first or damn near any of the second,' said Barny.

Philippa, listening to them talking, felt a thrill go through her. To all young women in England that winter, the RAF pilots had an extraordinary and painful glamour. People lay under bombardment in fear of their lives, but these young men rode the winds. They engaged, night after night, in deadly combat. They were heroic. Her eyes shone. What did it matter if they had not yet started to fight? They wore on their breasts the ominous silver wings.

The trio went into the dining room to have supper. During dinner, turkey and an unfamiliar cranberry sauce, she listened to them talking about their training. Chuck complained that they were making no progress and might as well be sitting at the corner drugstore. What use were they to the RAF? Finally they had gone to the CO in desperation to ask when they could start being trained.

Barny grimaced at the story naively told. It wasn't that simple, he said. The only instructors were pilots who were actually fighting – how had they time to teach?

'They go out at daybreak, return to base to refuel, then out they go again, day after day, night after night,' he said, 'They're dead beat. One guy who was supposed to be our instructor came back yesterday from France, went to sleep while eating his breakfast and waiting for his plane to be refuelled, was woken up by his engineer, and went off to fly again. Like a man moving in his sleep.'

'While we,' said Chuck, 'sit around fresh as daisies.'

They described the man who commanded the Eagle Squadron. He was an Englishman, a great flyer, who'd been until recently in the Battle of Britain. He could make a tactical report sound like a thrilling adventure story. But, there were a lot of buts. He was too keen on discipline. He made the Eagles stand up any time he came into a room. He insisted that they must learn how to salute smartly, that their uniform must be perfect and – to crown it all – that they must have a soldierly bearing, whatever in hell that meant. They had not come to England for such stuff.

61

Philippa wondered if she should spring ignorantly to the defence of their commander, but before she spoke Barny went on with the story.

'My pal here won't admit that our CO has some awful job,' he said. 'We aren't trained. We're wild with impatience. All we want is to get up there and win some glory. No, Chuck, don't interrupt! We're undisciplined, Flip. That guy has got to turn us into a fighting unit somehow. He has to cope with men like Tex who is a wild cowboy and has the idea that you just hop in a plane and have a go at the Jerrie, just as you would in a scrap on the ranch. If you did, you'd be shot down in ten minutes.'

But at last, Barny said, the CO was getting the time to lead them in the air. He was flying with them. During the last week they'd had fulltime training and what was more were finding out just how much there was to learn. They had to discover the way to make a plane do whatever they wanted. They must treat it as an extension of their own bodies, so that it instantly obeyed them. They must learn to make it twist and weave, to drop like a stone, to rise like a swallow. Pushing their coffee cups aside, they used their hands to illustrate what they were saying. When Philippa knew many pilots, she found that they all used their hands to describe flying, flattening and curving their hands like birds, swooping, rising, falling.

'We've got to learn how to stand a plane on its nose,' Chuck put it, 'or climb so high the thing is hanging on its propellers.'

They told her of studying detailed maps, of aerial photography, artillery shoots, long distance reconnaissance, air to ground Morse. The technicalities fascinated her. The jazz piano had started again, the dining room had emptied. She could have sat forever with the two young men. Finally Chuck looked at his watch and exclaimed that he must go. He was meeting some English friends 'on the other side of town'. He gripped Philippa's hand when he said goodbye, smiling as if they had been friends for years.

Barny and Philippa walked back to the room where they had sat before dinner. It was empty except for a pilot and a girl in a corner, talking in low voices. The music played on, but the door was half closed, the sound muffled.

'Chuck makes me feel old,' Barny said. 'Even the States that we come from are so different.'

He rubbed his nose.

'It isn't good to be old right now,' he said.

'We English are very old.'

He looked at her with eyes as dark as Trix's, but the quality of their glance was different, not fixed and brilliant, but tender.

'I've been thinking a lot about you. Every time the radio says a raid on London, I pray to God it isn't near St Helen's.'

'And all the time I'm safely tucked up under the billiard table and the corrugated iron ceiling!'

'So I'm not to worry,' he said, as if at a loss when faced by female courage.

They talked, then, of Chuck. He said that his friend's excitement about flying bothered him. Not that they were not all of them excited, but Chuck seemed uncontrolled.

'He swears that it is the *idea* which fires his imagination, and that he's perfectly cool in the air. I suppose I must believe him. He doesn't like discipline, though, he's worse than I am, and it certainly bugs me. The trouble with the Eagles is that we're just a bunch of American individualists. Flip? How do you find us?'

'I like you.'

'You do, don't you?'

It was long past eleven but there was still no Alert. Barny talked idly, his long legs stretched out, as relaxed as if they had been at a pre-war dance. Philippa's heart was full. If it had been before the war, how could she ever have met this man? Everything about him stirred her. His slow accent, his manner so much more gallant than her own countrymen's, his loose-limbed ease, even the exotic smell of his cigarettes. He came from a land where a single State was so large that you could lose the whole of England inside it. The animals and birds of Barny's country were different from those she knew, and so were the trees, the swamps, the snakes, the very air. She was physically conscious of him. Of his thick hair and the shape of his mouth. She wanted to step inside that male body, think with that mind, speak with that accent, learn to fly, risk her life.

She was laughing at something he said when he touched her.

'I want to kiss you.'

She stopped laughing.

'Come to my room. Just for a while.'

They went out to the hall, and up the staircase. She felt as if every person who saw them, a group of men in the hall, a maid in the corridor, knew where Barny was taking her. But nobody looked or paid the least attention. She was still in an agony of nervous embarrassment.

His room was on the top floor, very small and cramped, with a sloping ceiling.

'This one is a bad bet in the raids. That's why it's vacant. It's tough to get a room here unless you book in advance, and how can we know when we'll get leave? The only vacancies are always right up here. But it doesn't matter tonight, does it? Not while the Germans are trucing.'

'Do you really think they are?'

Her voice was forced.

'Honey, if the planes were coming, they'd be here by now.'

The room was as bare as a cell; nothing but a bed under a white quilt, a dressing table, a looking glass, an empty grate. On the mantelpiece was a candle in a china candlestick, with a box of matches. An expensive looking suitcase was in the corner and a clean blue shirt on the chest of drawers. It was just a room.

He moved over to her, narrowing his eyes, and put his arms round her. They stood, bodies touching, and he rocked her to and fro, and began to kiss her, forcing her lips with his tongue and exploring her mouth and running his tongue along her teeth. When she opened her eyes, she saw his pale face, eyes shut, wearing an expression as if in pain. She wanted him.

'Beautiful. Beautiful. Shall we lie down?'

Knowing that she shouldn't, she let him lead her to the bed where he lifted her and laid her down, and then shifted from being beside her, and lay on top of her as he had done that other time, his mouth on hers. He put his hand down her dress, found her breast and caught the nipple between two fingers, moving it to and fro. Still pressing her down and thrusting against her, he pulled up her skirts.

'Barny, oh Barny. I can't.'

He had been lost and dazed and intent, and he came slowly to himself. He stopped moving.

'Can't you?'

Because she was refusing him, she pressed closer.

'It's what I told you. I have never made love.'

He took his hand from her nipple and rolled off so that she was no longer lying underneath him. Sitting up, he gave a shudder.

'You must go.'

'Must I?'

He did not reply. Philippa could hear his thoughts as if he spoke them aloud. What do you expect? That you can stay here and I'll go on kissing you when I know I can't have you? Do you imagine I'm going on with such a farce? Yet she could break the horrible silence between them so easily, and change the shuddering expression on his face. She could throw a torch into the cold embers and light a fire fiercer than she had ever known – simply by telling him to untie her virgin knot. She couldn't do it.

He picked up her coat and put it round her shoulders. She leaned back to press against him, but he moved away. They went down the staircase and the corporal at the door said he would find a taxi. Barny politely waited with her. Neither of them spoke.

'Cab's here, sir,' said the corporal, returning.

Barny walked out into the street, opened the taxi door in the dark.

'Goodnight, Barny. Thank you for a lovely evening.'

There was no reply.

She cried as she was driven home.

Chapter Five

Early in February Elaine finally decided that she could not stay another month at St Helen's without doing some kind of war work. The half life, brought on by the blitz in a mixture of fear and boredom very like Philippa's, did not satisfy her. As her father said, human beings could get used to anything. There was nothing useful in simply putting up with the blitz like everybody else.

There had been the great fire of London at the end of December, after which the Fire Guard had been started. Elaine took her turn like most Londoners at sitting on rooftops in the freezing night, staring at the sky and waiting for the bombers to rain down incendiaries. But they hadn't done so again in d'Abernon Road. There were now a number of efficient local people fire-watching, and Elaine and Philippa were only needed about once in ten days. Somehow Trix was not asked.

What Elaine wanted was a job that would swallow up her time and tire her out and give her a feeling of belonging to the war. She wanted to be a Wren. But there was always the wild chance that Miles would get unexpected leave. If she were in uniform, that could be difficult. When she thought of him in the Atlantic, she was frightened by images of the terrible sea. She clung to an idea she had had which comforted her. Perhaps on his next leave she might succeed in becoming pregnant.

Meanwhile she was at St Helen's, keeping her father company when he was in, and bearing Miggs' appalling food. One evening after a dinner consisting mainly of potatoes, Theo was driven by disgust to take her into his study and give them both a strong gin and tonic. They listened to the guns.

Elaine looked tentatively at him. She knew although she did not approve of it that she was his favourite. Yet it was difficult to talk to him about herself. He was a man who thought people should solve their own problems. She rather respected his selfishness. After all, his three daughters were adults. His life was one of dedication, he risked it nightly in the streets. Why shouldn't he be free of the weight of his family? She was surprised when he suddenly remarked that she ought to get a job.

'I quite agree,' she said brightly.

'Do you remember a patient of mine, Captain Pendleton? Friend of your mother's family? He's by way of being a colonel in the War Office now. He called round to see me yesterday and asked me to dine. I couldn't accept, of course. We talked a little about you girls. He mentioned that the department he is connected with is very short of staff.'

'Which department is that, Father?' She had not yet recovered from the rare experience of her father interesting himself in her life, apart from smiling at family chat.

'MI5.'

She burst out laughing.

'Not the Secret Service!'

'Those ridiculous names from the *Boys' Own Paper*. Pendleton is in Counter Intelligence. Apparently a large section has been evacuated to the country and they're in dire need of secretaries. He actually remembered you went to secretarial school. Fellows in that sort of work train their memories, I suppose. Well? Does it appeal?'

She did not know what to say. In her own fashion she had a streak of the Tyrrell impulsiveness, as Philippa and Trix had, but she could control hers. Yet it was there in her nature, a dog straining at a leash. Working for the Secret Service did sound fascinating and unlikely. She had no idea what the work might be, and guessed that in spite of its alluring sound, it could turn out to be monotonous. Yet all the same, it *was* secret. The dog tugged at the leash.

Her father was looking at her affectionately. It had occurred to him once or twice lately that he did not do much for his daughters, apart from providing a home, and the small allowance from their mother's money. It pleased him to help her.

'I'd like to meet the colonel if he'll see me,' she said.

'Well done!'

When Elaine told Philippa about the possibility of the job Philippa merely nodded absently. She seemed, thought Elaine, to have lost her generosity. She had also lost weight and omitted to wash her hair. Her sister's gloom, Elaine had noticed, dated from the Christmas night when she had had a telephone call, and gone out with some man whose name she had carefully not mentioned. It was since then that there had been dark rings under her eyes.

What happened, wondered Elaine uneasily. She thought of the old rules that used to hedge young girls with safety. Blessed rules, where were they now? You might as well expect a wicker fence to keep back a tidal wave. Her sisters lived in a city teeming with men in uniform, strangers, foreigners whom their father had never met. The girls picked them up on the top of buses. The idea that Philippa had been seduced remained in Elaine's thoughts like a splinter she could not dig out. But she did not know what to do, nor how to ask Philippa about it.

Since it was clearly impossible to help her because Philippa wanted nothing but to be left alone to wallow, Elaine concentrated on herself.

Her father, still pleased at the rare sensation of helping one of his children, arranged for her to meet the colonel at a club in St James'. When Elaine arrived he was waiting for her in the hall and she recognized him. He was big and white-haired, with burly shoulders and a manner in which grandness was mixed with a somewhat lecherous gallantry. He took her into the enormous stuffy lounge where elderly gentlemen dozed, and talked to her in a low voice. He asked her a question or two in a perfunctory way. Then he told her that he would arrange an interview for her at MI5's country headquarters.

'Your shorthand and typing are still in good shape, of course,' said the colonel in a tone expecting the answer yes. 'Your father told me you are very speedy.'

He gave her a flirtatious look.

She returned it with a pleasant smile.

'I haven't done any secretarial work since I married, Colonel.'

'Skills like that don't rust, they never rust. And they're mighty useful to a young woman. There's a dearth, a positive desert of good secretaries in our department, Mrs St Aird. You'll be the most welcome applicant in Oxfordshire.'

Elaine's heart gave a dive. Oxfordshire! Where her in-laws lived.

There was no getting out of it now. The colonel went on to say that he would make the necessary telephone calls, and she

68

would be interviewed tomorrow. Desert or no desert, his manner said plainly that he had done her a favour. Elaine found it necessary to look deeply grateful.

Very early the following morning she arrived at Paddington. The February day was so dark that it seemed as if daylight was never going to come; the streets were dim with fog and the station was worse. Elaine found herself again in a packed and dirty train filled with troops and civilians. The train was nearly half an hour late before leaving Paddington, and she kept looking nervously at her watch. At last it started. The morning grew slightly lighter as she watched the suburbs going by, with long rows of houses in which there were gaps like missing teeth. Some streets seemed to have totally disappeared into a mass of fallen masonry. When the dreary streets and ruins were left behind, the countryside was misty and damp, the glimpses of the river grey and sad. She remembered going to Henley Regatta with Miles one summer day, and saw in an inward vision the jostling punts and bright dresses, hats wreathed in flowers, strawberries – and Miles' sweet laughing face.

Dragging herself out of the past, she looked round the compartment – she had been fortunate this time to have a seat. Everybody looked shabby and tired except for the soldiers. Pasted up on the wall were the instructions which were in every train compartment now, the target for a good many wartime jokes:

If an air raid occurs while you are on the train:
1. Do *not* attempt to leave the train if it stops away from a station, unless requested by the guard to do so. You are safer where you are.
2. Pull down the blinds, day or night, as a protection against flying glass.
3. If room is available, lie down on the floor.

It was the last instruction that made people laugh. Elaine recalled Miggs' account of a visit to her niece in Sussex. It had been at the start of the Battle of Britain, and the train had been attacked by an enemy plane which dived down and gave a burst of machine-gun fire. Everyone in the compartment scrambled down on to the floor. Miggs was in the bottom layer, with a stout girl of fifteen lying on top of her.

'I shoved her out of the way and crawled back to my seat. I'd rather be shot than squashed alive any day.'

The train was late when it drew up at Oxford. Elaine, joining the crowd leaving the platform, wondered if she would be met. The colonel had said a car would be waiting. Well, if it isn't I shall simply have to go home, she thought. She had no idea where MI5 was situated, and how could one ask? Even the idea was comic. At least, she thought, I look good if I do manage to get the interview. She had dressed with care, choosing her expensive suit, made for her in Savile Row before the war; it was in Glen Urquhart checks, tiny squares of brown and black on white, with a faint blue stripe. She wore a small brown hat tipped over her eyes, a blue sweater she had knitted herself, and Miles' diamond naval crown on her lapel. The day was cold and she had slung her camelhair coat round her shoulders.

As she came out of the station she heard a car hoot twice, and a thin bright-looking girl at the wheel of a Morris wound down the window.

'Are you looking for somebody?' she asked.

'Well – yes. I'm being met. Or I thought I was.'

'Could you identify yourself? Sorry, we have to ask.'

Elaine gave her name, address and – always thorough – produced a letter to prove it.

'Okay. I thought you were you. Hop in.'

The driver introduced herself as Marjorie Flower and drove off into misty deserted Oxford.

'Ah. There's the Keble bus,' she remarked, slowing down at a traffic light. There was a bus waiting outside the college, and about a dozen young women were climbing on board. Every single one was dressed like Elaine. There were a dozen Glen Urquhart tweeds, a dozen plain sweaters, and even at a distance Elaine could spot a dozen lapels pinned with badges of the Forces.

Marjorie passed the bus and drove on.

'I suppose they didn't tell you where we're going?'

Elaine, thoroughly put out by the girls' clothes, turned to her companion to reply. Marjorie Flower was thin and humorous, with a triangular face, a Robin Hood hat with a long feather, and the identical tweeds.

'We're off like the Keble gang to Blenheim. The palace, you know. Seat of the noble Marlboroughs.'

70

Elaine stared.

'How very extraordinary.'

'Isn't it? Not that it feels like a palace, as you'll see. Who recommended you, by the way?'

'Colonel Pendleton.'

Marjorie laughed. 'I always think he's like the major in the poem – the scarlet one who sends us over the top.'

The girls, like people playing a game of cards, put facts down for examination. They found that Marjorie's cousin Dick Polglaze had trained at Devonport with Miles. Marjorie was married, her husband was a doctor in the Army in the Far East. She had a small daughter whom her mother was looking after. 'That is Ma's war work. Which means I can have a job. I live at home with the parents now. Don't we all?'

She remarked that Blenheim might be thirsting for secretaries, but the fact still remained that only influence got you in.

'Everyone has to be recommended somehow. One of my friends was taken on because her aunt was having an affair with an MI5 officer.'

Elaine smiled somewhat frostily.

'Using influence always seems wrong to me.'

'Oh, I disagree. My father was in Crosse and Blackwell's and when we were children he used to bring us back enormous glass jars of sweets, like the ones you see in sweet shop windows. Samples. Influence is like that. Something special you only get by knowing somebody. Jobs in MI5 are the jars of sweeties. Not that the Blenheim jobs are any great shakes, the work is quite hard. But the food, believe it or not, is delicious. And the Duke's daughters serve behind the counter.'

Marjorie laughed when Elaine mentioned the Glen Urquhart tweeds.

'It's our uniform, isn't it?'

The car slowed down at two elaborate stone pillars standing on either side of tall open gates. In the distance Elaine saw the palace. In the thin winter mist it seemed to float.

'Are you nervous about the interview?'

'I suppose I am a bit.'

'Don't be. They need dogsbodies. And there is the morning busful of them.'

The Keble bus had rumbled up behind them and stopped, and the flock of girls jumped out and began to ascend a flight of steps to the palace. Marjorie and Elaine followed. Through great doors, they entered an enormous hall, lofty as a cathedral. In this place dukes had sometimes welcomed kings. Carpets like lakes of crimson had been thrown down to warm the marble floors, and exotic trees had stood about, blossoming and scented and bringing the winter indoors. Now the hall was filled with metal filing cabinets. Shabby, scarred and scratched, they were piled one on top of the other until they formed entire pillars, the highest almsot reaching the ceiling. It would be impossible to get at the top ones, thought Elaine, without a fireman's ladder.

The day outside was chill, but the palace was like a tomb, with an intense, penetrating, arctic quality of cold. All the girls wore boots and thick woollen stockings. Elaine shivered and pulled on her coat.

Like water into dry earth, the Keble girls began to disappear. Some went down passages on the ground floor, and others through double doors. Marjorie took Elaine up a staircase, along two or three corridors, and finally deposited her in a room containing nothing but four kitchen chairs. The window was uncurtained. The walls were covered with yellow damask.

Blowing into her woollen gloves, Marjorie said she would come back to collect her after the interview. She wished her luck.

Alone, Elaine went to the window and looked out. Below lay a cobbled courtyard overlooked by high palace windows. The courtyard was crammed with hideous army huts.

'Mrs St Aird?'

A dark woman with a face of an eagle stood in the doorway. She beckoned Elaine to follow her into an office next door. She sat at a table and indicated yet another kitchen chair. The room was marginally warmer than the rest of the palace, a little fire burned in a large marble fireplace. On the walls were portraits of sexy-looking men and women who gazed scornfully down at Elaine with worldly eighteenth century faces.

The dark woman picked up some papers and glanced at them.

'Recommended by Charles Pendleton. And you're Claire St Aird's daughter-in-law, I gather.'

She looked up with approval. Elaine thought her pleasant and alarming. Her glossy dark hair was coiled in a bun at the nape of her neck, not a tendril out of place. Her face was unlined and experienced, and looked as if it was scrubbed daily with Lifebuoy soap.

72

The questions she asked Elaine about her previous work were brief. She seemed pleased at her total ignorance of MI5.

'You can start at once, Mrs St Aird. Now, let me see. You're with your family in London at present. Many of our girls have digs at Keble. I'm afraid they complain a good deal. Particularly if there is any snow, as they have to cross the quad to have a bath. I've told them, surely it is worth the journey. However. We have a bus which passes quite close to Shelton. I imagine you will find it much more convenient to live with your parents-in-law?'

The eagle regarded her benevolently. Elaine saw she was not going to escape the St Airds.

Marjorie fetched her when the interview was over. She said mischievously, 'I bet she didn't once ask about your shorthand speed. When she saw me, I said I couldn't remember mine and *she* said We Will Call it a Hundred. Isn't she like a hospital matron?'

'I thought a headmistress.'

'Interchangeable.'

The girls went through green baize doors, crossed store rooms filled with more filing cabinets, and eventually out at the back of the palace, and into the stables. They were given an excellent lunch, mostly of vegetables but cooked with inspiration.

When Elaine was on the train on her way back to London, the thought that she was now being forced to live with Miles' parents hit her with its full force. How infinitely would she have preferred Keble's snowy quadrangles.

She did not, and could not, like the St Airds. Miles's father was a man who always reminded her of a duke in a Shakespeare play, expecting homage and giving nothing in return. But it was not her father-in-law who was the problem, it was Miles' mother. After the first welcoming meetings when she had clearly believed Elaine was bringing money into the family, Lady St Aird had become very cold. It was perfectly obvious that she did not like or admire Elaine, who was chilled and depressed by that. The irony was that she knew very well the St Aird's wouldn't hesitate when she asked if she could live at Shelton. 'Of course,' they would say. She was family. And when Miles knew that she was going to live there, he would be delighted, touched and happy. He loved his parents, Shelton, and above all, Elaine. He was convinced that they would suit each other wonderfully.

A raid had started by the time Elaine arrived at St Helen's. Both her sisters were out, and Miggs was in the cellar. Tired and depressed, she went into the kitchen and sat down, listening to the ground shudder with explosions, the strange whistlings, the guns. She thought of Blenheim floating in the cold mist. Of Miles in a ship plunging in the icy seas. Oh, this war, this war. It did not only kill people, and reduce poor homes to smoking ruins. It destroyed everything. Lovers were dragged apart. Families divided. It even took away a place where your thoughts could be at rest. A person could hide in the deepest Underground, she thought, or hurry to the loneliest part of the country. There was no shelter anywhere.

When Elaine left for her new job in Oxfordshire, Trix made a sudden dragonfly dart in the direction of Philippa. It had not escaped her black eyes that her second sister was depressed. Trix diagnosed love. She had seen the sickness too many times not to know the signs as accurately as her father recognized the measles. Trix had already coaxed Philippa to come out dancing once or twice, and the occasions had been a moderate success. She now decided that it was high time something was done about Philippa's appearance. She would find time to make her a party dress.

Trix was always busy, in and out of the house, whisking to the telephone ahead of Miggs calling, 'It will be for me,' and now also occupied with what she called her war effort.

Wrapped up against the cold, she dug up her mother's herbacious border, throwing away the plants in their winter sleep, and preparing the ground to sow vegetables. She had visited the local nursery, collected a good deal of information, and bought some stakes from the nurseryman. They were to be for beans.

'We will have fresh vegetables all next summer. So good for our skins,' she told Philippa. 'And the man is finding me a special rose bush. He says the flowers have a really strong scent. He said, "It'll do well for you, miss. I can see you're the sort whose roses always come out."'

As well as sewing for Philippa, Trix was making herself a dress copied from *Vogue*. It was of grey flannel, with white stripes as thick as if they had been drawn with chalk.

74

'Jan, my Pole, gave me the money – he's gorgeous. So gallant,' she said, neatly sewing.

Philippa raised her eyebrows but said nothing. She did not approve of Trix, but she had spoiled her since she was born.

Trix bit off her cotton.

'You are feeling ropey, aren't you?'

It was the RAF's now universal word.

'I'm perfectly okay.'

'Don't pretend, stoopid. I know you. The trouble with you is that you don't go around enough. You quite liked it when we went to Hatchett's, didn't you? Well, there are lots of boys about and we can get them to take us to movies at weekends, and then in the evenings – the blitz *really* isn't too bad, is it? – we'll go dancing. But we must do something about your clothes.'

Like a horse led to a high jump, Philippa was dragged along to her bedroom where Trix opened the wardrobe and threw all the clothes on the bed, commenting on each dress.

'Old-fashioned. That waist! Poor you. Let's give this one to Miggsy.'

The dresses lay in a heap, looking just what they were. Old clothes. Philippa could not think of a way to refuse Trix's offer to brighten her up. When had she refused Trix anything? Her little sister had been six years old when Philippa saved her pocket money to buy her an outsized teddy bear that her parents had thought unsuitably big. When Trix was eleven, Philippa did her homework and went to watch her riding in the Row. Elaine and Mary Tyrrell, never Theo, were interested enough. But Philippa was the fairy godmother.

Now Trix had apparently decided it was her turn. She spent unselfish hours remodelling her sister's dresses, spent money given to her by 'her' Canadian, Pole or New Zealander on knitting wool, burgundy and ice blue. Philippa must, she commanded, knit herself a sweater, half one colour, half the other, buttoning down the back. It would be *very* smart.

With Elaine away again, Philippa's life was altered by Trix. She was taken about, still resembling the horse led by a pert little girl. There were foursomes, and whoever the two men were who made up the party, they were admirers of Trix. While she danced with one, the other would order Philippa a drink, (she had never left so many rums and limes in her life) and watch Trix dancing.

75

'Isn't she a whizzer? What a girl,' the young man would wistfully say. Philippa agreed. While her sister danced she drew all men's eyes, seeming to have a light round her. Philippa watched too; she did not mind her sister being adored.

Her own boyfriends from the past had disappeared one by one. They never telephoned when they were on leave; or, if they did, they never took her out more than once. She discovered that if your mind is on another man, your male companion knows that by instinct. Was it the opposite of a mating scent? Men did not ask her out any more.

She knew it was ridiculous to have fallen in love with Barny Duval. She had met him three times in her life. But she could not see him in perspective at a distance, only close and out of proportion. He had come here with a few other men, scarcely fifty of them, to fight for England. She thought him one of the most romantic and reckless men in the world. Soon, perhaps now, he would be in the dark air over France or London or the sea – what was the RAF slang – 'dicing with death'. The words were flippant and true. Pilots did gamble with the dark opponent. Danger excited her. It made Barney sexually alluring and somehow unreal. When she had lain with him she had felt she was in the arms of a god. But she was a virgin and believed you must marry before you lie naked with a man. So she had lost him.

Her eyes were clouded with desire and sadness. She did not know how it was that she remained in love. She travelled to the Temple through the mess of bombed London, she worked, she went home to be pounced on by Trix. She sat in smoky ballrooms in the company of men who wanted her sister. She stayed miserably, passionately in love. She thought of Barny all the time. She thought of the country he had come from, about which she had such hazy ideas – of its swamps and rushing rivers, its orange groves and its huge deserts never as dry as her unhappy heart.

It had been her own decision not to make love. If they met again, and were embracing on a bed in the same way, would she behave differently? She had found that all the solemn warnings of the past against the lust of men had never mentioned how much a girl might want a man. I know that everything I want is wrong, she thought. I should never have him in my arms. Wanting him can only bring me pain. And even that he didn't

76

care for me. And yet – and yet – how he haunted her imagination. But I have never done it, couldn't he understand that, she thought. If you won't let a man have you, does he always leave you? Does it have to be so? Perhaps American girls sleep with their boyfriends. And if they won't, you are no good to them. That's a thought. No good.

One night when the blitz was slight, and she was not out with Trix, Philippa lay under the billiard room table, and lit the lamp, and wrote to him. It was a short enough letter, full of clichés. How was he? What news? Her own was slight, nothing much was happening except the blitz. Would he read what the letter did not say? She posted it to the Eagle Club, with 'Please forward, urgent.' on the envelope.

For weeks she hoped. She listened for the telephone, and ran to the front door to the postman. She had a hundred disappointments. Trix noticed. Kind-heartedly, she said nothing.

Philippa was not the only member of the Tyrrell family to be gloomy that 1941 spring. Theo was leading the most exhausting period of his life at an age when he should be slowing down. If Miggs took her daily queuing for fish and the steady reduction of unrationed food, with a grim, amused philosophy, Theo took his work with nervous determination. He was not as tough as he liked to think himself. The blitz showed no sign of abating; blast and collapsing houses and broken glass caused most of the casualties, but there was also the terrible danger of fire. Firemen on the top of ladders faced infernos. Injuries were terrible.

Although he worked part of every day at the hospital, and fitted in his private patients when he could, he was ready at any time of the night to go out with the rescue parties. He delivered a baby in a kitchen, with the warden holding a torch to shine on the mother while Theo, in rubber apron and tin helmet, stitched her up. Like every doctor, he had a carapace which protected him when he had to cope with the dying or the dead. But he never managed not to suffer when the patient was a child. Returning to St Helen's in the blitzed dawns, he was often in pain.

To add to a doctor's anxieties, there now began what the newspapers called 'the great drift homewards' of evacuated children and their mothers. 'Leave the children where they are!' shouted a government poster, with a Hitler figure in the background hissing 'Take them back'. Hundreds of thousands ignored the warning and poured back into London.

Short of sleep, working beyond his physical capabilities for his age, he confided in nobody. His favourite child was gone. He did have a sentiment which he never admitted was love for his old nurse, but Miggs was not the devoted slave she used to be. She looked at him sardonically. It seemed a long time since he had been admired. There was nobody in his family to talk to. Philippa was too like her mother, soft and sentimental. As for Beatrix, she was his child and must live at home if she chose. But he had never had a sensible conversation with her in his life.

He was unexpectedly involved in his two daughters' social life when the two Frenchmen from the Centre d'Acceuil reappeared.

'Guess who's turned up,' announced Trix to Philippa one evening. She looked at her sister's closed face and said, 'Ah well, no point in asking, it would bore you to answer. My two A's are here again. I thought they'd been posted. They've been away on some ghastly course, very hush hush. I met them in Kensington High Street. Alexandre was swinging along like something out of the *Prisoner of Zenda*, and poor Alain plodded with him, all dumpy. I told them to come round. If Pa's out, we can raid his study. My jewel-case key fits his drink cupboard. The luck! And I know his patients bring him black market gin.'

'He'd have a fit.'

'It's patriotic to entertain the Fighting French.'

Trix, who had been sitting on the arm of the sofa, jumped up and peered at herself in the glass over the mantelpiece. She frowned. She was her most severe critic.

'I do wonder if Miggsy can manage to give us all something to eat, don't you?'

'I suppose that means you want me to ask.'

'Oh Flip, would you? She's not mad keen on me just now. I used all her beastly butter ration for a cake for my Pole when he came to tea. He loves sweet things.'

Trix laughed at the old joke.

Philippa went to the kitchen. She found that Miggs was out of her disguise as doctor's receptionist – the starched coat hung on a hook behind the door. The boiler was well damped down, and Miggs, in her hideous puce apron, was peeling potatoes. She was watched by the unblinking gaze of a large ginger cat.

'Miggs! Where did that come from?'
''Tisn't a that. 'Tis a he.'
'Is he from over the road? Or the people at the corner?'
'Nobody's seen him before in their lives. Not the milkman. Nobody.'
The cat's green eyes were glued on Miggs.
'Outside the kitchen window all day yesterday he was. I was washin' up and there he was. Glarin'. I told him to get off with it. Half-hour later, back again. Starin' fit to bust. No sign last night when I went off to my shelter. This mornin', blow me down, back again in the pourin' rain. More than a body could stand, so I let him in.'
'But Miggs, you're not thinking – '
'Not thinkin' anythin', Miss Philippa. His fur was soppin'.'
Philippa felt bound to say that her father disliked cats.
'The doctor isn't goin' to know.'
Philippa did not argue. She wondered how a cat as large as this one was going to be concealed. But Miggs, it was only too obvious, had made up her mind. Philippa tentatively mentioned lunch for the Free French visitors.
Miggs held up a potato.
'Got some carrots and a heel of cheese. I'll make a veggie pie.'
'Poor things, they probably get that at barracks.'
Miggs sniffed.
'They *are* fighting with us, Miggsy.'
'Didn't see much of them at Dunkirk.'
'You know very well these Frenchmen came over to join us, risking their lives. We ought to welcome them. But veggie pie I suppose it will have to be.'
As Philippa left the kitchen, the cat began to purr like an engine.
Things did not work out the way Trix had expected. When the front door bell rang, she winked at Philippa and flourished a key. But then the girls heard their father's voice in the hall.
'Bother and blow,' whispered Trix, 'goodbye to the gin.'
The door opened to admit, not two people but four. There were Alexandre and Alain, a strange young woman they had never seen before and – wonder of wonders – Theo. Was he joining the party?
The Frenchmen introduced their companion, they did trust they were not trespassing on the doctor's hospitality? Theo

smiled benevolently as they presented Mademoiselle Ghilain. She was a little thing who looked like a bird. She had narrow feet in high-heeled shoes and thin legs and her black hair was as shiny as the wing of a crow. She was dressed in black and white. Alain explained that Annette was his cousin from Brittany. She had recently arrived.

'I am to work at the Centre,' said Annette, whose accented English was surprisingly good.

Alain explained that many Bretons were now arriving. He said this with sombre pride, and exchanged a look with Annette which seemed tender.

Theo bustled about with glasses, produced the gin – Trix and Philippa did not dare to exchange looks – and the Frenchmen presented their usual beer bottles of burgundy. There was animated talk. Philippa thought it very surprising of her father to remain. He talked a good deal to the French girl, and took her over to the window to show her the burned-out conservatory which had become a kind of Tyrrell landmark.

Trix, always indifferent to bad food, had expansively invited everybody to lunch. Theo and Annette Ghilain, still talking to each other, were not listening. But Alain, who had understood, said to Philippa,

'Could you tell your sister that we hope you will do us the honour of lunching with us?'

'At the Centre?' from Trix, when Philippa had translated, 'What fun.'

'No, no,' put in Alexandre, who never let a conversation continue without taking it over, 'Chez Prunier.'

Trix looked delighted. Philippa was embarrassed. She stammered that it was very, very generous, but was not Prunier's a little . . . she stopped, hoping for rescue. She knew, and so should Trix if she'd given it a moment's thought, that the two men hadn't a penny between them.

'But we have money,' said Alain seriously, looking at her through his spectacles. 'We have saved our pay. And there is some South American money Alexandre has changed.'

'Also,' put in Annette Ghilain who, with Theo, had joined them, 'my cousin has sold his watch.'

Horror from Philippa. Admiring silence from Trix.

Alexandre spread out his hands.

'We have money. We wish to use it up. Money does not

80

belong in the pocket. It must continue to roll. *Monsieur le Docteur*. We trust you will join us?'

Theo, who spoke good French, thanked them very pleasantly but regretted he was due at the hospital. Annette said that she, too, was expected back at the Centre and Theo said he would walk there with her. Annette looked gratified and they left the house together.

Miggs greeted the news that the girls and their visitors were lunching out with 'a good thing too.'

Trix darted up to change, coming down soon afterwards in a new dress she had made from some expensive pink crêpe de chine sheets she had bought in Bond Street. Perched on her head was a tiny hat, with a veil floating behind it like a pennant. She carried suede gloves with gold tassels. Alexandre admiringly watched her descending the stairs, and she jumped the last three steps into his arms. They both burst out laughing. Nobody was better at starting off for an expedition than Trix.

The quartet walked down St James', to stop and admire some potato plants growing in tubs which used to contain bay trees.

'What a marvellous idea,' said Philippa.

'The English have ingenuity,' said polite Alain.

Alexandre thought it a pointless gesture. How many pounds of potatoes would be grown from those? A plateful.

The two A's entered Chez Prunier like fish emptied back into a lake. They argued about the table given to them, studied the menu critically and disapproved of the wine. Everybody treated them with deep respect.

When the meal had been ordered to their satisfaction, they turned their attention to the girls. Their conversation, sentence by sentence, was translated by Philippa for her sister. Or rather, Alexandre's conversation. Alain merely listened with an occasional pointed interruption.

Although he was French, said Alexandre, he was not French. He had left his native land twenty years ago, only returning when war broke out and 'idiot that I was, I thought I would be needed.' He told his story to Trix rather than to Philippa, although Trix only understood the flattering expression in his eyes and the smile that flashed with gold.

His hunting ground, he said, had been South America. He had made and lost three fortunes. He had sold guns in revolutions to both sides, he'd helped a president during a *coup d'état* to escape in a motor boat upriver, where a half drowned forest under the water was more dangerous than enemies. He had been paid in suitcases which were filled to bursting with money, and lost it all in a month on gambling. He had returned to the gun-running and the smuggling, and to the company of the most beautiful women in the world.

'Their beauty,' he said, 'strikes the heart with fear. Their hair is so long and thick you cannot lift its shining weight. Their music forbids you to keep still.'

Trix did not mind such talk: it put her on her mettle.

Alain did not bother to hide the fact that the talk irritated him. Alexandre irritated him, he was a cork you could not keep below the water. But destiny had thrown the men together, and they were friends in spite of the laughable difference in their natures.

'Tell your lovely sister,' said Alexandre, 'that I have made a decision – never to go out with women unless Alain is beside me.'

'You're afraid we'll trap you,' said Trix, pleased.

Alain did not join in the laughter. He looked sombre, and Philippa wondered if he had left a girl in Brittany.

Counting their money to pay what Philippa read, upside down, as a very large bill, the young men declared they could afford a taxi back to Kensington. Trix was squashed between them on the seat. Philippa, offered a uniformed knee by Alexandre, preferred to sit on the folding seat.

The journey home was enlivened by an argument between the men as to which of them spoke the better French.

'The Breton of good education has no accent,' said Alain.

Alexandre scoffed. Why, he could distinctly hear the Breton note in Alain's voice, in the vowels and intonations. Even in the expressions Alain used. He was unmistakably from Brittany. Whereas he, continued Alexandre with a wave of one olive-skinned hand, had originally come from Burgundy, had spoken nothing but Spanish for twenty years, but retained an accent of perfection. His French was pure – not a shadow of regional sound. Speaking like an actor, he began to intone Racine.

'Oh Flip, tell them to stop arguing,' interrupted Trix, 'and what's more, tell them they are not to speak another word of French until we get home. They can jolly well have a stab at English. I shall help them.'

This silenced the dispute, and they obeyed her. There was laughter for the rest of the journey.

Released from the task of turning one language into another and back again, Philippa stared out of the window. A man in RAF blue was walking in Green Park – something in his swinging walk made her stomach turn over. Of course it wasn't Barny. But all the way home she looked into the streets, and three times more saw men in RAF blue, with broad shoulders and a relaxed, easy stride. It was like being haunted.

Chaper Six

Lady St Aird received Elaine at Shelton with her customary cold politeness. Elaine was given Miles' bedroom and dressing room. 'If you wish to invite friends to stay, please do,' said her mother-in-law. She spoke as if she still had a staff of servants.

Shelton was very beautiful and Elaine loved it, despite its owners. It had been built before the time when titled landowners had attacks of glory and meglomania. It was not a building to St Aird importance, but a comfortable Cotswold stone manor set in gardens, with a lake and a little wood. The family had lived there for generations. Before the present Shelton was built there had been a Tudor house on the same land. The remains of the older house, low rose-coloured walls, could be seen in the gardens.

Every day except on Sunday, Elaine travelled to Blenheim and back by bus. She had wanted a job to swallow up her time, and she had certainly found one. But even so, breakfast and dinner at Shelton were meals she did not look forward to, and the company of her mother-in-law on Sundays was something that had to be bravely borne.

Elaine was too much in love with Miles to admit a fault except that he was over-devoted to his parents. Once before they married he had said to her, 'I don't know a woman I would rather spend the day with than my Mama.' Elaine had felt jealous. Miles was also deeply fond of his father, whom he respected and admired.

St Aird was a tall white-haired man, with a well-trimmed beard and a long haggard face. He looked older than his years. He had been born at Shelton, grew up there, and left only when he joined the army in the summer of 1914. He fought bravely, won the MC and in 1916 was badly gassed – which explained his lined face and stooping figure. St Aird's meeting with Claire resembled a musical comedy of the Great War. He met her in the military hospital where he was taken after being gassed; she nursed him. But she refused to marry him until after the war ended: it would have stopped her from nursing.

When he was invalided out of the army, he returned home and began to paint. He had talent, took lessons, and one of the Shelton stables was converted into a roomy studio, given the necessary north light by a large new skylight. For twenty years, apart from occasional trips with Claire to Italy, St Aird painted.

The first time that Miles took Elaine to Shelton – it was after picnicking on the river at Oxford – he told Elaine that unless they bearded St Aird in his den Elaine would not get the chance to meet him. Miles took Elaine round to the stables, knocked at one of the doors and shouted, 'Father? It's me.'

St Aird opened the door and looked down at Elaine. She looked up at him as brightly as a robin, with the same quick inquisitive way of holding her head. He shook her hand and that was all. Miles asked if he might show Elaine some of the paintings. The elderly man pulled a few canvases out; they were stacked with their faces to the wall.

Elaine liked pictures and knew a little about them. She was very surprised by St Aird's. They were all of country subjects. There were winter skies and misty trees, smoky November distances, rooks. There were also rainbows, and tangles of poppies in flowering grass. The paintings had poetry and an instant appeal to the heart.

When she exclaimed over them, St Aird looked dark. She innocently asked if he exhibited at the RA. He said, 'No.'

He made it plain that he disliked talking about his work.

Later Miles told her that his father had never exhibited anywhere. He had once given a picture away – he had not wanted to do that but a relative had insisted. He had not sold a single picture since he began to paint.

'But that's unbelievable. They're lovely! Why not?'

'I don't know, poppet. He's a funny old stick, and they're his pictures. His sister Joan marched into the studio one day and said she wanted to buy one for her godchild's twenty-first. He exploded.' Miles burst out laughing, and added, 'He thinks selling things is vulgar.'

Now that she was living at Shelton, Elaine had become used to her father-in-law and his painting. If she was not meant to admire them or even look at them, that was his business. She was bright and polite, but rarely addressed a remark to him, although she always answered pleasantly if he spoke to her. Like a contrary dog, he occasionally advanced towards her and once actually asked her to the studio to show her a new picture. It was of the same horizon and the same wood in other pictures – but it was bleaker. All she did was to nod. He quite cheered up.

The trouble with Shelton was not her father-in-law, misanthropic, talented and usually invisible. It was Lady St Aird. Elaine tried to like her. She tried hard but she simply could not manage it. She and Claire resembled the queens of two islands, set close to one another but in a sea utterly impassable except to Miles. Only he could navigate it, land on either island and find fresh water there and food and welcome. But without him, the islands stayed within sight of each other and immeasurably distant, the sea between them boiling with whirlpools and monsters.

Elaine was perfectly aware of her mother-in-law's good qualities. Claire was brave. She had nursed right through the 1914-18 war in France, and been wounded by shrapnel. Miles told Elaine that his mother had a livid scar running the length of her left arm, and that was why she always wore long sleeves. Her courage was part of her, like her protuberant pale blue eyes. The photographs in the crested family album – Claire was the daughter of an Earl – showed a blank-faced young beauty under a hat stabbed with a large feather quill. Later the same beauty appeared in ugly 1914 nurse's uniform, and later still there she was on her father's arm in wedding satin.

Now Claire's golden hair was a clouded grey which she still wore in the frizzy style of her youth. Like Queen Mary, she stayed in her period. Her tweeds were old and fine, her jewellery was a choice of heavy yellowish diamonds and strings of large valuable pearls.

Claire's courage did not fade with age. Until the war she had hunted, jumping the highest fences as recklessly as a boy and contemptuous of any other rider who had nerves. Matching her courage was a deep unselfconscious patriotism. People in this war simply got on with the job. But Claire talked of England as of a lover.

Bravery, patriotism, and devotion to Miles were undeniable in Claire. But she was cold and snobbish. Elaine did not mind the coldness so much, she herself could be reserved. But she detested the snobbery. She found it hard to believe that it was possible to be such a snob in the 1940s. Surely nobody could treat such nonsense seriously? But Claire did. She measured people by her dusty, dated old standards, she spoke of The Family as a saint might speak of God. She knew the geneaology of the St Airds by heart, and had hung a painted family tree in the dining room, illuminated with shields and crests. Sometimes when she talked of a cousin or uncle or more distant relative, she reminded Elaine of Miggs. Miggs had a passion for the Royal family which was also very detailed. But Miggs' references, to Princess Victoria or Lady Mary Cambridge, were more exalted.

Claire had no critical faculty about the St Airds. Those whom Elaine occasionally met were nothing very exceptional. Most of them were boring or rather stupid, and all were as snobbish as Claire herself. But she shone at them with her pale eyes, and if the daily woman did not arrive on a day when she was entertaining, she cleaned the silver tea pot herself.

It was late in the spring, and the trees in the huge parkland at Blenheim were budding. Ducks appeared on the lake. At lunchtime, Elaine and Marjorie hurried through their good meal so that they could walk in the sun. In the distance, beyond a group of tall trees, the column of Marlborough's Victory rose against a blue and white sky.

The girls had become friends. Both were optimistic and matter-of-fact and they shared an interest in their work, and the fact that their husbands were serving abroad. Marjorie's humour was an antidote to Claire St Aird.

'My mother-in-law is up to her eyes in the WVS,' Elaine remarked, as they walked in the park, 'She lives in her green uniform. This morning she had breakfast in that hideous hat.'

Marjorie giggled. 'Do you realise the country's packed with girls like us, stuck with their in-laws. In peacetime one only has to see them at Christmas, and then they're improved by all the strong drink. But now! I know I'm lucky living with my own parents, but we have to keep *visiting* Bob's and that's torture. His mother is one of those patient women who complains in a gentle voice and makes you want to swear. And his father's a teacher who turns every conversation into a lecture. You may have the St Airds. How would you like the Old Pretender and the Jacobites?'

Escaping into the park was a brief respite for the girls during their days of grinding work. Over a thousand people now worked for MI5 in the palace. The hordes of girls who tripped up the ducal steps each morning, waving their passes, and clattering down again each evening, had signed the Official Secrets Act. The work was secret and dealt in dangerous matters. Yet the atmosphere at Blenheim made Elaine think of a large school. The senior girls who had worked for MI5 from the start of the war had previously been based at Wormwood Scrubs prison. A cell had been allotted to each girl. They spoke nostalgically of The Scrubs. At Blenheim there was no privacy.

The extraordinary place in which Elaine and Marjorie, and all the scores of girls, found themselves did not feel like a palace at all. Sarah Churchill had called it 'that wild unmerciful house', and there it was, Queen Anne's gift to a hero. Everything about Blenheim was on a gigantic scale. The emblems in stone and in marble, the hundred rooms, the lake and bridge and beech-woods all symbolic of battle and victory, the grounds planted by Capability Brown with avenues of trees to represent the Battle of Blenheim. But the noble rooms were divided up by matchboard partitions and metal files the dun colour of war hid the painted walls. The young women who worked in one of the strangest houses in the world scarcely noticed it.

There was no social life there. All day long the typewriters clattered and the place was full of voices. At night the girls went home on the Oxford bus. On their time off they went to London to see boyfriends or husbands. And the palace was not only unsociable, it was freezing cold. During the chill spring it remained an ice house. Marjorie worked in a hut in the Great Courtyard, and wore three sweaters and two pairs of stockings. The wall by her desk ran with damp.

Elaine's boss was a handsome grizzled ex-lawyer called Paul Goodier, who had been educated in Poland and spoke the language as easily as English. He had caught the formality of Polish people, and always said to Elaine when she gave him her work, 'Thank you *so* much.'

Goodier's section was concerned with the Poles who had come to Britain since war broke out – waves of refugees. He and his officers were on the lookout for enemy agents who could have been planted among the innocent. Elaine typed interviews and reports made from carefully sifted information. The work of spy-seeking was difficult: officers had to be judges of people under suspicion, or of the evidence against them. The curious thing Elaine found was that she could not remember a twentieth of all that she typed from week to week.

88

'I agree. I'm the same,' said Marjorie blithely.

'I suppose it is our subconscious working. We don't realize it, but we're deliberately making our minds blank because the stuff is secret.'

'Speak for yourself, Elaine. My mind's a blank anyway.'

Elaine worked in the first floor in a room much envied by Marjorie for its small coal fire. It overlooked a pretty terrace where she sometimes saw the Duchess of Marlborough walking up and down in the spring sunshine, pushing a pram. 'That baby,' said Marjorie who was always up-to-the-minute with palace jokes, 'is known as the Duke's war effort.'

Travelling to and from Woodstock, Elaine watched the slow spring begin. She thought of the shrubs in the garden at St Helen's which she had watched budding during her child-hood. She knew the corner where the snowdrops came up first. She missed her family. Telephoning them was unsatis-factory, for Trix was rarely at home and when Elaine did manage to speak to her, her conversation was about young men Elaine had never met. Theo was brief and monosyllabic. Miggs was the same. This left Philippa who was the warmest, but even she was not communicative. Elaine was delighted when Philippa actually rang her one bright evening to say she had some leave due to her and would it be possible to come to Shelton?

'I'd love to stay with you if it's allowed.'

'Lady St Aird said I could ask people. Hold on and I'll check,' said Elaine eagerly.

Claire was in the drawing room, listening to the wireless and knitting the usual sweater in khaki-coloured wool. She knitted or sewed at any time when her work for the WVS, or in the vegetable garden or with the chickens, did not occupy her time. She glanced up.

'My sister Philippa has a few days off from her work for the hospital,' said Elaine, spelling it out because she required Claire's approval. 'Might I ask her to Shelton for a day or two?'

Claire continued to knit so quickly that her body and the chair shook.

'I have told you that you may invite your family or friends at any time.'

She did not add 'except that young sister', whose appearance at the wedding had appalled her. She sometimes wondered how Elaine would take her refusal to receive Beatrix.

It was a relief to Philippa to leave St Helen's and take the Oxford train. She had not heard a word from Barny for nearly three months; it was two and a half since she had written to him. The silence was a knell. She knew she would never see him again. What made it worse was that Jane Alwynne, who knew everything about the RAF through her husband, an air vice marshal, had told her the Eagle Squadron was now operational. The following evening it was on the nine o'clock news.

'The Eagle Squadron took part in a sweep over the French coast, both attacking and successfully beating off the enemy.'

Philippa had left the room and rushed up to her bedroom, despite the blitz. It was terrible to know the Eagles were flying, that Barny by now was probably dead. She knew her feelings were exaggerated and out of proportion – what right had she to feel like a war widow? He had been an incident in the shifting patterns of the war. But there it was, the pain inside her that would not go away.

She enjoyed the few days with Elaine in Oxfordshire. Her sister prevented her from giving in to a gloom which seemed to Philippa to taste like a London fog. Trix's way of cheering her had been to set Philippa's hair in a pageboy bob, produce young men, and wink at her on the dance floor. Elaine merely chatted and smiled and kept her busy. Claire was polite. She had decided that the visitor was quiet and well-mannered, and that her clothes were passable.

The rambling old house was the right place for wartime domesticity. The sisters made jelly from the withered yellowish apples, the last from the autumn crop, which they found in an apple loft. They tried out Ministry of Food recipes, and made a cake with raw carrot, margarine and rum essence. They dug in the kitchen garden and in the evenings they darned the heavy linen sheets embroidered with oversized coronets.

They were restful together. Elaine never looked at her probingly with her gentle blue eyes, and never asked her hurtful questions.

Claire left them alone most of the time. She was much occupied with her WVS work, from peeling buckets full of potatoes to visiting sick young women whose husbands were in the Forces. During the day, when Elaine was at Blenheim, Philippa took the bus to Oxford. She went to the cinema, and browsed in bookshops. One afternoon she spent in the public library, reading about Louisiana in the *Encyclopaedia Britannica*.

Her last afternoon at Shelton was on Sunday. The sisters walked to church, then came home and decided to weed in the kitchen garden. As they came into the house, they heard Claire calling.

'Elaine?' The voice was soft but curiously brusque.

Claire was at her desk in the drawing room.

'Miles telephoned.'

Elaine went as white as a sheet.

'Is he all right?'

'Perfectly. He's in Liverpool. His ship is in for a boiler clean, apparently. He was in a fire raid on the docks last night, he said. Most exciting.'

Elaine was still as pale as death.

'Was his ship hit?'

'I have no idea. He couldn't give any details, of course. He said it was a lot of fun. There's no chance of his getting any leave. But one did not expect it. Well, now. Shall we have tea?'

Philippa said she would get it and left them.

The Shelton kitchens were large enough to cook dinner for thirty people. The floors were of brick, there was a black kitchen range, a scullery with a hand pump for water, a flower room with shelves of vases of every size, age and shape. The Tyrrells still had Miggs, but the St Airds had lost all their servants when war came; Claire encouraged them to join up. Elderly help arrived erratically from the village sometimes.

Philippa laid a silver tray, and made the tea in a silver teapot shaped like an Aladdin's lamp with an ivory handle. At Shelton the Minton china was used every day, and the Georgian sugar tongs, although the sugar ration was down to four ounces a week.

Elaine's cheeks were pink again when she came into the kitchen.

'Oh Flip. If only I'd been here.'

'But he's going to ring again, isn't he?'

'If he can.'

'When?'

91

'She didn't ask.'

At seven the telephone in the hall rang. The St Airds were changing for dinner, but Elaine and Philippa were already dressed and downstairs. Elaine started violently, and ran.

Philippa heard her sister speak in a voice she had never heard before in her life.

'Miles. My dear one.'

Philippa shut the drawing room door.

Philippa had been glad to go to Shelton for a change of scene and even more glad to see Elaine, but when she came back to London she found that she was not refreshed. The uncanny night silences of the country did not make for peaceful sleep to ears accustomed to the blitz. Philippa had woken more often at Shelton than during the deafening nights under the billiard table. And Elaine's serenity, a kind of settled spirit in her despite her not enjoying Shelton, had made Philippa more aware than ever of her own unhappy heart. Both the still midnight which had lapped round the old house, and Elaine's love for Miles, had disturbed her. She was in love too, but *her* love was absurd. All the way home she planned how she could soon escape into the WAAF.

When Philippa arrived at Chicheley Buildings the next morning, she toiled up the stairs, feeling very nervous. She tried to settle to work, opening a shabby ledger and filling in a few cheques which had arrived since her absence. Poor Princess Victoria Hospital was poor in many ways.

Mrs Alwynne arrived at midday, her arms full of files, followed by an elderly man weighed down with more. Jane had recruited him from the street outside – he had been pounced upon on his way to buy some sandwiches, and looked bewildered.

'Could you place the files on the table? Very civil of you. Many thanks for your kindness.'

He went out hastily, sensing that if he lingered he would be given further duties.

Jane, smiling at Philippa, marched into her office and called to Philippa to bring her book. Philippa thought the time did not look ripe for breaking bad news. But when would there be a time to tell Jane one wished to leave her? Jane Alwynne was a big, fat, wonderfully-bosomed woman with a noble face which would have suited a general. She had coiled grey hair, a straight nose and eyes as bright and sharp as gimlets. Her clothes were expensive, her blouses real silk, her RAF brooch winked with large diamonds.

'I want a word, Philippa – '

'Mrs Alwynne, may I have a word?'

Both spoke at once. They laughed.

'You speak first, child.'

'Oh no, please.'

'Very well. What I have to say is brief enough. Are you considering enlisting in the WAAF?'

Jane was uncanny.

'Ah. I see I am right. You've always had a penchant for flyers. I suppose you have been reading about the WAAF's glamorous jobs, working in the flying control rooms, air ambulances, radio location and so on.'

'They do marvellous work.'

'Certainly they do, I only wish I were in uniform myself. But where would my charities be if I let my heart rule my head? We must stop talking like a recruiting leaflet. I don't want you to leave and I don't think you should.'

'But there must be lots of other people you could get – '

'Nonsense. There is nobody. It was an answer from heaven when you agreed to work here. I have managed to keep you so far, but I know very well you are havering. Now. Let us talk.'

Jane talked. Her voice was youthful and full of vitality, the voice that forced people to give her money. Girls, she said, joined the women's services by the thousand and the recruiting for the WAAF was a runaway success, she had met one of the commandants recently. As for the Wrens, they were turning girls away. There was the ATS, of course. But she knew Philippa cared most for flyers.

'Now, child. You have been in our hospital. You know the straits they are in. Can you in all honesty say they do not need you?'

The Princess Victoria Hospital for Children, in Surrey, had been built in late Victorian times, opened by the old Queen's daughter. It had been a fine hospital then. But the years and lack of money had begun to destroy it. Kitchens were antiquated,

Out-Patients in a gloomy basement, lighting in disrepair. There were no dimmed lights in the wards at night, the furniture was old and difficult to clean, the children's cots heavy and nearly worn out, the cumbersome lifts went wrong. Philippa had been shown all these things.

'And you remember Sister's office!' finished Jane.

Taking Philippa to visit the hospital had been Jane's way of binding Philippa to the cause. Jane had many good causes. She fought to keep anyone who unwittingly strayed into her circle of good works.

'Say you'll stay at least for the next few months,' said Jane, fixing her with bright eyes.

Philippa was beaten.

It was true, she thought travelling home, Shelton had done her no good; it had not even strengthened her will against Jane. And after the country, London looked dirtier and more damaged than before she had gone away. When you were here all the time, you were used to the mess and greyness and looming danger. But after looking through windows at lawns and yew hedges, and smelling the green spring, your eyes were different. D'Abernon Road depressed her. And at home the burnt conservatory looked as grim as a gibbet.

Miggs was on the telephone.

'Don't forget to gargle with salt and water three times a day, Miss Bassett.'

Ringing off, she looked at Philippa guardedly.

'Your sister's out with some chap in the Black Watch. The doctor's on his rounds. Had your tea?'

It was as if Philippa had never been away. And there was no letter for her.

She felt restless and jumpy, she did not know why. The old house did not welcome her. Her sisters were not here, her father out, Miggs unwelcoming. She wondered if her nerves meant the usual expectancy of a raid. Perhaps this one will be it. Perhaps we'll be hit. Oh, stop being a fool, she told herself, and went up to have a bath.

Trix's extravagances – where did she get hold of all the things and who paid for them? – filled the bathroom shelves. There were unpatriotically expensive creams, geranium soaps, almost unobtainable shampoos. Philippa had a slow bath but it was only five inches deep. That was what the Government asked you to do, and what Trix never did. People said even the King and Queen had five-inch deep baths now.

She washed her hair, and rolled it in a towel before going back to her bedroom. The feeling of nerves had not left her, and the prospect of the long night alone, with her father out in the streets and Miggs in the cellar, filled her with a rare sensation of panic. She dressed again, and rubbed her hair dry and set it in the way Trix had taught her. But she had not enough grips. The essential little metal things had disappeared from the shops months ago: it was only Trix who had boxes of them.

Walking down the passage, she went into Trix's room. The place was wild with disorder, Trix had clearly left in a tearing hurry. Her wardrobe door hung open, a pair of satin and lace cami-knickers was on the floor among a heap of silk stockings. Her jewel case was open, its glittering contents scattered among the face powder on the dressing table. There was a box from Harrods on a chair. It contained, half wrapped in tissue paper, some pink French knickers. They were folded to show lines of embroidery in pale blue above one leg. The embroidered words, like a poem, ran:

> Oh please do not do that
> Oh please do not
> Oh please do
> Oh!!!

Raising her eyebrows, Philippa shut the box and the jewel case, and sat down at the dressing table to look for a box of hair grips. She couldn't find any. Her still wet hair was falling from the coiled towel. She sighed, weighed down by a depression like an intense headache.

The make-up drawer was crammed, not only with little pots and boxes, lipsticks, nail files and combs, but with letters. Some of them had H.M.Ships stamped on them. All were obviously from young men. Two or three lay on top of a silver-topped box of face powder, and Philippa picked them up to find the grips. Automatically arranging them neatly, she saw something. A feeling went through her that was so sharp she lost her breath. Swallowing, she looked again.

Among the letters was a bill. It was a hotel bill headed

Amesbury Arms, Buckinghamshire. At the head of the bill in ink was written: 'Room 24. Pilot Officer and Mrs Duval.'

She stared at it. For a while she was so stunned that it did not make sense. Pilot Officer and Mrs –

And then she understood.

But it couldn't be true. Trix didn't know him. It wasn't possible. The two names danced before her eyes, conjuring up such terrible pictures that she couldn't bear what her imagination created. Springing up with a groan, she fled from the room.

Chapter Seven

Philippa lay on her bed like somebody who is bleeding and terrified to move. She did not know how long she lay there. The raid began and she listened indifferently. Hours afterwards came the long level sound of the All Clear with its note of safety. She did not stir. The towel had fallen from her hair which, in untidy spirals, was bone dry.

She had the sensation that there was a stone in her chest, and that was what was making her bleed. When she moved it moved too, falling and crushing her ribs and breaking her veins. She kept thinking, 'I must talk to her. I must know the truth.' But she did know it. She wanted to hear it spoken, to be poisoned and suffer more.

Perhaps Trix would not come home tonight, she so often did not return. That seemed unbearable, and all Philippa did was to strain her ears for the sound of her sister coming into the house. At last, at about two or three in the morning, she heard a noise. It was a taxi stopping in d'Abernon Road. She listened. There was the faint sound of voices. A stifled laugh. A closing door. Then an interval. And then the staircase creaked.

Crawling off her bed, her eyes accustomed to the dark, she went to her door. A pale figure was coming toward her.

'Flip? What are *you* doing up at this hour!'

The whisper was friendly with recent kisses.

'I want to talk to you.'

'Sh! Pa may be home. Come to my room.'

Trix slipped past, carrying her shoes which she swung by the straps. The curtains in her room had not been drawn, and muttering 'Darn it' she tugged them close. She switched on a dressing table light.

'Golly, you're still dressed. Have you been on the tiles too?'

Trix yawned and grinned like an urchin. She wore a short dress of bright green taffeta, a black velvet ribbon trailed from her hair. Her face was pale with tiredness.

Philippa swallowed.

'I came into your room for some grips. I found this.'

Trix glanced at the hotel bill in her sister's hand and made a giggling face.

'Naughty. You shouldn't peek. I know I shouldn't keep things like that, but they do make me laugh sometimes.'

'*Barny Duval.*'

'Oh lor, are you shocked? I've often wondered if I should tell you and Elaine about my odd affairs, but you're both so funny if I mention sex. Are you upset? Honestly, Flip, it isn't important. Lots of girls now – '

'You mean you've done it before?'

'Now you never thought that Yank was my first? I only met him the other night by chance. He came around looking for you and found me instead. He's not bad, is he?'

Philippa ran out of the room to the bathroom and was violently sick.

Trix was surprised when her sister did not appear the next morning. She tapped on Philippa's door and called, but there was no reply. Standing outside the door, Trix wrinkled her short nose. She can't be putting on an act because of what I told her last night, she thought, that really is stoopid. Is she so prim? What an old stick-in-the-mud. Sex is going to rear its ugly head eventually, even with Flip. Why does she take my goings-on so seriously? I don't.

When she trailed downstairs in her dressing-gown, even Trix did not dare to appear in transparent chiffon with *Toi et Moi* embroidered on the naked bosom in front of Miggs, she told the old nurse about Philippa.

Miggs hobbled upstairs and banged loudly.

'Breakfast, lady! You overslept?'

A hoarse voice replied. Philippa said she was ill and would Miggs telephone to tell Mrs Alwynne she wouldn't be coming in to work.

'That's all very fine and large but what's wrong with you? If you're ill, I'll fetch the doctor,' shouted Miggs, offended at the locked door.

Trix went into the morning room, drank some black coffee, she was uninterested in food, and telephoned a girlfriend about the day's entertainment. After another good natured call through her sister's door, she went to bath and dress and left, en route for Harrods.

Miggs donned her white overall, answered the door and the telephone, and took up some tea which she put outside Philippa's door. 'Tea, lady.' The door stayed shut.

Returning to the kitchen and the company of the ginger cat, Miggs stood reflecting for a moment. Then she went to Theo's study. He was reading his morning mail.

'Want a word, Doctor.'

For one alarmed moment he thought she had decided to leave him and join the evacuees in the country. He had changed his mind about her going and had realized how much he relied on her. Then, with sharper alarm from his old childish love for her, he thought she might be ill. But she was her usual solid, if crooked-shaped, self.

'Trouble,' she said.

Relief made him angry.

'What are you talking about?'

'Your daughter's in some kind of pickle. She's locked herself in her room and won't come out.'

'Don't bother me, Miggs. Miss Beatrix is a silly child.'

'*She's* all right. Who's talkin' about her? Miss Philippa's the one.'

He looked astounded. 'Miss Philippa? Is she ill?'

He got to his feet.

'Perfectly all right when she came home last night. It's my guess she isn't ill at all. She's troubled.'

He sat down again, saying with asperity that Philippa was a grown woman and wouldn't thank him to interfere with her private business. It was some young man, no doubt.

'No doubt,' echoed Miggs, giving him a sharp look that Theo had seen when he was ten years old. She realized he was out of his depth. He gave orders and snapped people's heads off, and when the fancy took him he was very pleasant, but the only troubles *he* understood were those he diagnosed. He tapped a patient's chest or looked at the whites of his eyes. He took the pulse and blood pressure, and he asked, 'Where exactly is the pain?' Miggs wondered where exactly Philippa's pain was. She knew there must be one.

'Thought you ought to know,' she said, and left him.

99

Later that day there was another tap on Philippa's door, a brisk rat-tat-tat.

Philippa was worn out with thinking and sick of the room in which she had imprisoned herself but she still cried hoarsely, 'Miggs, go away.'

'It isn't Miggs. It's Elaine.'

Astonishment made Philippa unlock the door. Elaine, still wearing her camel hair coat with the collar turned up, did not wait to be asked in, but advanced slowly, shutting the door behind her. She took off her coat and sat down.

'Miggs rang Shelton. She said you're in trouble.'

'Why can't she mind her own business?'

'You locking yourself in is her business. And stop prowling about like an animal in a cage. Are you pregnant?'

'What the hell are you talking about?'

'I take it you are not. Then has somebody you love been killed?'

The questions disgusted Philippa.

'It's nothing like that. Nothing like that.'

Elaine examined her sister, whose crumpled clothes, ashen face and manner made her look slightly mad.

'I shan't go until you tell me.'

'It won't do any good.'

Elaine was silent. She saw that Philippa was trying to get the courage to speak. At last Philippa said, speaking fast, 'I went into Trix's room to look for some hairgrips. I found a hotel bill.'

'And?'

'There's a man I know. In the Eagle Squadron. I don't know why I didn't introduce you to him. I suppose I wanted to keep it a secret – being fond of him, I mean. He – he came here looking for me when I was at Shelton. Trix was here instead. She went out with him.'

She was too desolate to hear her sister's unsurprised sigh.

'What you mean is that she went to bed with him.'

Philippa shuddered and said nothing. Elaine leaned back in the chair. She felt tired. How often she had wondered about Trix since the time Miles put the idea into her head. 'I'm not at all sure I approve of your young sister,' he said. Later he spelled it out. Elaine had loyally denied it, but the words had stuck.

'We must talk to her,' she said at last.

'I couldn't bear to.'

'Somebody must. Does she know you're in love with this man?'

'Who said anything about –'

Elaine interrupted with exasperation. 'Of course you are, it's written all over you. Why else are you in this state? I'm sure it's been a horrible shock. But Flip – think! You must see it is not Trix's fault. She didn't know how you felt about him. How could she? Certainly it's her fault if she goes to bed with men. I only hope to God that Father doesn't find out.'

'You're very broad-minded all of a sudden.'

'Of course I am not. I am just facing unpleasant facts. How do you feel about him now?'

'I never want to see him again.'

I don't expect, thought Elaine, when he knows what has happened he will want to see you. In her mind she saw the American arriving here at the house, hoping to see Philippa. Whom did he find instead? A girl modelled on Hollywood, a fair-haired mantrap. Elaine saw that Trix could be irresistible if she set her mind to it.

'I must talk to Trix. Where is she?'

'How should I know?'

'Oh, stop being so *rude*. I came to London to help and that's what I intend to do, so just stop trying to make things worse. Miggs will know where Trix is, she always does. I shall see Trix and hear the whole story. I won't have you two becoming enemies. I refuse to allow it. You'll have to find a way of forgiving her, Philippa, and you must remember that she had no idea in the world how you felt.'

'I suppose she sleeps with everybody.'

'Perhaps she does,' said Elaine with a cold dryness like her father's. 'In which case it's time I knew about it. Apparently it's up to me to do our mother's job.'

She walked out.

She had an effect on Philippa, who washed her face, changed her clothes, and telephoned Jane Alwynne to say she would be at work the next day.

It was true that Miggs always knew Trix's whereabouts. The girl amused her. Miggs saw Trix as the *Belle Dame Sans Merci*, wreaking vengeance on the male sex. Trix's triumphs over men were also Miggs'. Pressed by Elaine, she said grudgingly that Trix would be staying at the Brevet Club off West Halkin Street and would be there 'sure as a gun' by six to change into her party dress. Trix was always at parties.

Elaine telephoned the Brevet, and was told that Miss Tyrrell was a member, and had booked there for tonight. Elaine then rang an uninterested Lady St Aird to say she would be back tomorrow, and would go direct to Blenheim Palace.

The Brevet Club was small and no place to be in a raid. It was a poky eighteenth century cottage that had once been occupied by ostlers. It stood in a cobbled mews. A similar house nearby had disappeared into rubble. There was a notice in the club's narrow entrance hall, 'Best Shelter is Knightsbridge Tube but you're welcome in our cellars. Bring your own blanket.'

The porter told Elaine that Miss Tyrrell was in and would she take the stairs? The lift was out of order for the duration.

Elaine found the door at the end of a narrow corridor and knocked.

'It's Elaine.'

The door opened and Trix, exclaiming, 'Of all the!' put thin arms round her and gave her a scented kiss.

'How did you find me? I bet it was sneaky old Miggsy. Why are you in London? Oh jeepers. You've heard the ghoulish news.'

Guilty and grinning, Trix returned to her dressing table and began to brush her long hair.

'Wasn't it,' she said, 'the damnedest luck?'

'*Trix*. I have not come from Oxford, leaving my job when they needed me, to have a jolly chat about luck. Do you sleep with all your boyfriends? Is that how you usually end the evening?'

Trix made a moue, turning her red lips into a kind of trumpet.

'I wish you wouldn't carry on as if I were the whore of Babylon.'

'Answer my question.'

'Okay, okay. Yes, I've slept with a few guys. You're going to say since when? Since three years ago, as it happens. So it's nothing very dramatic or new, is it?'

'*You were fifteen.*'

'No, I wasn't, it was my sixteenth birthday.'

Now that she was launched on the story, Trix thought she might as well tell it in full. Did Elaine remember all three of them being asked to a party at a house in Bray? A kind of birthday party for Trix, but the people were mostly friends of the parents, most of them quite old. There had been a solicitor. Trix couldn't remember his name. Skipton? Skeffington? He'd made a pass at her and wanted to dance with her all the evening, he had been jolly boring and she had cold-shouldered him. Well, that night very late he'd come into her room. It had not occurred to her to lock her door. She had been quite scared at first because he was so big and so drunk, and he'd caught hold of her and slobbered all over her and ugh! given her great wet kisses and he kept saying 'was that nice?'. When she tried to get away he hit her. She thought of screaming, but he put his hand over her mouth, and then she thought of jumping out of the window, but it was on the second floor and too high, and there was a stone terrace underneath, 'not even a rose bed to fall into'. In the end he'd sort of shoved her on to the bed and was on top of her and before she knew what was happening 'he'd done it.'

'But that is rape.' Elaine was cold with horror.

Trix gave her a candid look.

'No, I can't pretend it was, darling. I thought it disgusting, him grunting and heaving away, and then I began to think it was rather interesting. And I realized that with somebody I liked, someone young, you know, I was definitely going to enjoy it. Poor old thing, he was pathetic next day. And he gave me twenty pounds to buy myself something. After that, of course, there were others. I mean to say, why not? I was quite in love with Alastair. And my New Zealander was wizard. And Canadian Dave, oh, and some others. You mustn't think I let them do it all the time. Only when I like them. Love them, sort of. I know you and Flip think I'm dreadful and I'm sure Flip is a virgin, but I am *not* dreadful and lots of girls do the same. It's what happens now.'

Elaine said nothing. She was thinking of the middle-aged solicitor coming into her sixteen-year-old sister's bedroom and hitting her and 'heaving away'. What a description for love. The old virtues were falling into rubble too. Men soon to go into danger wanted to make love before the journey. Why shouldn't they take what Trix cheerfully gave away, getting in return the scent and meals and dances and £10 notes?

Trix was looking at her warily, waiting for the row. It then began to occur to her that there wasn't going to be one. She had been right to confess. And it was going to save an awful lot of boring old lies.

103

'You know I think it is very wrong what you are doing.'

'Sorry.'

'Don't be impertinent. You are not sorry. But there is nothing to be done about you. The harm is done.'

Trix's gardenia cheeks suddenly turned crimson.

'For crying out loud! You talk in a holy voice as if I were a fallen woman. I *knew* you would. I just wish you could hear yourself. What's so terrible about a bit of sex with someone you like? What harm, as you call it, does it do? It's good for the man and for me too. All my girlfriends do it.'

Elaine felt that Trix on morality was more than she could stand. She said coldly that they had talked about it enough. What Trix did was wrong and there was an end to it.

Trix furiously shrugged. She was not used to being told off. Her diet was thick sweet slices of sexual admiration. She began to brush her hair again.

'It wasn't my fault about Barny Duval,' she resumed in a sulky voice. 'You have to admit that. Flip never breathed a word that she knew anyone in the Eagles. He turned up one evening looking for her while she was with you. I didn't know he was anybody special. He just said she was a swell girl, and they'd met on the night of the fire. He hung about, and I gave him what was left of the sherry. Then he asked if I'd like to go for a drive, he'd got hold of a car and some petrol. So off we went. We drove to the country and had supper in a pub –'

She shrugged.

'You know how it is.'

'No, Trix. I don't.'

Trix threw her eyes heavenwards. She had always known that if ever her sisters found out about her sexual adventures they would disapprove and be pious and Victorian. It annoyed her. She found to her surprise that she disliked losing their good opinion. If only Flip had not seen that Yank first. Or if only, more to the point, poor virgin Flip was not so sentimental.

'So we made love. Of course we did. He's a pilot isn't he? He flew over France this week and almost bought it. He had *twelve* Messerschmitts on his tail. Poor Barny,' she said, smiling slightly, 'I don't like him more than other men. He's a bit slow tempo'd for me. Sort of drawling. Only sharpens up when he talks about flying. Do you want me to tell him I won't see him again?'

She looked expectant, anxious to do her good deed.

'No. If he rings simply say you have another date and don't mention Flip.'

'Okay. I bet she never speaks to me again,' she added, sounding like a child.

Elaine could not help marvelling. Everything that Trix believed was anathema to herself and Philippa, just as everything *they* believed she was sure Trix despised and pitied. All they had in common was the Tyrrell nose, a streak of impulsiveness from their father, the past, their parents. When she said goodbye Trix suddenly said,

'Swell of you, coming to town specially.'

While she was waiting for a bus at Knightsbridge, Elaine thought about her sister's life of casual sex with men who were almost strangers. She saw that Trix, who did nothing for the war except embrace its soldiers, had a curious quality of being part of everything that happened. She belonged to this war, moving confidently through the dark days and fiery nights. And she belonged to the men who were fighting. They were not like those chaste admirers who used to take Philippa and herself to Hurlingham. They were lovers. It is Flip and I who are out of date, she thought.

She found Philippa in the kitchen, stirring something in a saucepan, the two crescents of dark hair falling down and concealing her face. She did not look up.

'I saw Trix. She is very, very sorry for hurting you.'

No reply.

'Oh, stop doing that!' snapped Elaine, suddenly exhausted by both sisters. 'I was not supposed to take any leave. It was given to me as a big favour. You can at least be civilized enough to listen when I speak to you. I might tell you that nothing is worse than minding other people's business, it is boring and detestable. And don't say why do I do it. It's no pleasure to me. But Mother is dead.'

Philippa pushed aside the saucepan, and sat down at the kitchen table. The daylight was almost gone. The whitewashed walls, the grey of Philippa's sweater, the shine on Elaine's hair were fading.

'You think me unsympathetic. That isn't true. But,' said Elaine carefully, 'would it surprise you to know that he's by no means the first?'

'She said something about that. I wouldn't listen.'

'You should have. It has some comfort in it for you. It would be worse if she were in love with him. Don't shudder like that, Flip, we have to talk or it will go bad inside you. We're going to have to get used to Trix. She is not like us.'

'She's a tart.'

'What a word. She's eighteen and growing up at a time when nothing is as it was, and nobody believes the things *we* still believe. She's had a lot of lovers.'

'How revolting.'

'Why are you only against her? What about him?'

'It's Trix who catches people.'

'You used to laugh about that.'

Philippa looked down and the two crescents of her hair met across her face. When she glanced up again her face was so strained yet so expressionless that Elaine could have wept.

'I suppose I'll get over it eventually. At present I dread even looking at her. As for all that sleeping with men, I don't think it's right, I don't, I don't! Other girls have men wanting them in this war. They've kept their standards. Why can't she?'

Ah, thought Elaine. Now I understand.

She left St Helen's the following morning. As she was walking down the road she remembered something Miles had once said to her. 'Oh, you! You're the cement of the family.' The cement she'd been trying to spread was pathetically thin between the bricks. Was it any use at all?

While Elaine was on her way to Oxford, and Philippa at work, Trix was in her bedroom in the Brevet Club, drinking coffee and polishing her charm bracelet. She always took a duster wrapped in tissue paper in her suitcase for this purpose. She cleaned her bracelet daily, as a Guardsman did his buttons. The bracelet grew more crowded every week as, added to the gold pigs and horseshoes, the Eiffel Towers and Victorian seals, were buttons gallantly cut off their uniforms by Polish officers, New Zealanders, Frenchmen and Canadians. There was a pair of wings, and a naval crown with curved sails like the petals of an inverted tulip.

She stood up and twisted in front of the long mirror which was inside the old-fashioned wardrobe door. She straightened her stocking seams, added Vaseline to her dark lipstick. Her movements were leisurely but not her thoughts. Jingling and jangling

106

down the stairs, she liked her noisy bracelet, she went to the telephone in the passage and dialled a number. While she waited, she examined the toe of her cyclamen coloured wedge shoe.

'Mrs Mason? It's Trix. You very sweetly said that while Zena's on leave I could stay. Could I really? Today? That's lovely.'

Trix returned to St Helen's, packed a suitcase, gave her address and telephone number to Miggs, and said she'd be away some time.

'The Masons, eh? They're made of money,' said Miggs, approving.

The house had not felt exactly welcoming to Trix, particularly when she went past Philippa's bedroom. It was only when she was in the taxi and it had left d'Abernon Road and turned into Kensington High Street that she began to sing.

> If I only had wings
> One little pair of those elusive things
> All day long I'd be in the sky
> up on high
> Talking to the birdies who pass me by
> How the fellows would stare
> To see me zooming past them in the air . . .

The driver caught her eye in his driving mirror, 'Very nice, Miss. Going to sing for us on the wireless?'

Trix smiled prettily and finished her song,

> I'd be so careless and bold
> That when the story of my deeds was told
> I'd get my picture in the papers
> And it would proudly say
> The RAF and me had had another good day.

Philippa found a letter on her dressing table when she returned from work. The sight of Trix's bold illiterate handwriting made her feel slightly ill. The letter was brief.

107

Gone to the Masons for a bit, Zena's back and there'll be
parties. Anyway, you want a rest from me being around. It's
rotten and I'm ever so sorry. I do feel ropey about it. Luv – I
mean it –

                    Trix

It hadn't occurred to Philippa that her sister would swiftly
remove herself from trouble. At first all she felt was relief. She
had been dreading even seeing Trix, and as for hearing her speak
of Barny, it made her want to be sick. But when the relief wore
off, she felt dully resentful. The person who was tactfully absent
somehow put herself in the right. It was the one who stayed
behind who was left to wallow. Philippa hadn't suffered from real
jealousy before, she had no idea what a degrading experience it
was. And it was all the worse because she had been dotingly fond
of Trix, proud of her beauty and her conquests; now she saw her
only in the lurid light of hideous imagining. She saw Trix and
Barny naked together and it made her ill. When she managed to
conquer thoughts which resembled a Victorian engraving of hell,
she was jealous of less unforgivable things; of the hours they had
been together; of Barny looking with frank admiration at her
little sister, the sexy one; of Trix laughing and alluring. She
thought of the food they had eaten and the flirtation starting as
gradually as gentle music, leading at last to the right true end.

Miggs saw that Philippa was silent and self-absorbed, but she
did nothing about it. If Miss Elaine couldn't fix things up, she
certainly couldn't. Philippa looked peaky but she'd recover. She
was young. Miggs was more concerned with today's question –
would the cat eat whale meat?

Philippa made no effort to get over her masochistic jealousy.
Elaine would have done so and even Trix, supposing she were in
a situation where another woman supplanted her, would have
refused to brood. Philippa let herself suffer. She worked exag-
geratedly hard for Jane Alwynne, who merely egged her on.

In the past months, like thousands upon thousands of Londoners, Philippa had learned to sleep through the thump and
thunder of the blitz. People who had never lived through
bombardments had no idea how soundly one could sleep. But
now misery, not fear, kept her awake. The blitz was a background, like the roar of rough seas to a sailor. One night she
scarcely slept at all and when she finally dozed she woke feeling

108

very cold from having unconsciously thrown off a blanket. Her father was standing by the billiard table.

'I am sorry to wake you, Philippa.'

She sat up, yawning, and asked if the All Clear had gone. He said that it had. He had been in Shepherd's Bush where another pub, the third, had been hit. She realized through the haze of sleep that he had come in to tell her something. At this hour? She crawled out from under the table and pulled on her dressing-gown. She saw by the wall clock that it was half past five.

'Yes, Father?' She was awake enough to give her voice a note of resentment.

'When I got back to hospital there was a man in Casualty from the Welsh Guards. He said the Café de Paris has had a direct hit.'

'Oh God!'

'Does Beatrix go there?'

'Often. Oh God! What shall we do?'

She had begun to tremble. He put down his bag and calmly asked where Trix was staying. Philippa went into the hall and found the telephone pad. Her father took it from her shaking hand.

'She's with the Masons,' she said.

He dialled the number.

'Mr Mason? I do apologize for this early call but – yes – the Café de Paris. I see . . . yes . . . thank you.'

He replaced the telephone.

'Beatrix and her friends returned home an hour ago. They had booked a table at the Café de Paris. But changed their minds at the last minute and went elsewhere.'

He looked suddenly quite old.

'I must get to my bed. Tell Miggs to put off any patients until this afternoon.'

Philippa trailed back to the billiard room and lay down. For a few minutes she had believed Trix was dead, and that *she* had killed her. She had not forced her sister to go away, for when was Trix not out enjoying herself? What had made Philippa believe she'd caused Trix's death had been her own jealous hatred which had released the devil from the abyss. But Trix was alive. It was the hatred which was dead.

When she arrived at the office that morning she saw that Jane

Alwynne had been crying. Two of her friends had been at the Café de Paris, young Guards officers, both dead. Her niece had had all her fingers blown off. During the day Jane spoke again about the tragedy. Everybody she knew seemed to have had somebody killed or wounded there. The loss of life had been terrible for the place was packed with dancers. Only one girl at the party of Jane's friends had survived. She had been on the dance floor when the bomb burst, had been hurled across the room, her dress torn off, her hair burned, but she was completely unhurt. Blast was like destiny. It was inexplicable.

It was spring now, the daylight clear and pale, and that evening, saddened and subdued, Philippa walked home down d'Abernon Road. She felt worn out from lack of sleep. She stopped and looked over the gate of an old house. It was roofless now, but friends of the family's had lived there before the war. Children had played among the shrubs, and there had been a swing under the pear tree. Now the garden was going wild and branches were interlacing. By summer it would be a small jungle. On the unkempt lawn, she saw a patch of mauve crocuses. She trailed through the open gate of St Helen's. A figure in Air Force blue was sitting on the front steps. It was Barny.

Chapter Eight

He stood up and gave a mocking salute, his cap at a rakish angle.
She thought she was going to faint. She felt giddy, as if she were
falling. Before she had taken a few steps he had hurried to her
and seized her hands.

'Good to see you! I wasn't sure which of you girls I'd find. I
daresay Trix told you we met up when you were out of town. It's
so good to see you,' he repeated, gripping her hands and smiling
like a boy. She had no time to recover but managed to mutter
something about being surprised. He walked up the steps with
her to the front door. Still talking, he accompanied her into the
hall.

'I've gotten a forty-eight hour pass, I wasn't expecting it, on
my honour, that's why I didn't call you first. How've you been?
Ages since I saw you.'

'January.'

'As long as that? I suppose it must be. A lot has happened
since then. I'll tell you about it, but how are *you*?'

He squeezed her arm.

They went into the drawing room. With Elaine away, it had
returned to its wartime state, the dust was thick on the
furniture. Some flowers given to Trix weeks ago were still there,
roses in a bone-dry vase. Their heads had dropped off, they
were mummified.

'Sit down, Barny. I'll see if I can find anything to drink.'

'How about English tea?'

He leaned comfortably back against the sofa cushions.

Escaping into the kitchen, Philippa put on the kettle, thinking
desperately – I wish he'd go. I wish he'd go. I can't cope with
this farce. Shall I make him go?

The American voice called, 'Can I help?'

When she returned, carrying the tray, he sprang up and
exclaimed that she should not wait on him, it was not the way
things should be. Back home his sister would be shocked to her
soul. He took the tray and put it carefully down in front of her.

111

She poured tea and he talked about the Squadron being operational at last. Did she know? Wasn't it wizard? They were fighting the real war now. Recently they'd had their first scramble across the Channel towards Calais. It had been strange. There was the sea . . . and suddenly they were over France. But then a Messerschmitt 109 had come towards him and in a moment the sky had just been full of them. 'I had my hands full before I made it for home. I knew then just how green I was.'

He talked on, of his own inexperience and that of the Squadron. It showed up that first time. They'd been lucky to stay alive. Battles taught you something you could learn no other way. Then he said that two months before, while they were still training, one of his friends was killed in a crash. The weather had been dreadful. 'The sky became filthy grey in a few minutes, the clouds came up so thick!' His friend, he said, flying at 20,000 feet had gone into a steep dive. Barny and the others on the training flight had followed him, shouting over the radio transmitter, telling him to pull out.

'He couldn't. Perhaps he fainted or his oxygen failed. We saw him crash. Later we found out what had happened. His plane had gone into coarse pitch.'

'What does that mean?'

'The engine's out of control. You can't get her back again.'

She nodded. She didn't understand, but she understood very well. She wondered if that was what had happened to her. My heart's in coarse pitch, she thought.

He changed the conversation, as if guilty at asking for sympathy, and told her that now the Squadron was on ops, all the letters from home were 'full of hero rot. How we hate it!' Did Flip know that Hollywood was making a movie called *Eagle Squadron*? Could you beat it?

When he passed his cup, he put out his other hand and touched her.

'You look very beautiful. But very pale, honey. Your skin's honey-coloured. It's got just the same golden look of the blossom honey we eat at home. Blossom honey. That's you.'

She put down her cup and it rattled in the saucer.

'Barny. I must say something. Don't interrupt, please, just let me get it over.'

He raised his eyebrows and made a comic face. But Philippa did not look at him.

'What I want to say is this. I know about you and Trix.'

He started.

'Don't say anything yet,' she hurried on. 'Trix did not tell me. I found out by chance. I know it's no business of mine about my sister and you. But I can't pretend I haven't found out, or that it hasn't made me feel different. I can't be your friend any more.'

'How in hell – '

'I told you. By chance. Unlucky chance, you'd say, and I suppose Trix would too. But there it is.'

'She told you.'

'*She did not.* If you must know, and I don't understand why you do, I found the hotel bill in her drawer. It sounds like a vulgar divorce, doesn't it? When I told her she admitted about you and her. She would never have told me otherwise.'

He was horrified. He stood up and went over to the window, standing with his back to her. She wondered with dull curiosity what he would say next. She thought how beautiful his figure was silhouetted against the spring light. She imagined what it would feel like to stand close behind him and wind her arms round his waist.

He turned.

'Is your sister here now?'

'She's gone away.'

'Because of me.'

'I suppose so.'

'What did she say about me?'

Philippa blushed and burst out, 'What did you expect her to say? That you're marvellous in bed? I can't bear any more of this. What do I care if you made love to her? It's nothing, nothing, nothing to do with me except that I won't see you any more. I suppose you're in love with her like everybody else. I just don't want anything to do with it.'

She began to run out of the room but he followed her, caught hold of her and pulled her roughly into his arms. He began to kiss her savagely, forcing open her mouth, putting his tongue between her teeth, pressing himself against her and thrusting forward. Sobbing, she fought him. It was like being raped.

'Don't, don't! You don't care for me, it's horrible of you – ' she gasped, and was once again enveloped in the fierce open-mouthed kiss. Bending back somehow she gasped, 'Leave me alone. You're hateful. Hateful.'

113

She only managed to escape because he suddenly let go of her. She rushed out of the room, leaving the door open. He heard her running up the stairs.

He remained in the empty room, breathing fast. Then, with a fierce grimace, he picked up his cap and left the house.

She did not know what to make of her own feelings. She was disgusted at his taking her in his arms against her will. She remembered how she had fought him. It was indecent of him to embrace her after being Trix's lover. But although she felt a revulsion at his treatment, his brutal treatment, a part of her was excited by it. He wanted her still, in spite of the infinitely more desirable Trix.

The next day while she worked at Chicheley Buildings, staying as late as she dared, she kept wondering what would happen next. He would find out where Trix had gone. They would go to bed again. Apparently everybody who had Trix could have her again. Philippa supposed Barny would find Trix through Miggs.

She tried to envisage a time when Barny would be one of Trix's regular beaux, as she called them. He would appear when he was on leave, take Trix out, and finish in her arms. Suppose Barny were killed? Would Trix grieve much? The thoughts hurt so that she shook her head to and fro as if to get rid of them.

She felt wicked, though, to remember that she must have wounded him yesterday. How shocked and upset he had looked. He was a hero and she had been cruel to him and even now, as she walked slowly home in the rain, he might be over France – or wounded – or dead. How dared she think that her miserable little life was so important? But it was all she had. She had fallen romantically in love with him, and what he had wanted was sex. Trix had given him that. Philippa no longer hated her sister, but she still felt as if she had been very ill and was a long way from getting better.

She turned in at St Helen's gate.

The RAF figure was there again.

She stood rooted to the ground. He did not wave but came down the short drive fast. He said harshly, 'I want to talk to you.'

'Why did you sit on the step?' she absurdly asked.

'Mrs Miggs asked me in, but I wasn't sure you'd want me in the house. So I waited.'

114

She did not want him in the house and found no way of saying so. Five minutes ago she had thought he was over France – forgetting he was still on leave.

Nobody had been into the drawing room since they had left it the previous evening. The cushions were still squashed where Barny had sat. There was a cigarette end in the ashtray. She shook up the cushions as if to get rid of yesterday. Not asking him to sit down, she faced him, like a cat facing a dog.

'Yes?'

'How hard you look. You aren't, though.'

'What do you want to say? We said it all.'

'You did. I certainly didn't.'

He sat down, although she had not asked him to do so, squashing the cushions she had fussily shaken up. He lay back too far, as if trying to seem relaxed. But his olive skinned face was nothing of the kind. He looked unfamiliar because he did not look easy but drawn and tired. She had to harden her heart against that.

'Listen, Flip. And if you hate me after what I'm going to say, okay then you do and I'll have to put up with it. You said yesterday that I must be in love with your sister. I am not and never could be. Sure, she's glamorous and there isn't a guy in the country who wouldn't be proud to take her around. She's fun. And she's fun in bed too,' he added, staring at her fixedly, 'I can't say she isn't, though I wish in hell you hadn't found out. Do you know whom I'm afraid I *do* start to love? You, for God's sake. You said No to me when we first met, remember? I wanted us to make love but you didn't want me, something like that. I thought – hell, I'm not hanging around if there's nothing doing there. I daresay that sounds filthy but it's the truth. Guys feel like that. My sort, anyway. But then I wanted to see you again although you'd refused to let me love you. I came round here, and I found Trix. Can you blame me? Bud had been killed and I was shocked and unhappy, I guess, and she was good to be with. We got on fine. What we did that night was fine too for both of us, but no more than that. You don't understand any of it, do you?'

'No.'

'I didn't think you would. I don't blame you. But will you see me again? The Trix thing is over. It never started, except that one time. See me again, Flip.'

'I don't want to,' she said and began to cry.

He did not touch or go near her but stood up, looking at her in silence with his tired face. He pushed back his hair and said, 'I'll call you.' He walked out without looking back.

She did not go to the window or hear the door close. She sat down on the cushions as if taking possession of his warmth and his body. Leaning back, she closed her eyes.

In the days that followed she thought of him while she worked and travelled and fire-watched on St Helen's roof, with the sky crimson in the distance. Once she was in a daylight raid – it was early evening and the whole heavens seemed to roar with aircraft. Philippa ran into the garden to watch the waves of raiders coming over. Guns were roaring and as she stared up for a glimpse of English fighter planes she suddenly saw what appeared to be four enormous German bombers diving straight for the house. She fled indoors and down to the basement with Miggs. But the bombs that followed were a mile away.

She could not understand why she was no longer afraid for Barny. She had a certainty that she would see him again. Perhaps people in danger had meaningless superstitions and beliefs. She did.

Trix rang Miggs to say she would not be back for another week.

'Your sister,' Miggs told Philippa, 'is having a rare old time.'

'Good,' said Philippa, almost meaning it.

What she waited for happened. Barny telephoned her.

'I'm in town. You alone?'

'Yes, but – '

'Trix back yet?'

'No,' she said, deeply shocked at his mentioning her.

'Better if she isn't. Can I come round now?'

'I'm not sure.'

'See you in half an hour.'

She would not receive him again in a dirty room and hurriedly cleaned it before going to wash and change. With Trix away, Philippa's make-up had run out. She had no lipstick left and almost no face powder. She brushed her hair, looked at her face and remembered her mother's phrase. 'You look dingy.' I don't care. That's what I feel.

She heard the bell and ran to the top of the stairs, but Miggs was already in the hall, wearing her creaking white overall.

116

'I'll answer it. It's for me,' gabbled Philippa.

Giving her a look of sharp curiosity, Miggs disappeared.

Barny said, 'Hi,' easily enough, but they went in silence into the drawing room. It smelled clean. One of the windows was open and a bush of flowering currant, budding outside, sent in a smell of early summer. Philippa asked him calmly to sit down. She was slightly trembling.

'I keep turning up,' he said, taking his usual place and giving an automatic smile. He stretched out his long legs and looked at his black RAF shoes. They were dusty.

'How did you manage to get leave again so soon?'

'I haven't. I hopped on a lorry and must hop back in an hour or so. We're not supposed to play hooky but I'm not on call tonight. I wish,' he added without moving, 'you wouldn't look that way.'

'I wasn't aware of looking any particular way.'

'But you do. As if somebody had knocked you down. Hell, I suppose it was me. Don't you love me any more?'

The question made her desperate.

'I never said I loved you.'

'Oh, but you did. With your eyes. And the way you kiss. I suppose I can't kiss you, can I? I've only got an hour.'

'I'd rather you didn't,' she said, and stood up as if expecting him to go. But he got up and came to her and began to kiss her, passionately, differently, gently, strongly, holding her against him so that every part of their bodies touched. Moving away after what seemed a long time, Philippa said in a broken voice;

'Do you still want me? Then the answer's yes.'

What is the use of virginity, she thought, I could keep it and Barny might die. Better, oh so much better, to love him now.

He did not answer, but went on kissing her, breaking off to mutter indistinguishable words. After a while he picked her up and carried her to the sofa where they fell rather than sat.

Lying on the cushions she thought – will it be now? She wanted it to be now. But all he did was go on kissing her, hold her breasts, rub his cheek against hers so hard that his face scratched hers. Then he sat up and looked at his watch.

'Christ. I must go. Well . . . do you love me, then? I have a funny feeling that you do. What shall we do about it? I know what I want to do. Make love to you until we drop dead.'

117

'So do I.'

He wiped his hand over his face.

'Yeah. But we're not going to. What am I doing, feeling this way? I always said falling in love was for the other guy. I know I slept with that sister of yours. Don't look so frightened, I am not going to hurt you, I swear it. But I'd come to find *you*, and you were off God knows where and I hadn't heard a word.'

'But I wrote to you! I thought you didn't want to see me because you never answered.'

'I didn't get the letter. Hell. So what next? I'm not going to make love to you, Flip, though you so beautifully said . . . not to a girl like you. There's only one thing for it. We must get married.'

When he had gone and she was free of his physical presence, no longer the slave of her own helpless body, she knew the idea was mad. You couldn't marry a stranger. It was wrong. It was miraculous. She looked at the prospect, trying to grasp it. Barny, husband, lover, next of kin. Would he have asked her if she had gone to bed with him that night at the Wings Club? Or if she had not found out about Trix? She could remember nothing of what they had said after the extraordinary 'we must get married'. All she recalled was a haze in Barny's arms while she felt she would die of desire. What would become of her if she did marry him? Hopeless to ask the question. To try and use her head even now felt like coming into a room where a raving lunatic sat in a corner. You sat down very calmly and you took the madwoman's hand and you said, 'Let us be logical. Let us be practical'. All the poor lunatic could do was laugh and babble.

The moment that he had asked her to marry him, she had started so violently that he burst out laughing.

'Is the idea so terrible?' he said. Was it any different from an Englishman asking her?

'You might say we are made for each other or some damn thing.' He told her that marrying a pilot would take guts. And the other way round, because it took guts for a pilot to marry. Many of them wouldn't. In the RAF he'd heard pilots say it wasn't fair on the girl. Flyers buy it sooner or later, and then the girl would be a widow. Why store up misery for her in

118

the future? But he was not one of those. He wanted her for keeps. Even if the keeps was to be short, it was all that they'd got.

Before he left, he told her she must break the news to her family.

'And that is going to take guts too.'

It was never wise to speak about anything but the weather and last night's blitz to her father during breakfast. Silence was the best way to escape a glare over the top of *The Times*. But Philippa had never been a diplomat. She had the Tyrrell impulsiveness more than any of the three girls. During the meal she was too excited to eat, and waited for the non-existent right moment. She chose a time when Miggs was pouring the tea – Miggs might give her some moral support.

'Pa. Sorry, Father. I hope you'll be pleased,' she began idiotically, 'I am engaged to be married.'

Theo, who had been turning the pages of the newspaper, put it slowly down.

Miggs became frozen with interest.

'What did you say?'

'I'm engaged.'

A pause.

Her father said contemptuously, 'What tosh is this? And who is the man, pray?'

'You've met him. Months ago,' said Philippa. Her father looked pinched as well as angry; and why was he so thin?

'His name is Barny Duval. He is in the Eagle Squadron. He is an American,' finished Philippa bravely.

'*An American?*'

'Yes, Father.'

He seemed at a loss for words. 'Who knows about this? Your sister?' he finally said, meaning Elaine.

'No. I wanted to tell you first. Barny is very anxious to meet all the family. He did catch a glimpse of you on the night of the fire. But of course you don't know each other yet.'

He glared at her and Philippa added with more sang-froid than usual, 'He is looking forward to meeting you, Father.'

Ah, thought Miggs, a bit of gumption at last.

'This is no time to discuss the matter,' said Theo, with a haughty look at Miggs, as if she could be kept out of any family row. 'Come to my study later and explain yourself. I will make

one thing clear. I will not allow this marriage to an *American*.
Make up your mind to that.'

Philippa walked out. But only as far as the kitchen where she
sat by the boiler. A moment later Miggs joined her.

'You're a sly one. I thought that young feller was one of Trix's
hangers-on.'

Like a man who knows that if he doesn't jump the precipice he
is doomed, Philippa went at it.'He only took her out once
because I wasn't here. You'll like him, Miggsy. You always said
the RAF is marvellous.'

'Doesn't mean you've got to marry one, does it?'

'Yes, Miggsy. It does.'

'Really goin' to marry him, then?' said the old woman with her
intense, interested curiosity, 'That's a turn up for the book. You
were always reckless. Miss Elaine works things out and Trix
knows where she's goin' too. But *you*. That hot head'll get you
into hot water one of these days.'

Miggs chuckled at her own joke.

'The doctor's goin' to carry on somethin' chronic, we can make
up our minds to that. Think we can persuade him to give you
away?'

Blissful, excited, Philippa burst into all kinds of happy nonsense about love at first sight. Miggs listened and nodded and
thought that if she did manage to throw a drop of cold water on
the burning words it wouldn't do a bit of good. The fire would
just go on, hotter than before. The girl looked as if she believed
she could never be unhappy again. The very war seemed
forgotten. Drenched with happiness, Philippa was like somebody hit by an enormous wave, lying on the sand ecstatically
waiting for the next.

Miggs, making herself a fresh pot of tea, listened to the story.
She noted it contained no more reference to Trix. Miggs
admired Trix's success with men, but for once it looked as if
Philippa had got what she wanted. Talk of engagement rings
made it sound real. There was no point in recalling that
Philippa's chap had cast a quick eye over Trix first.

Drinking her tea and listening to the romantic story, Miggs
reflected that the girl had not changed since she was a child. This
was the Philippa who had made passionate school friendships,
written appalling poems which she used to read aloud to Miggs,
who had been bored stiff. Philippa was the one who had given

120

Elaine for a wedding present the only good piece of jewellery that she owned, a ring of her mother's. The jewels, diamond, emerald, amethyst and ruby, spelled 'Dear'.

It was exactly like Philippa to fall into marriage with a foreign pilot she had clearly only met a few times. People didn't change. 'Tell you, somethin', lady. Your sister had best come to town. You'll never get to organize your own weddin', sure as a gun.'

Even Philippa saw the sense in that.

Before she left for work she telephoned Shelton. Lady St Aird was very cold. Yes, Elaine was here. She would get her. The moment she heard her sister's voice she poured out the news, punctuating the story with laughter and 'I'm so happy.' 'You won't disapprove, will you?' she added eagerly. Elaine laughed too. She did not say it was very sudden and certainly rash. She simply said how glad she was and that she looked forward to meeting Barny and of course would get some leave and help with the wedding.

'Will it be soon? He'll have to get compassionate leave.'

'He calls it passionate leave,' was the maundering reply.

Elaine let her talk on. When Philippa was beginning to run out of steam she asked the only question not tied with white ribbons.

'Flip. What about Trix? I gather she is still away. Would you like me to tell her?'

'Oh. Would you? And – and I'd be so glad if she'd come home.'

'You might like her to be bridesmaid,' said Elaine. She thought wryly what a dreadful suggestion she had made. What would Miles think? An American stranger would soon be walking up the aisle, having had one Tyrrell girl in his bed and about to have the second.

'Oh yes, she could, couldn't she?' came the dazed, happy and boring reply from London.

'One last thing, Flip. Don't let Pa upset you.'

So he could have done at any other time. Philippa loved her father, whom she had so often tried to approach, always failing. He awed her. But another male figure dominated her thoughts, a graceful, lounging, youthful figure. Another voice replaced her father's abrupt English syllables, with a drawl and an accent of unexpected elisions, 'gotta', 'kinda', 'helluva.'

Her father was sitting at the old-fashioned desk in his study, which since Philippa was a child had always been heaped with papers which never seemed to grow less. The room had its wartime changes. The strengthened metal sheet fixed to the ceiling, and a pile of government health leaflets in a clip. On the wall in a rectangular frame were three photographs of his daughters. Elaine, at fifteen, was at the top, dressed in tennis white, smiling. Below her in the centre was Philippa, at eleven, sitting in the garden swing, serious. At the bottom was Trix, seven years old and wearing gingham. She was looking down at the toy dog in her arms. The frame had been there so long that every one of Theo's patients knew it, and his daughters were so accustomed to it that they no longer noticed it was there. But Philippa looked at it now. She saw for the first time that it was a symbol of paternal love.

Sitting facing him, she looked at him with her candid eyes. He returned the glance stonily. His conscience lately had been rather like a subdued recurring toothache. There had been some trouble with the girls, God knows what it had all been about, he had preferred to avoid a scene, and had deliberately not enquired into it. When Miggs tried to tell him, he had shut her up. She had then, high-handedly he considered, sent for Elaine. His eldest daughter had not informed him what had happened, which had been a relief. She was the one to tackle such problems, after all, it was up to her to take Mary's place. He had presumed things were settled. It now occurred to him that Elaine must have come to London to try and prevent this hare-brained marriage scheme.

'Well?' he said, swivelling round in his chair to face her, 'Try to tell me quietly what this is all about.'

She did try. She kept her voice as reasonable as she could manage, and with difficulty she avoided superlatives when mentioning Barny. She also attempted to make the decision to marry appear carefully thought out. Barny was writing to his sister and her husband, and so on. He had his pilot's pay, and his Squadron Commander had actually said that when Barny was married, Philippa would be allowed to live near the station. It was unusual, but permission had been given.

When she finished, Theo said, 'I'm afraid all this is out of the question. What do we know about this man? A foreigner. An American from God knows where.'

'Louisiana.'

122

He ignored that and went straight on.

'For all I know, he may have a wife in the United States. Things like that happen with men overseas. What you are suggesting is impossible. You are simply behaving like a young woman with a head full of nonsense. I refuse to give my consent.'

She was sorry for him, because he had used his authority.

'It's no good, Father. I don't want to cause you pain, and I know this will upset you, but Barny and I are going to be married. We really are.' She swallowed the words, 'And you can't stop us,' but they both heard it.

'I hope you will give me away on my wedding day.'

She went out of the room then without looking at him, sure that she had hurt him.

Trix had been the family pet for so long that finding herself cast in the role of villainness was very uncomfortable. She had pangs. Sometimes, remembering the look on Philippa's face, she felt quite miserable. It must be awful, she thought, to feel like that about a man. She never had. When Elaine telephoned from Shelton with the news, Trix was astounded and very amused. Wartime romance put everything right.

Unless she was pretty crazy about a man, which happened rarely, Trix soon forgot about the lovemaking. She had enjoyed her night of sex with Barny Duval, who had been energetic and enthusiastic and he'd had a lot of stamina she remembered with a grin, but he was definitely not very exciting. She vaguely recalled that he had woken her twice during the night for more. But she hadn't thought of that again and only about him because of Philippa. There were new men around who excited her far more.

What now filled her thoughts was the coming wedding. When Elaine had married in the winter of 1939 it had been unfashionable to wear white, it showed lack of patriotism. White satin and French champagne were definitely discouraged. Poor Elaine had worn a suit and carried some violets. It had all, thought Trix, been definitely dreary. But now it was not a question of patriotism but of practicality. Brides were delighted to wear white if they could borrow old wedding dresses preserved from before the war. Churches, of course, were boarded up. Confetti and rice were illegal. Trix considered the worst feature of

123

wartime marriage parties was the cake. Iced wedding cakes were now banned and everybody getting married had elaborate cardboard covers looking like the three-tier traditional cake, covering whatever poor rationed sponge could be offered. Trix had attended a wedding the previous month where, surrounded by wine, whisky or gin, the cake had stood in its glory, decorated with artificial flowers. Then the cardboard cover was whisked off, and underneath was a poor eggless thing tasting like sawdust.

Flip, thought Trix, wasn't going to have anything so phoney. The thing to do was to beg, borrow or steal extra sugar. Always part of the present, Trix turned overnight from immoral sister staying away from home to kindly bridesmaid planning to help a wartime marriage in the family.

Returning to St Helen's the day after she had heard the news, Trix rushed into the house, found Philippa upstairs and flung her arms round her.

'Delightful! Delicious! D'lovely!' she exclaimed, quoting a song. 'I've got some wizzy ideas for your dress and what do you think? We can have a *real cake*. Mrs Mason gave me two pounds of granulated sugar. You put it through the mincer and behold – icing sugar.'

Philippa had dreaded actually seeing Trix. What she had not realised was that Barny's kisses had healed her and wiped the jealousy away.

Barny had a special licence; the marriage would be in the same church, St Barnabas, where Elaine and Miles had married two years ago. Trix was up until three in the morning, finishing a dress for Philippa. It was cream-coloured silk, and had a pocket cut out of a piece of mink in the shape of a heart.

'She's wearing her heart on her hip,' said Trix.

Elaine, on special leave and at home doing the arrangements, was almost awed by her younger sister. She isn't sorry in the least either about all the other lovers or about Barny, she thought. She is simply glad we know the worst. But she *is* sorry to have hurt Flip and is doing her best to show it. Wheedling sugar rations from friends and making clothes is Trix's best. She is like the tumbler who did back somersaults in church, thought Elaine. It was the only way he knew how to pray.

The first thing Miggs told Elaine when she arrived from Oxfordshire was that Theo was not only refusing to give the bride away, he was also not coming to the wedding. Yes, he had met Barny. A pleasant-enough young man. It did not make an iota of difference to his decision that the marriage was totally unsuitable, hurried, and something he considered wrong for his daughter. He would not attend.

Elaine went into his study. He looked up from his desk, but neither greeted nor spoke to her. He was grim. She bent forward calmly and kissed him. As always, his expression changed. Something in her soothed him.

'I've told Philippa that I will not sanction it.'

She made a noise of sympathy. He began to tell her what he must have said many times before, to friends, to Miggs, to poor Philippa. He would not have had moral support from Miggs. She was enjoying the drama.

'You had met Barny before, you know, Father,' Elaine said mildly. 'Didn't he help put out the fire months ago? And Philippa said you and he got on perfectly well when he came to see you. Were you unwelcoming?'

'I didn't put out the red carpet.'

'But you liked him?'

'I know nothing of Americans.'

'You soon will. Now, darling,' she said – it was a rare endearment to him – 'You must come to the wedding. You must give her away for everybody's sake. For ours. For Mother's. Even for your own.'

There was a long silence.

'I don't know how you have the gall,' he said.

Despite the dark church, the wedding was a cheerful affair. Four members of the Eagle Squadrom, rangy Americans with easy manners, were present. Marjorie Flower managed to get to London and brought her cousin, Miles' friend Dick Polglaze. The two French A's had not yet been sent abroad and they arrived with a remarkable amount of beer bottles. Annette Ghilain came too, looking very elegant. Elaine saw her father's face brighten when he spoke to the French girl.

Philippa looked quite beautiful in the creamy dress made for her by Trix, and a little wreath of yellow roses. During the ceremony she was so pale that Elaine thought at one moment she was going to faint. Trix looked like a bluebell, even to a hat made of petals. At the reception she was surrounded by men.

Barny was taking his bride to spend their first and only night's

125

leave at the Savoy. They left St Helen's in a taxi. As Philippa leaned from the taxi window Trix sprinkled her hair with fragments of torn-up silver paper, and Philippa laughed and threw her bunch of roses to Trix, who neatly caught it.

'My third this year!' called Trix, 'I'm sure to be next.'

Chapter Nine

It was breathlessly hot that June. Trix sang to herself as she dressed to go out. She could not remember the last time she had been to Kew Gardens: probably not since Miggs took her in the bus when she was a child. They used to walk for miles, in what Miggs called bluebell time or lilac time. Miggs knew the names of every flower they saw.

Dick Polglaze had suggested he should take her there, and afterwards he'd drive her down to Wargrave to punt on the river. Goodness knows, thought Trix complacently, where the petrol was coming from.

The sun poured through her open windows and she fastened the shoulder buttons of a new white dress she had made from one of her mother's evening petticoats. It was very short, and had a blue silk sash. Her idea was to look about twelve.

She had first met Dick Polglaze at Philippa's wedding and had taken a fancy to him. But the Eagle Squadron had demanded her attention, and all four had declared that after the wedding she must come dancing with them. 'We will teach you to jitterbug. Know how? Good, we'll show you.' After Philippa and Barny had driven away, Trix, flushed with American compliments, had gone in search of Dick and found him in the dining room, quite alone and unselfconscious, sipping a final glass of champagne and looking at the garden.

'I'm being swooped away by the Eagles to the Dorchester. You come too.'

'Thanks, but I don't think I will.'

'Bother, you have another date. Cut it and come with us.'

'No date. Too much American competition.'

Trix pouted and looked at him languishly. But that did not work either. He bade her a smiling goodbye.

The Eagles all flew away after that. But Dick Polglaze wrote to her. He was at Greenock doing trials for a new ship, and he might be able to wangle some leave soon.

He telephoned her from Scotland, and Trix rearranged her

dates. She found that she liked him, although they had spoken so little at the wedding. It rather surprised her that she was looking forward to seeing him so much. The war had been on, it seemed to Trix, a very long time. Trix had been only sixteen when it began and when she had decided to be beautiful. From the moment she came out of her chrysalis she had collected men. She never expected not to be admired, given presents, telephoned, pursued, asked out and asked to bed. She did not necessarily say yes to the sexual invitation, and she had a rare talent for keeping as admirers the men she did not sleep with; she was so promising that perhaps they still hoped.

When her men went abroad, others appeared at once. Now Dick Polglaze had, as she put it, hove into view.

He was unlike other men she had known. To begin with he was short, scarcely five foot eight, and she liked her men to be tall, regarding it as a sort of compliment. He did not treat her seriously and she was accustomed to every man being at her mercy. He was teasing, highly-sexed, and tough. They went to bed after they had met once or twice. He had been lent a dilapidated flat over a gymnasium in Orchard Street. When they went up the stairs he remarked that if there was a blitz, they would not have a chance.

'Concrete is best,' he said, 'there's some stuff called vibrated concrete, whatever that is. Even your billiard table is all right. Sure you want to risk your lovely self in this rat-hole?'

'Certain,' said Trix blithely.

Up in the shabby flat they fell into bed. He was an exciting lover, quite silent, strong, and she sharply enjoyed him. He never said he loved her.

The omission piqued her. All her men declared their love, some in terms so extravagant that she smiled inwardly. When she thought about Dick, she was determined to make him fall in love with her. He ought to do so. Sometimes when she was in her room at St Helen's, she took off every stitch of clothing and dispassionately studied her naked figure. Her breasts were small and pointed, the nipples the colour of wild roses. Her waist was only twenty-two inch, her hips swelled out well and at the top of her long silky legs was a fuzz of hair a dark gingery gold. Really, she thought, looking critically at herself, I am not bad. Then, going close to the mirror, she stared at her nose, and turned sideways to catch a glimpse at her profile. Why didn't Dick say he loved her? Everybody else did.

128

Trix's taste in men until Dick came on to the scene had been predictable. She liked them big and tall, with heavy shoulders and what she called 'lovely muscles.' She preferred the sort of man who, like Rhett Butler, could pick her up as if she were a feather and rush upstairs to the bedroom to rape her. But it would not be rape with Trix. Dick was only an inch or so taller than she was, and although he was sturdy she very much doubted if he would make the stairs with her in his arms. More annoying still, he would not want to. She had an idea that he was not the man drawn to the big romantic gesture.

Elaine told her he was a friend of Miles' and that his parents lived in Cumberland and were quite rich.

When he was talking to her about his family once, he said vaguely that his father owned two companies in Lloyds.

'Lloyds of London? I saw a movie called that. Tyrone Power was in it.'

'Yes, featherhead. Lloyds of London. Nice work if you can get it but I am not at all sure it's my kind. However, not much point in bothering about that just now.'

'So your Pa is rich?'

'You could say that. Come and kiss me and stop asking silly questions.'

She liked Dick Polglaze. She even liked the fact that he was short. He was attractive. His looks were curious, he might have been an actor, his cheek bones were so high and his face was triangular. He had slanting eyes which were never serious. Very sexy, she thought his eyes were. His mouth was too thin, and when he set it in a certain way, she knew there was no point in wheedling. He was the first man to say No to her. She found that sexy too.

Sitting on bar stools at the Ritz – he liked expensive hotels – holding hands at the films – he liked funny ones – Trix learned more about him. His father was apparently a tycoon. His mother had been an actress but gave it up when she married. 'She was not very talented but had a pretty singing voice. My father was a sort of stage door Johnny really. He buzzed round backstage and asked her out. Rumour has it, I don't know if I believe the story, that he gave her some flowers with a diamond brooch popped inside.'

'Jolly romantic.'

'You don't think that at all. If it was your sister Philippa – well, yes. But there is not a romantic bone in your body, Trix Tyrrell.'

129

On the hot June morning she was ready long before he arrived. When she heard the bell, she tripped down the staircase to pose at the corner, her hand on the staircase nob, her head slightly on one side. Miggs opened the front door and Dick stood looking at her. With a sniff and 'leave it to you' Miggs disappeared through the kitchen door.

Dick grinned as he took Trix's hand.

'How glamorous you look.'

'Do I? Good. I've made us a picnic. Did you bring some drink.'

'Will champagne do?'

'Where *did* you get it? I won't ask.'

They went out into the blazing midday. A small car, a pre-war MG scarlet as a poppy, was at the gate. Dick settled her beside him, remarking that the way she did her hair was like Veronica Lake. 'But you're much prettier.' As they drove away through the deserted roads in the direction of Kew he asked her teasingly what she had been doing since he last saw her.

'Making the men suffer, I suppose.'

'Stoopid. I'm their ray of sunshine. Actually I was in bad with my father last night. Quite a row. I was so relieved when my date turned up to rescue me.'

'And what had you been doing? Unsettling the male patients? Any of them threatening suicide again?'

'All I did,' said Trix, opening her eyes wide, 'was to use some of my father's beastly gin. Well, it was the last drop in the bottle but honestly, so *little*.'

'My dear Trix, I had no idea you liked the stuff or I'd have – '

'Silly! It was to clean my diamond ring.'

His laugh was sudden, infectious, and sounded like a burst of machine-gun fire.

Trix liked to make men laugh. Looking at him from under her curling lashes, she wondered if she were falling in love? A new experience. Flip had once told her that there was an answer to that eternal question. Her sister had been talking about love. Trix had been scarcely fifteen, and Philippa was mad about some man or other who later vanished from her life. 'My theory,' said Philippa, 'is based on Watford Station.'

'What do you mean, Flip!'

Philippa explained that it was a test one could set oneself. If a girl was willing to take a slow, stopping and crowded train to

Watford Station, knowing that when she arrived the person she was meeting would only have five minutes on a draughty platform to talk to her – and if she eagerly went on the journey – that was love.

I can't see myself on the Watford train for you, Dick Polglaze, thought Trix.

They parked the car outside the high walls of Kew and went into the gardens. Dick carried the picnic basket.

'You are not supposed to carry anything when you are in uniform,' said Trix, 'the command's quite right, it ruins the way you look. A Naval officer, too. Let me have the basket. I shall look okay with it. I shall be little Red Riding Hood.'

'And I'm to be the wolf? Don't tempt me. The basket is too heavy, I can't have you with bulging muscles.'

'I have beautiful muscles.'

'Then we must keep them that way.'

The gardens still had some flowers, roses, scenting the air as they went by. The grass had been left to grow long, for hay. There were beds of symmetrically planted, curled green cabbages. None of the great glasshouses had been bombed – so far, and they shone like giant diamonds which had been cleaned with Doctor Tyrrell's gin, winking and sending back rays to the sun. In the distance in the blue sky, swimming, floating, was a long line of motionless barrage balloons.

'Come paint the dawn with dainty elephants

To graze upon the pastures of the sky,' quoted Dick.

'Do you like poetry, Trix? Somebody should write a poem about you.'

'Oh, they have,' she said, and he laughed again.

They picnicked under feathery trees more exotic than any English oak or beech. They drank the champagne. Trix took off her shoes and the sun warmed her long bare legs and pretty, narrow feet. She lifted up her face, thirsty for the golden light.

Propping himself on one elbow, he looked at her with his narrow eyes. His senses were stirred. The great gardens were empty and very still. No figure crossed the grass or walked under the trees. They could have been in Arcadia. He leaned over, put his arms round her and kissed her. She returned the kiss. He said nothing when they drew apart.

In the afternoon they drove down to Wargrave. At the river's edge by an old hotel there was a boathouse. Dick, who had come

131

often here, went to a cottage and persuaded an old woman to unlock the boathouse for him. For a pound she allowed him to drag out a punt.

Trix climbed into the long narrow craft and they set off along the river. Cows stood up to their knees in the water and stared mildly at them from the other bank.

Using a paddle, Dick steered his craft skilfully past deserted houses sleeping in the sun, and gardens where weeds grew among the delphiniums. He turned into a backwater, overhung with trees. There were forget-me-nots at the water's edge and little flotillas of moorhens. It was a world empty of people and smelling of flowers, filled to the brim with summer. Trix lay back on water-stained plush cushions and trailed her hand in the water.

The backwater at last joined the broad sweep of the river, and he finally moored the punt under an enormous willow tree. It was more than fifteen feet across, high, green, an ancient tent whose hanging branches swept the water. Tying the punt rope to a tree stump on the shore, he stepped back into the punt beside her. They were in a dim, green, watery light. The river gently slapped against the craft now and then.

'Shall we make love?'

She giggled in reply, excited. Lying down together, their movements rocked the punt. They made love for a long time. He was fierce and silent in lovemaking and when she opened her eyes to look, she saw a tranced expression on his face. Excited, melting, she was not as tranced as he. When it was over, he said, putting on his clothes, 'you're a luscious piece of female flesh.'

Still naked, she put her arms behind her head.

'I thought you were going to say that you loved me.'

'Did you?'

When he drove her back to St Helen's, gave her a brief kiss and said he would write when he was at sea – 'Lord knows when you'll get the letter, though' – Trix smiled airily. She waved, watching the short sturdy figure walking, with a light step, towards the gate. He turned and gave a salute.

She made up her mind to marry him.

After Philippa's marriage and its excitements, Elaine returned to the unchanging pattern of her life in Oxfordshire. She worked at

Blenheim six days a week, every evening was spent at home. She lived for Miles' letters. Apart from Marjorie Flower, she had made no friends. And her mother-in-law was far too busy to notice that.

Claire had joined the WVS before the war on the week that it had been founded. It was started with the aim of specialising in air raid precautions, but the Service's work since 1939 had steadily extended. Claire wore her WVS green tweed suit on every day except Sunday, it was as much her uniform as Miles' navy blue was to him. In the evenings, however, she still changed into pre-war lace dresses, floor length, and her string of pearls. But it was in the uniform, which she named her battle dress, that she looked her angular and energetic best.

She had learned to drive a lorry; she delivered food and baby clothes. She cooked (not very well) and knitted (excellently) and organized work parties. The WVS wanted salvage of every kind: Claire was one of its most pitiless collectors. She would cajole or shame women into giving up their precious aluminium saucepans, their children's metal tea sets, and sackfulls of magazines. Nobody in Claire's district had a spare blanket in the linen cupboard. She collected blankets and clothes, packed them and sent them to the bombed cities. Her work took her all over the country, and often when Elaine came home, the old house was empty. Lord St Aird, of course, was in the stable studio. Sometimes Elaine's heart would give a jump: there would be a letter on the hall floor. *On Active Service. H.M.Ship. Passed by Censor.*

Miles had been sent to Canada after the bombing of Liverpool, as part of the expedition crossing the Atlantic to collect the US destroyers. Roosevelt had offered Britain forty or fifty elderly ships in exchange for British bases in the Atlantic and the Caribbean and Churchill had accepted immediately. The destroyers were sorely needed.

Elaine received a letter from Miles when he had arrived in Quebec. Letters from him were usually written in pencil, at sea, on scraps of paper torn from notebooks. But this time he used rich-looking writing paper, at the top of which was the engraving of a gothic Quebec hotel.

The ship, he wrote, had been crowded to the gunwales with women and children, evacuees travelling to Canada. Praise be the sea had been calm, and the journey safe. There had been a lot of nervous faces. He had played deck tennis, walked for miles round the deck to keep in training and made a lot of friends. 'We subs hit it off pretty well,' wrote Miles in his optimistic way. 'And you'll be amused to know, darling, that the drinks really *are* duty free.'

Elaine read and re-read the letters. Sometimes she could not decipher a particular word, and was glad. It meant puzzling it out later on, and so getting something more. She was like a man half dead with thirst, licking the inside of his water-can.

Miles' parents received letters from him about the same time: he never wrote to his wife without writing to them.

Claire read paragraphs from his letters during dinner, including a description of Quebec.

'I simply can't imagine how he can like Canada, can you, Edmund? We couldn't stick it.'

'I recall that my grandfather enjoyed the salmon fishing,' said Lord St Aird.

He sounds, thought Elaine, exactly like an American's outdated idea of an Englishman. She was glad one of Philippa's Eagle friends was not present. Philippa had told her about the American prejudices about the English.

'I know it sounds ridiculous, but they come from so far away – most of the boys have never travelled before, and their ideas about us are archaic! They think all Englishmen are reserved, frigid and never see a joke. Worst of all, they are convinced the English feel deeply superior to boorish Americans. Of course I keep telling them they're wrong.'

Are they? thought Elaine. Perhaps the St Airds preferred the caricature. Her father-in-law put all his paintings with their faces to the wall.

The summer days were bright, and one early morning as Elaine was leaving for Woodstock, the telephone rang. Claire was in the fields at the back of the house feeding the chickens. Elaine answered it.

'Shelton Manor?'

'*Miles.*'

'Darling, what luck. I thought you would have left. I'll be home tonight, or tomorrow at latest. I must fly. Did I remember to tell you that I love you?'

Elaine ran. Her feet scarcely touched the ground as she flew out into the blazing sunshine. In the distance she saw Claire surrounded by a sea of brown chickens. She was sprinkling corn.

Dragging open the farm gate, tripping as her shoe caught in a rut, Elaine yelled, 'Lady St Aird. Miles rang! He's coming home tonight or tomorrow. Isn't it wonderful? Oh, isn't it wonderful?' She was running and gasping, out of breath, radiant.

Claire stood with one hand spilling corn. The brown feathered sea eddied round her.

'Good. Please don't shout, Elaine. I've told you that before.'

That day, her intense happiness scared Elaine. Her nature was balanced and preferred a chosen calm. The wave of feeling which kept seeping over her was so violent that she felt as if she were drunk. And in between a terrifying happiness she felt cold and her stomach ached. She told Marjorie the news at lunchtime. Marjorie beamed, laughed, exclaimed with pleasure, patted her shoulder. She did the things needed by a person suffering from bliss. She then looked observantly at her friend, and suggested they should go for a walk after lunch.

'Why not now? I couldn't eat a thing.'

'Elaine St Aird! I am starving. You come and watch and I'll eat anything you don't want.'

After the meal they went out into the hot sunshine. The fields were full of marguerites and a breeze made the forest of white flowers shiver. The palace towered. The lake had turned blue.

'I know how it is,' said Marjorie, 'pretty awful, hmm?'

'Awful and wonderful.'

'Of course. But you mustn't stare at the hour glass when he's with you. *Enjoy* his leave. My cousin Elizabeth was with us recently during her husband's leave. Elaine, she was frightful. She kept wailing 'only two days more' at breakfast and thoroughly depressing everybody. Her husband Ted is a cheerful soul, he loves a joke and a gin, and he looked positively hunted. You must find the way to enjoy Miles, at the same time blocking off the thought that he will soon be gone.'

'I suppose you know how to do it.'

'Of course I don't. Doesn't mean, because I know what is right, that I'm capable of doing it.'

* * *

135

The evening bus stopped on the corner by the Wheelwright pub. Elaine had a quarter of an hour's walk to Shelton. Miles hoped to be with her tomorrow. In twenty-four hours she would see him again. She gave a sigh of happiness. But as she climbed out of the bus she saw something that made her feel as if the blood was draining out of her body. Standing on the green by a gnarled tree which had a bench built all round it, was a figure. Tall, dark clad, narrow shouldered, a man with a brown face, wearing a shabby naval cap.

She began to run. He opened both his arms and she threw herself into them.

That evening St Aird brought out the 1912 burgundy, two cobwebbed bottles taken from the Shelton cellars. He poured out the wine slowly into heavy eighteenth century glasses.

Miles was delighted and astonished.

'Not the 1912. Really, Father, you shouldn't!'

'I can't think of a reason why not.'

Punctuating stories of his life in the Navy with bursts of laughter, Miles was full of talk. Dinner was festive. It was odd, thought Elaine, to see Claire actually smiling, to hear her short amused laugh. Her mother-in-law was in her best lace, and Elaine wore a new dress that Miles had bought for her in Canada. It was made of crêpe, very clinging and soft, the colour of a geranium.

'I forgot to tell you,' said Miles, drinking his third glass of brandy with relish after the humble dessert of stewed apples and custard. 'You are all going to laugh. I've been put up for a gong. A civilian one. For the shindig in Liverpool.'

His father's lined old face beamed.

'A decoration? You told us nothing of what actually happened in Liverpool, did he, Claire?'

He referred every question to his wife.

'Oh, I couldn't say much because of censorship,' said Miles, grinning. 'It was nothing to make a song and dance about. I told you on the telephone, remember, Mother? About the fires. There was a big blitz over Liverpool and I was on my way to barracks. I'd been to a movie. Hellish boring in Liverpool. The blitz was roaring away and as I was going down the road, carrying a totally unnecessary torch, suddenly I heard a voice – very loud and absolutely furious. It was a warden shouting "Put out that bloody light." That was a laugh, because the fires had

136

really got going in the docks, it was so light you could have read a newspaper by them. The sky was crimson.'

'I remember that at Amiens,' Claire said.

Elaine did not speak.

Miles said – 'I bet you did, Mother. I must say, it did look exciting. So I turned back and ran down to the docks. There were some ships burning, one worse than the others. Apparently it was just about to explode. There were two matelots still on board, both of them had been wounded. I got hold of the rope they'd used to pull off the others, and said I'd shin up it. Somebody shouted to me that I'd fall off – the men were on the top deck. I said, what the hell? I'll only get a wet shirt if I do fall. So up I went and got 'em. First one, then the other.'

'And came down the rope, carrying them,' said Claire.

'Yes, poor beggars. They both died later.'

'Worth a try, though,' said Claire.

St Aird sipped his burgundy.

'Good show. Nice try,' he said.

Elaine had never felt so distanced from them. She even felt separated from Miles. *She* wanted to cry out, to exclaim, to ask questions and let her feelings burst out like stars. She didn't dare. Instead, she managed to say with nearly as much coolness as Claire,

'What about the gong?'

Miles laughed again. 'Rumour has it that it's to be a George Medal. Look rather nice, won't it? White and purple. A bit like an MC.'

The evening seemed very long to Elaine. And Miles was so very nice to his parents. He went out in the dark to the studio to see his father's new painting. He admired his mother's WVS work charts.

'Good lord, Mother, you're going the pace. You're the one who should get the gong.'

Elaine jangled with nerves. To be alone with him. To have him in her arms. To make love.

At last they went up to bed. The old house settled down into its thrall of country silence, and she was in bed with Miles, close to him, feeling his warmth. They made love over and over again.

'Being away from you, sweetie, makes me very sexy.'

When they separated, he lay and held her hand. Letting his hand go, she got out of bed and pulled the curtains. The moonlight of early summer washed into the room. There he was, really there, she could see him in the shadows, a dark shape in her bed.

'Sleepy, poppet?'

'Oh no. Do you want to talk?'

'A little. I've got some news. I wanted you to hear it first and I've been saving it up. Best bit is that it looks as if I'm going to get quite a lot more leave. How you started! The fact is that the old destroyer we just chugged back over from the States is not exactly used to the rough Atlantic. She was happier in warmer seas. She is not, distinctly not, in good shape. She's in dock for repairs and our skipper's guess is that this is just the start. We'll be in and out of dock after every trip. So – more leave.'

Elaine looked at him. She could just make out the prominent bumpy forehead, two dark hollows for eyes, a thickness of black hair.

'Second bit of news. I'm taking you away for a naughty weekend.'

She was dumbfounded. Since when had Miles wanted to be anywhere but Shelton?

'It sounds wonderful. But are you sure, my darling? What about your parents?'

It cost her a lot to say that.

'Oh, I suggested it to Father this evening in the studio. He agreed. We ought to get away by ourselves.'

Oh did he, thought Elaine. Or was it that he would agree to anything asked by his son.

'I thought Brighton,' Miles said. 'We had fun there when I was at King Alfred. We must recapture the first fine careless rapture. Except that we've just done that.'

Elaine had to go to work the next morning. On her journey to Woodstock her thoughts kept returning to the astonishing fact that Miles was taking her away from Shelton for three whole days. How would his mother like that?

Yesterday evening, his first at home, when they had had dinner, and sat afterwards in the drawing room, Elaine knew very well how self-conscious and inhibited she had been. She found it impossible to be natural with Miles when his mother was there. Any sign of affection to him, even a 'darling', would be despised. Elaine knew Claire would think it very vulgar. She did not even dare to touch his hand. Was Claire jealous? Elaine

138

had had a strong sensation last night, as if there was a kind of invisible grabbing coming from Claire, a pulling of Miles towards herself whilst pushing Elaine away. Perhaps Miles had felt a little of that too.

Marjorie promptly said she would exchange some leave with Elaine to make the Brighton trip possible.

'Don't bother to thank me. You just wait until Bob comes home!'

'Then you can take all my Sundays.'

'You're right. I will.'

While she was packing, Elaine heard Claire and Miles talking on the stairs. Claire laughed, sounding like a girl. But when the taxi arrived, and Elaine came down the stairs, she saw that her mother-in-law was displeased. Her manner to Elaine was very cold, ridiculously so. She was all smiles to her son, who gave her a smacking kiss.

As they drove to the station the morning was grey. Summer was hiding in a white blanket and the wind was cold. By the time they arrived in London the day was drearier still.

'Do we care?' said Miles, giving her arm a pinch.

But when the train drew in at the station at Brighton and they stepped out, everything was blue and gold. The transformation was dramatic, it was as if they had walked inside a pre-war poster for the Cote d'Azur. Brighton was teeming with troops. There seemed to be regiments marching down every street, the pubs were so filled they overflowed, and troops went by in lorries. Miles and Elaine walked down the street towards the sea.

As they came to the front they saw that it was full of block houses, there were huge rolling barricades of barbed-wire, gun emplacements, and notices saying succinctly, 'KEEP OFF!'

They stood looking at the stretch of shingle, grey, white and brown. It sloped down to the almost waveless sea. They were both thinking of their wartime honeymoon. All they had had was twenty-four hours. But they had crept out of the hotel at midnight and swum. The water had been as warm as a bath. All the mysterious future was ahead of them, sprawling across the horizon. They had been too happy to look at it.

Miles glanced from the menacing beaches to his wife. She stood quietly, a small elegant figure, fairish hair curled under a hat shaped like a little wreath. Elaine's appearance, he sometimes thought, was a work of art as much as his father's pictures

139

were. Everything about her was perfect, the result of thought and design. He had never seen her look messy, or caught her with a smut on her face or a laddered stocking. She glowed with a kind of interior colour, as if the painting were lit from behind the canvas, her skin like a peach, her eyes steady shining blue. He marvelled at the difference between Elaine and her impulsive rather untidy sister Flip, whom he liked but did not admire. As for Trix, she was a chorus girl. But Elaine was his ideal. She was beautiful and collected, passionate when he wanted her, reserved at other times. She continued to fascinate him and continued to belong to herself.

As for Elaine, behind the cool façade she was hiding the very emotion Marjorie had warned her about – a consciousness of time running away like the sand in the hour glass. Its neck was so narrow that you thought nothing could get through it: yet the sand seemed alive, rushing downwards to the growing heap of yesterdays.

'What do you want to do this evening, sweetie? The cinema's only a step away from the hotel. I *think* it is a Will Hay.'

'Oh, do let's.'

The film finished on the stroke of ten fifteen. A notice on the screen announced To Patrons that the curfew began at half past ten, and would they please return home as quickly as possible.

Walking back to the hotel, they met only two soldiers, both hurrying, and a policeman.

'I never liked Brighton so much,' Elaine said.

The night was so quiet that after they had made love, when Elaine lay wide awake looking into the dark, she could hear the sea washing the shore. The waves broke and made a gentle, dragging noise. She wished it did not make her feel sad. 'Forlorn, the very word is like a bell, Tolling me back from thee to my sole self.'

'Are you awake, poppet?' said Miles in the dark.

She moved so that her shoulder pressed against his bare chest. He folded her in his arms.

'You smell delicious. Expensive. There is something I have to tell you. It won't happen just yet, there'll be more life on the ocean wave in that poor benighted US destroyer. But. I am thinking of volunteering for submarines.'

The silence was only broken by the sound of the sea.

140

'Well?' he said, pressing her close, 'are you going to ask me not to?'

'Of course not, if that's what you want to do.'

It was the most difficult sentence she had spoken in her life.

'You are wonderful, know that? I was afraid of a scene.'

'Since when, my darling, have I made one of those?'

'Never. There are never any at Shelton either, thank Allah. I had a girlfriend before the war. Very glamorous. But she enjoyed scenes. They made me curl up.'

'I've always known you felt like that.'

'It's strange. You know everything about me. Much, much more than Mother, and I always thought she and I were the same kind of people. Now I see the differences. Anyway, back to being a submariner. It's a grand life, you know. Interesting and difficult and technical. Fascinating stuff. I'm mad about going into submarines. A friend of mine, Allardyce, you haven't met him, you'd like him, has already volunteered. He tells me one gets danger money.'

What answer was there to that?

She heard the smile in his voice as he said, 'So at last I can buy you a really decent naval crown, with good-sized diamonds, not those chips you wear at present. Something worth looking at.'

Once before the war when she had been playing tennis and the game ended, she had jumped the tennis net. She had tripped at the top of the net and fallen forward, winded. She had the same intense stomach-ache now.

'When shall you go, Miles?'

'Oh, not for ages. First there's the next Atlantic trip. Then all the papers have to go through, and then there's the course at *HMS Dolphin* at Portsmouth. Allardyce said it's a pretty intensive course with lots of hard work. It will take three or four months. I shan't be going for a while, sweetie. You'll have to wait a bit before your husband is a hero.'

He talked for a while longer, and then he kissed her. Soon, with a gentle sound not unlike the waves outside, a kind of sigh, he fell asleep. She lay awake, her head against his chest, eyes wide open, in pain.

Part II

Chapter Ten

During the late autumn of 1941 the Tyrrell sisters saw nothing of each other. A giant hand had come out of the sky and shifted them, as it moved everybody in Britain, pawns in the game of chess.

Miles returned from the Atlantic and was sent to Portsmouth on the course for submariners. Elaine was not allowed to live near him, the area was prohibited. When he was given leave, which was seldom, she set off on one of the slow wartime journeys by train and cross-country bus to get to the village which was nearest to the line over which civilians must not cross. Here she and Miles met and stayed at the village pub – often only for a single night.

He had never seemed happier or looked more handsome. He retained a tan from months at sea, to his own surprise. 'I don't know how I manage it, we were below decks most of the time in the most filthy weather.' His grey eyes were so clear that the whites were blue, and his figure was as springy as steel. When she walked with him, she had to run to keep up. He was, he declared, a hundred per cent fit. It was his favourite joke, after making love to her a number of times during the night.

The course was taxing and some of it was technical, but it was also a big sharpening up, he said, of seamanship. Submarines were 'sensitive beasts'. They were difficult to handle and the seamanship underwater was more advanced than for a big ship. He learned of deep sea pressures, of keeping the submarine on course – a strangely difficult task – and of many kinds of attack and escape. He praised his fellow officers. He always did that.

When the hoarded leaves were over, she returned to Blenheim and Marjorie's acerbic company. Her friend reminded Elaine of the sweets that she and Philippa used to buy as children called Refreshers. They fizzed when you bit into them.

Elaine could never get to London now, since her time off had to be saved for when Miles was granted leave. She had to content herself with telephoning St Helen's. She rarely managed to get Trix or her father, but Miggs gave her the news. The doctor was taking out 'that French girl Gilling or whatever she calls herself' to dinner sometimes. Trix 'had her picture in the *Mail*, dancin' with some young chap.' Miggs's cat 'turns out to be a gentleman, so no kittens.'

Telephone calls were unsatisfactory but reassuring. Her family was still there, well, busy. And at last the blitz on London had stopped, so she need not worry over the night raids.

The member of her family most in Elaine's thoughts was Philippa. When she rang her at the cottage where her sister was now living, Philippa sounded happy. Elaine wondered how true that could be for a girl newly-married to a pilot on operational flying. Sometimes in the background Elaine could hear the sound of men laughing. Philippa said gaily, 'That's the boys. They've all just come charging in.'

Elaine's guess was right, Philippa's happiness was an act – in a way. When she had walked up the aisle on her father's arm and had seen Barny waiting for her, it had been like going towards paradise. She had scarcely been able to believe the wonder of it. Here he was, the man she adored, and she was to be his wife.

On her wedding night Barny made love to her, taking her virginity not gently but roughly. When he was asleep at last, lying against her naked body, his face buried in her neck, he breathed as peacefully as a child. And it was then that she saw for the first time what she had done.

When Barny put the ring on her finger that morning she had taken more than a husband. She had accepted ghastly company. From today it would sit down at her dinner table, stalk her, grin at her. When she was alone it would come up behind her and blow its icy breath on her neck as Barny now breathed his warm one. Her father had known all this. So had Elaine. Philippa never had. But now as clearly as the skeletons grimacing in plague paintings, she saw it. She had been given what her body longed for, a winged hero for a lover. In a dreadful exchange.

She was unlike other women married to fighting men. She was not destined to wait, to dread a telegram, to sleep with censored letters under her pillow, to live for a few pathetic days of leave. Compared to Elaine's life, Philippa's was infinitely better and terrifyingly worse. In many cases the officers in the RAF were not allowed to have their wives living near the station. CO's thought this pyschologically wrong. Other pilots without women

146

envied them. And the closeness of wives made the pilots themselves more conscious of danger, unsettled, uneasy. But Barny had been given permission, and Philippa lived ten minutes away from the Eagles' aerodrome.

They had arrived in the evening following the day of the wedding. The sun was setting as Barny unlocked the rickety cottage door. Just then there was a noise in the sky growing into a roar. Barny and Philippa ran into the overgrown garden and looked up at the sky – there they were, six, seven, eight Spitfires in tight formation, flying low, then steadily rising.

'They're off on the daily bus service,' Barny said. He looked at her and gave her a kiss. 'You don't know what I am talking about, do you? We fly over to France every day for a sweep. That's the bus service. Your husband will be up there tomorrow.'

And so he was. And Philippa must learn to bear it.

Within a week of her arrival at the cottage, Barny had brought all the members of his Squadron to meet her. Eighteen pilots visited her at odd hours, sometimes in a crowd which made the cottage bulge. When she heard voices, she threw open the front door and there were the Eagles, walking through the nettles towards her.

She was instantly and uncritically fond of them. They came from all corners of the United States – from Texas, Florida, Georgia, New England, New York. She could not distinguish which accent matched which State, although she could hear one lilt differing from another. At first she was hard put to it to recall who was Tex or Pete, who was Buzz or Andy. They had short names or nicknames, and they called her Flip the first time they met her.

They were Americans who described themselves as 'part of Lease-Lend.' Civilian pilots in American could earn thousands of dollars a year, but the Eagles were paid seven pounds a week. They belonged to the RAF, wore its blue uniform, and had adopted its lore and language. RAF slang coloured their talk. To be shot down in flames meant to be crossed in love, sprog could be a new uniform or a recruit, putting up propos meant being promoted. A favourite topic – it was the same with all RAF pilots – was the subject of gremlins. These were creatures of the upper air. One or two of the Eagles swore they had seen them – they looked like elves, or demons, or goblins. One English fighter pilot, the story went, had his own gremlin covered with fur like a mole. If stroked the wrong way, it rolled on the floor of the plane in rage. Gremlins plagued pilots. They shifted flarepaths, guided planes to the wrong aerodrome. One ground-based gremlin lived in the Central Registry and hid the files. It was agreed that the gremlins' greatest pleasure was to get pilots into trouble. The WAAFs disagreed. *They* loved the gremlins and said the little creatures protected pilots, cleared away frozen snow and sat on the wings of bombers to prevent the wings from shuddering.

Listening to the talk, Philippa was only half amused. Pilots were superstitious and she had already caught the feeling. To be lucky you must be cautious about invisible things. Who was to say that there were not elves, malicious or well-wishing, living in the icy regions of the upper air?

She did not know how she was going to manage when Barny was flying. She had dreaded discovering that she was too weak to bear it. But she found that she could. It was exactly the same as living through the blitz.

Barny was concerned at her being alone during the days or nights he was flying.

'But I'm sure I can get some kind of work,' she said vaguely.

He tenderly agreed. But he agreed to everything that she said, and she found his American way of spoiling her both beautiful and shocking. She wondered puritanically if it was bad for her.

She had scarcely settled to her life as a pilot's wife when the telephone rang one day.

'My dear Philippa, or do I say Mrs Duval?' said an energetic English voice. It was Jane Alwynne.

Philippa had left Chicheley Buildings in a daze a few days before her wedding. She was too far gone to notice that Jane had asked for the address of the station, and written it in a small note book on the cover of which, in her bold hand, were the words *Do Something*.

They exchanged politenesses. Philippa thanked Jane for her two wedding presents.

'Quite an interesting combination, didn't you think?' said Jane complacently. She had given Philippa an electric iron, and a copy of *The Forsyte Saga*.

'Well, now. Do you suppose you could find a typewriter somewhere?'

148

'A *typewriter*, Mrs Alwynne!'

'Certainly. There's usually an elderly one knocking about somewhere. Try the WVS. Or perhaps your husband might buy you one as a present. Americans are richer than we are,' said Jane. 'I wonder, you see, if you might consider working for the hospital again? I daresay there are times when you will be glad to be busy.'

An ancient upright typewriter was discovered in a junk shop; Barny bought it for her, and one of his mechanics put it in order. After that, with Barny away and her thoughts on him every breathing moment, Philippa once again began to work for Jane. She worked hard. She kept files, sent weekly reports to London, and thumped away at begging letters. Now and then she looked at her watch. At last the Squadron was due back.

She went out into the garden to watch for the planes.

Occasionally a girl called Joan Monteith, a WAAF at the station, called round. When they heard the sound of the planes they would go out and watch for them together. They always began to talk nervously and too much as the planes appeared, tiny dots in the sky. When they could make out the individual planes, Joan would say,

'There's Buzz.'

'That's Tex.'

'There's Barny.'

Both girls would relax and talk more slowly then.

Death did stalk the farmhand's cottage which was now Philippa's home. But she could face it. Sometimes she was strong enough to drive it out and slam the door. It was not only Barny's love which filled her with joy despite the spectre in the house; it was also being with the Eagles in a kingdom of the young and brave. They seized her in their arms and danced with her. They taught her to jitterbug, picking her up and throwing her round. They played Fats Waller until the record wheezed. They shouted with laughter and sprawled on the floor. She was one of them. She loved them.

'You know what you're turning into,' said Barny. 'A Yank.'

'Oh good.'

'It isn't good at all. I married a Limey. I can't have her losing the lime.'

At the time of her marriage, the Eagles had at last flown in battle, welcoming the chance with an eagerness amounting to

149

desperation. Wasn't that what they had come for? But before they flew on ops, two of their pilots had been killed in air accidents. The deaths had confused and depressed the Squadron. Suddenly, death was real. Barny told her about the effect this had had. It sounded crazy, but he thought none of the Eagles had faced it until then. They had come to England for the big show. What they all had in common was being in love with planes, speed, excitement – and danger. That was what being in the RAF meant. Quite a number of the Eagles, Barny said, had wanted to fly in the American Army or Navy, or in the Marines, but they could not pass the tests.

'Here in Britain it is a darned sight easier to get in.'

'That's because we need you.'

He smiled at the reply, but gravely. He returned to the death of the two Eagles. It was decided to give them State funerals. The coffins were draped in Union Jacks, and the Eagles marched behind the gun carriages to the eerie wail of the Funeral March.

'A lot of VIP's from the Air Ministry were there,' he said, 'And the whole Squadron. Officers lined up by the sick quarters, and we were all in service dress with black armbands. It was so odd, Flip. We marched in slow time behind the gun carriages and the music made the hairs stand up on the back of my neck.'

'I suppose it was a gesture to Anglo-American friendship.'

'Oh, sure. But it didn't seem to be anything to do with our buddies, you know. They would have laughed their heads off at the solemnity. One of the guys from Texas is an Indian, you know – you've met him – well, he just couldn't move to that slow tempo. He loped along the way the Indians did across the plains. Of course we were impressed by the British giving our guys a send-off. But – a State funeral, for God's sake.'

The farmhand's cottage, Philippa's first married home, was uncomfortable and poky. The front room was airless and hot in summer, its small window overlooking the garden full of nettles. The kitchen shelves were covered with cracked oilcloth, the brick-floored scullery was so narrow that three big Americans could not fit in it at the same time.

Being married to the Eagle Squadron was a revelation to the conventional English girl. She had only known life at St Helen's, with its middle-class formalities. Now she found her home treated as open house. Nobody telephoned, they simply turned up, called her Pal and gave her a hug. They brought American

150

magazines, Coke and packets of Lucky Strikes and shouted from the door, 'Hey, Flip?'

If she was washing her hair, they sat on the bath and talked to her. If she was ironing, or darning her precious silk stockings, they sprawled beside her on the carpet. If they found her busy with her hospital work, they demanded to help.

'Give us a job. Folding letters? Sticking on stamps?'

Nothing about these Americans was in the least like Englishmen. They thought it right to help in any domestic chore and enjoyed it, saying it reminded them of home. They had no ceremony, and would not know it if they met it. They were as casual as brothers. Sometimes they were rough and boisterous, at other times they quietly talked of their homes on the other side of the world. Of cattle ranching or growing timber, of days in the saddle and nights in the open. They told her stories of beaver dams and young pumas – they called them mountain lions – of raccoons and rattle-snakes, the howl of coyotes, and the slow walk of armadillos.

One of Philippa's closest companions was Chuck Greenfield, whom she had met with Barny at Christmas. Chuck was the youngest member of the Squadron, popular, shy and much teased. His family was wealthy and when cheques arrived from Rhode Island he spent the money as lavishly as the two penniless French A's who had decreed that money was meant to roll. Philippa was at home with Chuck. Yet she was as strongly drawn to the wildest of the Eagles. 'You like Chuck because he's like an English guy,' Barny said, smiling, but it was not so. She loved his candid face and truthfulness and a sort of innocence.

Barny did not share Philippa's admiration for Joan Monteith, a WAAF officer with whom Philippa had things in common – a widowed father and two sisters. Joan was too serious for Barny's taste. She must have guessed that, because Philippa often noticed how she made an effort to be bright when Barny lounged into the cottage and found her there. Philippa admired her – she was stage-struck about the WAAFs and envied her job.

The autumn weather, gold upon gold, went suddenly. The skies grew overcast and there were heavy rainstorms. When Barny woke one morning he went straight to the window, pulled back the curtains, looked at the sky, and returned to bed. Bad weather meant that fighter pilots were grounded. He loathed inaction. He was irritable all the morning, and when the duty officer telephoned to say there was a Recognition lecture, Barny left with alacrity.

Philippa settled down to her hospital cards. How quiet the cottage was. Petrol had become almost impossible to obtain now, and life in the country had returned to an early nineteenth century existence – it might have been Jane Austen's time. Nothing went by in the lane outside but the occasional clip-clop of a horse-drawn farm cart or pony trap.

She was surprised when the front door bell rang. Eagles ignored bells. The thin uniformed figure of Joan Monteith stood on the step.

'I did telephone but the number must be out of order. It was engaged for ages.'

'That was my boss, Mrs Alwynne, giving me orders. She goes on forever. How nice to see you. Let's have tea.'

Joan gave her curious almost embarrassed smile which made her look as if she might cry. When Philippa brought in the tea, they sat down in the stuffy front room on a sofa as hard as a stone. Joan talked of the bad weather – how the Eagles hated it – 'Eagles need clear skies' – she spoke as if of a flock of birds. Thank heaven for the lecture, otherwise they would simply hang round the mess playing poker or shove halfpenny, and getting steadily more jumpy and picking at each other.

'When I look at the boys sometimes,' she said, 'I think about all those American girls who write to them and send them photographs of themselves. They can't know what it's really like.'

'I don't know what it's really like either. I envy you. Being part of it.'

'But you're married!'

'That's not it, Joan. You know it isn't. Barny married me and I know he sometimes thinks he shouldn't have done. So many CO's think it is bad for morale to return from night fighting to home comforts. They don't believe a man with something important to do in the war should have the responsibility of a wife. Of course *I* never think we shouldn't be married. But some of his friends do. There are things they think and don't say.'

Joan looked at her for a moment.

'I suppose I do see. It's true you aren't part of it, on the station, working with them. For them, really. But don't envy us. We know them and we love them, although we try not to fall in

152

love with them. That's true. We try. The Eagles come into our mess, you know, just as they come here, and they sit and drink beer or grab us and dance. When that happens, they're just the same age as we are, they call us kids, but so are they. Then there's a call. And they go off to "receive further orders in the air" as it's called. Maybe the afternoon bus service to Abbeville or Lille. They go to the dispersal hut and into their planes, and we stand on the roof and count them as they set off. We wave. They might be setting off to some air circus to do aerobatics.'

'I don't think I could bear to stand on the roof and count.'

'We can't help it.'

Joan sighed. She said that she had disliked Americans before the war without knowing a thing about them. Her father still did. He hated foreigners and nothing would budge him about it. He'd been horrified when she was posted to the Eagle Squadron. She remembered that she herself had not been too pleased. She was ashamed to remember that.

Philippa wondered whether Joan's 'we try not to' really meant that she was in love with one of the Eagles. Which one? Did he also love her? She had the strong impression that Joan was already regretting having said too much. That happened. You said what was in your heart and then you wished you hadn't. Saying it aloud made it worse.

Barny was still the sweetest-natured man Philippa had met in her life, the most spoiling, the kindest. But the very times she thirsted for – when he was out of danger – were what made him very nervous. There was nothing he would not do for her, yet the only part of his life that truly mattered to him she could not share. For the first months of their marriage he told her almost nothing about flying and she knew she could not ask. The weather cleared, Barny kissed her, and swung away in the early morning with a 'goin' huntin'.'

But one night he came home in a state of exhausted excitement, his eyes blazing in a grey face. He took her in his arms and made love to her fiercely – she had the feeling that almost any woman would have done just then. But after he had slept, he woke and told her what had happened.

He had been over St Omer. The Squadron had been sent to escort the bombers, and after the bombs had been dropped Barny saw a dog-fight going on behind him. He turned to join battle, attacking a Messerschmitt which dived vertically towards

153

the ground. Barny dived in pursuit, but a second enemy plane came after him, firing in hard bursts. In a few moments Barny was at ground level, flying at 500 miles an hour right over the St Omer aerodrome with the enemy planes still hunting him. He was flying below the level of the trees and only glimpsed the enemy now and then in the plane mirror. He waited until the first enemy was in firing range, pulled the stick back and turned as tightly as possible – only to realize with horror that the enemy was turning too, inside his turn, and Barny was now the target. He couldn't climb . . . the Messerschimtt was above him.

'Suddenly I knew I was fighting for my life. It was a weird sensation, realizing if I didn't do something in that split second, I'd never see you again.'

By now he was a mere five feet from the ground, almost skimming the grass. He pulled the stick back so hard that he blacked out – it must have only been a second but it seemed like terrifying hours. When he came to he was twenty feet behind the enemy plane. He gave the plane a burst of fire and the enemy began to do extraordinary aerobatics, weaving, climbing, then streaking back to the aerodrome with Barny chasing him right down to the hangar, then across the flying field and back. The enemy was trying to get the St Omer ground defences to shoot Barny down. The whole thing was so wild, so quick, the planes moving so impossibly fast, and as the enemy plane in desperation turned on its back, Barny gave it a long burst – and found his guns were empty. He turned frantically for home, pursued for a while, and losing his hunters at last. He flew at hedge level all the way to Le Touquet, only rising when he reached the sea.

Philippa could say nothing when the story finished. She kissed him.

But the description of the fights stayed in her imagination and now her dark opponent was harder than ever to combat. She worked for Jane Alwynne when Barny was flying. She ran out of work and telephoned for more. Jane, delighted, asked if she could manage to do the hospital's financial records? They were in an appalling mess and she would be so very grateful. The trouble was the time it would take . . .

Philippa agreed. She would have agreed to dig the foundations of a new hospital wing single-handed, providing the work could be done near the cottage. She welcomed anything which kept her from seeing visions of planes skimming the grass, attacker and pursuer, both with death in their hands.

Now when she heard the planes coming home she ran out to count them. And if one or more was missing she sat, dry-eyed and sick, until Barny came home.

Often he returned to say they had flown on two patrols and seen nothing, nothing at all. The sea had been flat, visibility good, the patrol boring. Dreary.

'When damn all happens, patrolling is just hell. Battles are different. They're exciting.'

Days went by. Winter days when lovers in another world would have walked in the bare woods or climbed the low brown hills, or sat by fires in English pubs, eating bread and cheese. She couldn't believe there had ever been such a time, free of the dark companion. What was real was her life now, her life close to Barny, who lived in the sky and returned unwillingly to earth, an eagle well named.

'More patrols. Nothing bloody happening. Some of the boys swear they'll get out of the goddammed Air Force and I don't blame them.'

It was evening, and she went across the room and knelt down beside him. He put his hand up to her cheek. But his eyes were looking inward.

'Long spells without action do get us down, Flip. I know I griped when the weather grounded us, but patrolling is almost as bad. We want to be in battle. That's our job.'

'I know.'

'Do you realize that when I first met you that time I'd never been in a dog-fight? And nor had any of my pals. And even after our first go, when we were jumped by some Messerschmitts, we were so wet behind the ears, it was difficult for us to realize there was an enemy actually trying to kill us. Some guy up there stooging around waiting for the chance to give it to us if we weren't quicker on the draw and got him first. I remember the first plane I shot down. I was so excited and het up and everything happened so fast and I thought – Christ, it's him or me. It was a bomber coming straight at me. I fired a half second burst at about a hundred yards. I saw the bomber burst into flames and head straight into the drink. God, it went so fast, and it hit the sea and I reckon I killed the lot of them. I couldn't help thinking about it. Everybody at the station congratulated me, and the story was written up in the personal combat reports. The bomber was seen going down. I'd scored officially. But do you know, I couldn't help thinking about how that bomber had been *there*, in the sky ahead of me, and its crew had been alive and full of hope and excitement, just as I was. And the next minute there were flames and the huge splash, and a sort of mess on the surface of the sea. It's still the only one I remember.'

He had taken her hand and was examining the palm. She knew he couldn't see it.

'I suppose fighting men have always felt like that, Barny. If they had hearts, I mean.'

'We mustn't have them. That's the point.'

When the Squadron was moved – this happened three times – Philippa moved too. The cottage among the nettles was left behind, and she packed and travelled on, and quickly learned how to make a ramshackle lodging comfortable. She became a practised camp follower.

Months had gone since her marriage. The Eagle Squadron was extended from one to three, with more pilots, more Spitfires, more action. There were losses. Andy was shot down. Tex was missing, believed killed. He was never traced. And there were others. Young men who had hung round in the cottage, called her 'Pal' and sat drinking Coke or danced to the old records with her. They vanished as if they had never been, and more young Americans replaced them.

The Eagles talked of the dead pilots as if they had been posted abroad, matter-of-factly, without emotion. 'Isn't that Andy's favourite song?' somebody said, and 'Tex never believed that story of yours, Buddy.'

Philippa also lived in the present. She loved the Squadrons with a passionate partisan love. They were proud of their identity, wore English uniform, and were utterly, movingly, American.

Towards the end of the year it was bitterly cold. The fields were sprinkled with frozen snow and the skies were so low that the pilots were grounded. The Squadrons, and Philippa, were back at Martlesham Heath, where she had come first after her marriage. Barny managed to get back the same cottage, which had stood empty since the Eagles had been gone. It was odd to find herself back in the poky rooms where she had lived what seemed now to be years ago. She tried not to think of the lost friends who had filled its narrow rooms.

When Barny came home one bitter December night, she knew he was going to be gloomy and difficult. She left him to himself. She had lit a fire in the sitting room, and after giving her a perfunctory kiss he went to sit by it and listen to the wireless. From the kitchen, she could hear a measured English voice. It must be the nine o'clock news.

Suddenly there was a blood-curdling yell.

With a pang of sheer terror she rushed into the sitting room. He was staring at the wireless in stupefaction. He began to stutter –

'The Japs have attacked Pearl Harbour – they've b-b-bloody well attacked – *we're in the war!*'

Leaping up, he picked her up and swung her round.

'You were in it anyway, stupid Yank!' she cried, laughing,

'But this is different! The *US is in the war!*' he shouted back.

He hadn't stopped exclaiming when there was a thunder of knocking on the door which burst open and in pelted Chuck Greenfield.

'It was on the radio in the pub – what do you know – the Japs – '

It was a night of drink and song.

After the extraordinary news the Squadrons' spirits were irrepressible. They teased Philippa.

'It's our war now.'

'When wasn't it yours? You're in the RAF, aren't you?'

'Yeah, but now it's different.'

It never occurred to her, sharing their gaiety and the euphoria of the 'Here's to the good old USA drink it down, drink it down' that it was indeed different. Later news came from across the Atlantic that the Eagles were going to be disbanded. That was not the word used – it was called 'transferred'. The three squadrons were to be transferred out of the RAF Fighter Command to the United States Air Force.

When she heard that she knew that part of her life was over. She had, in truth, taken on Barny's life as if buttoning herself into his blue tunic, and because she wore it she had accepted the never absent dread and the more terrible visitor. But it had been a fair exchange. She had had Barny in her arms, and she had

157

lived among men who made Englishmen seem tame. When she first married, the Eagles had been boisterous and uncontrolled, keeping no rules, forgetting to salute, blowing off steam by crazy forbidden flying when on test flights. She'd seen them flying upside down over the tops of trees, or skimming the fields as if cutting corn. They had been excitable and excited, lovable and maddening.

But fighting had changed them. They'd started by thinking they had a birthright to behave as they damned well pleased. Weren't they individualists? Weren't they American? But they painfully learned that the old myth of the solo ace shooting his way through the sky was a dangerous myth indeed. They had to become professionals, to work and fly in formation. The very thing they resisted, discipline, was what brought them safety. They were veterans now. Danger had changed them, and the death of friends. During one terrible ten days, the Squadron had lost five pilots.

Barny had altered too. He was quieter and older. Philippa had a pain in her heart to remember the young man of last year who had been in the London fire raid with her. Would that young man ever come back? She didn't think so. Sometimes in his sleep he started and shuddered. Or he woke groaning 'Oh Christ.' And when he was sitting with her during the day, he would suddenly flinch.

She knew that *he* must speak about it and that she could not. Then one evening when he returned from a sweep over France and came into the cottage, his teeth were chattering in his head. He said he felt icy cold. She made him sit down, she fetched a blanket, and hot coffee laced with rye whisky. She knelt by him and rocked him in her arms.

He couldn't speak.

He leaned against her in the silence of the hideous little room. At last he drank the coffee and said, 'It's the flak. I dread it so. Even on the ground I keep thinking about it, imagining it, thinking I can see it. I'm not afraid of meeting the enemy planes, Flip, it's not that. It never has been. It's the flak barrage, seeing the shells exploding round you like – like giant black flowers all over the sky. And then the plane shivers and rocks about from the explosion and you can't control it. And while you're trying to get it back on course, the flak gets worse. There are explosive shells that the gunners shoot at the planes, which can burst in

158

the middle of the formation. They knock holes in the wings or the fuselage, or they hit the pilot, or the plane catches fire. Then you're trapped. It isn't the enemy,' he said again, 'You can see him and fight back. Flak feels like a hand reaching up to pull me out of the sky.' He paused and shivered again and said, 'Tonight there were shell holes in my wings.'

But he went on flying. And although his nightmare recurred, he never talked about it again. Philippa did not dare. Perhaps speaking of it would raise it like a demon.

Chapter Eleven

'Flip? It's Pa's birthday next week. I really think we both ought to make the effort to get home. He'll start thinking he only has one daughter. And I shouldn't imagine he sees much of her, would you?'

Elaine was speaking on the public telephone in one of the ground floor corridors at Blenheim. It was difficult to hear her sister's reply, there were footsteps and voices going by.

'Sorry. There's such a noise here. Did you hear me about Pa?'

Raising her voice, Philippa agreed that they should come to London. They arranged to meet at St Helen's on the day of their father's birthday which was in mid-January.

Elaine went back up the staircase from the Great Hall to her office. She sat down at her desk, on which reports lay waiting to be typed. Sensual-lipped eighteenth-century women in silks and pearls looked down at her from the walls. Things at the palace had changed since their day. Sighing, she began to work.

The Submariners' Course had ended and now, after more leaves than she had dared to hope for, Miles was gone. He was at sea. She found it hard to know nothing. When he had been on convoys, horrible though the Atlantic was, she had at least been able to imagine something of his sailor's life. But it was different now. Where had he gone? Husbandless, she was glad to work for more than nine hours a day. She had said that she wanted an 'eating up' job, and the description applied to her work at Blenheim. It consumed the uncounted days as if it were a dragon.

She still worked for the well-mannered and silent Captain Goodier. His reserve towards her was total. She could not remember him ever asking her a personal question. She supposed it was a change for him after the exhausting interrogations which were part of his work.

The one bright spot in Elaine's dull life was Marjorie. To Marjorie she could admit how painfully she missed Miles. Her friend's attitudes were her own. She could tell Marjorie things about herself that she would never tell her father or her sisters.

'You really hate Shelton, don't you?' remarked Marjorie, on the day Elaine had telephoned Philippa. 'I don't know why you stay. You could think up some straightforward lie, as we used to call them at school, and get digs at Keble. You could live with me, come to that. Why not? We'd have a lot of fun. You are an unnecessary martyr, you know. What can Miles possibly gain from you being stuck with those parents of his?'

She glanced at Elaine, who was walking beside her under the huge bare trees, the collar of her coat turned up. A scarlet scarf was tied round her neck, it trailed on to her breast. Marjorie said, laughing,

'You're a robin. Oh look! There's another.'

Elaine was not looking. She said humourlessly, 'You know quite well why I'm at Shelton. Because the *idea* of my being at his home makes him happy. He so loves it.'

'And you detest it.'

'The house is very beautiful.'

'Pooh. You know I mean your in-laws. What is the good of a mansion and crests on the family silver when you have a stone-faced mother-in-law behind the teapot?'

'She liked you when you came to see us,' said Elaine perversely.

'Stone-faced,' repeated Marjorie, 'I am middle-class and so are you, and the upper classes really make us feel it, don't they? They can't let go of their superiority. They have to grind down us peasants. Do you remember how Lady St Aird asked me about the Flowers when I came to tea. She positively grilled me. And then she discovered one of the Flower cousins nine times removed was related to that St Aird bishop. One had the feeling she had found an excuse for giving me tea. What it all boils down to is that if you're one of them you're fine, and if you are not, then you are out. Well, you married one, so you are in.'

'But she doesn't like me any more than I like her. And then there is Miles' father.'

Marjorie couldn't help laughing. St Aird, who had only appeared at the door at tea time and then, seeing her had promptly vanished, had taken her fancy. He was a kind of mad Mrs Rochester, wasn't he, she said. Except that he was in the stables and apparently knew how to paint.

'Or so you say. I wasn't asked to look.'

'He did look funny, standing in the door so suspiciously,' said Elaine, beginning to laugh too.

Elaine did not feel disloyal, smiling over the St Airds with Marjorie, because what her friend said was true. Elaine tried with all her heart to see with Miles' eyes and think with his thoughts, but now that he had gone it was becoming more and more difficult. There had always been differences in his way of thinking and her own; but his enchanting presence removed them or perhaps veiled them. When she was with him, she could see nobody else. She knew he was a snob: that made her smile. She knew that money – or to be exact the stylish signs of it – pleased him. Why shouldn't he look at things in that way? Miles was convinced, quite wrongly, that she would eventually love his parents and Shelton as he did. It was part of his deep family affection that he believed it, and Elaine stayed in his home just because of that. Sexual love between Miles and herself formed a kind of glue, which mended the ship and held it fast and made it seaworthy. Now that he was far away, there was the danger that the glue would melt.

Life at Shelton told on her nerves. There was the farce, every night, of changing for dinner when there was not a servant in the place. Claire was no cook, and the food was as bad as Miggs', but there was much less excuse, for in the country such treasures as fresh eggs and vegetables were commonplace. Elaine offered to cook the meal once or twice, but Claire had been so patronizing at the result – Elaine cooked beautifully – that Elaine realized it simply counted against her. To cook well was middle-class, or even common.

Usually serene and with a gentle philosophy, Elaine discovered in herself a temper she had not known she possessed and which needed to be kept in check. She lived in an ancient house with a dreamy English feel about it which soaked into the very walls. The bedroom smelled of lavender, the windowsills were broad enough to sit upon, the parquet floors were the colour of honey. From every window she could see a garden overgrown and wild, but lovely yet. In the dining room enigmatic St Aird faces looked down at her during the ill-cooked meals. How much more did she prefer the Blenheim portraits, all of them sexy, some positively vulgar. If it were not for Miles, she thought, I wouldn't stay here for five minutes.

The St Airds had few visitors. But the weekend Elaine had

arranged to go to London for her father's birthday she heard that Claire had invited her elder sister to stay.

Breaking the news of her coming absence, Elaine felt very guilty. Who would help to cook for Lady Agatha, she wondered.

At Elaine's hesitant and anxious manner, Claire raised pale eyebrows, 'My dear Elaine, of course it is convenient for you to go. Edmund and I are taking my sister to dine at The Bear at Woodstock.'

Never once since Elaine first came to Shelton had they taken her out for a meal, despite the Government positively encouraging people to eat out as a way of improving the meagre weekly rations.

Lady Agatha arrived before Elaine left for the station. She was older and plainer than Claire, very stout and slow. Even during tea she had begun to drone family litanies.

'I saw Cousin Robert at Eastbourne, Claire. His three boys are at Eton now.'

'Rachel is in the Wrens. She's engaged to a lieutenant commander, one of the Eynshams. You remember Michael Eynsham? He married . . .'

Refusing a second cup of tea, Elaine escaped to finish her packing. The round winter sun had begun to set. It shone through her bedroom windows, and when she looked out, the gardens were lit with a dying orange light. The yew hedges which had been shaped like peacocks and urns when she came to Shelton in peacetime summer had lost their identities now. They were simply green bushes. The lawns were like winter fields.

There was a tap on her door, and Claire walked into the room.

'The postman has just come. Two letters from Miles. One for you.'

She handed Elaine the letter with *On Active Service* stamped across it, and stood in the doorway, reading her own letter.

Elaine tore hers open. And found something in the envelope which was not a letter at all, but a square about five inches in size; Miles' letter had been photographed. His writing, never easy to read, was rendered miniscule.

'My darling. Here I am and this will be a dull letter due to dull routine only enlivened now and again by moments of happy oblivion due to the local drink. You'll be amused to hear that it

163

is cheap and very plentiful. Do you remember in Brighton, my darling, what a great event it was for us when we actually got hold of a bottle of white wine? Here it flows like a river . . .'

Elaine gave a little gasp.

Claire looked up from her own letter and said sharply, 'What is it?'

'He's in Malta.'

'So he says. Well?'

'Oh,' said Elaine weakly, 'it seems so far. I wonder when on earth he will be back.'

'Very likely not for a year or even two,' said Claire in a voice of an admonishing headmistress. She put her own letter into the bead handbag which she carried about with her, like a girl going to a ball. At the door she turned and looked at Elaine. The last sunlight shone on her, making her handsome and old.

'Our submarines must be based at Malta to patrol the Med. They are needed and the more there are of them the better. I trust,' she said, turning to go, 'we are not going to be sorry for ourselves.'

Marjorie was in Oxford on a shopping expedition, and she arranged to meet Elaine and see her off. She was in good spirits.

'Keep your eyes peeled for a lipstick for me, *please!* Any colour, any price, and as black market as you like. My face is looking khaki now my lipstick is down to the metal edge. And it's jolly painful putting it on, I might add.'

Elaine had been prepared for London to look dirty, but her country-accustomed eyes were shocked by its battered, dusty, wrecked appearance. It was a city of ruins which had not settled to be just that. There was a thin fog in the streets and it was nearly dark though not yet blackout time, when she walked up the short drive to St Helen's, letting herself in with her key. She put down her suitcase, pulling off her hat which had flattened her hair. The kitchen door opened.

'You're back, then. Like a cuppa? Sailor and I are havin' one.'

Wondering what matelot was sharing Miggs' strong red tea, Elaine followed her into a pleasantly warm kitchen. The split in the boiler was wider and through it she could see coke glowing almost white. It made a dull roar. There was nobody in the kitchen but Miggs and the ginger cat. It, too, had grown considerably.

164

'I call him Sailor because of the way he strolled in here. Casual-like. Quite settled down, he has.'

'How does Father take him?'

'Pretends not to see him, of course.'

Nothing in the kitchen had changed. On the mantelpiece so high that Miggs had to stand on a chair to reach it, was a black marble clock with a brass plaque: it had been presented to Miggs' great-uncle in the Royal Engineers when he left the army. Its chime, on the quarters, was like Big Ben's and it was the only clock in the house to keep good time. The dresser was built against the wall, and stacked with white china patterned with red, blue and yellow plums, a design called Imperial Fruit. It had been a wedding present to Theo and Mary – thirty-six of everything. A surprising number of the dishes still remained, considering how many Miggs smashed, shouting, 'God damn it!' as yet another soup plate crashed to the ground.

On the bottom shelf of the dresser was a large basket for Sailor. Miggs's sewing box was on the table, with some socks of Theo's. The three ration books were nearby, fastened with an elastic band.

Pouring tea, Miggs looked approvingly at Elaine. She had a soft spot for the eldest daughter, often remarking that Miss Elaine didn't let you down. And she liked Miles. Miggs had finally grown accustomed to Philippa's Yankee husband, but still sometimes remarked 'How do we know there isn't a wife in Hollywood or wherever he comes from?' Her prejudices had not died because America was now an ally.

'Up for the doctor's birthday? I hope you're not plannin' a dinner at home. There isn't a blind thing in the larder.'

She gazed into her teacup.

'Blow me down, another stranger. Must be a new young fellow of Trix's. That'll be no surprise. Who keeps an eye on her now, I ask you, Miss Elaine? Nobody. Not your job or mine either. It's the doctor's and he's too busy to see what goes on under his nose. Not that I blame her,' added Miggs with a swerve of attitude, 'for makin' the young chaps dance. But nobody could say she's doin' her bit, could they? Ah. There goes the surgery bell.'

She donned her creaking white overall.

Upstairs, Elaine thought how small her bedroom looked after the high-ceilinged spaciousness of Shelton. She was unpacking

165

when she heard her sister's voice and called out, 'Is that Flip? I'm in here.'

A second later Philippa rushed in headlong, to throw herself at Elaine and hug her tightly. Elaine, embarrassed at any emotion except between Miles and herself, laughed.

'Oh, darling!' cried Philippa, 'What an age! I've sure missed you – let me look at you! Glamorous as ever.'

Elaine was wearing one of the suits she had had made for her before the war; it was a milky brown and with it she wore a white silk blouse. As the nearest thing to uniform, such clothes were fashionable. Philippa was dressed in a purple, green and white checked shirt like a cowboy's and a pinafore dress of dark brown with metal clasps on the straps. Her hair was glossy and fell in its two crescents as always, but her eyes were too large for her face.

'Flip, you're very thin. I am not sure it suits you.'

'I measured my waist. It's nearly as small as Trix's. Less than twenty-three inches – imagine.'

'Sure you get enough to eat?' said Elaine disapprovingly.

Philippa laughed. Of course she did, more than enough. Why the Eagles were sent lovely boxes of American food, chocolate and biscuits and a wonderful cake made of things called pecan nuts and great big sticky cherries. It was a miracle that she was not as fat as a pig.

'By the way, Barny sends his love. He's got a weekend pass and please God will be here on Saturday.'

'How lucky you are to have him in England!' Elaine exclaimed without thinking.

Her sister did not answer but sat down on the bed and asked about Miles, about Blenheim and Shelton. The questions were perfunctory, and soon she began to talk. She had so wanted to see Elaine, she said. She had so much to say. She had tried to write, but somehow things looked melodramatic when you wrote them down.

The summer had been tough, she said. The patrols had been sent out over France every day. Then the offensive had begun and the bombers went out in large numbers and of course they had to be protected by the squadrons of Fighter Command, which included the Eagles. Big groups of fighters always guarded the bombers. First there was the advance guard – 'Their job is to try and sweep the enemy fighters from the sky,' she said. Then came the bombers with their escorts, fighters who flew

166

beside them and in the rear and above, making a kind of protective wall. Escorting was the hardest job for fighter pilots, they were not allowed to leave the bombers, they had to stay in their exact positions.

'You see,' said Philippa carefully, 'they must not break away and attack the enemy, even if he's trying to get through the wall. The only action an escort fighter ever gets lasts for an instant – it's never a real fight to the finish. Escorts can't have the fun of the chase. The position they *do* like is being above the bombers, it's like the man in the crow's nest of a ship on the lookout. Pilots prefer that job because there's the chance they'll be ordered down to attack.'

She talked on. Of the comradeship between pilots and their technicians, the signal operators, the engineers. Of how on duty most pilots drank nothing and 'ordinary people' didn't know that, and thought them hell raisers. She talked of battles, chases, of planes hunting and planes vanishing, of baling out and landing in the sea, of a bullet hitting Barny's compass, and how one of his friends flying to France lost his way and came home and how horrified he was. The air was filled with Spitfires in her talk, the sea with ships. The Eagles often said 'A Spit's more sensitive than a dame.' And the other thing they were always telling her was 'Those Krauts sure can fly.'

Her language was littered with slang unfamiliar to Elaine who knew nobody in what Miles called The Royal Advertising Force. Philippa talked of stooging and weaving, peeling off, snaking about, hedge-hopping. To parachute into the sea was to brolly hop into the drink. The slang was flippant, her sister's face tense.

'One of the Eagles wrote a love song to a WAAF I knew,' she said, 'it was called "You Shot me Down in Flames".'

She sang the refrain in her hoarse voice.

Then suddenly,

'I'm so selfish. Why do you let me go on like this? Forgive me. It's just so good to be able to talk. Not to have to watch my tongue.'

'With Barny?'

'With everybody, Elaine. They're so different now. The war has changed them. Changed Barny. When I first got married and met them all, they were just a bunch of wild boys. Their CO told Barny he thought they would never make a proper squadron, they just didn't know how to think as a team. That's very

167

American, you see. Not toeing the line, no obedience, things like that. They changed because you have to. They're experienced pilots now and they're tough. They joke about getting killed, about who'll be next. I think they make themselves feel that death is for the other guy. It won't happen to them.'

'Do you manage to feel like that?'

'I only pretend, Elaine. And there's something else. The three Eagle Squadrons are to be disbanded. Not right away, but it is going to happen when the Americans come over here. All the Eagles are quite excited about it, really, even Barny. I mean, their own people here and not on the other side of the world, not understanding a thing that's going on. But I *hate* it. Knowing the Eagles won't be in the RAF.'

She sighed and stood up, saying – an old panacea of hers – that she would go and wash her hair.

As she left the room she said, 'Do you like my pinafore dress? It's called a lumberjack. Barny's sister in Louisiana, Mary-Lou, sent it to me. Wasn't it swell of her?'

Elaine, who disliked it, agreed about the kindness of the American sister-in-law. For a moment she imagined Claire St Aird, in her trailing pre-war lace and pearls, faced at dinner time with a girl dressed as a lumberjack.

Miggs was doing the blackout. Theo was still at the hospital, and there was an hour before the family would be leaving to dine out. The girls went into the drawing room and sat by a miserable one-bar electric fire, talking of small things. The food at Blenheim, served by the duke's daughters, Philippa's hospital work which had recently raised two hundred pounds.

'Elaine? Flip?'

A metallic little voice called. In darted Trix.

'Together at last!' She ran over to kiss them both, squatted on the floor between them radiantly smiling. Her hair seemed longer and fairer, she still wore it in the Veronica Lake style, hanging on her cheeks and hiding one dark eye. Her pale blue skirt was short and pleated like a kilt, and a fine silk blouse was of a darker blue, with antique silver buttons engraved with daisies. Her smile was as gamine, her face as flawless as her sisters remembered. But it was more secret.

'Fun to see you,' she said, 'I begin to forget that I've got two big sisters. Of course I tell everybody about you both, but I don't think they believe me any more. I suppose you're up-to-the-

168

minute with each other's news, and all I shall get is the fag end. Well, girls? What's been happening?'

She looked charmingly from one to the other.

Philippa glanced towards Elaine, almost for rescue. She hoped Elaine would speak, for she herself still found it quite difficult to talk to Trix about Barny. It was foolish and unsophisticated, and she had been married for nearly a year, but there it was. Trix and Barny had made love. Why couldn't she forget it? Elaine, always quick, began to talk about Miles and Malta and Blenheim. She also described the St Airds and Trix listened and laughed.

'Flip will fascinate you about the Eagles later,' finished Elaine casually, 'but what we both want to hear is about *you.*' She sounded like their mother when she added, not without severity, 'You never write to us. And when we telephone, where are you?'

'Dynamiting the West End, I guess,' said Philippa.

Trix gave her a friendly look.

'That's Yankee talk. I like it. Yes, I do a bit of dynamiting but lately perhaps not as much as usual. The fact is – '

She paused for effect. She wound a lock of hair round her finger, and then arranged it on her shoulder.

'The fact is, girls, I am married.'

Chapter Twelve

'You're what?'

Two horrified voices spoke at once. Trix looked delighted. 'I thought I'd knock you out. Yes, I am a married woman. Have been for two whole weeks. We were married by special licence at Caxton Hall. I told Pa I was at the Masons as per yuge, but actually I was with my *husband* at the Ritz. He got passionate leave to marry me and then after a glorious night of love, off he went back to his ship.'

'To his ship,' repeated Elaine who had gone pale, 'Who is he?'

'Wouldn't you like to know?'

'Trix!' shouted Philippa, as red as Elaine was white, 'You are under age, you had no right – poor Father – '

'Poor fiddlesticks. What does he care? Particularly now that boring French girl is hanging around. You remember her? Mademoiselle from Armentières. One of the two French A's stupidly brought her here, she's Alain's cousin. Miggs simply can't stick her and neither can I. Anyway, if you must know, I married a guy I met at your wedding, Flip. He is a friend of Miles' and *you* know him, Elaine. You invited him as a matter of fact. I am married to Dick Polglaze.'

'Marjorie's cousin!'

'That's right. He often tells me about the Flowers in Oxfordshire and says I must go down and meet them. Well, he's had a bit of leave, not much, his ship was due for a boiler clean and . . . and . . . off he took me to Caxton Hall. I must show you our wedding photographs.'

Elaine and Philippa stared at her. She had never seemed so much a stranger, so far from the little girl who had sucked sweets and failed examinations, the child whom Elaine had worried over and Philippa had petted.

Both sisters continued to look at her, as if waiting for something she was not going to give them. Philippa automatically put her hand into the pocket of her pinafore dress and pulled out some Lucky Strike cigarettes. Elaine refused, wrink-

170

ling her nose, but Trix accepted. They smoked for a while in silence, the room filling with the foreign scent.

'Do you love him,' asked Philippa at last.

'Of course I do, stoopid.'

'Are you having a baby?' said Elaine suddenly.

Trix really laughed at that.

'How old-fashioned you are. Why should I be preggers if I don't want to be? Not that Dick would object, he said I'd look quite sweet, one baby pushing the pram of another. But of course I am not.'

'Then I don't understand and I'm sure Flip doesn't either. Why rush into marriage exactly as if you *were* pregnant and didn't dare to leave it another week? Why the haste and secrecy? Dick Polglaze is a nice man. I can't imagine what he was thinking of.'

Trix stretched her legs and wiggled her toes in the toeless pink and blue shoes. She seemed as if she were reflecting, a rarity with Trix. Philippa saw that although Trix had expected their reaction, and had been prepared for it and even amused at it, she still found her sisters hard to cope with. She might be casual and airy about them at a distance, but Elaine in particular impressed her. Far more than their father did. Perhaps, thought Philippa, that is because Elaine loves her. Trix is not sure that Father does . . .

'Dick's ship is back on Atlantic convoy now,' she said, 'we thought we'd take the jump while we had the chance.'

It was a sentence to move the hardest heart, and it certainly reached Philippa's. She looked kindly at her little sister.

'Are you very happy?' she said in a soft voice.

'It's lovely fun being married,' said Trix, seizing on the sympathy and affection, 'Why didn't you tell me what a lark it is? I would have rushed to Caxton Hall ages ago.'

'Scarcely with Dick Polglaze, since you only met him at Flip's wedding. And he must have been at sea most of the time since then,' said Elaine very coldly. She had no sympathy at all, and Trix was getting on her nerves.

'Oh Elaine! What I meant was supposing I had met Dick sooner, of course. Anyway, it was love at first sight. Isn't my ring wizzy? Little sapphires, because Dick likes me in blue. It's an eternity ring, of course; he got it at Asprey's. He's going to get me a diamond one next, he is *so* extravagant.'

Turning her black eyes on her elder sister, she said in a wheedling tone, 'Elaine . . . one thing . . . '

'I know what you are going to ask me. About Pa.'

'Darling, it *would* be better if you told him.'

'Trix!' exclaimed Philippa, sympathy oozing away, 'That is pretty monstrous of you.'

'Oh I know. But I am.'

Elaine did not know what to answer. She saw in Philippa's face as well as Trix's the belief that she would do it. They were as bad as each other. They leaned on her as if she were quite old. They demanded that she would take their mother's place. You are the strong one, their silence said. She did not feel strong. Miles's absence had weakened her. She had the sensation that it would be easy for anybody to pull her down. She had lost the certainties of peacetime, the old moralities and standards. She resented her two sisters looking at her like puppies waiting for a biscuit.

'Very well,' she said, after a pause, 'I will do it. But not for your sake, Trix. If you are old enough to marry, you are old enough to do your own dirty work. I'll do it for Dick. Because he is Miles' friend.'

She walked out of the room.

Free of Elaine's coldness and disapproval and seeing how passionately interested Philippa had become, Trix told her in colourful detail the story of her wedding. She had worn a new dress from Harrods (she wasn't going to say how much it cost), and Dick had bought her white orchids to carry. They had had champagne cocktails, and the best man had been somebody from Dick's ship, he was called Lofty because he was six foot five, and he was *so* funny. They had had a lovely party, the three of them, at the Ritz after coming back from Caxton Hall.

'It was just gorgeous,' finished Trix.

A strain of impulsiveness, of precipitate haste, ran through the nature of all three Tyrrell girls. It had been in Theo when he was young: it was in Trix and in Philippa. They let theirs rip. Elaine had hers under control, but this evening she gave way to the Tyrrell lust to get things over. She marched straight into her father's study when his last patient had left. She met Miggs sidling out, unbuttoning her white overall. Miggs whispered, 'So she's told you.'

'*You knew!*'

172

'She never said. I found out,' said Miggs succinctly. 'I suppose you've got landed with the job of tellin' the doctor. Typical.'

Theo was at his desk, taking the wrapping off a weekly medical journal. He looked his usual immaculate and tired self. When he saw her, he stood up.

'Father.'

She did not, this time, back away from his kiss but stayed close to him and shut her eyes. He smelled of eau-de-cologne and disinfectant as he had always done. She liked it.

'A happy birthday, Father. We're going out to dinner, you know. *We* are taking *you*.'

'That's very nice of you, Elaine.'

He gave her a kind smile.

She sat down, drew a breath and said,

'Before we go I have a shock for you.'

Theo stiffened. He thought – it can't be Miles, she is too calm.

'Trix is married,' she said baldly. 'It was my idea to break the news to you before we go out. I think you should know right away. But I don't want you to quarrel with her. Listen, please! She is impulsive and hotheaded and all the rest of it, but people do things like this now. The man she has married has rejoined his ship and is in the Atlantic. God knows when she'll see him again. They didn't tell their respective families, they simply didn't have time. They just upped and went to Caxton Hall.'

'*Caxton Hall*. Why not a church?'

He actually looked angrier at that than when she first broke the news.

'I know, Father. A civil marriage of all things. I dislike it as much as you do. I suppose they chose it because it was quick.'

He looked, she thought, as hard as Claire.

'And who, might one enquire, has she married?'

'Someone you know. A friend of Miles' who was at Flip's wedding. Dick Polglaze.'

Hearing the name, a faint change came over her father's flinty face. I'm through the worst, thought Elaine. And perhaps he will get closer to Trix now that she is married to a man he likes. She remembered her father's pleasant way with Dick at the wedding; there was no mistaking it when Theo liked somebody.

He asked one or two questions, sounding calm. He even smiled, a sign that ordinary life had returned. From now on, she thought, he would think of Dick Polglaze as a son-in-law and

173

when Dick finally appeared at St Helen's, Theo's imagination would have turned him into a member of the family.

'You will be nice to her, won't you, Father?' said Elaine, sensing an advantage.

He replied with a dry smile that it did not look as if he was going to be given much choice. But her advantage was not so very strong after all. When she suggested that they should open the bottle of champagne he had been saving for the end of the war, he refused.

He did not speak to Trix about her marriage when they all left for their dinner in Knightsbridge. During the meal she kept darting expectant looks at him. He did not meet them. With their father present, there was the usual constraint on conversation between the sisters. Elaine talked of Miles in Malta, and Philippa told her father about the Eagle Squadron's exploits at Dieppe.

'Do you know, Father, nearly one-third of the pilots whose planes were shot down at Dieppe were saved. Barny said that's because the designers of the Spits had planned a proper exit.'

Trix, competitively, weighed in with something about Atlantic convoys. Her father merely nodded. Apart from offering her a second glass of white wine, he did not address a word to her. Trix was not sure whether to be relieved or annoyed.

When they came home, their father thanked them warmly for the dinner and bade them goodnight. The girls exchanged glances. Trix and Philippa wandered into the kitchen to make a final cup of tea. But Elaine, also saying goodnight, went up to her room. Her sisters' company oppressed her. Philippa was foreign and sentimental and Trix, the moment her father had gone, would start to show off again.

Elaine felt slightly sick. Her period was a fortnight late. Could it be herself and not Trix who was pregnant? She certainly did feel sick and rather ill. She had not wanted to go out to dinner, and had had no appetite.

She was already in bed, trying to read and feeling wretched, when there was the ghost of a knock. A grizzled head came round the door.

'Have a nice time, did you?'

'Very nice, Miggsy, thank you.'

'And how did things go with the doctor and the news, lady?'

'Not too bad. Better than I hoped.'

Miggs stood in the doorway, her hands in the pockets of her red dressing-gown.

'She can thank her stars that you were here, that's all I say. You're the only one with a bit of tact.'

Miggs turned to go, but suddenly gave a laugh which sounded like the snort of a pony.

'One thing I will give Trix. She knows when it's wise to look slippy. But she cut it pretty fine, didn't she?'

Elaine did not know what she was talking about, unless it was pregnancy again. She said shortly that there had never been any question of her sister *having* to get married. She did not spell it out. Miggs had offended her.

The old nurse impatiently shook her head.

'I'm not talkin' about bein' in the family way, Miss Elaine. She's a sight too smart for that. I'm talkin' about the call-up. You surely heard of *that*, down in the country? Girls in the Food Office told me today that it's the first time it's happened in history, callin' up unmarried women between the ages of nineteen and thirty. They got to go into uniform, or they got to go into factories. Well. Your sister wouldn't have liked either, would she? Not with those long finger-nails.'

Elaine went to see a doctor when she returned to Oxfordshire. He was the St Aird's doctor, who lived within walking distance of Shelton, a sharp-featured elderly man with a faint Irish tang in his voice, and a surgery out of a Victorian novel. He was very kind to her and confirmed that she was pregnant.

The news made her deeply, overwhelmingly happy: so much so that when she told her mother-in-law she almost felt she would enjoy being kissed. But that would be going too far.

Claire smiled, refusing to be surprised, and said excellent, excellent. Miles would be delighted and it would be sure to be a son. There was a 'preponderance of boys' in the St Aird family. She ignored the fact that Elaine was one of three girls. Claire also added that she would inform her husband. Elaine was not too starry-eyed to miss what Claire meant, which was that if Elaine told him St Aird would have been shocked to his soul at such middle-class lack of propriety.

The feeling of bliss, not unlike that which drenched her after Miles' lovemaking, did not last. She was regularly sick every

175

morning before taking the Blenheim bus, and sometimes sick
again during the day. There was a lavatory at the end of the
corridor near her office, to which she gratefully retired, returning – just like the old days of proposals of marriage – with a rosy
face. Captain Goodier surprised her by saying she looked well.
She had not told him yet.

'Suppose,' remarked Marjorie, 'you were working in the
despatch department. They have to walk miles. You'd never
make it.'

Marjorie made up for Claire by her unaffected delight at
Elaine's news. She was knowledgeable about pregnancy, lent
Elaine a brown smock with a pale blue collar, and offered a
wardrobe-full of baby clothes which she was keeping for her own
next child. When would that be arriving, she said. She hoped
she would not be too old to conceive by the time Bob came home
from the Far East.

The girls also talked over Elaine's other piece of family drama
– Trix's marriage to Marjorie's favourite cousin. The suddenness
of it was not what surprised Marjorie who said Dick Polglaze was
a man who made up his mind and then carried out his decision
without hanging about. It was his marrying at all which was so
unexpected. Marjorie had never thought he would: he had too
many affairs.

'How do you know?'

'Because he's told me about them. What a face, Elaine! I do
believe you are a prude. He doesn't go into the details, you
know, but he always confides in me because he knows it makes
me laugh. He says I do as a sister. There was a girl in
Cumberland who worked in a factory. Very tarty, she was, I
have a vague notion she was his first (he wasn't hers, which was
the point). They made love in a boat on the river. Dick likes
boats. For about a year there was a Wren, Rosy Whitlock, he
said she was lovely. They spent bits of his leave at expensive
hotels: Dick's a great one for hotels as well as boats. He took his
wife to stay at the Ritz, didn't he? He runs true to form. There
were others too, only I forget their names. Dick is a sexy old
thing.'

'My sister is not exactly the virgin bride.'

'That must be what they have in common. Sex is the strongest
bond.'

'In the long run?'

176

'What long run have we, Elaine? Any of us?'

Marriage had apparently changed Trix for the better. She telephoned Elaine two or three times to report that she had received letters from Dick. She also described the appearance in London of Mr and Mrs Polglaze who had come down from Cumberland specially to meet Theo and herself. Mr Polglaze, she said gaily, was short and grizzled and exactly like an old bear. And his wife had a big bosom and a huge diamond brooch which she assured Trix would be hers one day. They had had dinner at Brown's, and Trix had dressed for the part in her dullest clothes. They had been very nice to her, so she thought she must have been a success. Elaine, who had seen Trix put herself out to charm, was sure of it.

Marjorie was eager to meet Dick's wife. When Elaine said this, Trix sounded pleased. She obligingly travelled to Oxford one Sunday in the usual unspeakably crowded train, and met both girls for luncheon at The Mitre. Trix had enjoyed the journey. She had sat, all the way, on the knee of a Scots Guard sergeant.

The lunch went well, but Elaine did wonder if Marjorie had expected anybody quite so startling to look at as her younger sister. Everybody in the dining room, everybody male, that was, stared. Trix seemed unaware of the sensation she caused. She was friendly to Marjorie, talking about Dick and asking lots of questions. Did Marjorie know what was his favourite food? What did Marjorie think was positively the best Fortnum's parcel to send him? She had forgotten to ask him if he liked dried figs: she had been given a whole box of them.

When Trix was once more on her way to London, perched upon another stranger's knee, Marjorie saw Elaine to the bus stop.

'She's gorgeous looking. Do you think she'll stay the course?'

Trix enjoyed being a married woman. There was a song she often sang, 'Kiss the Boys Goodbye'. Before Dick went to sea he had told her that she could 'kiss the boys hello', as long as that was all she did. She had agreed solemnly. And when she was out and about in London now, expertly keeping susceptible men in order, she often said to them, 'Of course, Dick always comes first.' 'Of course,' they agreed. With Trix, they agreed to

177

anything. She no longer went to bed with the boyfriends who attracted her, but their number did not grow less. She was wonderful company besides being the best-looking girl in a restaurant, and the lightest dancer on a dance floor.

Her twentieth birthday had come and gone. It was the summer of 1942. To Trix, London was home. It was a city which she could never remember as not dusty and shabby and crammed with troops. There were the Commandos in their green berets, the Poles rakishly wearing their dark blue ones. There was English khaki and Naval blue with gold lace, and Wrens wearing hats which made them look like Nelson, and Land girls, and Philippa's beloved RAF with their romantic silver wings.

Suddenly, quite suddenly, London was invaded. The Americans arrived. Pearl Harbour had been months ago, and of course everybody knew they were coming. But when the American troops actually began to pour into London it was very extraordinary. They appeared overnight in their thousands. It was impossible to estimate how many Americans there were. London was engulfed.

Americans were not strangers to Trix. She had had one or two admirers in the Eagle Squadron, had gone out with them now and again, and lost touch with them. She had no close American friends. There had been the incident, conveniently forgotten with Barny. But Trix liked Americans and Canadians. She liked their accents, familiar from the films, and she also liked the idea of America. That summer – there they were wherever she looked. When she walked down Bond Street, or danced at Hatchetts, or glanced from taxi windows she saw them. They had done something no other foreign troops had done. They had changed the face of London.

They sat on the steps of stuffy antiquated houses which had been the guarded mansions of the aristocracy. They lounged at Rainbow Corner in Piccadilly where the American Red Cross had set up a club for GI's, including a canteen and a theatre. At the back of Knightsbridge, the Berkeley Gardens hotel, shut since the outbreak of war, was opened. The Stars and Stripes hung outside it – it was now a club. American troops went in and out of its swing doors in a stream of pale coloured khaki.

If Trix was conscious of the young men now swarming over the great dirty city, the Americans were even more conscious of

Trix. Before they had arrived in England, a place which apart from the language, and there were pitfalls in that, was as foreign to them as Peking, they had been given instructions by the War Office in Washington. These had been in the form of an 'Introduction to Great Britain' and began 'YOU are going to Great Britain as part of an Allied offensive – to meet Hitler and beat him on his own ground. For the time being you will be Britain's guest. The purpose of this guide is to start getting you acquainted with the British, their country, and their ways.' It did not mince words. The British were reserved but not unfriendly. There were differences in the language that it was necessary to remember. British people did not say bum or bloody and a GI must never say that the USA won the last war. They must not brag. US pay was the highest in the world. They mustn't say so. 'Don't make fun of their accents, you sound just as funny to them but they will be too polite to show it,' said the instructions severely.

The instructions were actually orders. Having had them dinned into their heads, the Americans were wary. In many cases they found their worst fears confirmed. British people *were* stuck up. Their accents *were* ridiculous. Their food *was* filthy. And a large number of British troops resented them. It was not long before the Americans heard the jealous joke against them, that they were over-decorated, over-paid, over-sexed and over here.

And then, as their eyes wandered through the mass of uniformed or drab strangers, they suddenly saw Trix. She was the epitome of the beautiful blonde. She was Betty Grable and Veronica Lake and Alice Faye. She was a knockout. It seemed impossible that she could be British.

'Aren't you really an American?' was the question that Trix was asked daily. She smiled delightedly, lowering her eyelashes over her black-treacle coloured eyes. Did they really think she was? Surely she looked like a Londoner, for that was what she was. There would follow more admiration and more assurance of the positively American style of her good looks.

Trix met them on dance floors, they stood beside her and her friends in the bars of expensive hotels. Sometimes, like the two French A's now vanished from her life, she picked them up on the tops of buses. But 'Dick always comes first', and she did not invite them home. Yet they fascinated her. She would have

179

liked a passport into the new American world of occupied London.

Of all the people to provide such a passport, her father proved to be the man.

The blitz was over. The sound of the Alert was rarely heard now and Theo had returned to concentrating on his private practice. Many of his patients who had fled from London had come back, and his telephone and waiting room were busy. He was also seeing something of the young French girl, Annette Ghilain. She was working as a secretary at the Centre d'Acceuil. He took her out sometimes for a meal in the West End.

Trix did not like Annette much. She thought her a gold-digger which Trix herself had never actually been. She certainly wouldn't go out with somebody her father's age just to be given a meal. But she did not wish Annette ill and had once said to a shocked Philippa, home on a brief visit, that anybody who could make their father spend his money was jolly clever.

'Of course most of it is Mother's money, but still. I take my hat off to her. They went to the Dorchester twice. Imagine that.'

'Do you think he may be in love with her?'

'For Pete's sake, Flip. He's over sixty.'

Refreshed from undisturbed nights of sleep, enjoying the summer and the occasional company of someone young and attractive, Theo was quite pleasant nowadays to his married daughter Beatrix. One evening he found her watering her row of lettuces in the garden. She was still a fervent follower of the Dig for Victory campaign.

Her father stood watching her. The air was filled with the smell of wet earth and birds were singing in the pear trees. For the moment he remembered his youth; he had brought Mary to see St Helen's before he had bought the house and Mary had said, 'Why, look at the pear tree, Theo. All that blossom. Just like a bride.'

Now the tree was hung with small greenish-brown fruit.

He pulled up a deck chair and sat down in the deckled shade under the tree. Behind him was the skeleton of the conservatory which had never been pulled down, but had become a part of the landscape, a familiar ruin. The burned frame was green with moss and lichen, weeds grew in the cracks. and a buddleia with long purple flowers had managed to take root in the roof.

Trix finished her watering and sat back on her heels.

180

'Have you *seen* how many Yanks there are in town now, Father?' They're simply everywhere. Poor things, I bet they are homesick. We ought to ask one or two of them round for a meal,' she added, remembering a brief flirtation on the top of a Number 73 bus.

'It would be better if you did some work for them,' replied Theo. 'Do you remember Mrs Alwynne? I met her recently at a dinner party. Philippa still works for that children's hospital, you know. But Mrs Alwynne has taken on some new tasks, it seems. She is working for the Americans. Apparently there are clubs for the American troops opening up all over London. And they're crying out for help.'

He was accustomed to Trix, although he never used the idiotic name. He scarcely noticed his youngest child's dyed silvery hair, her strong scent, or heard the little voice quacking on the telephone. He was used to seeing her dart through the house busy on her own devices. In a way he loved her. She was his child. And she did not need him: she was a married woman and an adult. He was glad to give her a home while her husband was at sea, but she was Dick's responsibility. Looking at her with slight irony, he waited for her to refuse to do some war work. Even unobservant Theo had noticed that Beatrix never worked.

She put down the watering can and clasped her hands, exclaiming eagerly that she would love – simply love! – to do war work for the Americans. Could he possibly arrange it?

Theo felt the same unfamiliar fatherly satisfaction which had come to him when he helped Elaine to get to Blenheim Palace.

Anyone willing to work for Mrs Alwynne had no chance to change their minds. The telephone rang next morning while Trix was in the bath. Miggs shouted for her. Trix dashed down in a négligé so transparent that Miggs averted her eyes and retreated to the chaste company of Sailor.

'Mrs Polglaze?' said a lively commanding voice, 'Jane Alwynne here. Your father tells me you have most generously . . . know your sister, of course . . . sterling work . . . the club is at Knightsbridge. Yes, I shall be here. Could you come at six this evening?'

Unlike Philippa, Trix did not realize that when she agreed to meet Mrs Alwynne at the club, she had taken on the job.

She dressed thoughtfully for what she believed was an interview. She decided on a new clinging crêpe dress. It was white,

181

one of her favourite colours, and had the fashionably large padded shoulders embroidered with gold beads. She blued her eyelids, brushed her hair energetically, and when she was ready picked up a flower made of stiffened white lace. She put it on top of her head and looked at herself. Yes.

The evening was still hot and sunny when her taxi drew up at the Berkeley Gardens hotel. The Stars and Stripes hung limply from its pole without stirring. The hotel's flight of once-white marble steps was so dirty it had turned almost black, and all the way up were soldiers, sitting like debs at pre-war dances. All the way up Trix was given whistles of approval.

A harrassed woman at the reception desk said that Mrs Alwynne was in her office, the second on the left. And – 'Yes, Lieutenant, what is it that you want?' to a young man waiting to catch her attention. Four others waited behind him.

Trix found Jane Alwynne sitting in a small office crammed with baskets of clothes and box files. She was dictating to a cowed-looking girl.

'Oh, sorry. Am I interrupting?' said Trix, knowing that she was.

'You must be Mrs Polglaze. Come in, come in. You can run away, Betty, I will send for you when I need you.'

Jane looked at Trix and hospitably patted the vacated seat.

Inwardly, Jane was having a good laugh. Who would have credited Philippa Tyrrell with having a sister like this one? If I had knelt down to pray for a helper in this place, thought Jane piously, I could not have been sent anyone more fitted for the work.

'Well?' she said briskly, 'One night or two?'

'Oh, more if you really want me.'

Trix had enjoyed the wolf whistles.

'Shall I put you down for four? You can shout if you find it is too much. The hours are six until midnight, if you can keep awake that long.'

'I'm sure that'll be okay.'

Jane paused diplomatically. 'Of course you know that it is voluntary. This is war work, so there is no pay, naturally.'

Trix, who had vaguely imagined generous pay since it was for the Americans, replied that she had never imagined being paid.

'Good, good. I'll get Betty to take you along.'

'What would I have to do, Mrs Alwynne?'

Trix spoke in the conditional tense. She felt she was being rushed. The lace flower had become unpinned, and she made a dab at securing it.

'All the girls here are cooks and bottle-washers. They dish out the Coco-Cola and the coffee and the fruit juices and so on. Not demanding work, you know. But it is important to look after our Allies, isn't it?'

Trix most earnestly agreed.

Jane's cowed secretary, who looked as if she could do with a good night's sleep, took Trix down the corridor. A group of girls far less pretty than Trix were hard at work in the hotel's big kitchens which were filled with steam. Three girls at the sink were standing on the wet linoleum floor.

'Thank goodness, more help,' said a lanky girl with spots whom Trix thought should be introduced to that wizard lotion from Harrods. 'Take this tray out to them, will you?'

She picked up the heavy tray and put it into Trix's hands. 'The boys sitting are waiting for hamburgers. The ones by the bar want Coke. All right?'

The tray was excessively heavy, thought Trix, but at least she was escaping the steam. The smell of cooking was unpleasant, and she recoiled at the prospect of having to put her clover-tipped hands into water slimy with soda. But she liked Americans.

The room into which she carried her tray had been a spacious hotel dining room. Now it was the club room and had a dance floor. Two GI's at two pianos were playing a duet of 'Kiss the Boys Goodbye'. Hearing it, she grinned. At her entrance, thirty or forty pairs of eyes looked across the room. And thirty or forty men thought – so they make 'em this way over here after all.

She moved among the tables, smiling at the compliments, stooping to put down plates, then shaking back her glittering hair. Wherever she went there were the wolf whistles again. She was enchanted by her success, and was at her most fascinating and confident when a tall man put his hand on her arm.

'Good to see you again, Trix.'

She looked up, surprised. She did not recognise him but saw that he wore wings.

'Again? We haven't met, have we?'

'Sure we have. At Flip's wedding and afterwards we took you dancing, remember? I'm Barny's buddy, Chuck Greenfield.'

'One of the Eagles!'

She turned the full ray of her smile on him, to the envy of a tableful of admiring GI's.

'Will you dance with me, Trix? I'd like that.'

'But I can't, Chuck. I am working,' said Trix for the first time in her life.

'Not allowed to say No to an ex-Eagle, didn't they tell you that?'

She stood holding the tray, tempted and tempting. He lingered beside her. He had a most particular smile, it was mischievous and intimate and trusting. It was as if he loved the world. Trix had known many men. Conceited men and clever ones, sexy men and shy ones, confident Frenchmen and serious Dutchmen and Guards officers with handsome faces and not a word to say and wild New Zealanders. She had never met anybody as innocently friendly as Chuck Greenfield.

He gently took the tray out of her hands and put it down on the table. Then he led her to the floor where a few couples were dancing. The music changed to a slow tune. 'That Lovely Weekend'.

'"The two days of heaven you helped me to spend,"' sang Trix, and he put his arm round her and danced in the swaying American way, cheek pressed against hers.

When the dance ended he said, 'You're like a leaf.'

'Thank you, kind sir.'

'Don't you dare dance with another guy. They only just got here. I had a claim on you when I arrived in 1940.'

'Were you in the Battle of Britain?'

'Not quite, but we were *here*, weren't we? Waiting to join in.'

'Flip says all the Eagles were heroes,' said Trix winningly.

'Don't know I can live up to that!'

The music began again and they danced again. He told her he had already been transferred, he called it pitchforked, into the US Army Air Corps. They'd made him a temporary instructor. The job was 'all talk and no do.'

'I bet you're a swell instructor.'

'I do my darndest,' he said, looking down at the sympathetic beauty in his arms, 'but teaching's so dull. We study air battles, analyse mistakes that were made on both sides. That's called learning tactical awareness. I sure would prefer being in the old squadron dispersal hut, waiting for a scramble signal.'

184

He told her that it only half amused him to receive letters from home complaining of the terrible privations they were now suffering. All they were allowed now was a pound of sugar a week, just imagine that. And forty-six gallons of petrol a month, how did they manage?

Trix listened and smiled and liked him. She thought it very attractive that he wore two pairs of wings, the RAF wings on the left of his tunic. He was a prize and she wanted to go on dancing with him. She also wanted to avoid the kitchen but thought it wiser to be seen there, at any rate tonight. So, with a lingering goodbye to Chuck, she returned to the kitchen to carry more trays and to help with the disgusting washing-up. At midnight the club closed. When she came down the hotel steps, her face freshly made-up, the white flower bobbing on top of her head, she was not even surprised to find Chuck waiting for her. He had a driver and a jeep. Trix had never ridden in a jeep before, and stood for a moment admiring the great heavy automobile. It was painted dark khaki, built like a tank, and on the bonnet was WHATAGIRL!! in thick pink lettering. Stepping over the word, wearing French knickers and nothing else, with enormous breasts crimson-nippled, was the figure of a girl. She wore high heeled ankle-strapped shoes and carried a parasol.

'The boys call her Rita Hayworth. She's not near as pretty as you,' said Chuck, giving Trix his hand. She climbed into the jeep, showing yards of silken leg.

When they stopped at St Helen's it was dark and moonless. Telling the driver he would not be long, Chuck walked with Trix to the steps of the sleeping house. She turned to say goodnight. For a moment or two he hesitated, taking her hand and pressing it. But something in the way she stood, something in the very air made him know he could kiss her. He put his arms round her and kissed her so passionately that she could scarcely breathe.

'Beautiful. You're beautiful. Don't you forget me, now. I'll call you.'

Chapter Thirteen

Summer was hot. Day followed cloudless day of blue skies, and when the clouds did appear they were fine weather mountains of gleaming white. In the park at Blenheim the hay was cut – it was bone dry in a few hours. When Elaine walked home in the evenings, the hedges were alive with birds and the strong-smelling meadowsweet had grown four foot high.

She used to love the summer. But her pregnancy was not easy, she felt rather ill most of the time and although she determined to go on working, the journey to Woodstock and back was long and made her ache. She had another worse pain. She found that she missed Miles more than ever before. Was it because she was pregnant that she felt this dreadful and unceasing want, a yearning that never left her? How long was it since she had seen him – seven months, twenty-nine weeks. Marjorie had not seen her husband for over two years. I suppose it is what Claire calls my condition that makes me miss him so, she thought. She wondered where her serenity had gone.

He wrote to her as often as he could and he was overjoyed at the news of the baby. But the letters did not bring her very much comfort for there was not the least chance of his being posted home. Watching the ebb and flow of the war, she saw that for Miles to come home from the Mediterranean now was impossible. The war was going badly, the Eighth Army in the Western desert was in retreat, and the terrible Russian war did not abate. What could *she* expect? She was one near-invisible dot on the huge bloodstained map of the world.

Sometimes Miles's letters had references to his work, vague references, but she never managed to create what his life was like in Malta. He had no gift of description. He said the job was hellish difficult and very absorbing. He said he'd made good friends. Miles always made those. She tried to imagine the life of a submariner. But she had been afraid of the world beneath the sea since she was a child. When she learned to swim she would never swim underwater. The thought of Miles, fathoms deep,

186

scared her. Everybody needed courage now. The families who had faced the blitz, the troops sweating in the desert, the men in Japanese prison camps, the friends like Dick Polglaze sailing the cruel Atlantic. But soldiers, sailors, pilots, civilians, could at least use their eyes. They could *see*. The world Miles had chosen was in the dark.

Every day and every night of her life she thought about him. The child stirred and jumped in her womb. Would it be a son? Would he have Miles' grey eyes and that dent in his chin? Miles's face, arrogant and movingly young, came to her. There was a photograph of him in a silver frame in the drawing room, and a badly-painted portrait in the dining room. It had been one of his father's failures: St Aird was no portrait painter and had done the picture entirely because Claire asked for it. St Aird had painted Miles in uniform, with an almost black sky above him, and the dim shape of a surfaced submarine in a dark sea behind his shoulder. Elaine disliked the painting. The man looking out with painted eyes was not Miles but a waxwork hero. There was no mischief or humanity in the face. It was a poster for a flag day.

Avoiding the eyes of the portrait and the stiff photograph, Elaine took Miles with her, as she took his child, wherever she went. He was part of her. She had a real photograph of him in her room. Theo had taken it at St Helen's just after Miles had gone into the Navy. He wore matelot's uniform and was laughing like a schoolboy.

Captain Goodier actually referred to Miles one day. As he never said anything personal to her she was very startled.

'I gather your husband is a submariner in the Med., Mrs St Aird.'

Elaine wondered what was coming next.

'They're doing important work out there, you know. Now that Crete has gone, we are using Malta as our bastion. As a matter of fact, we ourselves are using the island for some of our work at present. I mention this because you will see it in my next report. It is Operation Ali Baba.'

He gave her a dry smile.

'The submarines are running our agents into the Middle East at convenient moments. It is a most useful way of delivering them,' he added. He made the submarines sound like suburban trains.

The weather grew steadily hotter, and Elaine in her eighth

month felt the heat more than ever. Her hands had become slightly swollen and so had her ankles. She did not mention this to anyone, even Marjorie. Talking about aches and pains embarrassed her, she had always been physically reserved. She supposed the swelling was usual when one was dragging about with so much extra weight.

One evening which seemed hotter than the rest she walked back to Shelton after the oppressive bus drive. She was sweating. She kept thinking about the river which lay behind a distant row of willow trees. Months ago before her pregnancy she had asked Claire is one could bathe there. Claire was dumbfounded.

'Good gracious. Only factory girls do that.'

Elaine hadn't the spirit to disobey. Probably Miles would think it common too.

But now the idea of the river, across the hot fields of dusty stubble, haunted her. She imagined what it would be like to be immersed in the cool water. She could feel the silky mud as she waded in, and smell the green scent of rushes . . .

One day Miles and I will take a punt from Oxford and go down the Cherwell, Miles promised he would take me there. We will have strawberries and champagne, and then we'll swim, and then we'll lie in the punt under a tree and kiss and kiss.

The old house dozed. Its stones were hot to the touch, the rooks croaked in the high trees behind the house – caw-caw-caw. The St Aird retriever lay prostrate under a crab apple tree. When he saw her he raised his head and lazily thumped his tail, not bothering to come and welcome her.

In doors there was a cool spell of silence. Nobody was about, and she supposed that Claire was out on her unending work for the WVS. She automatically looked at the salver in the hall where Claire left her letters, but there was no envelope with HMS Ship on it. The drawing room door opened. Claire stood there.

She had a piece of paper in her hand.

'Miles's submarine is missing,' she said.

Elaine stumbled up to her room and slammed the door and fell on the bed. She began to cry violently, her sobs a dreadful sickening kind of cough as she groaned aloud like a woman in her death agony. Oh Miles, Miles, dearest, dearest, you can't be dead, I won't believe it. I want you, I need you for always, I need you now. There's a baby inside me, you can't have left me, you never would, you never would. How can I live if I'm never going to see you again? Never. Never. Never. They don't only sail in the dark, they die in the dark. If you're in a ship and you're hit there's a chance, but not in submarines, and nobody knows whether it's quick or slow or where the ship is somewhere in the black water, fathoms, fathoms deep. Miles's submarine is missing.

Lying on her face, coughing and groaning, she did not hear the door opened so roughly that it hit the wall.

'Stop that.'

The voice was so loud that Elaine did stop for a second, losing her breath, rising up and turning a face distorted with crying.

Claire walked over to the bed and took her by the wrist.

'How dare you have hysterics? How dare you behave like this? And in your condition too. What would Miles think if he saw you howling like a servant dismissed for stealing? If my son is dead, and I don't think there's the least hope he has survived, then he's done his duty. Died for his country like other men before him and other men will do in the future. In the last war they were cut down in their hundreds of thousands, left to drown in the mud. Do you suppose their women acted like you? You make me sick.'

She walked out, slamming the door so hard that it reverberated through the house. The sound of Nemesis.

Elaine began to vomit in the night, and could not stop. It went on all night long and the whole of the following day. Claire finally telephoned the doctor, and when he arrived said contemptuously to him that she presumed it was shock. The doctor took one look at Elaine and rang for an ambulance.

At dawn, in a Banbury Road nursing home, Elaine went into labour and the child was born. She had been suffering from toxaemia for some time, which explained the swollen hands and ankles. She had never visited the doctor while she was in that condition and it had worsened. The child was born dead. It was a boy.

Philippa sent her flowers. White roses whose petals dropped in the heat of the bedroom, making it smell of their sharp scent. The nurses were jarringly kind. Elaine asked the matron to telephone her family to say she wished to see nobody. And would she please give the St Airds the same message. The matron tried to dissuade her, but Elaine was perfectly calm and perfectly cold. She looked dreadful. A priest called to see her, but she would not see him either.

She lay in the hot room, with the blinds pulled down but still blazing white from the sun outside and wished that she was dead too.

When she was well enough, she returned in a car to Shelton. Neither of the St Airds spoke to her about the loss of the baby. Claire avoided her as much as she could without making it too obvious. Elaine knew she had not been forgiven. She felt that Claire also blamed her for the death of the child, believing – although the doctor would have told her otherwise – that Elaine's paroxysms of grief had brought on a stillbirth.

The week after she came back from the nursing home, Elaine received a letter from Miles. She had been expecting one and through her dulled misery it was the only thing that she thought about, the only thing to live for. But when she actually saw it on the salver in the hall, she could scarcely pick it up. She thought she was going to faint.

The house was empty. She took the letter and walked out into the gardens and up to the coppice at the top of the hill. Here alone she groaned aloud as she opened it, her voice making the same hoarse sound she had made in labour.

It was not a photographed letter. That might have kept him at a distance and have been easier to bear. But the letter was real, it was a piece of paper that Miles' hands had touched, scrawled in pencil on a sheet torn from a Services notebook.

'*I have,*' he wrote, '*for some unaccountable reason a desire to write to you, my darling, and keep on writing as if to rid myself of an intangible sadness that seems to be all round me. I keep feeling that I'm being prepared inside for something to happen. That I must lose something. It can't be you, the best and dearest thing I have, I know it can't be you. And surely it can't be my life because I don't care a damn about that.*'

She read with the tears pouring down her face and when she saw that sentence she sobbed 'How could you think that, write that? How could you *not* care for your life when it was all I had to live for?'

During the two months that she remained at Shelton the loss of the submarine was confirmed. There was no more news. Perhaps they would never be told what had happened. Had there been a sea battle? Had the submarine hit a mine? The

190

Admiralty might know or not know: they would tell the St Airds nothing and the St Airds accepted that in silence. Miles went so quietly. And took his son with him.

Claire was unsurprised when Elaine told her she would be giving up her Blenheim job and returning to London. What went on in Claire did not show, even in her pale eyes. Sometimes when Elaine looked at Claire she had a kind of longing. She is Miles' mother, she thought. She is his flesh and blood, all that's left of his reality. Why can't I love her and feel a shared sorrow? But it seemed to Elaine now Miles was dead, and she was no longer carrying his child, that in an extraordinary way she had evaporated as far as Claire was concerned. She had been turned into a ghost. The St Airds now thought she was nothing to do with Miles any more. There would be no child to carry on the name and title. It would go to a cousin, towards whom Claire now began to offer an interested friendship. Elaine still had Miles' name but she was not a relative: merely a widow.

On the afternoon that Elaine was finishing her packing, Claire came into the bedroom. She had not entered it since the night of the telegram. She stood for a moment in silence, looking vaguely round the room which was filled with Miles' possessions, school photographs, books. Glancing up at her, Elaine could not see a trace of grief. Perhaps she had learned that in France in the 1914 war, she thought. Perhaps it is the only way she can bear things. It is brave and it makes me shudder.

'I've been wondering if you would like anything of my son's, apart from things that he himself gave you.'

'I have all I need, thank you, Lady St Aird.'

'Do you want this?'

Claire held out a small cardboard box. When Elaine opened it, she saw it contained a child's metal watch of the kind that small boys wear at school. The strap was worn, the holes much enlarged, and the back of the watch badly dented.

'We gave it to him when he was at prep school. For his tenth birthday. I found it just now among some old things. Well?'

'Can you spare – '

'I was going to give it to the WVS jumble sale.'

Elaine took the watch and fastened it on her right wrist. She already wore on her left the gold watch her father had given her. She wound up Miles' watch and put it right. It didn't go.

The day that she was leaving Shelton dawned hazy and

autumnal, the leaves had begun to turn and fall, many of them were already scattered across the unkempt lawns, yellow, brown, crimson. Claire had lit a bonfire in the field and the pungent smoke floated in bars upon the still air. When she was ready, Elaine went to the stable studio and knocked.

Her father-in-law opened the door, said nothing, and stepped back for her to enter. She saw that he was working on a landscape: it was the river scene he had painted often before. But in this new version the water seemed to have no light, and the dark sky was filled with rain.

'I am sorry to disturb you, Lord St Aird. I came to say goodbye.'

He wiped his hands on a paint rag. He stood looking down at her, his bearded face guarded. He stooped more than he used to do.

'Going to London, are you?'

He never called her by her name.

'Yes, I've asked to be transferred. They say it can be arranged.'

He nodded, saying, 'Good.'

She wished, suddenly, passionately, that he looked like Miles. He put out his hand and shook hers formally, as if they had only just met. Then he saw the child's battered watch and a grimace of pain went across his face.

'Goodbye, Lord St Aird,' she said.

Elaine was ready long before the taxi was due. She wandered into the dining room to look at the painting of Miles. It was as meaningless as it had always been, the painted face was not his. But the prophetic menace of the submarine behind his shoulder made her look away.

When the taxi drew up at the door, and Elaine had shown the driver where her suitcases were stacked in the hall, Claire walked in from the garden. She stood watching the driver stow the cases into the taxi. Elaine hesitated for a moment.

'Goodbye,' said Claire, 'I hope the train journey won't be too tedious.'

'I don't expect it will be.'

Claire did not shake hands.

She stood, in her green uniform, with Shelton a painted manor behind her, watching as the taxi drove away. As it turned at the gates, she called the dog and went indoors.

*   *   *

Philippa's heart went out to Elaine. She kept thinking about her sister. She wrote to her. But she did not telephone Shelton. What could one say? And in a dreadful selfish way that she despised in herself, Elaine's loss frightened her, as if destiny were whispering 'your turn next'.

The autumn had its own blow for Philippa too. When she had first heard the news that the Eagle Squadrons were to be disbanded, she had felt a chill as if a splinter of ice had entered her breast. She had been part of the Eagles. She had secretly been proud of the fact that all the time she'd been with them, even though she was only a civilian, she had done the Squadrons credit. She had almost seen herself as an Eagle too, having known and loved them all and borne their sufferings as stoically as they did. She had the sensation that she herself had been with them on their sorties over Germany and France.

And now the three proud Squadrons were to be disbanded. They would no longer be part of RAF Fighter Command, they were to join the United States Army Air Corps.

She began to dread the day when all this would become official, and found herself saying 'it's over a month before it will happen', and then 'a week' and then 'a whole day.'

But at last on a day of pouring Sepember rain, only two weeks after Elaine lost her child, the Eagles mustered at their aerodrome. They stood smartly to attention together with a unit of the RAF Regiment, lined up in a hollow square. Philippa and other RAF wives watched from the barrack window: it was raining much too hard for them to stand out in the open.

On the platform were Sir Sholto Douglas, the C-in-C of RAF Fighter Command, and two commanding generals of the American Air Force. And there in front of them were the three Eagle Squadrons 71, 121 and 133, on their final day as members of the RAF.

Sir Sholto made a wonderful speech, Philippa thought. He said that during the two years they had been flying, the Eagles had destroyed the equivalent of six squadrons of the Luftwaffe, and probably many more.

'There are those of your number who are not here today – ' he said – 'those sons of the United States who were first to give their lives for their country.' He went on to say that the Eagles who had fallen would remain the honoured dead of two great nations.

'Goodbye. And thank you, Eagle Squadrons of the Royal Air Force.'

Behind the pilots were the ranks of English mechanics, riggers, fitters, radio-men and armourers who had kept the planes flying, who had shouted 'Good luck' as the Eagles set off, who had run across the airfield to greet them when they returned.

Philippa looked at the Eagles standing to attention, camouflaged buildings behind them, forming a quadrangle round the parade ground. There they stood, the young men who had meant everything to her, the Americans who had come over to join an English war.

The rain hammered down on the figures in blue. The Stars and Stripes was slowly hoisted next to the RAF's blue flag. The two hung side by side, but there was no breeze to make them shake out their bright colours and snap and stream.

'Good hunting to you, Eagle Squadrons of the United States Air Force,' said Sir Sholto. The Eagles marched slowly in review – out of the RAF.

Barny and Pete Jansen, one of the 1940 friends, wandered back into the mess when the ceremony was over. They were very wet. New uniforms had been laid out for them – brand-new uniforms, of fine brown twill with a gold US on the lapel and wings on the breast.

They stood staring at them critically and Pete scratched his nose. He glanced from Barny's shabby tunic to his own. The elbows were patched with leather, the wings were worn and dirty.

'Know what these need?' Pete said, pointing at the perfect uniforms, 'a bit of mud.'

Barny returned to the cottage in his unfamiliar uniform, and Philippa – waiting eagerly – hugged him. Her face shone with the determined optimism she had burnished all the morning. The ceremony had been wonderful, she said. She did not admit she had wanted to weep. She had convinced herself that now she would give her love and loyalty to the American squadron. Why not? Many were friends. All were Barny's countrymen.

But it did not happen like that. The US Air Force recognized the value of seasoned veterans. Some of the Eagles were posted. Some had already gone, including Chuck Greenfield who was a temporary instructor to new pilots.

194

Philippa guessed that the new squadrons with the Eagles' name would be moved – it always happened like that. Some weeks after the handing-over ceremony Barny told her that the Squadron was going elsewhere.

'This time we've had it, my honey. You won't be allowed to come too.'

He put his arms round her tenderly. But she could not relax and lean against him. She was stiffened in pain.

'Darling Flip, you mustn't mind so much. Your days as a camp follower have been good, haven't they? Now kiss me and stop being so brave and quiet.'

Her eyes brimmed as he gently said that it was not as bad as all that, she mustn't fret. There was a town near the aerodrome, and he was sure she could 'put up at a hotel' now and then. There would be leaves. Even sleeping-out passes.

'Isn't that what we need, my honey? Lots of sleeping-out passes?' And he laughed.

She longed to burst into passionate argument. To say it was unjust to send her away, and that she had proved her worth in the dangers of the past.

But she didn't dare to.

Chapter Fourteen

There had been too little sympathy for Elaine at Shelton – but there was too much at St Helen's. Miggs and Theo were unnaturally kind to her, and she caught them looking anxiously at her when they thought she was unaware of it. They got on her nerves. All her clothes had been dyed black while she was at Shelton, and although they said nothing about that, she knew that the sombre figure she made startled them. Nobody went into mourning now.

She was listless and easily tired, had no appetite and slept badly. Her father did not need to be told any of this and suggested she should postpone going back to work, at least for the time being. She must get back her strength.

Ignoring his kind advice, she went to MI5's offices in St James' Street. The tired-looking woman who received her and knew of her work at Blenheim said they were no longer recruiting in Counter Intelligence. The direction of the work was changing, she said. But Elaine could work in Special Operations.

It was the other side of the Intelligence coin. At Blenheim they had been combating enemy agents in Britain. At SOE the job was to send allied agents into enemy-occupied Europe.

Elaine went to the headquarters near Baker Street and to her own dulled surprise was given a job. I wouldn't employ somebody looking like me, she thought. But she knew people were needed, even widows as thin, unimpressive and indifferent as she was.

Drifting home, and trying to keep her mind on the idea of working again, she thought about Marjorie. She missed the only real friend she had made in this war. At St Helen's there was her old sardonic nurse and there was Trix – neither replaced a dear friend. Her young sister's sympathy had been demonstrated by a hug, a kiss, and a promise to make Elaine a new dress.

'Oh golly, you're in black. Never mind, I can make you a

marvellous black dress with lace round the neck. I've got some white lace. I'll dye it.'

Trix made clothes for people in a way a child offers a loan of his teddy bear.

The offices where Elaine now began work were in an ugly pre-war block; the rooms were the usual wartime jumble of partitions. She compared the place to Blenheim. Here were no panoramas of the changing seasons outside the office window, no flash of lakes, no sulky Marlborough beauties pouting from the walls. She no longer arrived through vast gates to see the ponderous building floating in the mist of its curious past. And there was no narrow-faced, teasing friend to walk with her under the trees.

Her new boss, Giles Seton, had been wounded at Tobruk and invalided out of the army. He was lame and like many crippled people contrived to walk fast with a sideways swing. He had ginger hair and a curling handlebar moustache and despite being ex-Army, used the kind of RAF slang Elaine had heard from Philippa. When Elaine arrived at the office every morning he would say 'Good-oh. Now we can get weaving.' Sometimes he suggested they should 'bale out for coffee'. His highest praise, of course, was wizard, and his lowest disparagement was ropey. But despite the affectations he was tough.

Seton's office was next to the operations room, on the wall of which was an enormous map of Europe. The map was covered with flags, each representing an agent working underground. When the map was explained to her, Elaine asked why there were no flags anywhere in Holland. Seton looked grim. Recently the entire Dutch Resistance had been penetrated by the enemy. Every one of the agents was dead.

It was through Seton that agents were despatched to training centres where they learned the strange craft of being a spy; they were taught to parachute, to use short wave wireless, their skill at language must be faultless, their knowledge of the country to which they were bound must be full of the most elaborate detail. When the agents left London and were dropped into Europe, it was often too dangerous for them to contact London. They were on their own.

From the first day that she began to work there, Elaine found the atmosphere as matter-of-fact as an office in peacetime. Seton and his officers sent men on missions as if they were dealing with a team of door-to-door salesmen. There was no sense of danger. SOE had an enormous – and odd – staff working in and out of London. There were people skilled at creating false passports, craftsmen who knew how to make specially constructed suitcases, deliberately seeming old and battered, to contain wireless transmitters. Seton had an office drawer filled with lethal pills which he gave to the agents before they left London. If an agent was caught and felt that he might betray his friends, he could use one. In one corner of Elaine's small office was an old sewing machine. It was stuffed full of American dollars and was destined to be dropped by parachute for an agent in France.

Lysanders took off at night to ferry the agents to the remotest districts of France, returning with news of the Resistance. Giles Seton called the flights 'our Lizzie Landings.' Secret armies lay waiting for the Lysanders. They set out lights in deserted fields, in a pre-arranged pattern for the pilot to recognize. The Lizzie landings were mostly in France which was large and in places wild and uninhabited. Holland, Belgium and Italy were harder to penetrate.

Staff at Baker Street office were a motley crew, markedly different from the officers and upper-class girls at Blenheim. There were men and women of many nationalities and countless curious realms of knowledge, from those who knew precisely what labels to sew in an agent's clothes if he were to be dropped in Marseilles to the correct cigarettes a workman would smoke in Antwerp. RAF pilots came to the office too: their job was flying the Lysanders across the shrouded darkness of Europe.

Elaine was good at her job, which was demanding. At night she returned home, listened to the wireless, went to bed early to read and not to sleep. Marjorie telephoned and invited her to Oxfordshire. Elaine lied, saying she could not get away. She shrank from being forced to behave like a real person again. She fended off affection and got through her life like an automaton.

In January the London raids began again. On the news there was triumphant talk of huge waves of bombers over Germany. Twenty-four hours later when Elaine was home from work she heard the unfamiliar banshee wail over London. Hearing the sound of planes, she ran to look out.

'Quite like the bad old times. You just come indoors,' shouted Miggs on her way to the cellar.

Elaine ignored her and stood watching the enemy bombers

going over, and the flares in the sky, and hearing the thunder of explosions.

During the January raids she never slept under the billiard table. Totally lacking fear, she did not care if she were killed. She went to bed and lay thinking of Miles. Sometimes the thought was so clear that she could see him, young and beautiful and sexy and brave. She could remember just how he made love, once, twice, three times. She saw his large grey eyes shining as he lay with her. Once, after they had made love, he was silent for a long time and Elaine snuggled up to him, tenderly asking what he was thinking about.

'I was thinking what I'd choose for breakfast if peace suddenly broke out. I decided. Haddock kedgeree and coffee with cream.'

She slapped him.

'What was that for? No, on second thoughts, I'll have bacon, eggs and fried mushrooms. Or kidneys. Bulldog Drummond always had those.'

He rolled over and leaned on his elbow and said, 'Want to hear a joke?'

'Must you?'

'Yes, I must. There was a Polish general and he said to one of his officers "Have you any children?" "Oh no, sir," was the reply, "my wife is unbearable".'

'Miles! That's as old as the hills.'

'Ah, but there's more. "Surely, Lieutenant" said the general, "you mean that your wife is inconceivable". The officer answered, "No, no, General, I do not say it right. I mean my wife is impregnable."'

Miles burst out laughing. He liked the silliest jokes. Sometimes in the beloved lame letters he sent her, he copied out new ones to amuse her. When the Americans had begun to arrive in England last summer, Miles put a *P.S.* on his letter.

Have you heard the new description for Utility knickers? One yank and they're off.

That night, there was no raid. Elaine lay reading and rereading her packet of letters, and the joke caught her eye. For a moment all she thought about was Miles' mischievous face. Then for the first time since he had died, the selfishness of grief left her. She thought about somebody else. Trix. Trix had left this evening as always for the Berkeley Gardens club and what she now called 'my war work'. Trix was on her way to show her paces

199

to a hoard of susceptible and lonely Americans. Trix had yanked off some far-from Utility knickers often before her marriage – once for the man whom Philippa had later married. Trix talked fondly of Dick. Sometimes she fished letters from her handbag and read aloud boring passages, punctuated with 'Isn't he sweet?' Whenever she went out with a man, she earnestly said to Elaine before leaving the house, 'Of course he understands completely that with me Dick always comes first.'

The man about whom Trix now talked, rather more often than about Dick, was Chuck Greenfield, the ex-RAF Eagle and friend of Barny and Flip. Trix quoted Chuck a good deal. She used his expressions – his friends were 'a bunch of palookas'. When she came home with spoils, they were always gifts from Chuck.

Coming home one snowy night, Elaine found Trix playing a record. It was 'Whispering Grass', and Chuck had bought it for her. Singing with the music, Trix was on the floor by the electric fire, surrounded by tissue paper.

'Chuck wrote to his folks in Rhode Island,' she said, 'Look what they sent! Have you *seen* these stockings? They're the newest thing, made of nylon. Look, they absolutely float if you blow them. Chuck asked for four pairs. And ciggies for Pa and candies for Miggsy. I thought you and I could share these!'

Scrabbling in the paper she held up a squat, striped box tied with shiny ribbon in the shape of a twelve-inch high lipstick. She opened it to show eight lipsticks arranged in colours, from pale pink to crimson.

'Aren't they wizzy? Which will you have?'

'Trix. I want to talk to you.'

The girl's face clouded. She took the lipsticks out one by one and painted them in stripes on the back of her hand. She looked up warily at Elaine.

'Chuck Greenfield seems to come into your conversation a good deal.'

'He comes into the club a good deal. Whenever he has a bit of leave.'

'You know perfectly well what I mean.'

Trix continued to stripe her hand with crimson. She sniffed it and said, 'Delicious.' Then, irritably, 'Give a dog a bad name. Sure, I see Chuck. I can't very well avoid it, can I? I'm at the club and he asks for a Coke or a dance or something. Anyway, Dick *said* it was okay because I asked him before he went to sea. Could I go out occasionally, I said.'

'Occasionally!'

Trix opened her black eyes very wide.

'Yeah, that is what I said, occasionally. Dick just laughed. What he said, if you must know, was "you can kiss the boys hello". He knows me. He doesn't expect me to stay home and die of boredom. *Or* watch my father with that French witch cluttering up the place.'

'There is nothing wrong with Pa taking Annette Ghilain out now and then.'

'I never said there was. She's *his* war work, isn't she? Anyway, she was supposed to like Alain. What happened to him? Imagine preferring an old man.'

Elaine ignored the rudeness, and returned to the point which she saw Trix was trying to avoid.

'Your husband is away. When he does get leave – '

'Then I'll be thrilled to bits,' was the snappish reply. Picking up her parcels, Trix flounced out.

After her sister had left for the club, Elaine went up to her room, passing Trix's. The door, as usual, gaped open, and she noticed that there was a very new, very large photograph in a white leather frame on the dressing table. She recognized the young man, she had met him at Philippa's wedding. He was very young, wearing his Mae West, flying boots, and holding his helmet. *All love, Chuck* was scrawled across the picture. He looked as insouciant as Miles.

Elaine scarcely remembered him, she had only spoken to him for a moment of two at the wedding. And, although he came so often into Trix's conversation, he never appeared at St Helen's. She decided that Trix was keeping him out of the range of sisterly disapproval.

Spring came. The wild flowers on the bomb sites began to blossom in mauve and white, their leaves and buds thick and healthy. On the bomb site near Bruton Street, Elaine saw that a little poplar was growing, it was nearly three feet high. There had been a jeweller's shop where the tree flourished now – Miles had taken her there to buy her a naval crown. It was the same all over London. You looked at a place which had been a friend's house, and the burned wreckage sprouted with flowers. In the

201

place of a familiar shop there was a reservoir. Trees and weeds had turned dead places green.

The raids had not stopped, and one April evening when Elaine had just returned home after a long and hard day of work, the Alert was wailing. Miggs was nowhere to be seen. The brown teapot and tea caddy and the cat's basket were missing. Her old nurse must be in the cellar with Sailor for company. Listening to the raid tuning up, Elaine sighed. *Must* she shelter? The idea bored her, but when her father returned from his rounds he would only scold if she did not.

As she went through the drawing room, on her way to the billiard room, she heard an unfamiliar sound. It was her father's laugh.

'Is that you, Elaine?'

Theo was installed under the table. The scene was festive. A half bottle of gin, two glasses, lime juice, American cigarettes, and a plate of digestive biscuits. Keeping him company was Annette Ghilain.

'Coming to join us?' he asked.

'But of course you must shelter, madame, or your papa will be anxious,' from Annette.

Elaine could scarcely refuse. She was hospitably offered a gin and lime.

'Share my glass, madame. On this side I have not drunk.'

It was, thought Elaine, rather like being offered a sip from a loving cup.

She made an effort to be pleasant to the French girl, whose narrow foxy face resembled a Delacroix painting of the figure of Revolution. She only needed to grasp a tricolour and wear the cap of liberty.

'Have you seen anything of Alain and Alexandre?' asked Elaine. 'It is such a long time since they've been here.'

Annette's expression which had been pleasant enough, changed. She looked as if she resented the question.

'Alexandre is with General de Gaulle. For my cousin, I cannot say.'

'Surely he is with the General too?'

'I do not know. He wished to join the British. There was some dispute about it.'

She was brusque enough to be almost rude and Elaine said nothing more. But Theo, smoothing things over, said that

202

Annette had heard arguments between the two men. General de Gaulle wanted all Frenchmen to serve under him. Some, Alain among them, chose to go with the British.

'He told Annette it was from gratitude.'

Changing the conversation, Theo began to talk to Annette. His manner was doctorly. Was she sure she had enough to eat at the Centre? She had lost some weight. A good diet was essential, and even in wartime not difficult to obtain. 'The nation's health has never been better,' he said sententiously, 'and strain is more easily borne on a full stomach. Your work is taxing, my child.'

Annette's smile was forced.

'I am thinking of my silhouette, *Monsieur le Docteur*. The empty stomach is flatter than the full one. It is the same with warm clothes in winter. You scolded me because I shivered. But at least I do not wear clothes so thick that I do not look *bien*.'

'My dear child, I have never seen you look anything else.'

Raids or no raids, Annette was a constant visitor to St Helen's. Sometimes Elaine heard her voice coming from Theo's study. Sometimes, on raid-free evenings, she met them leaving the house to go out to dine. Occasionally Elaine found Annette seated in the drawing room as if she owned it, reading a French novel, with her feet up on the sofa.

When she had first seen Elaine after she returned from Shelton, Annette's manner had been solemn. It was as if the French girl had hurriedly pulled on a black armband and a face to match. But seeing that Elaine never cried, and talked of Miles in a normal manner, Annette relaxed and became her real self. She criticized everything.

'This dried milk that the Americans send us, it is *dégoutant*.'

'How can one dress well when all one's coupons buy but one pair of silk stockings?' exhibiting a thin leg. If was a waste of breath to contradict her or resent her attitude to her host country. She was more scathing about France. It anyone mentioned Occupied France, she exclaimed, '*Lâche, Lâche*'. When there was a reference to the Free French, she remarked that they were all sex mad, which Elaine took to mean that she was constantly fighting for her virtue at the Centre. Even her Breton home came in for no praise. 'It smelled of fish.'

Theo heard her pronouncements with exaggerated laughter

203

and a flushed face. Elaine disliked seeing her father excited by
a girl who was two years older than Trix.

Summer came. The Allied victory seemed nearer, the dark
mood of last year was fading. But not for Elaine. What happened to grief? You grew used to it. But it did not leave you,
and you did not want it to do so. What else had you?

It was late one summer evening when Elaine went upstairs
to find Miggs doing something very unusual, she was giving
Philippa's room a desultory flick with a near-bald feather
duster.

'Haven't seen Miss Philippa for a month of Sundays,' said
Miggs in a disgruntled voice. 'Why can't she get home to see
her own folk now and then, that's what I want to know? Those
Eagle Squadrons, they've been disbanded, haven't they?
Doesn't that give her a bit of time to come up? Anyway, she
rang today, wonder of wonders. Said she'll try and come this
weekend. I'll believe that when I see it.'

She continued to flick the duster here and there along the
top of Philippa's bookshelf. Her back was turned to Elaine. It
looked more crooked than it used to do.

'What's the matter, Miggsy?'

'Dunno what you mean.'

'Yes, you do. You're worried. I wish you'd say why.'

'You got your own cross to bear.'

'Like thousands of other women. It's Trix, isn't it?'

Miggs turned round in plain astonishment.

'What's *she* got to do with anythin'? Yes, I'm worried and so
should you be. Know what the doctor wants to do? Give that
Frenchwoman my job. Miggs, he said, Miggs, I think Miss
Whatsit will do very nicely as my receptionist. The practice has
picked up since the big blitz, and a lot of patients have come
back to London. Miss Whatsit hasn't enough to do workin'
where she is. (Why hasn't she, I ask myself? Isn't there a war
on?) She's been good enough,' finished Miggs savagely, 'to say
she'll work for us. *Us!*'

Elaine was as dismayed as her old nurse.

'He can't mean it.'

'Oh, but he does. And a foreigner. Takin' away an English-
woman's job. And more than that. You've seen the doctor with

204

her. Gigglin' like a silly kid. There's no fool like an old fool. Beg pardon, lady.'

Elaine was not sure whether to make matters worse by agreeing.

'But Miggs, what can we possibly do about it?'

'I can do somethin' and pretty sharp too. I'll go to my niece in Ditchling.'

'*Leave us*?'

'That's about the size of it.'

Annette's constant presence continued to disturb Elaine. And there was now a new visitor to the house, who up until now had been kept out of the way.

Chuck Greenfield was being what was called 'rested up' after working as an instructor for some months. He was due to go back to active service, and in the meantime had been given generous leave. He had time to call, now, very often in the hope of finding Trix. Nowadays she was always in. He collected her and bore her away for a day, or an afternoon, or an evening. Returning, Trix was in the sunniest of tempers. Elaine never remembered hearing her sing as much as she did now.

Elaine could not stop herself from liking Chuck. He was the friendliest and most uncomplicated man she had met in her life. When she compared him in her thoughts to Miles she saw that her husband had had tensions, paradoxes and reserves. From the little Elaine knew of Barny, he was not easy either, despite an American openness. But Chuck was a man of simplicities.

He never arrived at St Helen's empty-handed. She sometimes thought that Chuck would consider not arriving with gifts an impossible discourtesy. He simply had to give. He epitomised the extraordinary, unaffected American generosity. He took Elaine's breath away. He brought tins of coffee and butter, real oranges the peel of which Miggs later preserved to flavour cakes and puddings. He brought boxes of every kind of chocolate bar, which he called candies. There was scented soap for Elaine, tinned jam for Miggs, Bourbon whisky for Theo. He never came without a long pack of cigarettes under his arm – Lucky Strikes marked *For the United States Services Overseas*.

He reminded Elaine of a boy at school, a prefect or the head of a cricket team. His figure was loose-limbed and young, his eyes filled with tears when he laughed. His hair sprung up in a wave above his forehead, he couldn't make it stay down no matter how much he slicked it with a wet comb.

Sprawling in the house or on the burned-dry grass in the garden during the hot early autumn weather, he could not take his eyes off Trix. He had the look of a man seeing a vision. When she was near him, he linked his arm in hers or held her hand, her long thin fingers interlocking in his own. Every now and then they looked at each other, their eyes half drowned, and it struck Elaine that it was possible to kiss without moving a muscle.

She was moved and disturbed by the emotion there seemed to be between them. Aware of his eyes, Trix went through her paces, dancing on the lawn, sitting on the arm of his chair, playing records and singing all the words.

When he spoke about Trix to Elaine, Chuck sounded as if he were talking of royalty. He seemed more American when he spoke about Barny for whom he had a boyish admiration. Barny sure was a brilliant flyer, just brilliant; there was nothing that guy couldn't do with a plane, he could make it sit up and beg for him.

Who could resist Chuck? Yet Elaine found her sister's intimate manner with him hard to bear. Trix knew she was being disapproved of and put herself out to please her big sister, using a coaxing charm.

On the last day of his leave Chuck managed to get some petrol, and he and Trix planned to go out to the country. They were going to lunch at the Compleat Angler at Marlow. Giving Elaine a scented kiss, Trix left with Chuck, her long hair shining in the sun, a new handbag with TRIX in gilt letters slung over her shoulder.

It was a day for couples to leave the house. Theo and Annette also went, they were bound for luncheon in Soho. The sight of them did not worry Elaine as much as seeing Chuck and Trix, although the behaviour of her father did put her teeth on edge. As Theo had come downstairs he had seen Annette waiting for him by the front door. She was wearing a navy blue dress with a broad sailor collar and a pleated skirt, and a little straw hat perched over her eyes. Seeing the fresh pretty figure, he had blushed the colour of a beetroot.

There was no escaping the fact that the point of command at St Helen's had moved. Annette had left the Centre, and now sat during the week at a desk in the hall – the desk, a handsome

206

Sheraton piece, had been moved from the drawing room specially for her use. Miggs said no more about leaving, and at present satisfied herself with a war of attrition. She omitted to tell Annette if a patient telephoned when she was absent. She hid the tea. The threat of her going was not overt, but Elaine could hear it rumbling like thunder on a sultry evening. She wondered what St Helen's would do without its spirit, its grudging laconic witch with cat? She could not imagine life without Miggs, or think how to prevent losing her.

Alone in the shabby old house, with the sun unpleasantly hot, Elaine went out into the garden and found a deck chair. All the garden chairs were pre-war and had begun to split. She sat down gingerly under a tree. The garden was dull with no flowers but a few seeded michaelmas daisies. The freshest things were Trix's lettuces standing in crisp green rows: her sister always watered those. Sitting in the shade, Elaine closed her eyes. Birds chirped. Next week was the anniversary of the day the telegram had arrived: a whole year since Miles' death and the birth and death of their little son.

1943 had changed the spirit and feeling in England. There had been the conquest in North Africa, victories in Italy, and now the great US raids on Germany. Sometimes in broad daylight the planes flew over London in their hundreds, squadron after squadron of huge dark Flying Fortresses filling the air with their roar like enormous birds. People in the streets stopped and looked up and admired. There they go, good luck to them.

There was a feeling of hope now. But not for Elaine. With her eyes shut she thought of Miles. Thinking, loving, longing, grieving, ah, those were the things that made her weak. What had Marjorie said before they parted in Oxford. That grief was not like an illness, it *was* an illness. You were sick and you had to wait until you got better. I am not better, Miles, and I don't want to be.

There was a sound on the terrace by the French window; she heard it through her reverie and slowly opened her eyes. In a terrifying moment like an ecstasy she thought she had raised a ghost. It was a man in naval uniform.

Dick Polglaze came running across the grass.

'Elaine!'

She sprang up and he took her in his arms, holding her close

207

and kissing her. He had never done such a thing before and she understood everything he meant by the embrace.

'Beautiful sister-in-law,' he said after a moment, as he let her go. 'It is so good to see you. And where is my beautiful wife?'

'Oh, Dick. Why didn't you let us know? How awful – she's gone out.'

She was still shaken by that first moment of seeing him, and now a feeling of desperate anxiety flooded through her.

He laughed.

'Silly of me to imagine she'd be home. I did try to ring but I couldn't get through. From Scotland.'

He threw his cap aside, and the sun shone down on his cropped curling fair hair. He was sunburned and he looked handsome and confident. He met her eyes just then, and said matter-of-factly that he had never written to her about Miles. He hadn't heard for a long time, letters arrived in batches. And by the time he had known, it was too late.

'It would only have been one of those letters.'

'I liked those letters.'

'Hell. You're right. I'm sorry, will you forgive me?'

'I expect so.'

Leaning on his elbow as he sat on the grass near her, he began to talk about Miles. He talked of when they had been in the Lower Deck together; of Miles' astonishment at having to do his own washing, and the 'make do and mend period' when the NCO would shout 'Settle down, you men,' and huge stokers would begin painstakingly darning their socks. He made Elaine laugh. For once she felt that the hideous word 'widow' was not pinned to her like a label on an evacuated child. He seemed unworried by Trix's absence, saying how he had wished he could let them know. His ship was having a refit.

'Glorious, isn't it? Nearly two weeks' leave'. But he had thought he was going to be duty officer for the first couple of days.

'I rang, as I say, but no luck. It's my fault, rolling up without warning. Of course she's out. Is she as beautiful and run-after as ever?'

'Oh, you know Trix,' said Elaine, smiling. She thought – but do you? He smiled back at her with his narrow eyes. His English voice sounded unfamiliar, after Chuck's drawl.

He talked about the recent months at sea. He was in a Hunt

Class destroyer, and they had been on convoy, bringing ships over from America and Canada. He couldn't tell her where except that the ships had come to Scotland.

'It was so strange, Elaine, this huge sheltered bay filled, packed, crammed with liberty ships. I went fishing in the loch for mackerel with some mates – we dragged pieces of silver paper behind us on lines and we got scores of fresh fish, delicious. When our boat went near an American ship, the Yanks leaned over the side and threw us chocolates.'

'That's so exactly like them.'

'Yoo-hoo? You in the garden?' called a voice gaily.

Elaine went cold. She waited to see Trix appear in the French window hand in hand with Chuck. Trix was alone.

'*Sweetheart!*'

Dick sprang to his feet, rushed across the garden and picked her up, to swing her round like a child, pressing a kiss to her mouth as he did so. He was laughing as he set her on her feet.

'Dick, where on earth have you sprung from?'

'Leave! Isn't it marvellous? Our ship's in trouble and needs a refit, poor thing, I've got *days*. Let me look at you.'

Grabbing her hands, he held her at arm's length, taking in the extraordinary beauty.

'More gorgeous than ever, isn't she, Elaine? Two lovely Tyrrell girls. Are you both coming to dinner with me at the most expensive place in town? I've months of pay to waste.'

To Elaine's nervous relief, Trix behaved just like a wife whose husband has returned from the wars. She let herself be kissed a good deal, and waited, smiling, while he fetched his bag and produced presents, scent and soap and silk stockings. The gifts were less than those Chuck brought, and Elaine's heart hurt her.

Trix opened the bottle of Jean Patou scent, rubbed it on her freckled arm and said that it was her favourite. And what wizzy soap. Did Dick know the beastly government had rationed soap now? They wanted us all to be filthy.

Sitting on the grass with him, she looked calm enough when he put his arm round her.

Elaine refused the invitation to dinner. She thought Trix insisted too much, but she stood firm. It was Dick who accepted her refusal, saying affectionately that there was lots more time and lots more pay. He gave her hand a casual kiss before he and Trix left in the evening.

She watched them walking towards the gate, Trix with her long-legged strut, her skirts short and full as a ballerina's, her legs in American nylons. Dick whispered something to her, and Elaine saw her sister slightly move away.

They did not come home. Her father returned late after supper, yawning and saying he was going to bed. She was not inclined to ask him if he'd had a good time: he wore a most self-satisfied expression. When she told him Dick was home on leave, he said 'good, good', scarcely listening.

Elaine did not go to bed. Dick was staying the night at St Helen's and she told herself that there was absolutely no reason for her to sit up for them, as if she were a maiden aunt. Trix was with her husband and everything was as it should be. At last, tired out with her own anxiety, she went to bed.

She woke suddenly, knowing somebody was in her room. A faint greyness came through the drawn curtains. It was dawn.

'Elaine?'

'What is it?'

Her voice was frightened and she heard Dick say, 'Sorry.' It was not an apology. 'I woke you.'

'I was awake,' she lied. 'Don't put on the light. Pull back the curtains.'

He went quietly over to the windows, a dim figure, and pulled the curtains gently as if anxious to make no noise. More grey light came into the room. He was in uniform. Already dressed? Still dressed?

He stood at the foot of her bed.

'No,' he said, meeting her eyes, 'I have not been to bed. Trix has. She is asleep.'

He had the look of exhaustion which makes a face appear dirty, as if smeared with dust.

'She wants a divorce.'

Elaine gave something between a gasp and a shudder.

'Surprised?' he said in derision, 'I imagine you have known about it for months.'

'What do you mean! Of course I didn't know.'

'About Greenfield, the American? She's sleeping with him. Don't tell me you didn't know *that*, because I shan't believe you.'

'I don't care if you believe me or not. I didn't know.'

He shrugged and folded his arms.

210

'I don't see that it matters. She wants a divorce. "I don't love you any more".' He mimicked the metallic voice. 'She's made up her mind. And as you know, when Trix wants something, she sure in hell gets it.' This time he mimicked an American accent.

Something in him, cruel and savage in its pain, dried her sympathy.

'She's overwrought. She's only a child still.'

He gave a violent laugh.

'Don't laugh like that!' she said angrily.

'Why not, don't you think it's funny? You expect me to behave well, don't you? To agree that she's a child. I don't agree and why in God's name should I behave well? Oh, of course, the Flight Lieutenant is a hero, a pilot, and what is more a fully-fledged Eagle, an American who came here to fight our war. Nothing's too good for him. He must help himself to my country, my hospitality, and of course my wife. Indeed, why not. She's common property.'

'*Stop it.*'

'Why?'

'Because all you are doing is revenging yourself on me. I won't have it. What did you say to Trix?'

'A good deal.'

'Surely she saw reason?'

He gave another imitation of a laugh.

'Oh yes. She cried and carried on. I suppose I agree with you in a way, she was like a child, a disgusting spoiled child. A greedy child who isn't used to being called names. She makes me sick.'

'And the divorce?'

'Let her have it.'

Elaine was shocked to the depth of her soul.

'But you've only been on leave a few hours. How can you and she decide anything so – so terrible. She is twenty, Dick, not thirty. The Americans have gone to her head. Yes, she is spoiled. We've spoiled her. You have. But she is your wife.'

Putting up both hands, he pulled his hair, viciously tugging it. She scarcely recognized the enchanting man who had sat on the grass this afternoon. He looked merciless.

'She is not my wife and now I think about it I see she never was. It was her idea that we married. She got it into her head and I agreed. I was in love with her. I thought her the most beautiful sexy thing I'd seen in my life. And I believed she was in love with me.'

'So she was – don't laugh like that, I hate it – and will be again.'

'Oh – ' he stopped himself, and then went on, 'I won't swear in front of you, I'm sure you've never heard bad language in your life but there's a dirty word for Trix. I was the sucker who married her, so it's my own bloody fault. However. I'll fix up the divorce. It'll take time, as I'll be at sea, but I don't suppose that will worry her much since she is fu-sorry, making love with that American anyway. I just came to tell you,' he said, turning away, 'that I don't expect I'll see you again.'

He walked to the door.

She climbed out of bed, ran across to him and caught hold of his arm. For a split second she felt his body react towards her. It was as if by touching him she had made him human again. But when he looked at her, his face again wore a vicious smile.

'Please give it time, Dick! Give *her* time.'

'Trix doesn't want me to give her time. She doesn't want me to give her anything. Except the certainty that she won't set eyes on me again.'

He looked at her for a moment with his iron face. Then went out, closing the door so carefully that she thought she would scream.

When Elaine arrived at the office she telephoned St Helen's. She rang twice, but both times Annette told her that Trix was asleep. On the third call Trix answered, yawning.

'Yeah?'

'I want you at home when I get back tonight. Don't go to the club. I have something to say to you,' snapped Elaine.

'It won't do any good.'

Elaine had been growing steadily angrier all the morning.

'I shall expect you there when I get back.' She slammed down the receiver. She would have liked to box her ears.

When she came home, Trix was in the sewing room. The battered nursery table was covered with yards of slithering oyster satin. Trix was cutting out a pair of cami-knickers. As Elaine walked in, Trix looked up. She, too, was in a temper.

She went on cutting out.

'Stop that and pay attention.'

Trix gave an exaggerated sigh. But she put down the scissors and sat waiting, and there was something, even in her way of sitting, which made it impossible to be angry with her. She looked so young and so absurd. As swiftly as a puppy knows its mistress has stopped being unkind, Trix lost her ill temper. She put her chin on her hand.

'I know what you're going to say, but it truly isn't my fault that I've fallen in love again. How can you control a thing like that? I'm just unlucky not to have met Chuck sooner, before I married, I mean. You were absolutely right,' she added solemnly, 'I never should have rushed into it.'

'Now you propose to rush into something worse.'

'Oh no! Chuck and I are wonderful together. I can't tell you what it's like, Elaine. Him and me.'

It was only too clear she was talking about sex. 'You know, he's really honourable,' she went on. 'That's rare, isn't it? He believes in behaving well. He is a guy who wouldn't do a dirty trick to a living soul – '

'But he's breaking up your marriage,' interrupted Elaine, finding it hard to listen.

'That's the *point*, Elaine. He feels the way I do. That this is it. Love.'

Trix gazed at her across the table covered with bride-like satin.

Elaine answered carefully, trying to explain that what Trix wanted to do was mad. Sudden, mad and cruel, and she would regret it. It was Trix's turn to look as if she could not bear to listen. She fidgeted and sighed and tried to interrupt, while Elaine who was out of her depth droned on, using cliché words like infatuation.

'You must see what you want is impossible,' she finished.

'You don't understand anything!' was the sudden fierce reply. 'I told you. Chuck and I are getting married. I shan't listen to another word.' Putting her fingers in her ears, Trix began to hum. Elaine leaned over to unstop her sister's ears, but Trix dodged, humming more loudly. Deeply offended, Elaine stood up and began to walk out. The humming abruptly stopped.

'Don't go!'

Trix began to talk very fast, words of resentment and self-justification tumbling out in a flood. In her voice Elaine heard the frantic selfishness of passion. How *could* she stay married to a man she didn't love? If she went to bed with him she'd be sick. Dick had taken her out to dinner last night and the moment they sat down she told him right away. She hated lies and couldn't go on acting. She had said she was in love with Chuck, and Dick must give her a divorce. It had been awful at first, because he had thought it was a joke and burst out laughing. But then he saw she meant it, and when she was explaining about Chuck he took her by the arm, really hurting her, and sort of dragged her out of the restaurant, paying a lot of money although they hadn't had a single thing to eat. He walked her round and round St James' park arguing and pleading until she thought she would go mad. Then he pushed her in a taxi and brought her home.

'He made me creep up the stairs and he kept sh-sh-ing me and saying we'd wake everybody. *Stupid.* What did it matter if we had? Then when we were in my room he started all over again, going on and on about staying married and loving me and then he began to kiss me,' said Trix shuddering, 'and begging me to do it with him, do it *now* and it would all be okay, and then when I said I wouldn't he slapped me across the face.'

'Trix, stop. I shouldn't hear all this.'

'Why not if it's true?'

'I can't listen. I'm sorry.'

Elaine left the room.

She stood staring down the passage at the staircase and thinking of Dick walking so quietly so as not to wake the sleeping house, and shutting her door this morning in the same awful, careful way. And she thought of his life in his ship facing the fatal seas where many men drowned and ships sank in flames and smoke. She thought of the cold and danger, and how all the time he had carried Trix in his thoughts as a beautiful secret. And here instead was a girl with a white face and black eyes who looked like a witch.

The Tyrrell passion to get things over, even if doing so was idiotic, was strong in Elaine during the weeks following Dick Polglaze's dawn exit from St Helen's. She knew it was her duty to tell her father – or to be exact it was Trix's duty to do so, and the sooner the better. But Trix was keeping out of her way. When Elaine saw her she was pale and snappish, only brightening up

214

when Chuck managed to get some leave. He was now back on ops. If the telephone rang Trix ran to it so fast that Elaine pitied her, and pitied her more when the call was so often not from Chuck.

He came to the house one day expressly to see Elaine. At breakfast Trix had said abruptly, with a warning glance in her father's direction, 'Chuck may drop by this evening. Shall you be around?'

'Yes. Why?'

'Could you look after him for me. He surely wants to see you,' said Trix whose vocabulary became more American every day.

Another look towards her father, who was deeply engrossed in *The Times*.

Chuck arrived early in the evening. The weather had been muggy and there had been a slight fog all day. Now the temperature dropped sharply, and the fog thickened. From the window Elaine saw a tall figure in uniform looming out of the mist. Why did Americans move so differently to Englishmen? Everything about them was easier and looser. Was that, she thought – displeased at the idea of the coming interview – the trouble with them?

She went to the front door to let him in. He greeted her with his pleasant politeness, and left a package in the hall for Miggs. Elaine wished he had not done that. He followed her into the drawing room in silence, and sat down, placing his hands on his knees.

Elaine looked at him earnestly, trying to see why Trix found him irresistible. There he was, handsome in a clean-cut boyish sort of way, with his shining hair and beautiful unmarked skin fresh with youth and health. He still made her think of a school prefect, or perhaps the head of the school team. He was like an eager boy who was ready to run faster and jump higher and win the most games. Yet he was as eager to make the loser feel it was only a game after all. Chuck was nothing if not gallant. But he was neither as odd nor as fascinating as Dick Polglaze; and it was for this pleasant boy that Trix was behaving with such cruelty.

'Are you very sore at us, ma'am?'

'I am afraid I am.'

'Of course you must be. I respect you for it. I can't apologise

215

for loving your sister or be sorry that she loves me. But I sure don't think,' he finished sadly, 'I play an honourable part in all this.'

'Trix plays a worse one.'

He was shocked. He was an American and his girl was perfect. He begged Elaine's pardon but he must disagree. She should not put the least blame on her sister who was wonderful, and most unhappy over what had happened.

He did not say that what had happened was simply that Trix had fallen into his bed and in his turn Chuck had fallen passionately in love. She was the girl desired by all men and married to an Englishman fighting the war at sea . . . yet she had chosen him. It was miraculous. He told Elaine how much he loved and longed for Trix, adding gravely, had Trix mentioned that he had re-named his plane TRIX?

'No, she didn't tell me.' Elaine could not think what to say to that.

As she listened to him talking of Trix and himself, it was as if he were talking of two people struck by an act of God, an earthquake or an avalanche, in which the helpless victims were hurled down by the force of mighty Nature. But just as Trix had some spell which weakened and finally erased condemnation, so had Chuck. Hers was caused by beauty, his by honesty. He talked of Trix with love and simplicity. His voice was reverent. Against her will, Elaine was moved.

'Of course you know we're out of the RAF now and part of the US Air Corps. It makes a mighty big difference,' he finished.

'Flip told me things had changed.'

'That's what I'm coming to. Now that Trix and I are engaged – '

Is that what they call it? thought Elaine.

'She won't be able to follow me around. They just won't allow it. Flip made a fine job of it when we were in Fighter Command, but that's all over. Maybe for the best. I know I couldn't fly as I should if I thought of Trix hanging around near the station, miserable and at a loose end. Maybe Barny's getting to feel the same. Flip's being sent home. Did she tell you?'

'She wrote something about it.'

'Well – '

216

He gave her a beseeching look.

Elaine said slowly, 'You mean that you want Trix to remain here at home.'

'Please, ma'am.'

The cement of the family, thought Elaine. What have I got myself into now?

'But my father is against divorce and she hasn't told him anything about all this yet. I should think she daren't.'

'Trix mentioned that your mother was a Quaker. Some of my folks are too.'

'My father isn't. He is scarcely an active member of the Church of England,' she said dryly. 'He only goes to church about twice a year. But his principles are those he grew up with. They are there. Immovable. He detests divorce and will not accept it.'

'Yeah. She said.'

'The point is,' said Elaine, meeting the serious eyes fixed on her, 'there will be an almighty row when my father finds out what is going to happen. It *is* happening, is it? I mean you have both quite made up your minds to marry. I know she said so, and her husband told me the same thing. It all seems very reckless and sudden.'

'No question. We are going to marry as soon as she is free.'

'But you want her to remain here.'

He was leaning forward, his elbows on his knees, his large graceful body anxious and unrelaxed. They treat me as if I were their mother, she thought with resentment. Trix. Dick. Even this American. Now that Miles is dead, is this all I am to be for ever? Somebody who minds other people's business.

She said, after a pause,

'If you are not allowed to have Trix with you, and I understand that when you're on ops, I suppose there is nothing for her but to stay. But I don't think my father should be told anything about the divorce.'

He looked surprised. Relieved and surprised.

'Are you sure you can manage that?'

Now you are going to be dreadfully grateful, she thought, and resented him more.

'It seems underhand to conceal the divorce,' she added, 'but if Father found out he could refuse to have her here.'

'Some people back home are like that.'

She had an irrational desire to exclaim, 'Then why don't you see that this is as a disgraceful mess and you are as much to blame as Trix. And what about her husband, for God's sake?' But instead she stood up and so did he, looking about for his cap which, like his uniform, was too crisp, too smart. She preferred the old shabby RAF blue. Putting out his hand, he gripped hers painfully. He muttered something about it being impossible to thank her, she was the soul of kindness, and other things she did not exactly catch. She thought there were tears in his eyes. She even thought she heard him say she was like a mother to Trix. That, as Annette Ghilain would say, was *le comble*. Elaine did not want to hear any more of the muttered speech, and went to the door with him, bidding him a most matter-of-fact goodbye.

Turning at the gate, he gave her a salute.

There was a jeep waiting.

Chapter Fifteen

Knowing that her father was safely out of the house at the hospital, and Annette had gone shopping in Kensington, Elaine telephoned Philippa the moment that Chuck left. She began by asking if Philippa were really coming home.

'I'm glad you called up, I keep meaning to,' Philippa said. 'But there's such a short time left. And it goes so fast. Bloody, having to leave him, isn't it?'

Elaine scarcely paused to be sympathetic before she gave the bad news.

'I've had one of your ex-Eagles here today. There has been a lot of drama. Trix is getting a divorce from Dick and marrying Chuck.'

She waited for her romantic sister to be astounded and fascinated. Philippa was furious.

'*Chuck Greenfield.* Do you mean to tell me . . . and divorcing Dick. How disgusting.'

'Isn't he a friend of Barny's? You are not going to be beastly about Chuck, I hope. Everything is bad enough at this end, and I haven't dared tell Pa.'

More than Elaine had done, Philippa had absorbed her parents' attitude to divorce. Divorce happened to film people and in 'Society', about whom ludicrously snobbish gossip was dished out in the Sunday newspapers. Philippa thought divorce a dreadful thing: she also thought it *déclassé*, despite it being usual among the aristocracy.

'Chuck had no right to break up the marriage.'

'Flip. What's the good of being censorious? You know what she is like. Dick has been away so long and London is swarming with Americans. She's been mad about everything American since she was ten years old, She fell in love with it when she started going to the films.'

Just as you, thought Elaine, fell in love with flyers. She remembered the old scandal of Barny and Trix. Of course, Barny had been Trix's first lover from the United States . . .

219

Both her sisters had a strong sexual urge towards an idea which excited them. They had had preconceived images in their heads. It was as if the men they chose stepped into canvases in which the background had been painted in advance. She remembered the horribly black sky and surfaced submarine in Miles' ugly portrait. For Philippa the background had been a sky full of vapour trails, bursting shells and Spitfires. For Trix, the vast sprawling continent of America.

'Barny will be as shocked as I am,' said Philippa in a grating voice.

Elaine tried to keep her temper. She wanted to be rude, but it would do no good. She had lost her influence over her sister now – Philippa was in a world she knew nothing about, with different laws and a different language. Leaving aside Philippa's declaration that the divorce was Chuck's fault, which was patent nonsense, Elaine said coldly that she had decided to keep their father in the dark.

'The child must live somewhere. And she won't be allowed to join him when she *is* married to Chuck, just as you are no longer allowed to stay with Barny.'

'She isn't a child and she isn't married to him yet. All I can say is I hope his CO doesn't find out. There'll be a God almighty row if he does. Americans are not encouraged to break up British marriages.'

'Stop talking in that disagreeable voice, and stop being so unrealistic! Just speak to Barny quietly. Chuck is a nice man and a vulnerable one, and he is behaving as honourably as he knows how. Talk to your husband. He'll tell you to shut up,' said Elaine and rang off.

Still red with anger, Philippa sat by the telephone in her hotel bedroom. She was going to ring back and go on ar guing: when furious she always did that if the quarrel was on the telephone. But the door of her room opened, and Barny put his head in. She had expected him, but some hours later. She rushed to him, filled with the bad news and her righteous indignation.

But before she had said three words he told her that he knew. Chuck was back with the Squadron. He'd talked to him yesterday about it, and asked him not to mention it yet to Philippa.

'He was going to see Elaine and he wanted to get that settled. He's very fond of your elder sister. I'm sure she was good to him. You must be the same.'

'Good to him!'

She was just going to burst into a long righteous speech about men stealing the wives of other men away at the war. She was going to flay wives who were unfaithful. Old resentment flooded through her like a poison. But Barny looked so tired. He sat down on the bed.

'Do you think they'd bring us up some horrible English tea?' he said, and then he added, 'You must do as I say, Flip, my honey. Be kind to Chuck. Feelings are the devil, they can throw you right out. Feelings can affect your flying.'

It was the sentence which frightened her most.

Philippa did not receive her marching orders for a while. Barny and his friends had become part of the American Air Force and the operational experience of the Eagles was very valuable. But it had not occurred to Philippa that, for that very reason, some of her friends would be transferred. She had simply imagined them in a different uniform, continuing the Eagles' tradition.

A few days after the transfer, Barny came home to the hotel where she had been living for some weeks, and told her that he was being sent into another Fighter Group.

'I have to retrain,' he said, walking round the hotel garden with her.

'Retrain. How absolutely ridiculous. You're more experienced than any pilot they've got. They're lucky to have you.'

He squeezed her arm.

'What a partisan you are. I have got to retrain, Flip, because I'm not to be in Spits any more. I shall be flying a P38 Lightning fighter in the new squadron. They tell me it's very much faster.'

Retraining was to be at the same station, so Philippa need not leave just yet, he said. 'I guess learning the new plane will take a couple've weeks.'

She did not see him at all during the course, but he managed to get a sleeping-out pass when it was finished. He looked tired and pale, he had had his flak nightmare again.

Determined to switch his mind away from that, she eagerly asked about the new plane.

'Well. It has advantages. It's a lot bigger, twin-engined, and it's mighty fast. Utterly different to fly. The trouble, for me anyway, is that it isn't as nimble as a Spitfire. I miss that reaction of the Spit's, the way it answers to you – as Chuck used to say, you can make it sit up and beg.'

He would be back on active service again at the end of the week, his Squadron's job was escorting the Flying Fortresses into Germany and back. Late that evening, lying in bed beside her – they had not made love – he began to talk of how it felt to be in the American Air Force.

'My God, Flip, it's different to the RAF. Much more different even than the Lightning and the Spit. All our pilots are fully trained, of course, and real keen. That's the trouble. The mess is full of guys all talking at once, just screaming for action. They keep saying how they can't wait to start knocking off the enemy, and how those Krauts aren't going to believe their eyes when *they* come zooming in.'

He was silent, and then added.

'If only they just wouldn't talk so big.'

'The Eagles used to be like that.'

'Yeah. I know. Sometimes they're uncannily like we were. It's as if I hear us talking. But I keep thinking how they've seen nothing, and can't know what it's going to be like. They've had no fighter experience, never seen their pals going down in flames, never had flak through their wings. Do you know what they call the Battle of Britain? The last war.'

He knew he sounded old, faced with the spirited young. Had he caught something of the English reserve, the much-mocked stiff upper lip? Yet there were times, he told her, when he felt at home with the noisy young pilots and the very sound of their voices was a marvellous relief after the clipped tones of the RAF. But then the innocence of his companions would suddenly irk him. They hadn't lived with death.

'But they will, Barny. That's what is so awful. And so inevitable. It's all in the future for them. Don't grudge them a short time of ignorance now.'

He sighed and took her in his arms, looking down at her sweet, familiar, vulnerable face.

'What would I do without you?'

'Get another girl. Much prettier.'

'Don't fish.'

Two days later he telephoned her from the station to say that he had received his posting, and that she must leave.

'I don't know if I can make it tonight or tomorrow, but I'll be along. Just get packed.'

It was brilliant October, sunny crisp days following each other

222

in that autumnal beauty which pretends it will never end. Philippa began to pack up her few possessions. She felt extraordinarily bereft to think she must leave him.

On a sunny Saturday morning, lovelier than the rest, Barny's Squadron went out on a daylight patrol in advance of the big bombers. At 12,000 feet over the Channel they met a flight of enemy fighters coming straight at them. Barny's plane was hit. He managed to climb out before the fire was too fierce: he parachuted into the sea. A rescue boat spotted him and reached him. But the Messerschmitt which had shot down Barny's plane suddenly dived downwards over the boat as Barny was being hauled on board. The deck was sprayed with bullets.

They thought he was going to die. He was in a coma from loss of blood, wounded in leg and hip in four places. They managed to get him to a coastal hospital, he did not die on the way, and was operated on at once.

Barny's section commander was his old friend Pete Jansen, who came to the hospital to tell Philippa.

He took her in a jeep a long way across country, into an area forbidden to civilians. When they arrived at the hospital he couldn't stay, he was on duty that night.

'I'll be thinking of you both, pal.'

He pressed her shoulder before striding away.

She sat in the hospital corridor. She did not know how long she waited, she was told later that the operation had lasted for four hours. At last a small man with grey hair came towards her through the swing doors. He wore a white coat.

'Mrs Duval? I'm John Murdoch, your husband's physician. He stood up to the operation pretty well, pretty well. We'll just have to see. We had to limit the anaesthetic we gave him, you understand. Because of the condition.'

Philippa did not understand. And could not ask.

The weeks that followed for her were spent in limbo. She was allowed to move to a seaside hotel, it was almost empty and within reach of the hospital. One night, returning after sitting with Barny, she had looked up 'limbo' in a battered dictionary she found in the lounge. It said that limbo was a region on the borders of hell.

Taking limbo with her, she travelled every day from the big,

223

shabby hotel where only some servicemen were staying, to the hospital six miles away. A taxi came for her at the same time every day, driven by a taciturn old man who said nothing but good morning. Each day she was allowed to sit by Barny's bed. He was still in a coma and she knew, although they did not tell her, that there was a possibility he would never emerge from it. Comas were, in a way, inexplicable things. People could remain unconscious for weeks, even for years. It frightened her. The hospital was big and full, for although the area was forbidden to visitors, people living on the south coast, the old and the very young, were patients here, and there were two wards of American casualties, ground staff and pilots. Philippa did not know any of the men who lay in the rows of beds. Sometimes they smiled at her.

Barny's bed was at the end of a ward containing forty beds, twenty on either side, arranged in lines so straight they could have been drawn with a ruler. The green screens round his bed made it into a sort of private room.

The weather had suddenly turned freezing cold, it was getting on towards November, and the wards were also very cold. There was not enough coal to keep the radiators comfortably warm. Nurses rustled up and down, carrying hot water bottles and scarlet blankets which they offered to the patients.

'Now are you sure you are warm enough?'

Each of the Sisters was named after her ward. Barny was in David Ward, and every morning Sister David sent a nurse to Philippa with a scarlet blanket. She was instructed to wrap herself up well. If she caught cold she would not be allowed to visit her husband. The nurses also brought a mug of hot cocoa.

Sitting in her blanket, watching Barny, Philippa did not feel strong enough to ask Sister David any questions. Her moral courage had deserted her. Elaine would have done so – she couldn't. Besides, they would never tell her, would they? that Barny was going to die. And in any case they did not know. Nor could Sister David or the doctors tell when he would emerge from that sleep so like the sleep of death. They would only give her half truths and cheerfulness. But she knew that the longer he stayed unconscious, the more he was in danger.

Every morning she walked down the aisle of David Ward between the rows of beds, where pyjama clad men lay patiently, and she went behind the screens, and sat in the chair by Barny's bed. The nurse arrived with the blanket, and Philippa thanked her, and wrapped it round her waist. She always said, 'How is he?' and the nurse answered, 'Not too bad,' with an upward note in her voice.

When she was alone with him, Philippa leaned forward and looked fixedly at the unmoving figure, and touched the dark hair so tidily combed, and took his hand, and wondered if she was ever going to look into his dark eyes again.

The only person she spoke to during her lonely ordeal, apart from the nurses, was Pete Jansen. He was a tall rangy man, older than the other Eagles who had been Philippa's friends, Pete was twenty-eight. He had thick hair that was so fair that it was almost white, and large blue eyes. Everything about Pete was on a big scale, his hands, his voice, the country he came from, Wyoming. Now and then, with a few brief hours of leave, he drove out to the seaside hotel to have dinner with Philippa. She was desperately glad to see him and – since the news of Barny was not good and limbo was around her – she forced him to talk about himself. She would listen with concentration, keeping her mind away from the bed at the end of the ward behind the screens.

'You cetainly make a fellow talk,' Pete said one evening, smiling at her thoughfully. She knew he guessed why and that *he* knew it was a way of helping her.

He told her about his State, which was 3,000 feet up, bitter cold in winter, roasting in summer. In the distance, he said, there were mountains with snow caps, and names like Cloud Peak and the Big Horns. In the deserts huge cactuses grew, 'big as houses. No, castles more like.' Pete's family bred horses.

'We breed 'em, train 'em, and sell 'em,' he said. Once a year he and his father rode into Cheyenne to the fair to sell their horses. It was the year's great event for the Jansens. Peter had grown up in an enormous and lonely country – sometimes his family did not see their neighbours for a month.

'When I got to England, Flip, I thought I'd never seen so many people in my life.'

She was glad to see him. She leaned on him. He was tough and had a stubborn kindness and even his silences were comforting. He was the only person she wanted to be with: she scarcely telephoned her family.

In December it began to snow. The snow looked dirty as it came flying down across the grey waste of the sea. When

Philippa came down to breakfast in the hotel dining room, where a few officers at the far end of the room talked in low voices, she saw that the snow was already lying thickly on the bushes in the hotel gardens. Suppose the taxi could not come. Suppose the road to the hospital was blocked. Her anxiety was out of proportion, for she knew it made no difference to the poor sleeping figure if she was there or not. But being with Barny was all she had. She could not eat, but kept going to the window to look at the snow.

The old driver did arrive after all, somewhat late and looking disagreeable. He drove at five miles an hour to the hospital, grumbling. The snow was slushy on the road but still piling up on gardens and hedges. At the hospital door, he said he would return in an hour. 'Can't leave it more than that.'

She went into David Ward and behind the screens and sat down. The nurse gave her the blanket. When she was alone, Philippa leaned across and took the pale clean hand lying on the bedcover. It was inert in hers. She looked at Barny's hand. It was thinner, and had the fineness of a sick person's hand, it felt like silk. This hand, she thought, has touched me in sexual love, and it has controlled the guns of a plane and it has killed people. It looked like a child's.

Very faintly, it moved.

She had a wave of something as sharp as fear. She could scarcely look up. His eyelashes were fluttering, and then, drowsily, he opened his eyes and said so softly that she only just heard it, 'Honey.'

When she returned to the hotel she rang Pete and Elaine – Sister David had been so pleased! – it was a wonderful sign! But her joy was short-lived for although he had now returned to consciousness he was very ill. His foot had been badly burned. Fighter pilots wore long leather gauntlets and knee-length boots for protection against flames, and their large goggles were shatterproof and covered their foreheads below their helmets to protect foreheads against fire. But while he had struggled to escape he had literally not known that his foot was burning, he had lacked the automatic violent physical reaction against the flames. So they were worse.

When he was well enough to travel by ambulance, he was moved to East Grinstead, where an operation was carried out on his foot. Another followed. Philippa left the hotel by the sea and tried to find somewhere to live near East Grinstead. She finished up in a guest house full of middle-aged women preferring to be out of London in a place where there was good food and a few luxuries. She missed Pete Jansen more than she could say.

She was not allowed to visit Barny daily or sit with him for hours. Nobody wrapped her in a scarlet rug. She had to make the best of an hour three times a week. Barny was feeble and quiet, and although he held her hand sometimes and smiled when she kissed him, he slept most of the time.

It was deep winter now, and dark at four in the afternoon. On a day darker and colder than the rest Barny told her he had seen the surgeon who was 'quite pleased' with his wounds. He was to be sent to an American convalescent home in Surrey.

'So I'm moving again. It's getting to be a habit with us both,' said Philippa, touching his arm. She had learned to use the upward lilt which was always in nurses' voices.

Lying against a high pile of pillows, he frowned.

'I'd like for you to go home, Flip.'

'Of course I won't, darling. I want to be near you and see you every minute I can. All the time until you're back flying. Then, since they say I can't be a camp follower, I must lump it.'

'It's swell of you . . . spending all these weeks . . .'

'*Darling, I wanted to!*'

'But I don't want you to,' he said in a fretful tone. 'Sister says the place is about thirty miles from London. You can come by train sometimes.'

Love made her obtuse. She bent towards him, her face alight with energy and devotion, her good health an exhausting loud presence in the room. She laughed and argued. It was so like him to think of her, as if she'd care about moving to another dreary hotel. Nothing mattered but Barny, his health, his convalescence, she would love to live in Surrey! Even her eyes looked hot to the man lying in the bed.

It took her a long time to realise the bald truth. He did not want her with him. Her absence would be a release.

He did not suggest that she should come down during his first days there. It would be better if she waited for him to settle. A week, maybe. Or two.

Before she left the hospital that afternoon, Philippa was called into Sister's office. This lady, her name was Glenn, was quite unlike the fat and motherly Sister David who had sent Philippa blankets and cocoa. She had no easy smile and apparently no sympathy. She was thin and small and looked like an elderly nun. A mass of stiff organdie frills was anchored on the top of her head, her starched blue dress reached just above her ankles.

'Mrs Duval. Sit down, please. Nurse has made us tea.'

Philippa sat down obediently. She was wearing a dark fur coat which Barny's sister Mary Lou had somehow managed to send from America at Barny's request last year. The rich glossy fur emphasised her pale face.

'Flight Lieutenant Duval tells me you are returning to your family in London,' said Sister Glenn, pouring tea with a rock-steady hand. 'That's sensible of you.'

'But Sister, I don't want to go at all!' burst out Philippa, imagining she had found an ally. 'I *tried* to explain that I don't mind a bit staying near the convalescent home. He wouldn't listen.'

Sister Glenn had interviewed many service wives in the last three years. It was not only patients who suffered from shock. There were young women who took bad news like dumb animals in stupefied silence. There were silly girls who had hysterics if she allowed it, and brave ones who seemed already practised at a kind of art of suffering. There were women who were so aware that you needed to tell them nothing. This dark young woman was none of these. Apparently she had character but no trace of instinctive understanding. A sad lack. If a person does not see for herself, she thought, you had to make her.

'You wish to be with him, Mrs Duval. I realise that. But he needs time to himself. He has not only been very ill, but the pace of his life has stopped, perhaps for good. He realises that he will be grounded.'

Philippa drew a breath in shock and shame. She had never thought of that.

Sister Glenn read her face.

'You've been too worried to realise that would happen, I expect. But the wounds in his legs and thigh are considerable. He wouldn't be passed fit as a pilot, let alone as a fighter pilot who needs every bit of co-ordination of hands, feet, eyes – every instantaneous reaction. He realises all that. He is deeply depressed.'

The elderly woman went on talking. She'd known many pilots

228

and nursed them, and their life as fighters was intense, a strain which they themselves did not realise was almost impossible to maintain. Barny had survived 'a long, long time'. Even without the crash it had been catching up with him. Hadn't Philippa noticed that? He had lived at top pitch, going into battle day after day. Philippa must have lived at top pitch too. The pace stopped pilots from thinking about life and the risk of death. 'If they did, they wouldn't be able to fly. Now he's being forced to think for the first time.'

'I suppose I ought to be grateful that he will be safe.'

'Perhaps one could say that,' said Sister Glenn politely.

St Helen's comfortable old presence welcomed Philippa but she no longer thought of the house as her home. Miggs had given her room a winter clean. Elaine put some bare twigs from the garden in a vase on her dressing table. Trix added a small bottle of *Moment Suprême*.

Her sisters were kind to her. At first Trix rather avoided her, she was expecting to be reproached about Chuck. But Philippa was miserable, and aware of her own empty heart, and had no stomach for moral issues she had once been fierce about. She was pleasant enough to Trix and Elaine. But gloomy.

Elaine considered she was behaving badly. She disliked Philippa's silences and her inward-looking expression. Philippa had grown thin and looked rather plain: it was also the first time that Elaine could remember her being totally selfish.

I was supposed to be the selfish one, thought Elaine, who had believed it. In their adolescence the sisters had acquired labels pinned on them by their mild mother, Miggs, and each other. Elaine was selfish, Philippa was sentimental and generous, and Trix was an addle-pate, an antique expression of Theo's.

Nobody's label suited them any more. Philippa was wrapped in her own anxieties, Elaine had been forced to take their mother's place. Even Trix laughed and sang less. Elaine missed the metallic little voice, word perfect in the newest dance numbers. The most recent one was 'Don't get around much any more.' It was true, even for Trix.

Phillipa knew she was not behaving well and longed to stop, but Barny filled her thoughts. She had seen the Eagles change, and gone on loving them. Now she had lost them. She was not thrown into the desolation of widowhood like Elaine – but she was in a wingless land. She did not know what to feel or think. She'd realised that Sister Glenn had seen and despised that. She was ashamed that she had actually felt angry with Barny, and had in her thoughts used schoolgirl adages. He must stop being sorry for himself, pull up his socks, make an effort, show some backbone. The phrases were those she and Elaine had used when playing netball. And it came to Philippa with a sense of pain that *she* was the one who should do all those things. Not Barny who lay like a wounded bird fallen from the sky.

When she had been at home for about a week, Elaine suggested one evening that she should telephone Jane Alwynne.

'You mean you think I ought to work.'

'That is exactly,' said Elaine, with a level glance 'what I mean.'

Philippa turned her head away. She wanted to be angry because Elaine had coldly refused her sympathy. But in her heart she knew she hadn't the right to that weakening comfort. She said, with a visible effort, that she would ring Jane in the morning. Elaine said nothing to that.

Jane Alwynne was enthusiastic.

'My dear Philippa, good to hear your voice. Your young sister is doing such excellent work at our club, you know.'

Actually Trix, with kindly tact, had said nothing about it. 'She's one of our stalwarts,' went on Jane, 'so willing. There is nothing she won't do for our American friends. Well, now, are you free tomorrow? Could you come to a little mews off Berkeley Square on the left? Thurston Mews, and I am in Thurston House. Did I tell you poor old Chicheley Buildings had a direct hit some months ago? Nobody killed, thank God, just a heap of burning rubble. My poor files!'

Jane sounded as powerful as a river in spate.

Thurston House was a small block of flats built in the 1930s on the site of a seventeenth century garden. Philippa found Jane installed in an office which had been the bedroom of a flat. Rosy and plump, and wearing her usual expensive style of suit, Jane pressed Philippa kindly to her bosom.

'I am so glad to see you, child.'

Jane was not alone – she never was. A stooping man, skeleton thin, was busy with some box files. After politely shaking Phillipa's hand, he left the room.

'Dear Andrew,' said Jane, when the door had closed on him, 'a

230

treasure. The poor fellow was invalided out, he's had consumption. On the mend now, and we must be thankful for his misfortune. Well, that's not very kind, let us say we must be grateful that in his misfortune he came our way. He is magnificent with my charities.'

Jane inquired kindly about Barny. Philippa had not told her that Barny had been shot down, but Jane's information service was always efficient. Philippa was determined to sound cheerful about his convalescence. Jane asked one or two questions – there was nothing she did not know, apparently, about pilots in hospital, even to the names of the doctors.

Having made sure Philippa had no other work and could therefore belong entirely to Jane, the lady rattled off her requirements. Her kingdom was spreading. There were American charities, the problems of evacuated children, war widows, a club for the Poles, and of course, a new one for the Americans. 'We have to keep them amused, poor things, so homesick.' As an afterthought she spoke of the Princess Victoria Hospital.

'You'll be pleased to hear that what with your splendid efforts and my own little contributions we can relax. They have just come into a considerable sum of money.'

Jane described Philippa's new job as 'a secretary on all fronts'. Ever the opportunist, Jane said, 'Take your hat off, and be comfortable. We may as well get through a letter or two.'

She handed Philippa a fresh notebook.

When Jane was preparing to leave for a meeting at the American Embassy in Grosvenor Square, she wrapped a fur stole round her shoulders and said, 'The old Eagle Squadrons are quite famous now, aren't they? I dined with Sir Sholto Douglas the other night. He said that the RAF couldn't have asked for better companions.'

Not missing a certain brightness in the girl's face she added, 'The American and British squadrons are flying together now. When we watch them going over, we can't tell which is which.' Then, changing the subject with wartime briskness, 'It's really first rate of you to work for me again. I've missed that pretty smile, let alone the excellent typing. I'll see you at the end of the week. My taxi, Andrew? Many thanks. And if you find yourself running out of work,' she said, turning at the door to look at Philippa, 'just telephone Andrew. He will always find you a little bonne-bouche.'

The next day Philippa was going to visit Barny at the convalescent home for the first time. It was dark, foggy and freezing hard. She squeezed herself into the usual crammed train which travelled at what seemed like five miles an hour. She thought she would never get to Guildford. She had told Barny on the telephone that she would be with him by midday, but it was after half past one when she crawled out of an antiquated taxi at the door of the convalescent home. The fog was very thick, muffling the grounds and turning a high barrier of rhododendrons into a looming cliff. The driver ground away into the obscurity.

Through the swing doors she was again in the only world Barny now knew, a world which separated him from her more completely than the silent fog outside. The hospital echoed with voices and smelled of antiseptic and furniture polish.

Men in dressing-gowns went by. One gave her a lopsided grin. He had the lumpy, shiny, crimson face of a pilot who has been burned. Another, on crutches, said 'Hi.' Philippa smiled brightly. When she got to Barny's door, she gave the six raps she always used. But before she could open the door it swung wide, and a figure in brown American Air Force uniform threw his arms round her and kissed her as the Eagles used to do. It was Chuck Greenfield.

'Pal! Barny told me you were coming. That husband of yours kept looking out at the fog every darned minute!'

He gave his boyish grin and said, twice, 'Sure good to see you.'

Oh, thought Philippa, her heart filled with emotion, you were an Eagle and I love you. Just for a moment, just while you stand there, dear dear Chuck, it's like it used to be. How could I have been angry *at* you, as you'd put it?

She ran over to kiss Barny, who was at the window, dressed and in uniform for the first time.

'Do I look okay?'

'Wonderful!'

'It's hanging off me. It'll need tailoring.'

'I *like* you so thin. It's romantic!'

Chuck's presence changed the feeling, the very scent of the room, it smelled of Camel cigarettes and hair lotion and crowds of people and reality.

'What do you know?' drawled Chuck, 'I brought that palooka a

232

great bunch of pink carnations. I felt pretty silly carrying the thing, and of course, I left them in the jeep.'

'I never liked pink anyway,' said Barny, laughing.

The trio talked a little. Chuck said he had a packet for Trix, would Philippa give it to her? He hoped to be able to call her tonight, 'if she can wait up that long.' While he was there, Barny was almost natural. But when she touched his hand, it was cold with sweat.

Chuck finally said that he must go. He kissed her again.

'You have forgiven us, haven't you? Trix said you've been real nice to her. And here's the packet. Two. One for Trix, and one for you and Elaine. Nothing much . . .'

He went over and put his hand on Barny's shoulder, using an expression Philippa remembered.

'Well, old buddy.'

He left them.

The silence which followed was like looking down a precipice. She lifted his cold hand and kissed it.

'How are you, my darling?'

She was never sure what he would say and she was always afraid.

'The doctor says I can work again.'

In a moment of unthinking joy she blurted it out,

'Fly again!'

'Hell, no,' he said furiously, and she dropped his hand; he clutched at it as if he would fall.

'The medic report has gone to the CO in charge of my old squadron – Pete Jansen. But it'll go further up than that. Chuck didn't come here on a sick visit, he came to tell me the news. I'm to be grounded. You must have guessed, although you've never said. They're putting me into Intelligence.'

'Is that so bad – '

'What do you think? Hell, what do I mean, I talk to you as if you were a flyer yourself. Yeah, it's bad. A wingless wonder. Christ.'

Chapter Sixteen

Two days after the 1943 Christmas, Elaine went to Shelton. She had told herself that she would never go back but this proved to be untrue. Two or three times a year she telephoned Claire, and then made the weary journey, returning home tired and oppressed. Neither of the St Airds had the least idea why she came. They accepted her visits with an adequate politeness and never suggested that she should come again. But she did.

When she telephoned Claire to ask if she could come, Claire said 'Of course', and re-arranged her WVS appointments. But after giving her tea, Claire would glance at her watch and excuse herself. She would go out to feed the chickens, or to make a telephone call. Later when Elaine said it was time for her to catch her bus, Claire obligingly walked with her to the bus stop; sometimes she even managed to get a friend to give Elaine a lift to Oxford. St Aird in the stable studio was less crudely pleased to see her leave.

Elaine did not go to Shelton to see the St Airds. She went because the beautiful old house had been Miles' home. When Claire left her, Elaine always went up to Miles' bedroom. The house was very quiet, in winter the silence seemed to ring. And if Elaine kept very still, sitting on the bed and waiting, she could hear Miles laughing. Miles' things were in their unchanging places: a shelf of silver cups for cricket and boxing, small cups engraved 'Miles St Aird, Egg and Spoon Race', 'St Aird, Monkey Race'. They were dazzlingly clean, almost blue. Did his mother clean them? The cap he won as a member of the school cricket team hung on a hook. It was red and white velvet beginning to turn yellow, and had long silk tassels.

Elain had not taken Miles' books with her when she left, and now they had become part of the spotless room. They looked as if they had been glued. *Swallows and Amazons. Kim. The Seven Pillars of Wisdom.*

234

In this room, keeping very quiet, she could still hear him. Perhaps it was wrong to go to Shelton and listen. She could not help it.

The end of December journey had been at Claire's invitation for the first time. She telephoned to say that Miles' trunk had finally been sent back from Malta. Would Elaine come and cope, as she put it.

Elaine had sometimes wondered about Miles' possessions. She thought it impossible for them to be returned. Why should the Navy take precious ship-space to send back the pathetic things left by men who were dead? News that the trunk had come home was a painful shock.

When she arrived at Shelton in the little winter afternoon her mother-in-law was not there. The trunk had been taken up to Miles' room. It was locked, and the key was on the dressing table.

There it stood, a black tin trunk painted with his name. She knelt down as if to pray and opened it. She began to tremble. The contents of the trunk were in a perfection of order, everything skilfully folded and packed. There were a dozen white shirts, silk pyjamas, black socks, and his uniforms. The arms of one of his jackets was creased on the inside by the elbow. There was shaving tackle in his initialled leather box and two photograhs of herself – looking very young. And at the bottom of the trunk were all her letters. He had kept them in date order, fastened by rubber bands which the Maltese heat had rotted.

She knelt in front of the open trunk, his clothes round her, and crouched down and put her face into the creased uniform. It smelled of him. She burrowed into it and there it was, faint and clinging, the smell of Miles, of his skin and his hair . . .

The journey home was long and cold, and she was glad to toil up to the blacked-out shape of St Helen's. Dazzled by the lights as she walked into the drawing room, she found Trix on the floor, hunched by the fire. Elaine asked why she hadn't gone to work at the club tonight. But she knew why. The pattern of closeness between the sisters had shifted: Trix often sought her out. She had been waiting for her.

With Tyrrell suddenness, not bothering to ask Elaine about her day, Trix wailed, 'Oh Elaine, I couldn't work, I feel so low. I wish, I wish, I *wish* the divorce would at least get started. Dick

235

said I could have it. But he's at sea and you have to go through all that faked rubbish about being seen at a hotel. Chuck was so glad when Dick said he'd do his stuff. He hated me being the guilty part – you know how Chuck is about women. He *respects* them so. I went to see that stupid solicitor and he said he can't do a thing. He kept mumbling, "it's up to your husband, Mrs Polglaze." I hate that name, it isn't me. And there's another thing. The silly fool rang here this morning and Annette took the message. Pa gave me a funny look when I came home this afternoon. Do you think he knows?'

'How could he?'

'I wouldn't put it past that nosey French bit to listen at doors. Imagine doing such a thing. Disgusting.'

'Trix. You know quite well Miggsy has listened at doors since we were born. Anyway, why should Annette bother?'

'Because it would put him against me. She's that sort. Oh, what a worry everything is. If I were Chuck's wife it would be so wonderful. I'd be safe.'

Elaine had never heard her speak with so much feeling – certainly not when she'd startled them with her sudden marriage, like a conjuror merrily producing a bouquet of paper flowers. Now she was anxious, vulnerable, and real.

'You know when Chuck was rested up and he took me away for a few days? I was jolly ill actually, I had a kind of miscarriage.' Elaine gave an exclamation, and Trix, satisfied at getting an effect, went on, 'Chuck was off his head with worry. He's so loving. Swell. Just marvellous. I was ill and my stomache has ached ever since. Do you think there's something wrong with me? It still hurts.'

'You must see a doctor.'

'I did. Today. Chuck sent me to the best specialist in Harley Street. I didn't like him too much. He said my stomach ache is nerves. Lots of girls get it now when their men are in danger, you see.'

Listening, Elaine thought, it's as if my darling Miles had never existed. She has utterly forgotten. Is that how it is with all my family? They just forget the dead.

Trix went on talking about love. She had never felt like this before. It sounded like the words of one of the tunes she used to sing. She'd always been fond of the men she slept with, she said earnestly, but it had never been like this. 'Why, when Chuck

and I meet, we've got to have each other right away. Like that!'
She clicked her fingers.

She went to the country sometimes and stayed at a pub near
the Squadron's aerodrome. It had to be a secret because
girlfriends and wives weren't allowed. It was bad for the pilots.
She didn't like to say where she was going, in case Philippa
heard. It might depress her because of Barny. Trix's voice had
no trace of triumph, she felt for Philippa. Sometimes Chuck got
away for an hour, she said, and couldn't Elaine guess how they
spent *that*. The other night he'd been able to stay with her until
five, he was on a dawn patrol. After he'd gone, Trix lay in bed
and listened to the planes leaving for Germany. It had been
rather wonderful. And awful.

Bending her head so that her hair covered her face in a golden
curtain, she played with her bracelet, moving the charms round
to find Chuck's US button. She looked like a man counting
money – but Trix was counting pigs and horseshoes and buttons
cut from young men's uniforms.

January was bitterly cold. One evening when both her sisters
had stayed up late to hear a play on the wireless, Trix returned
from the club looking brighter. She announced that she had
been given a part in a film.

'There's a guy at the club, a real film director who's making a
movie at Pinewood. It's called "They Flew into Danger" and –
guess what! – it's about the Eagle Squadron. Chuck was so
embarrassed when I called him up. Flip, do you remember the
Hollywood movie, "Eagle Squadron", which made all your
buddies squirm with embarrassment because they loathed being
called heroes. Didn't they all boo? This one's going to be good.
I'm to be a Waaf like the one in John Pudney's poem. "The Ash-
blonde Waaf makes tea". I'm being paid twenty-five shillings a
day.'

'But how can you get out of doing your work at the club?'
asked Elaine innocently.

'Stoopid. London's crawling with girls just begging to wait at
table for the Yanks.'

Considerably more cheerful than she'd been recently, Trix
pranced into the kitchen to ask Miggs to wake her at half past
five. A car was coming for her. It was the first time since she had
been born that Trix was willing to wake at such an hour.

Miggs was old and found no difficulty in rising on the dot.

Wearing her flannel dressing-gown, she hobbled into Trix's bedroom. It was cold and pitch dark. She cruelly switched on the lights, and when the girl did not budge, took a sadistic glee in shaking her.

'You gotter get up for this lark of yours.'

Trix, groaning, dragged herself out of a deep sleep. She washed her face and dressed and stumbled down into the blackout where a car was waiting. Round her weary head she tied a pale blue and pink scarf on which was printed *We shall fight on the beaches, in the streets, and on the airfields.*

She came home that night exhausted. She was not the girl who strutted off every evening to the American club. Her face was plastered with brown make-up as thick as mud, her eyes painted purple, and she was too tired to eat. For the next ten days she left at the same ungodly hour and returned, said Philippa, looking as if she'd been put through a mangle. Trix hated filming. The hanging-about fretted her, she was unused to being patient, she disliked the boring repetition of her few little scenes. For a show-off, filming simply did not interest her. Star-struck about everything American, there never was a girl less film-struck than Trix. On the last evening she came into the drawing room at St Helen's, waving an envelope.

'Never again. But I've earned thirty pounds. That'll buy this baby three new frocks.'

While her sisters worked, each chained as she slightingly described it, to a typewriter, Trix chained herself to the family sewing machine.

The life Elaine and her sisters now led at St Helen's was not a natural one. Married women who returned home to their parents never comfortably settled. Elaine could not go back to the old, easy, submitting and daughterly frame of mind. She was independent and had only lived at Shelton because it was convenient, and would have hurt Miles had she not done so. Disliking her in-laws, she never felt imprisoned.

Now it was different because she was forced to live at home. She had little money, her salary was meagre, and she certainly couldn't afford a flat of her own, unless she was willing to make do with far less comfort than at St Helen's. Her nature disliked the idea of deliberately choosing to be poor. Besides, she would be lonely. Who had she, apart from her family? Her few girl friends in London were not close to her. Her dearest friend, Marjorie, was in Oxfordshire. The Baker Street job, despite its strangeness, was monotonous. And she discovered with a chill of the heart that she was not attracted to men since Miles had died. She supposed that happened with some women. It was a kind of psychological suttee.

There was a flu epidemic in January, and just after her birthday she caught it from someone in the office. She had to spend three days in bed. She had not been ill since she lost her baby, and a temperature and solitude combined made her feel low-spirited.

The fever was gone by the weekend: she would be well enough to return to work on Monday. On Sunday evening she was alone in the house, as she often was nowadays. It was dark and cold and very quiet, except for the noise of rain. She was dressed and lying on the sofa in the drawing room, trying to read. The family were off on their own devices. Miggs was in Sussex with her relatives. Theo had taken Annette to stay the weekend with his friends in Hertfordshire. Trix had gaily left on Friday night.

'I won't kiss you, darling. Suppose I caught it and gave it to someone we know!'

And Philippa was with some American friends at the Embassy in Grosvenor Square. She would not be back until midnight or later, she had said.

Elaine felt melancholy, listening to the rain. Is it the noise, she thought, which makes me feel so sad? She picked up her book again as the telephone rang. She gave a sigh. It would only be an American from the club, Trix collected them from habit. They were so friendly, and they deserved better, thought Elaine, than talking to me.

'Is that Elaine?' said a voice with a distinct actorish pitch.

'Dick! Are you on leave? I'm afraid Trix isn't here.'

She heard him laugh.

'I'm not ringing for my ex-wife. As a matter of fact I hoped it would be you. I'm in town. A very short leave. I couldn't persuade you to come for a drink, could I? Now?'

She opened her mouth to refuse. But didn't. He must be coming to talk about the divorce and since Trix was so anxious about it, Elaine supposed she must see him. She did not want to.

She hadn't forgotten their last interview, when he had come into her room in the small hours of the night Trix threw him over. Elaine had been desperately sorry for him, but his behaviour had shocked her. Jealousy and anger made him vicious. He wasn't a man who believed, as Miles had done, that there were standards, and in bad times you owed it to yourself to be civilized.

Hearing the taxi, she put out the hall lights and opened the door to the pouring wet night. Dimly, she made out a figure running towards her. When he was indoors and the door was safely shut, she switched on the light. He laughed, pulling off his greatcoat and cap. Rain shone on his clothes and curling hair.

'Hello, Elaine. Long time no see.'

She gave an embarrassed smile. He was tougher and more formidable than she remembered.

'There's nothing to drink in the house except what Father locks up in his study. I'm so sorry. Will coffee do?'

'But I'm taking you out, remember? Great luck, finding you at home when I rang.'

'I usually am at home,' she said with a little meaningless laugh.

In the drawing room they stood by the fire, and Dick looked at her appraisingly. Something in the look reminded her of an expression she often saw on Miggs's face. Disapproval.

'I see you are still in black.'

Nobody remarked on this, and if they had she would have shut them up. He put one foot on the brass fender.

'When do you plan to come out of mourning?'

'I don't know. I like it.'

'Miles wouldn't. He was all for you looking beautiful.'

'I'll get the coffee.'

She had forgotten that he had refused it. Then she remembered, but still crossed the room to get away. He reached her before she was at the door.

'Elaine. Don't be angry. You mustn't mind, you know, if I tell you the truth. Would you prefer a lot of stupid stuff you couldn't believe? Don't run away.'

He did not say he was sorry, but took her hand and led her to a chair. Then he sat down, his arms along the top of the sofa, looking at her with his fascinating eyes. His face was like a satyr's. It was hard and laughing.

'Trix is away,' she began but he interrupted.

'I told you. I didn't come to talk about her. I'm not avoiding the subject, but the divorce has only this minute started because I haven't been able to do a thing until now. Your sister's solicitors (which mine call 'the other side') have been asking if we can hurry it on. Is she pregnant?'

'Of course not.'

'Don't be uppity. I wouldn't put it past her to make sure of her American lover. Of this one, anyway.'

'How cold you sound.'

He scratched his nose.

'Do I? Well, I am not cold. Not at all. It is simply that I'm not one to hang about when not wanted. One refusal, and you don't see me for dust. I'd like to hurry on the divorce myself. What is the American like, by the way?'

'Very nice. Very gentle.'

'Poor old him.'

'Sour grapes.'

Instead of being annoyed, he burst out laughing, with a rat-tat-tat as sudden as machine-gun fire.

'You must believe me, Elaine, I am quite recovered. It was like getting over a bad go of measles. There was a big depression for a while and I needed a tonic, Navy rum did the trick. It's wonderful stuff, thick and dark and strong. Delicious. We have a ration every morning. We line up and are given a tot in a pewter measure. My heart wasn't broken, you know. Just bruised. I was more furious than sad.'

'You certainly were.'

He looked at her with friendly eyes.

'I was rude, wasn't I? So unkind. Why was I unkind to you, when all you did was to be your sweet self? I felt a beast later. I wanted to write and apologise, but then I thought you had enough to cope with at home. You would only have written back, saying I hadn't been rude at all. We both know that was not true, but you're a girl for the courtesies.'

He seemed to know a lot about her.

'What happened with your father?' he went on curiously. 'I remember Trix told me that he is serious about religion and dislikes divorce.'

'He doesn't know.'

'*What!*'

241

'We have managed to keep it from him so far.'

He looked as if he found it hard to keep a straight face. He annoyed her. It was one thing to be good to a broken-hearted ex-husband, quite another to be faced with a spirited man trying not to laugh at the family's troubles.

'You can't keep his daughter's divorce a secret for long, Elaine. He is certain to find out. Then he'll be angrier still at being made a fool of. This sounds like one of Trix's dotty ideas.'

'It wasn't,' said Elaine coldly, 'it was Chuck Greenfield who asked me to let her stay. It is true, Father does disapprove of divorce. He might even refuse to let her live at home. He can be very difficult and where would she go then?'

'Aren't all Americans rich? She could live in some luxury hotel somewhere.'

'I have no idea if Chuck has money or not. I am simply looking after her until he can.'

Dick continued to regard her with his odd, slanting eyes. He remarked that keeping secrets was the devil. She replied that she was used to it, because of her job. He shrugged. Those were official secrets, we all kept them. Family secrets were something very different. They were to do with hurting people. Being forced to keep them made one nervous.

'Trix is very nervous,' admitted Elaine, calming down now that he had stopped looking as if he were laughing at her.

'I daresay she is. But the reason *you* feel anxious is from family affection, whereas Trix just wants to stay put while it suits her. Hell, am I being rude again? She is lucky to have such a champion,' he added. 'I salute you.'

Later, sheltered by one of Doctor Tyrrell's pre-war black silk umbrellas, Dick accompanied her out into the blackout on their way to the Hogarth. The rain hammered on the umbrella, the darkness was complete. It was, he said, holding her arm, like swimming. They ran, arriving breathless and dripping at the pub.

The Hogarth was in a square of old houses. On the winter's night, it was loud with voices, most of them American. The place was crowded with United States officers and their girls. Dick bought the drinks and took her over to a window seat in a corner. The pub was dark, panelled and old, and the walls were covered with the Hogarth cartoons. Above Elaine's head hung the dying gallant in *Mariage à la Mode*.

Dick looked round at the girls roosting on bar stools and flirting with their escorts. He observed dryly that all the women in London appeared suddenly to be blondes.

'I suppose American men choose girls with fair hair.'

'Charitable Elaine. What about peroxide on the black market? *You* are the only natural blonde in the place. Your hair's so pretty. Like golden feathers.'

She wasn't used to compliments any more, and did not know what to say. She smiled nervously.

He talked about the Navy. He was on Dover patrols now, the weather vile, the job boring. Then they began to talk about Miles. Not the dead hero, but the young man whom Dick had known before the war. Once after a party, when they were both driving home, Miles had said to him, 'Tell you what. Let's go to Scotland.' They had driven all night up the A1, stopping at Scotch Corner for porridge and bacon.

'Miles said we were characters in the first chapter of a John Buchan book.'

'Oh, he told me about that. It sounded such fun. It was before I met him, and he said we'd do the same thing, just drive and drive until we got to Scotland!'

A warmth went through her, sitting with this man. He had a kind of magic because he had known Miles. In his mind, as in hers, Miles still lived. He had not shuddered away from his loss, but sat there with her remembering him. She smiled, and Dick took her hand and give it a casual kiss.

When they walked back to St Helen's the rain had almost stopped. They went up to the house and he lingered for a moment, as boys used to do with her in innocent peacetime.

When she said goodnight in her resolute little voice, he suddenly said, 'Elaine. I forgot. I meant to ask a favour. Would you think it very unattractive if I asked for a book which I lent Trix ages ago? If she still has it, I really would like it back. It's my illustrated *Treasure Island* which I had when I was twelve. When I lent it to her, like a fool, I believed she would read it.'

'Perhaps she has,' said Elaine automatically.

'Don't kid us both, Elaine. You know she only reads *Vogue*. Well? Do you think we might at least see if it is in the bookcase?'

'Of course.'

They went indoors. She was pretty sure he would find his

book, for Trix's shelves were crammed with books lent to her by young men and never read. They remained there like trophies.

They climbed the stairs. Elaine put on the light as if to chase ghosts.

They went into Trix's bedroom. It was in its usual mess, drawers gaping, the wardrobe ajar to show dresses as bright as the costumes at a carnival. The air was filled with strong, evocative scent.

'Same old Trix,' he said, stepping over a pair of pink wedge-heeled shoes.

Elaine did not reply. There was no point in pretending Trix was not appallingly untidy. He went to the bookshelf, raised his eyebrows and said 'Henry James! What simpleton thought she'd read him? Ah. Here it is. Good-oh.'

It was a large handsome book lettered in gold.

'I'm really glad to have it back. Such an old friend. Thank you, Elaine.'

They walked down the passage. He stopped at the open door of her own room and peered in as if amused at the comparison. The room was spotless, tidy, a bunch of jonquils on the dressing table beside a photograph of Miles and Elaine at their wedding, looking at each other and laughing.

'I've never seen that before.'

He went over to pick it up, smiling at the smiling faces.

'How pretty you are.'

She gave a little empty laugh.

'I was.'

Putting the photograph carefully back, he turned to her.

'That's a silly thing to say. *You are* just as pretty now. Changed, yes, but it only makes you more beautiful. Surely you must know that?'

He pulled her gently towards him.

For a second her body stiffened, she resisted. But then, ah then, something inside her which she believed was made of iron and fated to keep her always imprisoned seemed to break. Her whole body melted. Not letting her go, he moved her towards the bed.

'No, no, I mustn't.'

'Of course you must. You're so lovely. So sweet. So beautiful. Don't waste it – '

Scarcely knowing that she was lying down, that his body was

244

urgent against hers, she only felt his racing heart. When she opened her eyes, his were closed and his face was changed, almost as if he were in pain . . .

When he had gone she lay in the bed where they had made love and fell into a dreamless sleep. She awoke late the next morning, and for a moment forgot what had happened to her. She was only conscious of a delicious sweeping languor that she had not felt for two years. And then she remembered.

Chapter Seventeen

'Elaine?' said a voice on her office telephone.

She answered in a low voice, 'How on earth did you get this number – '

'You gave it to me.'

She heard the laugh.

'I – I don't remember.'

'It's true. You were very sleepy.'

Alone in the little dark office, she blushed a miserable burning red.

There was a pause.

'Elaine? I'm standing in a freezing telephone box at the other end of nowhere. You are there, are you? You haven't died?'

'I'm here.' Another pause. 'Did you – did you want anything?'

'There's a question. I rang to say goodbye again. I keep having a funny idea you are feeling guilty this morning. Are you?'

'I can't talk now.'

She tried to collect herself, but couldn't.

'You see. You are feeling like that. Well, don't, Lovebird. For my sake. I'll write, I promise. Well? Are you going to say goodbye nicely?'

'Goodbye, Dick.'

'Do you never say "darling?" It's a shame to tease you. Goodbye, *darling* Elaine.'

When she thought about the conversation all that day, she did not know what it – or he – had meant. She did not know him at all – except in the flesh. She had never made love to any man but Miles. Now she had been unfaithful to him. She felt guilty and deeply shocked at herself. She had not known it possible to want a man again, as she had wanted Dick. When he had taken her she had thought she would die of physical bliss. He had made love strongly, fiercely, tenderly, for a long time. He had even stopped before it ended and said – 'Let's wait. Lovely torture to wait', and so they had, but it had been impossible to stay apart for more than a few minutes.

246

Now he was gone.

I suppose he rang me because *he* felt guilty too, she thought, and remembered the laughing voice and knew that was nonsense. She could think of no other reason why he should bother to speak to her from that freezing telephone box. And why had he called her by that sweet, stupid name?

She did not tell Trix about his visit. He had not asked her to, had twice said he hadn't come to talk about Trix. Elaine was glad she need not mention him, and ashamed of the pleasure of thinking about him. It couldn't be right to feel like this about her sister's soon-to-be-divorced husband. But when he came into her mind, so often! her heart still turned over. She remembered his face, narrow-eyed, clever and alluring. She remembered her sexual joy, and longed, literally longed, to see him again. Perhaps I never will. Is that what happened in love affairs? She was ignorant of the way men behaved who made love to you outside marriage. She wondered if quite often they never returned.

Trix was still gloomy at times about not yet being Chuck's wife, but one morning her whole manner changed. She was radiant. She had received a letter from the solicitors to say that the divorce was being given priority 'under the circumstances'. Chuck, she said, must have pulled strings.

'His CO doesn't approve of him being worried over *me*.'

She took to singing again, left for the club with her old swing and spring, and actually wrote to Chuck every day. She brought him tediously into every conversation, using American words. Petrol was gas, leave was furlough, and nobody was annoyed, they were fased.

During the bitter winter, Philippa once more had reason to be grateful to Jane Alwynne. When she had been part of the Eagle Squadron, the banging at the ancient typewriter had almost drowned the noise of the planes leaving for France. Now once again, Jane's shameless use of every moment of her time stopped Philippa from brooding. Barny had begun his work as an Intelligence officer, and telephoned her whenever he could. But she knew she must not ask when they were going to meet. She had discovered the curious truth that courage only grows if you nurture it.

Elaine and Trix were matter of fact about Barny. They asked how he was getting on, but never if he was due for any leave.

247

Trix, who had moments of perception, made encouraging remarks about his new work.

'That's a real tough job he's taken on. Specially when the pilots get back and report, and one of them really *believes* he's scored. And the Intelligence guy finds out that he hasn't. Imagine going up to a pilot and having to tell him. That takes guts.'

At last Barny telephoned to say he had some leave and she could come to Sussex for the weekend. 'I've booked us a room at The Dolphin. I'm just longing to see you, honey.'

There was fog at Chichester station. Muffled in her fur coat and an old knitted Eagle Squadron scarf, she shivered with cold and nerves. Carrying her suitcase with numbed hands she walked down the platform. The smoke from the train made the darkness deeper. There were only thin beams of torches, figures dimly seen. Had Barny not been able to come? Where could she find a telephone?

Suddenly a voice said, 'There you are,' and she was lifted off her feet, and hugged so tightly that she lost her breath.

He shepherded her out of the station, saying that the hotel was only a few blocks away. He held her hand tightly as they walked through the unlit fog where figures loomed and vanished like ghosts. Philippa tried to hear in his voice if he were himself again. She thought he sounded strained, although he laughed now and then. She was so nervous that she was still shivering. As they crossed a blank mass of fog which was a street, he put his arm round her shoulder.

'You're very cold. Never mind, we're here.'

A moment later they were in the dazzlingly bright woodsmoke-smelling hall of the hotel.

Barny took her straight to the bar and ordered them some rum, drawing up a bar stool for her and sitting facing her.

'Now drink that up. It's good for that old unheated train feeling. And that old unheated train feeling's good for nothing.'

They looked at each other then. He saw how thin she was, and that there was a shadow on her charmingly-shaped face. He thought she looked *triste*. The thinness made her more beautiful, in a way. She was no longer the plumpish candid English girl whom he had married, she looked as if she had secrets. But everybody did now. She wore the old pinafore dress his sister had sent her, and the bushranger shirt, and her Eagle Squadron brooch. He bent and kissed her cheek. She smelled of scent and

248

of her own smell which he always thought was like biscuits. She moved him. He was the reason for that thinness. He felt guilty and resented the guilt. For one terrified moment he wondered if he could bear so much love – and was the more afraid that she might guess what he was thinking.

As for Philippa, she looked at his olive-skinned rather triangular face and black hair, at the new lines under his serious eyes. He was more like the Barny of old.

'Let's go upstairs,' he said, after he had made her drink a second rum because of the cold night.

They walked up the stairs, passing ancient walls that bulged, and stooping under low ceilings in the quiet deserted corridor. We're going to make love she thought. She was nervous, because it had been so long since they had. Before his crash his lovemaking had been violent, exhausting, almost impersonal. She had had the recurring thought that any woman would have satisfied him.

Unlocking the door, he took her into a room with walls crisscrossed by black beams, and an oak floor which sloped. There was an ancient double bed, with slots at its four corners where the posts of the four-poster had been. Locking the door behind him, he looked at her with heavy eyes.

They began to undress in silence, throwing their clothes on the floor. When he began to make love to her, it was slow and delicious. She did not feel violated, she gazed up to see the face above her tender and lost.

It was over and they separated. Barny was wet with sweat. He bent across her to find a cigarette. Then, with his arm round her, for the first time since the crash he began to talk. It was as if he had been under a spell, literally struck dumb until now. He described how the plane had been hit, and the sound of the Messerschmitt diving towards the ship, and the moments of excruciating pain before he had fainted. That pain returned in nightmares.

Then he began to speak of what he said had been worse.

'Being grounded. It was as if I'd been a goddammed bird, you know? As if I'd grown wings and they'd hacked them off. I didn't want to see you when they did that. I was maimed and useless and no good. Even when I began to work again, I felt ill, not being able to get up there with the rest of them, having to stay *here*, on earth. The aerodrome was bombed one night. There was a hangar on fire, and a lot of stuff coming down, and I was pretty well in danger of being killed. I remember thinking "this is life." Isn't that something? This is life.'

He covered her with the eiderdown, carefully tucking it in.

'I didn't want you with me when I was like that. Who was it talked about the dark night of the soul? Mine was black as pitch. Well . . . I've gotten used to my job now. I don't do it badly, and I can help the guys I look after, because I've been there. I still want to fly but my reactions are too slow. *This* machine,' he looked scornfully at the long scars on his body, 'isn't in flying order. But the work – Intelligence officer – means I can make the boys go out to battle with confidence. That matters, doesn't it?'

He described how he briefed the pilots before they went on ops. They met in the Intelligence room where wall maps were set out and the course drawn. He showed each man how to fly on a certain course, how to avoid ground batteries, telling him to fly around or in between the ack-ack guns. He briefed the Squadron about the purpose of the flight. Sometimes they were escorting the big bombers, at other times sweeping out over Occupied France to challenge the enemy to come up and do battle. 'Lucky beggars – that was the job I liked best.'

When the planes returned, he was on the field waiting. 'I have to look at the planes after they've taxied down on the runway, to see which of their guns has been fired. Remember I told you that, Flip? There is adhesive tape across the muzzles to keep out the dust while the planes are on the ground. How it used to bug me when the Intelligence guy came looking at the muzzles of *my* guns. Didn't he believe that I'd fired them, for Christ's sake? Now that's my job. So there I am with the boys, listening to their stories, hearing about battles and narrow escapes – they're so excited – '

'You always were.'

'Was I? I don't remember. They all talk at once, swooping and turning their hands about to describe the flights, and I have to wait to quiet them down. Finally I write up the account of the day's fighting. The official report.'

He put out his cigarette, looked at his watch and exclaimed that she had had nothing to eat, she had been travelling for hours, and all he'd done was to make love and talk for too long. They must go down to supper.

His leave lasted two days. They met some young pilots at the Dolphin on the following day. Barny was glad to see them. It was very strange how the boys treated him with deference. Nobody called her Flip either, and that was strange too.

In the afternoon, with the fog thinning and a hard frost Barny took her for a country walk. Now and then the sky overhead roared with planes. They stood and watched the great dark flocks which filled the air with their steady roar before vanishing towards France.

'Fortresses, Flip. Did you ever see so many?'

'Never.'

'Things have changed a bit since the Battle of Britain, eh?'

Yes, she thought. And so have we.

When the sound of the Fortresses died away, they walked on in silence. The hedges were bare and thorny, the grass thickened and flattened by the frost. Along the edge of the road were little pools which had frozen, and she ground her heel into one to see it turn into stars. He watched her unsmilingly, and then said, 'There is something I want to tell you. No, don't look scared. Just give me your hand. When I was at East Grinstead there was a doctor called Wheatley. I told you about him.'

He had not told her, but Philippa said nothing. She thought with anxious love that he was like a sick animal, who will only eat and drink if you hold the dish with a motionless hand.

'Wheatley talked to me a lot. That's not true, I talked to him, because he wanted me to. About my parents dying. How they'd hated for me to fly. The Eagles. You. The future. I thought it pretty dumb, talking of the future slap in the middle of a war but he said that was the time to talk of it. He wormed out of me that I'd always wanted to write. I even showed him those poems I wrote when the Eagles first began to fight. Remember those?'

'They were beautiful.'

He looked at her and just for a moment he seemed young again.

'Honey. I'm glad you remember them. So – I've started to write again. I've done about a third of a book. You needn't ask what it is about. You know it can't be anything else.'

'The Eagles.'

'Got it in one.'

251

'Oh Barny! I suppose you wouldn't let me see it before it's finished?'

'How did you guess?'

Quite suddenly the blitz started again over London. Once again people heard the whistle and thud of bombs. Red hot shrapnel poured into d'Abernon Road, hitting and splitting the tiles on roofs. The February raids were heavy and so was the thunderous barrage of the guns. The night skies were full of the rapiers of searchlights and the sudden violent flash of flares. On one night in late February, a power station was hit and St Helen's – and miles of London homes – were plunged into blackness. But Miggs knew where the candles were.

Nobody in St Helen's, nobody in London, had the heightened energy and courage which had come in the 1940 blitz. The war had changed. It had become a vast conflict all over the world and there had been victories, and would be more. There was strain and resentment during the new blitz, instead of the old stubborn patriotism. People flocked down into the Underground again. There were many horrible fires burning in the streets.

By far the most nervous person at St Helen's was Annette. She would not go home to her lodgings a few streets away, but spent hours under the billiard room table, and usually refused to accept the All-Clear. 'Another wave of bombers will come. They always do.' Sometimes she was right.

Her exaggerated fear surprised Elaine, for the French girl must have been very courageous to escape from Brittany and make her way across the Channel. Elaine was sorry for her. Philippa, nervous because she knew the blitz alarmed Barny for her sake, pretended to be cool. But like the rest of Londoners she was not as strong as she had been the first time around. As for Elaine, she felt nothing but curiosity. Often she crept out of the house in the cold dark to watch. Now and then the old house trembled when a bomb fell. When she looked up at the sky, it was filled with golden-white flares and the stain of fires, it was split with flashes or the unearthly glow of phospherous bombs. Curious flaming blobs, like the stars of the most expensive fireworks hung suspended in the air. She thought of all the people in danger, and of those who would be killed tonight. She did not care for her own safety. Perhaps Dick, her fascinating

252

lover of a single night, might be sorry if she were killed. But she herself was like Siegfried, immune because he had bathed in the dragon's blood.

The blitz went on until March and when it ended, and sirens no longer wailed, London was filthy. Dust was everywhere. Dust from fires, explosions and the wrecks of houses. Everybody developed a sore throat, and Elaine's was so bad that although she went to work, she could scarcely speak.

Spring came. The nights were peaceful again and one sunny weekend Trix, all smiles, told Elaine that Chuck had rung and she was allowed to visit him for a twenty-four hour leave 'somewhere in England.' Everything was very hush hush, she couldn't say where. It looked as if the divorce would soon be final.

'Imagine. I'll be Chuck's wife. Oh brother.'

When Philippa came home from work that evening, the sun was still shining as Trix was walking through the open gate. She wore a new black and white striped dress, and a tiny hat with a spotted veil was balanced on her blonde head.

'Hi. I'm off to see Chuck. Shall I give him your love? He's always telling me how much he misses Barny. They were real buddies, weren't they. I'm sure they'll be together again sometime soon.'

Trix, happy, flowered with generosity.

Philippa couldn't help smiling.

'Give him both our loves,' she said and meant it.

Trix waved and tripped away on the lookout for a taxi.

Philippa sighed as she went indoors. She often envied Trix these days. There was an extraordinary quality about her young sister. Who else had the ability to walk, light as a feather, through the war? But Trix had known no other adult life but this; she grew up to the song of sirens. She had adapted to food shortages, air raids, dirt and danger, to divorcing an English husband and acquiring an American one. She was up-to-the-minute even when the world she lived in was a terrible one. When she talked of air battles and death at second hand, what she spoke about was often, almost always, tragic. Did she listen to what she herself said? Her voice rang with more reality when she spoke of her own magical knack of having fun.

The next day was still sunny, and Philippa brought home some of Jane Alwynne's work to finish on her father's typewriter. The telephone rang. Annette was out, and Philippa heard Miggs answering with the old familiar chant, 'Doctor Tyrrell's residence.'

There was a pause.

The old woman spoke again.

'My poor child. Come home.'

Philippa's heart turned over. Miggs came into the drawing room.

'That young chap of Trix's was killed this morning. Poor kid. Sobbin' her heart out.'

Both her sisters were waiting when Trix came home. They heard the taxi, the slam of the front door. They both wanted to rush out. Neither moved. When Trix came into the room she looked as if she were in a trance, and her face was so pale that it looked green. It was blank until she sat down, when she grimaced.

Elaine said, 'Is your stomach hurting?'

'Like hell.'

Philippa sprang up and ran over to clasp her in her arms. Trix clung. They broke away and sat down, and Trix slipped to the floor, where she crouched with her arms round her shoulders as if she were freezing cold.

'Isn't it awful? Oh, isn't it awful? Do you know he was with me until half past five this morning. I had him *in my arms*. We were together all last night, making love over and over, and when he left this morning he gave me a huge kiss and said he'd see me tonight and we'd fix the wedding for when he had his next rest period. Then he went and I fell asleep after I'd heard the planes go over. I don't know how long I slept but there was a banging on my door, and the porter was there and said someone wanted to see me. I was so frightened my legs gave. He came into my room, one of Chuck's friends, Ray. Oh, he was so upset. He could scarcely speak and we both began to cry even before he'd told me. He saw Chuck's plane go down near Amiens. In flames. He hadn't parachuted. There wasn't a doubt that he was lost.' She repeated, 'Not a doubt about it.' And rocking to and fro 'What a bloody war. What a bloody, bloody war.'

She was ill for two days, doubled up with stomach cramps and unable to eat or sleep. Sometimes in the night she slept for an hour and then woke crying and trailed into Elaine's bedroom in the dark. Elaine woke to find her standing beside the bed, just as she'd done as a child with earache.

She looked dreadful, she scarcely spoke a word. Neither Elaine nor Philippa, one widowed, the other knowing the anguish of a wounded husband, considered that Trix should not give way to sorrow. They put no time limit on her behaviour, as they would have done on themselves or each other. They gave her no stoic advice or fierce despising, as Claire had thrown at Elaine and that she, in turn, had pitched at Philippa. It seemed there were different rules for Trix. Just as in the war, where every other woman, even those over sixty were working, Trix never did a thing.

For Philippa, Trix's loss was a dreadful kind of bond. She suffered with her because she loved and understood pilots and their brief dangerous glory. Philippa's old protective love for her young sister filled her heart when Trix talked of Chuck. It was only then that Trix's dull eyes brightened. Chuck had taken her to dance to Glen Miller. He had asked his mother to send her a whole box of real nylon stockings. Then there was a faint light in her lightless face.

Her father did not ask her what ailed her. He sought out Elaine.

'The girl looks ill. I think I should take a look at her.'

Elaine was reminded of Miggs's proverb that the shoemaker's children were the worst shod in the village. She said that Trix had caught some kind of flu, and wanted to go to the country.

Theo, relieved, agreed and asked no more questions.

One of Trix's girlfriends in the ATS, who had heard the news, invited her to stay with her and her parents in Leicester.

'I may as well go,' Trix said indifferently.

When she said goodbye to Elaine, she began to cry.

After Trix was gone, Elaine noticed something very odd. The young men whom her sister admired began to disappear too. There were no longer crowds of GI's lounging in Piccadilly, or sprawling on the steps of what used to be the mansions of the aristocracy. The Americans seemed to drain away from the great wartime city. One day they were as familiar as the scarlet buses. The next day they had vanished from London.

There was a nervousness in the air as summer began. People bought more newspapers and switched on the wireless more often. They were waiting for news of the Second Front.

Philippa was not allowed to see Barny again, but he telephoned her whenever he could. He had been stricken by Chuck's death and had written to Trix. But Philippa knew that her sister had not opened any of the letters about Chuck. When they spoke on the telephone, Barny said very little. How was his book, she asked. 'Okay, but I can't get around to it now.' Philippa told Elaine that it felt as if their conversations were censored.

'Everything is a secret now,' said Elaine who lived in no other atmosphere. 'He can't tell you where he is or what is happening. But how did he *really* sound?'

'Staccato.'

One warm June night the sisters woke to the roar of thousands of aircraft. They both ran down in their nightdresses out into the garden. The sky overhead was thick with stars, and against them they saw line after line of powerful winged shapes in formation. The planes never seemed to end.

Next morning Miggs heard on the eight o'clock news that the BBC were quoting German reports that the Second Front had started. By half past nine, it was official.

Theo said, 'Thank God.' Philippa said, 'At last.' Elaine said nothing. Curiously, nobody was excited. When Elaine travelled to work, nobody talked eagerly in the bus or the Underground. And at the office it was the same.

She thought about Dick and wondered if he would be part of the great new movements of the war. When she thought of him her heart ached. She told herself she was being foolish. I meant nothing to him, so I suppose I must find a way of making him mean nothing to me.

She began to type the bills of lading. They were for guns, plastic explosives and ammunition. Yet it was like typing lists of tinned foods, she thought. She was told nothing about the work and was not allowed to ask. This morning she suddenly decided to risk it. Her boss was in his office talking in French about the daily list of messages broadcast to the French resistance. The messages always intrigued Elaine – who invented them? They were in the oddest kind of code. Giles Seton was repeating 'Yes . . . the umbrella dies of love. I've got that. The umbrella dies of love. Good. What? Ah, yes. The kangaroo has five children. The kangaroo has five children.'

'Wizard show,' he said as usual, seeing the coffee.

'Captain Seton,' said Elaine after a moment. 'Won't our job soon be finished?'

He daintily wiped his ginger moustache.

'One of these fine days, Mrs St Aird. It will all be mopped up, tidied away and finished.'

'But surely – '

'While there is a single enemy remaining in France, we've got a job of work here for the partisans. Which reminds me. There's a batch of new complaints about the equipment being too heavy. One of our SOE chaps is over and insists on seeing me. Stall him a bit, will you? He's due soon and I've some calls to make.'

Elaine left his office resentfully. Keeping official secrets was one thing. But now the Second Front had begun, the partisans must be joining the allies, area by area. She saw the invasion as a flood, with the resistance fighters scattered across France like small rivers and lakes waiting to be engulfed in the huge victorious tide.

She returned to her own desk in her box of an office which overlooked the well of the building. She was collecting her lading bills when the door of her office burst open. A man came in. He wore shabby foreign civilian clothes, patched and dirty. It did not need more than a glance to see he'd come from France. He carried a revolver and a canvas bag.

'I have a rendezvous with Captain Seton, mademoiselle – '

He stopped.

She stared.

Without a word they rushed into an embrace.

It was Alexandre.

They hugged and laughed and kissed, both filled with the sharp, intense joy of wartime reunion. It was as if they had both returned from the dead. When he released her, he held her hands and looked at her at arm's length. They looked at each other. Both saw faces that the war had changed. With his sharp eyes he saw that she must be a widow. There were new lines in her face and round her mouth, and her glow was gone. Elaine saw more dramatic changes. He was as thin as a skeleton, his bones stuck out, his lustrous eyes were staring and smudged with shadows. He looked dirty – and there was something dangerous about him.

They had only just started to talk when Giles Seton came in, to find his secretary and the French partisan holding hands. He ignored that, and breezily invited the visitor into his office, observing that he gathered there was a little matter of an official complaint. Alexandre caught Elaine's eye and winked.

'Yes, Captain, I have a strong complaint to make. But excuse me – ' he broke off and turned to Elaine. 'May we lunch? It has to be today.'

She nodded, and he turned back to Giles saying loudly, 'We know all about your tests on the weight of our equipment, Captain. We are told that it is *not* heavy and that we make a great fuss. We are absurd. You tell us that an officer here in London wore the equipment for an entire day and declared it perfectly satisfactory. Light as a feather. You did *not* tell us that this man was *un arrimeur*.'

The door closed. Elaine couldn't help grinning. It was true, there had been a man here doing the test – a huge man who in peacetime had been a stevedore.

They lunched in a small deserted tea shop in a mews near the office. Alexandre was in excellent spirits, having won his argument. With a touch of his old boasting he told her he had recently escaped from a German prison hospital.

'I had appendicitis. I escaped with the stitches still in my belly! The good British sewed me up.' He had been a partisan in Burgundy in the forests, and it had been there that Elaine's containers with their guns and explosives had been flown on some of Giles' Lizzie Landings.

Alexandre talked about himself in the old expansive way.

'I was sent to train as an agent. Parachuting. Ugh, that I detest. Combat. *That* I enjoy. For a time I flew a plane. You remember never had I flown one? I am,' said Alexandre with simplicity, 'a natural pilot. But our Halifaxes were crude. They were carcases of raw ironwork menacing our heads. Utility planes, cheap as the cheapest cigarette lighters. Two days ago, Elaine, I saw an American Liberator. Never had I seen such a thing. Engines that never break down, ash trays, leather seats, even soundproofing. Gadgets to bring cold or hot air to suit each man. Combat helmets. Bullet-proof vests to protect against flak. I was envious.'

'Were you, Alexandre?'

'You are perceptive, Elaine. No, I did not envy them. I feel that our planes are more in the spirit of the poverty of my nation than if I flew in one of those luxurious weapons of war. Our merit is not diminished. We will not achieve less than our American friends.'

He leaned across the table saying how quietly she listened and how glad he was to see her.

'You have suffered and you, too, are in the spirit of combat. After this war, perhaps I shall fall in love with you. You are very beautiful. Your sisters were lovely, it is true. You, the loveliest.'

When he left her at the door of the office near Baker Street, he kissed her. She stood and watched him swinging away. An invisible cape still seemed suspended from his shoulders.

Chapter Eighteen

There was no out-of-the-sky victory after the Invasion started. At home Philippa was very quiet, for Barny had been posted with his Squadron to France. Elaine lived through the first days after the Invasion with the curious sensation that she was gradually coming alive. Was it a process which had begun on the night Dick had made love to her? She felt like a creature protected for a long time by a repulsive chrysalis who was now crawling out of it. She felt weak and curiously lonely.

Returning home after a day at SOE she thought – what am I doing here at home? She was a widow of thirty-one with no future and nobody to care for. Even when Trix had been struck down by sorrow she had not needed Elaine.

The following morning a letter arrived for her. The stamped words on the envelope were hideously familiar – HM Ships. When she opened it, Philippa, sitting opposite her at the breakfast table, began to giggle.

'That isn't a letter, it's a doily.'

The thin blue paper was perforated with holes, varying from a slit or a small circle to a gap two inches wide. The censor's scissors had reduced the letter to paper lace.

'It's from Dick.'

Their father had left the room and Philippa murmured, 'I suppose the divorce is through. Not that poor Trix will care.'

Elaine began to read.

'Yes. He says it is. But he has not heard that Chuck has been killed. I must write and tell him.'

Philippa scraped margarine on her toast.

'Do you realise something odd, Elaine? They could re-marry. Trix does need a man. It is not impossible that they might get together again.'

'It sounds like a stupid Hollywood film,' said Elaine, upset to find how much she minded the idea. The doily had said little enough in between its gaps. The sea was hellish. Dick had bought her some French scent. He had thought about her a lot. At the bottom of the pierced page was scribbled, *I hope you are out of black*.

It was not an important letter and she did not know why she carried it all the time in her handbag.

Trix had been away for weeks. When she telephoned, she sounded unlike herself.

'But she won't grieve for long,' said Philippa after one of the telephone calls.

'Surely you don't want her to?'

'Elaine, what a thing to say. I want her to be happy.'

'Trix is like a boxer,' said Elaine, after a moment, 'she knows how to bend when the blow comes.'

'She's been so lucky until now. I always thought her luck would hold. She hasn't been like some of us – spending our lives expecting our man to be shot down.'

She did not add – or whose man was drowned, and Elaine thought again that her family had forgotten Miles. Or was it that Philippa remembered, and set herself up in a sort of contest of courage, with Elaine recoiling from the sea, while Philippa dared not look up at the sky?

Trix arrived home unannounced one hot evening. Her beauty had returned. She still talked of Chuck and smiled over things he had said. Sometimes her black eyes brimmed. His photograph in flying jacket and Mae West was on her dressing table. But she began to work at the club again, and she spent a good deal of time polishing her charm bracelet.

Later that week all three sisters were at home and in bed when there sounded the old familiar wail of the Alert, followed by thundering guns and distant, shattering explosions. As Elaine sighed and pulled on a dressing-gown, Philippa stood in the doorway.

'Boring. I suppose we'd better go down. I'll call Trix.'

'I'm here. Back under the old table. Golly, I thought we'd had all that,' said Trix, floating in clad in one of her indecent nightdresses. She looked aggrieved when Elaine sharply told her to fetch a dressing-gown: but obeyed.

The trio trooped downstairs, carrying pillows. They settled under the table.

'Elaine?' Theo peered round the door, grey hair on end like the crest of a parrot. 'Do you notice anything curious

261

about the noise? It sounds different. Want to come and have a look?'

Elaine scrambled out and followed him. Across the summer sky was a long straight trail of smoke stretching from the direction of Earl's Court. It was followed by what looked like something belching smoke and flames. There was a loud clattering sound.

'What the devil's that?' muttered Theo. A few moments later there was a loud explosion.

'Good,' said Elaine, 'They hit it.'

The raid went on all night. The girls were asleep when the All Clear finally sounded at half past seven, and when they saw the time, Elaine and Philippa rushed to bath and dress. Before they were ready another Alert wailed out.

'Damn and blast,' said Philippa, as she and Elaine both ate their breakfast standing up. Miggs waited on them.

'Doctor's out. House in Strickland Road's been hit, the milkman said. He told me somethin' else. That wasn't an ordinary blitz last night. They're usin' planes without pilots. Robots, they're shootin' at us now.'

Like the rest of the Londoners, the Tyrrells detested the flying bombs. The war had been on a long time and they had become like soldiers in the trenches – war-weary. The Second Front had given everybody a great surge of hope and a look towards the extraordinary possibility of peace. Now the flying bombs sputtered over London. They sounded as loud as airborne lorries and their tails flamed. In the House of Commons it was announced that if a bomb was overhead, the moment that the light in the tail went out, an explosion followed between five and fifteen seconds later.

In the past the civilians under bombardment had known they were being attacked by living men who risked their own lives and were in mortal danger from the defending guns and fighter planes. But now nothing could be done when the robots came over, except to wait until the light in the machine's tail went out before throwing oneself to the ground.

During the first two weeks the bombs, called variously buzz bombs, doodlebugs, fly bombs or bumble bombs, flew over London night and day. Anti-aircraft defences were ordered not to fire on them. If the gun did hit one, it would do just as much damage as if it simply landed.

In SOE headquarters, in Philippa's Mayfair office, in Trix's club – now noticeably thin of US troops – nobody talked of anything else but the bombs: there were stories of dreadful damage and there were jokes. Londoners finally became used to the things. Elaine heard one sputtering overhead when she was at the hairdresser's. Trix went shopping in Bond Street with one eye on the sky, where the familiar shape was whirring with its tail aflame. She waited for the light to go out, but it didn't. The bomb sputtered away towards Regent Street.

Rumours also flew across London. It was said that the RAF planes could get close enough to the flying bombs to tip the angle of their wings so that they fell harmlessly into the sea. The bombs, said some people, were radio controlled. Other said they were jet propelled. Most dramatic was the rumour that the Germans had discovered a way to use the earth's magnetic field, and that *we* must hurry up and find a way to upset that.

During the new blitz hundreds of thousands of houses disappeared into black smoke or were damaged beyond repair. There were no official figures given of the dead and wounded.

Both Elaine and Philippa acquired steel helmets in which they went to work, and Trix looked enchanting in her GI's helmet, her fair hair flowing from below the chin strap. There was an advantage to the bombs, she said. She'd been to Harrods and – imagine! – had been offered a choice of *four* different bottles of French scent. Elaine watched her young sister returning to her butterfly self. She envied her; it must be wonderful to be so resilient.

After thinking about it a great deal, Elaine made up her mind that she must tell Trix that she had seen Dick. One evening during an All Clear she found her sister in the garden. Trix was on her knees on the parched grass, admiring her row of well-staked and ripening tomatoes.

'If you pick this little bit in the crook of the stem, see? you get another tomato. How gorgeous they smell.'

Elaine sat on the grass. She wore a turquoise coloured pre-war silk dress which suited her. Her black clothes had been packed away at last. Trix was in white cotton, polka-dotted with scarlet. A ribbon trailed from her hair.

'I had a letter from Dick the other day,' began Elaine casually.

'Oh lor. Ropey news,' sighed Trix. 'What does *he* want? It would be the limit if he expects parcels from Fortnums from me now we're divorced.'

'Of course he doesn't. His parents can do that.'

'I should say so. They're filthy rich,' agreed Trix amicably. 'It was jolly nice, me not asking for alimony. I could have done but Chuck said no. I said – but American girls do, and *he* said "Stay as sweet as you are". Darling Chuck,' she added and returned, tearless and pretty, to the tomatoes.

'Dick didn't write about you, as it happens. And he called round some time ago.'

'Did he? And you coped? Good-oh. I s'pose he was hoping to see me?'

'Not particularly.'

'Wanted to know if I'm okay, so round he comes to see Little Mother Kitty. Remember that bit in Angela Brazil that Flip used to quote? "Little Mother Kitty, What would we do without you, You're the salvation of our family, she said with a happy sigh." If you do write, you can tell him that Chuck bought it. But I absolutely don't want to see him, per-leeze.'

Summer went by. News of the war in Europe was of victories but the flying bombs went on. And now the V2's were a new fear. They were mysterious rockets and did more terrible damage. People said they came down from the sky coated with ice.

The person who took the blitz the worst was Annette. She was plainly terrified, rushed out the moment an Alert sounded to listen to the distant putt-putt-putt, then ran to the billiard room to shelter. She would not answer the telephone to patients. The more nervous she grew, the more smug Miggs became, again wearing her creaking white apron. Annette was too alarmed to notice how often Miggs took over the telephone and showed patients to the waiting room.

Matching the raids, another kind of bomb burst inside the sheltering walls of St Helen's. One afternoon, with Miggs out shopping and Annette under the billiard table, Theo himself answered the telephone.

It was Trix's solicitor asking if Mrs Polglaze could call at the Temple about some matter concerning the decree absolute.

The moment Miggs came in through the back door, Theo stormed into the kitchen. He had had an hour to get steadily more furious. His face was a dull crimson.

264

'Do you know what I learned on the telephone!' he shouted. 'That there has been *a divorce* in my family without my knowledge.'

He continued to rant. Nobody had told Miggs about the divorce but she had known from the first. There was nothing about the family she didn't know, and what she did not gather from listening at doors she seemed to absorb through the pores of her skin. She filled the kettle.

'Hadn't you best calm down? You don't know the half of what happens to your children, and you never did.'

He went out, slamming the door.

Miggs waited. She knew the three separate ways that the girls opened the front door and when she heard Elaine come in, she bobbed out into the hall.

'Game's up, lady. The doctor's found out.'

'What on earth are you talking about, Miggs?'

'Save your breath, Miss Elaine. I know all about the divorce. Knew the marriage wasn't any good long before the poor Lieutenant came on leave and she gave him the boot. The one who looks like gettin' the boot now is Trix. Unless you stand up to the doctor. He's fit to be tied.'

Why, thought Elaine, should we imagine she wouldn't know about it? The old nurse then told her, not without a relish at the drama, of the solicitor's telephone call.

Theo was in his study dictating letters. Annette only incompetently wrote them in longhand, but he was patient with her. He was smiling. His face changed when he saw Elaine.

'May I have a word, Father?'

'I will leave you,' said Annette, showing by her expression that she, too, knew what had happened.

As Elaine sat down, her father looked at her as if at an enemy, and went into the attack.

'It appears that you decided to keep me in ignorance of the disgusting matter of my daughter's adultery with some American or other.'

He had at last put two and two together, she thought.

'You know very well that Trix was fond of poor Chuck Greenfield who was shot down last month.'

She hoped to shame him into charity. She failed.

'Very tragic. What has that to do with Beatrix? Where is her husband?'

265

'Dick is at sea. You know that too. He's been away almost continuously for two years. Anybody could see they were becoming estranged. Trix is so young.'

'Indeed. What you say appals me. You condone your sister's adultery, I take it.'

'I do not. But I can understand that it might happen – that it does happen, because of the war –'

'Don't use that excuse to me,' he interrupted savagely. 'I saw scores of people die in the last war, and I've seen them die in this one too. Brave men and respectable women. You are saying that separation turns women into whores. I am sorry the young man was killed, but I feel no more, perhaps less, than for any man dead in the blitz. What I do feel is disgust at Beatrix. I won't have her living under my roof.'

'Father!' cried Elaine, scarcely able to believe the iron prejudice and lack of pity. 'You can't mean you'd refuse to have the poor child here. Where would she go? She has nobody but us.'

'To my recollection she had a husband. Make up your mind to it. I won't have her here.'

She ran out of the room.

Both her sisters had come home and Miggs must have told them, for they were waiting in the drawing room, their faces wearing the same tense large-eyed anxiety.

Trix said, 'He wants me to get the hell out of here.'

'He'll come round,' said Elaine.

'No he won't. Okay. I'll go.'

Trix was white. She said, staring to the ground, 'I'll find somewhere. I could write to Chuck's parents for some money. Or there's a guy in the club who –'

'Trix!'

Both Elaine and Philippa burst out at the same time.

'I suppose he called me a whore,' said Trix, 'I don't care. He always hated me.'

'He is angry because he is fond of you, for heaven's sake,' said Elaine. 'Of course he won't turn you out.

Philippa was looking fixedly at Elaine. Her loyalty and love were all unswervingly with Barny, and now because of Chuck's death, Trix belonged to the old lost Eagle world.

'Pa can't turn her out, Elaine,' she said carefully, 'because he is doing exactly what he blames her for.'

'What are you talking about?' said Elaine sharply. Her sister's voice sounded ominous.

Philippa hesitated, then said in a rush, 'I wasn't going to tell anybody about it, but now I must. Annette was coming out of his bedroom the other afternoon. She didn't see me, because I dodged behind the door. And once I'd seen that I suddenly realised that they were having an affair. It is written all over them.'

Trix burst into an angry triumphant laugh. Neither Elaine nor Philippa smiled.

Elaine gave a long sigh.

'What a thing to speak of to my own father.'

All three sisters knew that the task would be hers.

But Theo did not send for Elaine and demand that Trix should pack her bags. There was no showdown. He was brusque with all three girls, and spent his time when not at work trying to soothe Annette who, hearing the rattle of flying bombs, was hysterical. Perhaps Theo realised that something in the atmosphere had changed. Or perhaps Annette did not want any trouble and consequent attention shifted away from herself. Trix was allowed to stay.

The flying bombs continued to land, people became fatalistic. The summer crawled by, the invasion news was good. Paris would soon be liberated. 'And when,' said Miggs, complaining that the milk ration had been cut, 'are we goin' to be liberated? That's all I want to know.'

One Sunday, weeks after Theo's discovery of the divorce, he asked Elaine to come to his study. Her heart sank. It was all going to start up again, and faced with the degrading prospect of counter attacks against her own father, Elaine felt a revulsion against them all. Why, she thought, must it always be me?

But Theo, looking unusually stylish in a new shirt with a thin blue line, and a blue silk tie Annette had clearly chosen, asked her to sit down quite pleasantly. He was in the old swivel chair, which twisted and turned for a moment. As she waited, she thought that her father's Julius Caesar face looked relaxed. Perhaps there would be no trouble after all.

Finally he said, 'Annette is very upset over the flying bombs. One understands it with such a highly-strung temperament. She's a Latin lass.'

'Yes.'

267

'The strain is bad for her. Very bad. I've decided she must go to the country. Remember Colonel Pendleton who gave you the introduction to Blenheim? He and his wife are living in Hertfordshire and most kindly say that Annette may stay with them until things have quietened down.'

'Miggs can help you while she is away.'

Her father was not listening.

'I have some further news. Annette has agreed to be my wife.'

Elaine had a moment of sheer astonishment. Her mouth fell open. Her father was marrying a girl of Trix's age. A French girl who did not like his daughters any more than they liked her.

'I know it must be a surprise to you,' said her father boyishly, 'but you must have seen that I admire her. We have grown very attached.'

He began to talk of Annette and himself. He used language which dated back to the time when he was young, to the romantic years of Edwardian courtship. It was odd to hear him. He said he was deeply honoured at her consent, that her character was exceptionally fine and he considered she had true nobility. He made the match dignified, even serious. Elaine produced some clichés about being sure they would be happy. He gave another of his boyish smiles, saying he had told Miggs, but would Elaine tell the girls?

'We will be married in Hertfordshire, I think, from the Colonel's house. Annette does not wish me to wait for her for long.'

You haven't, thought Elaine, waited at all.

With Tyrrell impulsiveness she ran straight up to the sewing room where Trix was helping Philippa shorten a dress.

'Pa's marrying Annette!'

'She got him in bed,' said Trix. 'He's nothing but a dirty old man.'

'Shut up!' exclaimed Philippa. 'He's our father, for God's sake, but what do we know how he feels? He's never been close to any of us, even you, Elaine. He doesn't understand us, and I'm sure it isn't his fault. He's reserved, sort of closed with us and always has been. When have we tried to understand him? Perhaps she does.'

Trix's pale face had the witch-like look which Elaine had seen before.

'How can she bear to marry somebody old. It's because of Mum's money.'

'But it is left to us in trust,' said Elaine.

268

'Pa's got it until he dies. She'll make the best of it while she can,' said Trix. 'She might even get the will changed. French-women are clever.'

Elaine might have guessed how her sisters would take the news. Philippa had returned to her romantic self. Trix was spiteful with revenge.

But what of Miggs? Among the family, it was Miggs who loved him and had known him since he was born. She was not all that much older than Theo, sixteen years was less of a gap between people of their age. And she could not stand Annette. But when Elaine went into the kitchen, Miggs did not even scowl. She was squatting by the giant basket which contained Sailor, listening to him loudly purring. She looked up.

'He told you, then.'

'And you too.'

'Didn't surprise me, lady. I know him like the back of my hand, daresay I knew what would happen before he did himself. There's no fool like an old fool, Miss Elaine, and that's a fact. We don't need to be botherin' about the orange blossom, that's a blessin'. She's off to the Colonel's and she'll be livin' the life of Riley.'

'Pa says they will marry soon.'

'He's not the boss any more, is he?'

Miggs stood up, grimacing at the pain of her rheumatism, and limped over to lay a tray. The Alert had begun to moan.

'The day she comes into this house as missus, I go out. Miss Philippa said I can go with her when peace comes. To America. Don't fancy it, but it's a sight better than puttin' up with that sharp little madam.'

One of Theo's patients had an appointment on the morning that Annette was leaving London. She had arrived from her digs with three large suitcases which were left by the front door. Theo was taking her to the station. Elaine came down earlier than usual, to say goodbye to Annette. She was surprised to find her in her white overall, at the desk in her old place.

Annette smiled.

'Old Lady Leveaux is coming to see Theo this morning, and she is very fond of me. I shall work until she has gone. It will please her.'

'That's kind of you,' said Elaine since it was expected of her. 'We haven't talked much lately. I'm not sure that I have congratulated you.'

Annette fiddled with a ring on her left hand. Elaine saw that it was one of her mother's, the emerald and diamond half hoop.

'Theo will make me happy, I am sure,' said Annette.

The comparison between her and Elaine was very marked. Annette looked young, handsome, confident. Her hair shone like the black wings of a bird.

She said suddenly, 'Alexandre told me he saw you at your Bureau. We dined that night. He always sees me when he is in London. He gives me news of my village. He obtains it through his secret work.'

'He shouldn't tell it.'

'To me. *Tiens*. I left France as Alain did.'

'I was very grieved when I heard that Alain was dead,' Elaine said impulsively. It was something she had known, through SOE, months before. 'I felt unhappy that I could not tell you.'

The serious young Breton had been a partisan. He had been shot.

'But I knew of it. I knew when it happened,' said Annette flatly. 'It is for him that I wear the cross of Lorraine. I have told Theo that it will stay on my neck until I too am dead.'

The words were dramatic, the tone the opposite. Annette tidied some papers on the desk.

'Did Alexandre tell you that Alain and I were betrothed? No? He could have done. Alain kept it a secret at the Centre d'Acceuil, he did not wish people to know of our love. That was why I came to England. Because he did. Not for patriotism, what is that? For love.'

It was impossible, thought Elaine, to say anything to the girl now wearing her mother's ring. And besides, Annette preferred to talk than to listen.

'Alexandre gave me the news that my parents are dead. They were killed in a British raid. How stupid the British are, what did the bombing of our village achieve? We did not even have a factory. I have some cousins who live there, but I do not like them. That is all. There is no reason for me to return when victory comes. Your father and I need each other. I do not believe in attaching myself to the past.'

'I am sure you will be happy,' said Elaine, and there was a faint tone of wonder in her voice.

'I will make him a good wife. We will have children. Theo needs a son.'

Thinking about Annette after she had gone, Elaine could not find a single thing that she and her sisters had in common with their future stepmother. Annette's affection for their father was probably genuine now, but it was based on commonsense, and when had any of the Tyrrell girls loved for such a reason? Annette was conceited in her polite way, and even Trix, the beauty of the family, had not a trace of conceit. She shared her beauty with people as if it were a kind of gift.

What the sisters did have was something in common with their father. He had fallen in love with a young girl over thirty years his junior and he had not hesitated. He asked her to be his wife. The family impulsiveness was in him still.

Elaine gathered, talking to the omniscient Miggs, that Annette was settling down well with the Pendletons. Perhaps she had decided to use some Gallic charm for a change. It seemed that she had taken over the cooking. The Pendletons were delighted with her, and thought the unsuitable match most suitable. Theo travelled to their Hertfordshire house to spend every weekend.

With Theo away a good deal and Annette gone, a blitzed calm descended on the old house. Elaine received more letters from Dick. Fortunately, Trix was rarely up at breakfast time and always missed the arrival of the morning post. She would not have cared that Dick was writing to her sister, but she might have laughed. Elaine was glad she did not know.

The letters were friendly and funny. They began *Lovebird*, and ended *All my love, Dick*. She read them over and over again. She was like a woman searching in her lap for a needle. She did not find it.

Chapter Nineteen

The war was dragging to a kind of close, but the foggy 1944 Christmas came and went, and it was not ended. The blackout was lifted. It was called a dim-out, and should have been cheerfully welcomed. But after five years in the dark, the lighting seemed abnormally bright to dazzled Londoners. Trix disliked it, it was unromantic. 'What about goodnight kisses now?'

Paris had been freed at the end of August, while London was still under bombardment, and the stories and pictures of its joyful liberation told on Londoners' nerves as they went their stubborn way to work through new ruins. Now in the winter the tales filtering through from France were of Paris, already its brilliant self, with money spent like water, not a single ruin from bombs, people dancing until four in the morning and cafés full to bursting point. That did not please Londoners either. They were envious and irritable.

Philippa had seen nothing of Barny. He had not stayed long in France after the first months of the invasion, he was back in England. But every time there was a big American raid, and the never-ending Flying Fortresses blackened the London sky like giant birds, Philippa wondered which of the planes were protected by Barny's fighters. Sometimes he managed to telephone. Telling her nothing.

One evening the telephone rang, and Miggs came into the drawing room.

'Your husband, lady.'

Philippa flew.

'Honey? Like to come up for a couple of nights? It's permitted.'

'*Would I!*'

'Grab a train to Chichester. I'll have a jeep meet you. And bring a party frock. It's Pete Jansen's birthday, he's thirty, would you credit it! Another thing . . . I've been thinking. Howsabout bringing Trix with you?'

She was very surprised.

'We're short of pretty girls,' he said. 'And besides . . . Chuck would've liked it. Okay?'

When Philippa told Trix, it was the first time she'd ever seen her young sister blush.

A heavy open jeep, with RITA HAYWORTH on the bonnet, was waiting for the girls when they arrived. It was already January and freezing cold. But the girls were too excited to notice the knife-sharp air as the great automobile thundered down frosty roads. There was a winter moon, and the headlights were now only half-masked. They shone on high glittering hedges and stretches of fields hard under the frost. Trix chattered gaily. But Philippa thought the metallic little voice sounded unnaturally hard. She wondered if the thought of being at an American air station again, seeing pilots again, would hurt. Yet Trix had accepted the invitation almost feverishly.

The girls were set down at the entrance of a big rambling old house round which a series of ugly army huts had been built. The Stars and Stripes hung above the doorway, stirring in the icy winds.

Through the door, they found themselves in a high-ceilinged entrance hall, facing a double staircase. Portraits hung on the walls. This had been somebody's home, once upon a time. Now it teemed with American troops; the noise of men's voices was loud. Every soldier going by stared at Trix who automatically shook back her long pale hair.

Suddenly Philippa saw Barny. How long it was since she had seen him, weeks, months. She simply ran, and he put out his arms and caught her and kissed her as if they were alone in the house, in England, in the world.

'Flip. Honey.'

'Oh, my dearest!'

Then he drew away from her and said, 'Is Trix around?'

Still holding her, he looked beyond her and Philippa saw him give an odd smile. She turned round.

There was her sister looking curiously small, despite her high wedge heels. Her head was tilted upwards. And, fairer than she, looming over her like a giant, was the broad figure, wings on his breast, of Pete Jansen.

* * *

273

Elaine was the only one to stay at home in St Helen's on the day which was called VE Day. It was not a complete peace, for there was still war in the Far East. But in Europe it was over.

'Our war's finished,' Philippa said, and it set Elaine's teeth on edge to hear it given the kindly pronoun.

In the house, in the garden, she could hear bells and car horns. Now and then laughter went by in d'Abernon Road, and somebody sang. Or there were shouting voices. London had turned into a river of people, arm in arm, arm round neck, slowly drifting towards the West End. They were bound for Downing Street to cheer Churchill. Then to the Palace to cheer the King and Queen. Londoners always went to the Palace when they felt happy.

Miggs had tried to persuade Elaine to go too. The old nurse never missed being part of a celebration.

'I remember the old Queen's funeral, all those kings walkin' behind the coffin. And I was in Trafalgar Square for Armistice Day. Then there's all the Royal weddin's and funerals. I can't miss this,' said Miggs, who had fished out a pre-war white straw hat, with daisies round the brim, from a box under her bed. After vainly trying to get Elaine to join the jollifications, Miggs left the house alone. Probably, thought Elaine, to get a lift to the Palace in somebody's taxi.

Philippa and Trix had risen in the dawn to walk to the Wings Club where Barny and Pete were supposed to be arriving as so on as they could. 'We must,' declared Trix, 'be there first.' Trix was quite out of herself, as Miggs described it, since Pete had asked her to be his wife.

'I always knew,' said Trix to Elaine, waving a hand decorated with yet another (larger) sapphire, 'that I'd marry a Yank in the end.'

Since Philippa had taken her to the American air station in January, Trix's recovery had been complete. Like a child at the edge of the sea waiting to tumble in, she had fallen in love again. Her sisters congratulated her, Elaine was introduced to Pete, and an atmosphere of romance – Trix was shopping again – invaded St Helen's.

Philippa and Elaine had supper one night at home, and afterwards went into the sitting room to sit by the fire. The day had been cold. Trix's plans, Trix's bliss, Trix running up and down stairs, waving new satin petticoats for admiring approval,

274

talking on the telephone to girlfriends, playing new American records, had occupied the entire week. A kind of lull had fallen as the two sisters sat looking into the fire.

Elaine finally said,

'I like Pete Jansen very much. But . . . do you think they are going to be happy, Flip?'

She turned to Philippa for enlightenment. Her sister understood Americans.

Philippa made a rueful face.

'Barny and I are slightly bothered. Barny more than me, really. You know Pete's from Wyoming. It's such a *huge* state, really enormous. Some of it is nothing but a great desert. Barny says there's nowhere else like it in the whole of the United States. Pete's family live their entire lives in the open.'

'But Trix knows all about that.'

'Yes, Elaine, but has she really grasped it? Has she actually realised that there is not a city for four hundred miles from their ranch?'

The sisters looked at each other. They had a vision of frivolous little Trix setting off blithely towards a life about which she had not given one serious thought. Elaine with her steady soul, Philippa with her full heart, might just have made so extreme a choice and succeeded by sheer love. But how would Trix endure such a life? Not because she wasn't young and strong, but because she wouldn't try. What Trix thrived on, what made her beauty glow, was pleasure. At present, with an American flyer making passionate love to her, she was in a dream. When she finally arrived in Wyoming, that fierce sexual bond between Pete and herself must hold for a while. Even the land itself, with its vast and harsh simplicities, might touch her imagination. But for how long?

Elaine and Philippa arrived at more or less the same moment at the same conclusion.

'Oh Flip. What will happen, do you think?'

'I suppose she'll leave. She'll never stay the course. Poor Pete . . .'

Elaine reflected.

'Perhaps he'll be relieved in the end.'

'That's what Barny said. He said any girl who marries Pete had just better come from a farm.'

There was a little pause.

'I'll tell you what,' said Philippa suddenly, 'I can't imagine her ever coming back to England, can you? If she leaves Pete she'll pack up, and she might even go so far as to buy her ticket. But she'll never come home – '

'You mean because she'll find somebody else.'

They were silent again, thinking of their sister.

'I suppose we ought to be grateful,' said Elaine finally, 'that whatever happens, she will be all right.'

'I don't know why we're so certain of that. But I agree.'

Trix herself talked knowledgeably of Wyoming and the ranch, for some mysterious reason called a spread, and the breeding of horses. She was sure Elaine knew how she'd always longed to ride again but Pa had refused to pay for it after that time she used to ride in the Row. He'd said it had become too expensive.

'Pete says I'll be able to ride again in three hours. He says you never forget and that I'm naturally graceful. But he also said the only way for me to ride *there*, quite different from here, is to learn from him and that I've got to do what I'm told. He makes me behave,' she added, speaking as if she and Pete were united in controlling a horse or a dog which was out of hand.

A month after Trix had 'met up' with Pete, as she called it, and Elaine supposed they must have gone to bed, Trix grew noticeably quiet for a few days. She was very pale and looked stricken. One night her colour and vivacity were back. She came into Elaine's bedroom. Remembering her sister's dislike of her naked nightdresses, she wore a modest négligé of white organdie threaded with blue ribbons.

'Oh Elaine. I'm so relieved I could cry. I had to come and tell you. I thought I'd lost him.'

'*Flying?*'

'No, no, he's not flying just now. It isn't anything to do with that, it was something I did. Oh, it was awful. God, I'm glad it's okay again.'

And out came the story in Trix's now completely American voice.

'It was last weekend when he called me up and said I could come to the station, and he'd gotten hold of a flat over a boathouse on the river. Well. Pete took me there. We had a night together. It was . . . well, it was just so wonderful, he's the most marvellous lover, oh Elaine, he's the best. Then Pete said next day why didn't we have his Captain over for tea. I thought it

276

would be good because although he'd seen me around, and must have guessed Pete and I were crazy about each other and everything, I'd never met him properly. I'm sure he is fond of Pete. After all, Pete's a star flyer, DFC in the RAF and all that. Anyway, the Captain (that's what they call them in the US Air Force) came to tea. I bought some buns,' said Trix solemnly.

Listening, Elaine could not imagine what was going to come next.

'He was swell, I sure did like him. He was funny and relaxed, you know? We talked about English antiques, and I told him how I'd bought a chest of drawers, you know the one, when Chuck and I – well, I didn't mention poor Chuck but I said that *when* Pete and I married, I was going to take it with me to the States. And I was dying to live in the US of A.'

She sounded uncannily American.

'The captain laughed, and then he said how he'd have to get back. I was quite glad. Because Pete was looking at me in a kind of way and I knew what *he* wanted and so did I. Then I had a brainwave. I was nice. I mean, I *can* be, can't I?' she said earnestly. 'I said something like Oh, Captain, there's one little thing I'm dying to say and that is – isn't it time Pete was rested up? He's pretty tired, and he's done ten sorties and his squadron and his folks keep writing me to know if he's okay.'

Elaine stared.

Trix made a face.

'It wasn't so terrible, was it? He had done more flights than a lot of other guys. But the Captain looked murderous. He didn't say a thing. As for Pete, he practically jumped out of his skin and he just said "*shut up*" and then said something to the Captain about me acting hasty and he didn't know what had gotten into me. Then he and the Captain went down the stairs, it was a kind of ladder thing leading into the garden, and Pete saw him off.'

She fidgeted with her bracelet. It clinked.

'When he got back, Elaine, he was *awful*. He yelled at me. He said I was nuts and he hit me. I don't expect you remember, but Dick slapped my face that night we parted. I mean that stung. But Pete hit me real hard, and I spun across the room and fell against a chair and banged my head. I saw stars. Then he picked up his jacket and walked out and didn't come back. I called up the station four times. They said he wasn't there. I didn't believe them. I had to come back to London. I hung about at home, you saw me, didn't you? I was so scared. I was sure I'd lost him. He's the real one, you know. The real one. In the end it was me who called him again – I've never done that before. I thought he'd refuse to speak, but then this time he did. He just said "never interfere with my job again or I'm through. I'll never see you again." Wasn't it awful? I'm still frightened, sort of. But I swore I'd never do it again, and then he let me come down to the station and we made love. And it was all wonderful again.'

'It was all wonderful again' was also the burden of Philippa's song. The book that Barny had written about the Eagles had been sold to an American publisher as well as to an English one and, Philippa said with shining eyes, Barny knew what he was going to be. A writer.

'We'll be going to the States pretty soon – there are no more U boats, haven't been for months, so we'll be getting a ship. Oh Elaine! I shall miss you! But I can't help being excited, you do understand, don't you?'

What answer was there to that?

Philippa continued to talk in her old, impulsive, romantic way. She talked of Louisiana where she would be living and of the letters she had received from Barny's sister Mary Lou. How kind everybody was! She showed Elaine photographs of a white house set among strange, drooping trees. Wasn't it wonderful to think that Barny was going home, and she would be with him, and – imagine! – Miggs had agreed to come too.

'Of course Miggsy is very funny about America. She keeps saying she is sure they won't like her, when what she means is that she won't like them. But she and Barny get on so marvellously. He spoils her and she pretends to think he is silly when really she's thrilled. Barny did say the other day that he was dreading going home. In a way, you know, because nobody there knows what it has been like. But we have each other. And Miggsy will be our bit of England. And maybe we can have a baby soon.'

Philippa gazed at her sister, seeing only joy.

Trix. Philippa. They had become part of the American invasion, thought Elaine. And then she remembered Alain and Alexandre, and the girl now married to her father. They had brought a French invasion to the old house, and changed her father's life.

278

It rained heavily last night, and VE morning was dull, damp and grey when Elaine went out into the garden. The coarse unkempt grass which had once been a lawn was drenched. She fetched a raincoat, and spread it on the wooden bench by the syringa tree where her mother used to sit and sew before the war.

All over London, all over England and France, and the great map of Europe pinned to the wall in the Baker Street office, people were running into each other's arms. They were laughing and kissing and dancing and making a noise. Happiness makes people want to bang drums and sing, she thought. They want to be part of a crowd, and sharing. Even Miggs.

What is there for me? She remembered talking to Dick at the Hogarth on that wet evening. He was so very fond of Miles that she had felt she could tell him almost anything. She had said how she had often thought that a dreadful day might come when she would wake up and find Miles did not love her any more.

Dick had given her an odd look with his slanting eyes.

'Yes. Lovers always think that. But it would be much much worse, Elaine, if you woke up one day and found you couldn't love.'

Perhaps that has happened, she thought, and even if I could, I'd be afraid to love. She pushed the thought of Dick's lovemaking away. Thinking about him hurt her. She began to think, instead, of Miles. In a wave of sorrow she heard his voice, felt his thin cheek pressed against hers. Is Claire feeling like this? On a day of such happiness, this is when it is worst.

She leaned back against the seat, looking at the tangled grass and hearing the distant tumbling of church bells. Suddenly in the garden a blackbird began to sing his heart out. He sounded just as her sisters did – free and blessed.

Philippa and Trix shared all the joy that was flooding through London, and soon they, and the Americans, would be gone. They would cross the Atlantic and become part of the country which had grown so close to England during the long, long war.

Father will sell this house. Annette doesn't like it because we all lived here together before she came. Miggsy will be gone.

She shut her eyes, listening to the blackbird, and did not hear the footsteps on the wet grass. Somebody touched her hand and she opened her eyes.

'Dick!'

'Elaine!' He took her hands and stood looking down at her. A rush of dismay, of love, of embarrassed love, went through her. She returned his look with her old bright reserve. Even her voice was brittle when she said,

'What a surprise.'

'I couldn't get to a telephone. The queues! I thought it quicker just to come. I'm ridiculously optimistic,' he went on lightly, 'I kept hoping you hadn't gone out to celebrate.'

'I suppose you thought I wouldn't want to.'

'Something like that,' he said, still looking at her very thoughtfully.

He had not kissed her. He sat beside her on the bench. Then, after a moment he said,

'Will you answer me something?'

She did not know why she was frightened.

'What?'

'Don't look like that. Answer me bravely. Did it worry you – that we made love?'

She was so embarrassed that she could not answer. He leaned towards her, and she recoiled.

But he ignored that and put his arms round her.

'Lovebird. Don't move away from me. Stay close. Now listen. I know, I knew, even when I left you after all that beautiful sex, how you'd feel. Sweet girl. You never had an affair, did you? Only Miles whom you loved. When we were in bed, and you were so gorgeous, I did remember that. But you thought that for me it was just one night of love, didn't you?'

'I don't know. I – I suppose I did. Marjorie once said you have lots of affairs.'

He laughed at that.

'My lovebird. How could *you* be an affair? Don't you know I worship you? That night was like stars. Dear love. Beautiful Elaine. Come closer. That's right. That's right.'